CUTANDRUN

Also by Jeff Abbott

Black Jack Point
A Kiss Gone Bad

Jeff
Abbott
CUTANDRUN

ORION

First published in Great Britain in 2004 by Orion Books
an imprint of The Orion Publishing Group
Orion House, 5 Upper St Martin's Lane, London WC2H 9EA

A CIP catalogue record for this book is
available from the British Library

ISBN (hardback) 0 75286 092 5
ISBN (trade paperback) 0 75286 093 3

Typeset at The Spartan Press Ltd,
Lymington, Hants

Printed and bound in Great Britain by
Clays Ltd, St Ives plc

For William

Ellen who became Eve

This is how you disappear.

First you make sure you don't go anyplace where you ever went before, if you can help it. You like Vegas? Forget about slots and Wayne Newton for the next five years. Love shopping in New York? Uh-oh, no way, baby, your shadow don't darken Broadway. Because when you step out of life, when you step away from the world you made, you don't step back into any old footprint. No. That's where they look first.

So those many years ago, when I left Babe and my sons behind in Port Leo, I went to Montana. I can't stand cold weather, never liked it. I'm a coast girl, love the kiss of the sun on my skin. But coasts were forbidden to me right off. Babe knew I loved to fish and lie on the warm sands. I don't think I had ever said the word 'Montana' out loud before I ran. Not sure I could find it on the map, although I wouldn't mix it up with Wyoming, because I know Wyoming is square.

I changed my hair color to red, because back then nobody ever thought you dyed your hair red on purpose. You usually dyed it brown to get away from red. And I dropped the Texas drawl, fast. Tried to talk like a newscaster. Said 'you guys' instead of y'all, which was harder than it sounds. Told people I was from California, because it's full of people originally from somewhere else. And hid a loaded gun in an old suitcase because insurance is a necessary evil in this world.

Jim was useless and he didn't like the cold. He said it made his balls hurt. He was afraid to look for a job, saying that the Dallas papers would have put his face all over the news wires and the TV. I sure never saw jack-squat about him in the Bozeman paper.

Twice I drove over to the university library, where they took the *Dallas Morning News,* but after the first week of headlines like MISSING EXEC ALLEGEDLY EMBEZZLED HALF MILLION there was no talk of him, no pictures of him. The one picture they ran of him was when he got made SVP at the bank and his smile's too tight, his hair a little too big. And never a word about me. The library didn't take the Corpus Christi paper, where I might have been mentioned. So I wrote the headlines in my own mind: MOTHER OF SIX MISSING. It's less glamorous than embezzling. And ten times worse.

But, in those Dallas papers, never a mention of me in connection with Jim the embezzling banker. Which was how I liked it.

After reading the paper in Bozeman, I would drink a cup of coffee and smoke and try not to think about the boys. Not think about my four oldest going off to the movies with my friend Georgie, me kissing them for the last time and them not knowing it. Not think about my littlest babies, Mark and Whit, running around in the backyard, chasing each other and laughing, trying to get them settled for a nap in their beds, Whit standing on the stairs, saying he didn't want to nap, asking me where I was going. I put him back in the bed and I didn't look back. Cried once on the drive north, for twenty minutes, all I allowed myself.

If Whit had asked once more where I was going, maybe I would have stayed. I thought walking away from the boys would be easy, the shackles of their grasping little hands falling off my wrists and ankles. Hardest thing I ever did. I wanted for one terrible second to take one with me, take Whit, he was standing right there, a little mirror of my face. Finally one who looked like me after five copies of Babe. But then the police and Babe never would have given up on looking for me. Ever. And Jim wouldn't have wanted a toddler making the most of his terrible twos with us on the run.

Popping out six, you think that'd be seared into my head, pain and happiness hot to the touch, but with each passing day they seemed more like little ghosts, boys that belonged to someone else. I tried not to remember them because it's easier. I had a new resolve to make my life easier.

But easy was not Jim.

He started drinking one afternoon in my motel room, crying after the fifth of whiskey was half gone, moaning and bitching about missing the warm sun of Dallas, missing his favorite Mexican restaurants, missing his big-ass house in University Park, missing his old comfortable life he'd stolen from himself.

I watched him sip his whiskey. I lit a cigarette. I quit smoking when I had the boys and now I liked a little knife of flame in my hand.

'Shit, shit, shit,' Jim said. He had the soul of a poet.

Jim lacked, always, a certain self-control required for living in the world. He stole a half million from his bank, and now was too consumed by guilt and regret to move. If you're gonna take an action, be ready for your own reaction. I'd agreed to go on the run with him and I'd left a family behind. He'd left a coke-snorting bachelor life behind. I was coping a lot better than he was.

'I got to go in a few minutes,' I said. I worked at an old neighborhood bar, serving beers to Bozeman's inert. Nothing to do with money or bookkeeping, my old job from before I got married. My bar-crows were not question-askers. I liked it. Gave me a few hours' escape from Jim and his moods.

'Go,' he said. 'Go and I'll be fine.'

'Fine at the bottom of the bottle.'

'I'm depressed, Ellie.'

'I noticed.' I got up and made instant coffee for him, knowing he'd let it cool in the cup and then pour it down the sink.

'The money,' he said. 'I didn't just steal it from the bank.'

I waited, the instant coffee jar in my hand.

'I stole most of it from the Bellinis,' he said. 'Sort of.'

'Who are the Bellinis?'

'People I worked for. On the side. They're from Detroit.' He swallowed hard, ran a hand along his lips. 'I cleaned up money for them at the bank.'

'People from Detroit,' I said, 'with an Italian surname. You better be kidding me.'

'I'm not. They're gonna be looking for me.'

I sat down on the mattress. 'Why didn't you tell me this before?'

'I . . . thought you wouldn't come with me.' He took a deep

swig from the whiskey bottle, left a little amber drop sitting on his lip. He had the palest lips I'd ever seen on a live person.

'The money was evidence,' he said. 'Of me making it legit for them, transferring it through a series of accounts. The Feds would have nailed me. So . . . I took it.'

'Jim, maybe we should go back to Dallas, then. Give the money to the Feds. The mob's gonna chase you harder than the Feds ever will.'

He looked at me, and an ugly silence hung in the air and the frown on his face turned mean. He grabbed my wrist and flexed his thin fingers back and forth, digging his nails into my flesh, my veins and bones.

'Jim, stop. That hurts.' I kept my voice calm.

'You want to go back to Texas? That what you saying, Ellie?'

'It's one option. Let go of my hand, please.'

'You know what Tommy Bellini will do to me?' He tightened the vise grip on my wrist, grinning, like nothing would give him more pleasure than to break my bones. 'I won't be a smear on the wall when he's done.'

'Please let go.'

'You don't give a shit about what happens to me.' He pulled me into his sour breath. 'You missing those brats of yours?'

'No.' A cold sharpness slid along my ribs, my guts.

'You are,' he said. 'You're missing those brats of yours, you want to go home. You go home, you're gonna talk. About me.'

'You're drunk.' I grabbed the bottle of whiskey to bring it down on his head.

He stood, yanked the bottle away from me, let go of my wrist. Pushed me down onto the bed and I thought: *This doesn't do, not for one goddamned minute.*

'You get this straight, Ellen,' Jim said. 'You made your choice, you aren't going to see your kids again.'

'I know that.'

'You more than know it, you live it.' He took a hit from the bottle, worked the hooch along his gums and teeth like mouth-wash, and he looked so sad and ugly and pathetic I nearly laughed at him.

4

'I don't want nothing to happen to those kids,' he said.

That burnt-smell silence got thick again. I quit rubbing my wrist.

'You threatening my kids, Jim?' I said it soft like I didn't quite understand, like it was an idea too left-field for human talk.

'You get an idea, Ellen, about calling the Feds, going back to Texas, I call a buddy of mine in Corpus. He's good at' – a pause – 'creating situations. Beaches are real dangerous for little kids. Cramps while swimming. Riptides.' He even gave me a smile, the drunk.

I may be a bad mother, but I'm still a mother, and I stared at him in rising horror as I rubbed my wrist. 'Don't do that, Jim. Please.'

'Then don't you screw with me, okay?' he said.

I let him believe I was afraid of him. 'They're little kids.'

'And you're the mother of the year.' Now I heard a twitch in his voice, shame that he'd had to resort to threatening children. He favored himself with another big gulp of Tennessee juice. 'So don't talk Texas. We stay here. The Bellinis aren't ever going to find us here.'

'Okay,' I said. But not okay. I headed for work and left him drinking. I wondered, what if he's not bluffing. The thought preyed on me like a fever. I decided to call Babe, tell him to take the boys away from Port Leo. Picked up a pay phone, dialed. No answer. I couldn't decide if that pissed me off or not. Shouldn't they all be sitting at home, waiting for me to call? I hung up, went to the bar, the start of one piledriver of a headache working underneath my forehead.

I didn't want to deal with Babe. You should solve your problems directly. That night was quiet at the bar and I had time to think, to construct four different plans and decide on one while I collected beer mugs and ignored a Giants baseball game showing on the television through a thin haze of cigarette smoke.

I returned to the dumpy motel, smelling of cigs and beer. Jim wasn't in my room. We have separate rooms. I insisted on it, trying to keep our new identities separate, too, but he liked to lie on my bed and wait for me.

I had a key to his room. He lay sprawled on his bed, passed out, reeking of whiskey and onion and hamburger. A globby mess of French fries, greasy on a paper bag, lay on the table.

'Jim,' I said. 'You awake?' Poked at him with my fingers. In his cheek, his throat, his stomach, his crotch. Let my fingers linger on his sweet spot, see if there was any response to my tickle.

Nothing; a little dribble of spit tracked down from his mouth, drying on unshaven cheek.

'Don't you threaten my kids, you asshole,' I said.

He didn't move, gave off a rough, sour snore.

So I went back to my room. I opened the little suitcase under the bed and got the gun I'd bought on my way to Dallas from Port Leo, paying cash, using an assumed name. Wiped the gun carefully with an old T-shirt, then wrapped the material around the grip but not the barrel. I walked back down the hall. The silence of the motel pressed against my ears, the quiet of empty rooms. I stuck the gun in his slack, open mouth, nestled it between his teeth and gave the trigger a little squeeze.

I jumped at the sound, more than he did.

I carefully put the gun in his hand, unwrapped the T-shirt from around it, pressed his fingertips on the grip. I went back to my room. It was one in the morning. I waited for someone to respond to the shot, but the motel was still.

No distant whine of sirens approached. I took a shower, washing the bar smells out of my hair, and packed. We'd paid cash for the rooms, a week in advance each time, and were still good for two days. So I took the money Jim stole from the bank and the mobsters, and I drove the car we'd rented to an all-night diner. I ate fried eggs and toast heavy with strawberry jam, and drank coffee, watching the night against the windows go gray, then orange. Pretty, but not as pretty as the sun rising out of the Gulf. Once I thought I saw my sons' faces in the glass, little ghosts again, but it was all the nerve juice pouring through me. Missing the boys really badly but at the same time not wanting to see them, knowing that chapter of my life was closing. I smiled at the boys and their little blank faces vanished in the dark glass.

At seven that morning I drove to the Bozeman airport, left the rental car in the lot. On the radio there was nothing about a suicide

– or a murder – at the Pine Cone Motel. Jim is apparently sleeping in late. The maid won't show up to straighten the room until ten or so, and I'd left the DO NOT DISTURB hanger on Jim's door. She won't knock until two. Perhaps not until tomorrow. Our maid was not the poster child for initiative.

An hour later I was on a plane, flying to Denver under the name of Eve Michaels, the name I'd used since leaving Texas, with five hundred thousand in cash in my checked luggage, praying to God they don't lose my suitcase. It's mostly businessmen on this flight, not as crowded as I would like; I might be remembered more easily. A gap-toothed man next to me asked me what I do, flirting way too early in the morning. I want to say I abandoned my family and killed my rotten mean lover and stole his money. You? You sell insurance? That's fascinating.

But I don't, of course. I said I work in a bar and I'm flying to Denver to see my boyfriend, who's on the semipro wrestling circuit. Gap-tooth lost interest and I closed my eyes. Part of me still wanted to go home. Part of me didn't. And part of me worried that the men from Detroit Jim stole that money from won't stop because Jim's dead. They could come after me. It's funny, looking back now, I wasn't really too worried about the police. But this Tommy Bellini guy Jim was afraid of, he scared me.

A half million is a lot of money. But not enough to live on for the rest of your days, not in style. So I wonder if there's a deal I can cut that will open the right door for me, into a life a hell of a lot more up my alley than raising six kids.

I sat that whole flight with my eyes closed, playing out the different twists and turns my life could take in the next few days.

I didn't stay long in the Denver airport. Grabbed my precious checked bag and fixed my makeup, and rented a car.

I headed east through the morning Denver traffic. For Detroit. Babe and the boys know I hate the cold. But the cold's where Tommy Bellini's at. And I needed a new best friend.

Thirty years ago, I thought Montana would be the last time I would ever need to disappear. I was wrong.

1

'Stop the search, Judge,' Harry Chyme said. 'That's the best advice I can give you.'

Whit Mosley wrapped his fingers around his bottle of beer, felt his friend Claudia Salazar inch closer to him in silent support.

'I don't give up easily,' Whit said. 'Are you telling me you've hit a dead end?'

'No,' Harry said. 'I'm telling you that finding your mother might not be a good idea. It might be, well, dangerous.'

'Dangerous. You're kidding, right?' Whit asked.

'I don't often deal in hunches but I have one about where your mother ended up. But I need to know how risk-tolerant you are before I proceed.'

Claudia put her hand on Whit's arm. 'Whit's tough, Harry. Throw your worst at us.'

Harry dragged a hand through his short, dark hair. He didn't look the part of a private investigator: bespectacled, wearing a tweed coat and a yellow silk tie, with the casual rumple of an English professor. Harry had a kindness in his face Whit trusted, and Harry had been Claudia's instructor at the police academy before she joined the Port Leo police department. Now he sipped at his iced tea and set the glass down, studied Whit as though measuring his strength.

'You may not like what you hear, Judge. This information gets out, could be you don't get elected next time around.' His voice lowered. 'And I know the situation with your father is delicate, but . . .'

'Harry,' Whit said, 'the doctors give my dad four months. For years he's wanted to know what he did to drive my mother away, to make her leave a good life and six sons who loved her. I want you to find her so I can drag her sorry ass home to face my dad before he dies. I want her to explain herself. I don't care if she's got a perfect life now and I mess it up.'

They sat in a back corner at the Whitecap, a small seafood restaurant overlooking Corpus Christi Bay, and in the midafternoon of a February weekday, the restaurant was empty, the sky the color of burned charcoal. The bay lay empty before them, windwhipped. The restaurant was a converted bright yellow house, the tables close together, but they were alone in the back, the lunch crowd evaporated back down Ocean Avenue to the small towers of downtown Corpus Christi or to the regal mansions that lined the street.

Harry Chyme spread files on the restaurant booth's table in a loose jumble. 'Okay then,' Harry said. 'I know your father hired investigators to look for her for several months when she initially disappeared.'

'Yes,' Whit said. 'Then he started drinking and stopped caring.'

'The investigators weren't terribly creative in their search.'

'Harry's got game.' Claudia smiled. 'You found her, you genius.'

Harry ignored the compliment. 'Your mother's disappearance was treated, for the most part, as that of a woman who was simply tired of being married, tired of having six kids to raise.' Harry folded his hands on a folder. 'They looked at her as a woman who had packed a bag, hired a lawyer to end the marriage, and driven off. To have a calculated break from her life. But even a divorce meant she might want to see her kids again. And when she didn't come back and she never got in touch again, then something bad must've happened to her. That theory's crap,' Harry said. 'Because she didn't leave alone.'

Whit shook his head. 'No one else took off from Port Leo the same time she did, or from any other nearby town. She didn't run off with a boyfriend.'

'I looked at every person in Texas who went missing the same month your mother did. There were nineteen people, not counting Ellen Mosley. Fourteen turned up later, safe and sound. The other five didn't turn up safe. Two were kids, kidnapped and killed, one in Fort Worth, the other in Houston. A third was a young woman in Texarkana, raped and killed and found on the banks of the Sabine River three months later. A fourth was an elderly man with senile dementia who wandered off from a nursing home in El Paso and was found dead in the desert from stroke. The fifth was James Powell.'

'I don't know that name,' Whit said.

'James Powell was a Dallas banker. He embezzled over a half million in cash from his bank and ran. He committed suicide three weeks later in Bozeman, Montana. He actually disappeared the week before your mother did.' Harry Chyme opened a folder. 'James Powell fished regularly in Port Leo.'

'Lots of people do,' Claudia said. 'What proof of a connection do you have?'

'The woman who was living with James Powell in a Bozeman motel and took off after he died matches your mother's description, except for hair color.'

Whit thumbed the base of his glass. 'Really.'

'So I started going back through the files, in Dallas and in Bozeman, about James Powell. He'd told a friend at the bank he'd gotten involved with a married woman. Said nothing about Port Leo. But he fished in Port Leo nearly every month.'

'A woman with six young children hasn't got the energy for an affair,' Claudia said.

'Six kids underfoot could give her every reason for an affair,' Whit said. 'We were left to our own devices a lot, Claudia. Or left with our grandmother or friends. My mother could have met up with a guy now and then. But it would have been difficult to keep it quiet for long.'

'But easier with it being a tourist,' Harry said. 'Much less chance he'd be recognized. He could stay at different hotels, or stay in Rockport or Port Aransas or Laurel Point, where Ellen would not be recognized or known.'

'This James Powell. No question it was a suicide?' Claudia didn't look at Whit.

'That's a nice suggestion,' Whit said.

Harry pulled a photocopy of a faded police report from a file.

'There was no sign of struggle, and he was drunk according to the tox reports. No prints on the gun other than his.'

'Did that half million turn up?' Claudia asked.

'No. That obviously concerned the investigators.'

'And this woman who was with him was never a suspect?'

'Sure she was. But the trail died. She and Powell weren't actually living together. They were renting rooms in a dive motel, her room down the hall from his. She arrived at the motel a week after he did and, according to the motel maid's statement at the time, they seemed to not know each other and then hit it off. The maid saw them going to each other's rooms a couple of times. But no proof that they had a connection beyond acquaintance. The stickler is this woman – her name was Eve Michaels – left the night Powell died.'

'Eve Michaels. Ellen Mosley,' Whit said.

'Yep. According to the investigator files on Powell's case, a woman named Eve Michaels bought an airline ticket to Denver from Bozeman. Rented a car in Denver, used a fake credit card. The car was found abandoned in Des Moines, Iowa. Then the trail went cold, and the Bozeman police didn't have luck pursuing it further.'

'So my mother, if she's the same woman, is a killer and a thief,' Whit said. 'I think I know enough now.'

'But maybe she isn't,' Harry said. 'Here's the second part of my theory, and it gets ugly. James Powell cleaned money through his bank for a couple of small businesses in Dallas that were fronts for an alleged organized crime family in Detroit. The Bellini family. The money he stole was from the accounts he'd set up for them. These guys might have caught up with him in Bozeman. But being mob, they would have roughed him up before killing him. No sign the guy had been beaten or tortured.'

'Unless there was no need,' Claudia said. 'They found the money, took it, and killed him.'

'A faked suicide's not their style,' Harry said. 'And unlikely they would have left the body in the motel.'

Whit pulled the old police report across the table and studied the description of the woman. Five-foot-six, around 140 pounds, attractive face, green eyes, red hair. No picture attached but a sketch. It sort of looked like his mother. 'It says she had a bartending job at a beer joint. Why would she work if they had a half million in cash to blow?'

Harry said, 'She wanted a cover. Not draw attention to herself.'

'And she had red hair. My mother was a brunette.'

'Safe to assume she would change her appearance if she was on the run, and with an embezzler,' Harry said. 'Do you remember anyone else asking about your mother after she vanished? Strangers?'

'No. My father would know.'

Harry's face softened. 'How's he doing?'

'The chemo is hard.' Whit glanced back out at the bay, no longer empty in the winter afternoon. One brave sailboat plied the waves, racing along the edge of the bay in a sweeping turn, its wake a slurry of white foam and gray water. 'So he feels horrible, he knows he's dying, and I tell him my mother ran off with a Dallas embezzler with mob ties who ended up dead?' Whit shook his head. 'Maybe the Bellinis caught and killed them both but dumped her body elsewhere.'

'And a woman who looks like her happens to leave Bozeman the same day?' Claudia said gently. 'Let's say she took the money. She killed Powell, or guilt or fear ate him up and he killed himself, and so she ran with the money.'

'Yes,' Harry said. 'Great minds, Claudia. She had a few choices. One, come home.'

'She didn't do that,' Whit said.

'Two, run. Always waiting for the Bellinis to catch up with her.'

'That seems the logical choice,' Claudia said.

'Yeah, and y'all might never find her again,' Harry said. 'Or three. She went to the Bellinis to return the money, to take the heat off of her, to cut a deal.'

'Huge risk,' Claudia said.

Harry slipped another set of stapled papers from a file. 'Yes. Tony Largo was a loan shark in Dallas who'd been close to James Powell. He turned to the Feds about ten years after Powell died. Said word on the street was the Bellinis were looking for Powell but never found him. And the Bellinis fell from power a few years back.' Harry opened another file. 'The Feds could never get the hard financial evidence against them for racketeering charges. Big Tommy Bellini, the head of the ring, cleans up after himself better than an anal-retentive maid. The meanest, baddest, most vicious SOB in Detroit crime circles, but the one who maintained the lowest profile. Until two years ago. Then he kills another boss without permission, books himself on freaking *Good Morning Detroit* and disclaims any knowledge about the killings. Grabs way too much attention. So he basically gets kicked out of the mob. The other families can't whack him, but they can't work with him any further because he's damaged goods. His wife used to be a Texas debutante, came from old money, so they head back to her home turf in Houston. He sets himself up as an importer of fine textiles, rugs, art, and so on. Totally legit, and he was being watched very carefully. He's probably importing white powder and hash, but what do I know? Houston police roughed him up once, and he sued their asses into the ground, and he won a million-dollar settlement, and so I don't know how hard they looked at him afterwards.' Harry pulled out a newspaper clipping. 'A month ago he had a stroke at the wheel of his Jaguar on the Gulf freeway and crashed. Badly. Two of his buddies were killed. Tommy Bellini's been in a coma ever since.'

Whit tore the wet napkin under his beer in strips.

Harry leaned back. 'Eve Michaels' car ends up in Des Moines. It's on the way to Detroit from Denver. She wasn't running away, she was running *toward* something.'

'Or the Bellinis caught up with her and killed her,' Whit said. His voice was hoarse.

'And she's long dead. Or they might be grateful to her. And possibly she wanted something from them,' Harry said.

'What?' Whit said.

'A new life,' Harry said. 'You want me to see if there's a connection between Eve Michaels and the Bellinis? It's a thin chance, but it's about all I got left to check.'

'This could be worse than Pandora's box,' Whit said. 'The mob. Jesus.'

'I'm not afraid of these people, Judge,' Harry said. 'Okay, well maybe a little. Because I'm not foolish. I can go to Detroit tonight.'

'Detroit? What about Houston?'

'She might have stayed in Detroit once his organization fell apart there. But I'll try Houston as well.'

Whit nodded at Harry. 'Find her. Please.'

On the way back to Port Leo, they stopped at the Nueces County morgue for Whit to pick up autopsy results on a drowning victim who had been pulled from St Leo Bay. As justice of the peace for Encina County, Whit also performed coroner's duties, ruling on cause of death and conducting death inquests, but the autopsies were performed by the pros in nearby Nueces County. Whit read the report as Claudia navigated through the traffic heading north out of Corpus Christi. The dead man was Lance Gartner, a young grad student from Austin who had gotten raving drunk visiting cousins in Port Leo, taken a rowboat out in the bay in the middle of the night, freebased heroin, fallen overboard and drowned. He was twenty-three. A life wadded up and thrown away.

'Shame about that man,' she said as he put the autopsy file away.

'Yes. I don't think his family knew about the heroin use.' Sad silence hung between them. 'Busy day tomorrow. I've got a full docket in small-claims court and then two days' worth of juvenile court coming up this week. Get to have surly teenagers attempt to explain idiot behavior for hours on end. Time I could be spending with my dad instead.'

'I know. Why don't you take time off from work, be with him more?'

Whit said, 'And not waste time trying to find my mother.'

'Your father only has a while, Whit. Who cares about your mother? She's hardly more than a concept to you,' Claudia said. 'If Harry's theory is true, she was bent if she wanted a life with embezzlers and mobsters. If she is still with these people, then she won't want contact from you and they won't want you bothering her. She's not worth five minutes of your time.'

'I don't care what she or anyone else wants,' Whit said.

'Whit, end this now. Tell Harry you changed your mind.'

Now he looked at her. 'I have to know, Claudia.'

'You're up for election in another couple of years. You want the voters knowing your mother might have been involved in a murder?'

'Are you going to publicize it? Fast way to get a fresh face to work death investigations with you.'

She gave him a quick sideways smile. 'I would never breathe a word. But you know politics.'

'If someone else wants to run inquests and juvenile court and small-claims court that bad, let them splatter me with mud. But that's not what you're worried about, is it?'

'Promise me,' she said. 'You'll wait to hear from Harry before you do anything.'

'You're afraid I'm going to run up to Houston, check out the Bellinis. See if I can find her myself if Harry backs out?'

'I know you. Let Harry handle this. Be patient. Stay out of it, Whit, please. Promise me.'

'My family was never much good in the promises department,' Whit said. 'But I won't do anything you wouldn't approve of, okay, worrywart?'

Claudia knew it was all she would get, and she silently wished that Harry found no trace of Eve Michaels.

2

When the strippers showed up, Eve Michaels knew the business deal was done and the Bellini family was going to get burned.

The negotiation dinner in one of Club Topaz's private suites started winding down early, about ten, not nearly soon enough for Eve. She was bone-tired and ready for the deal to close. She suspected Paul Bellini was ready, too; she saw as the table was being cleared that the two strippers, fresh from performing downstairs, were waiting outside the suite. It was a subtle difference between Tommy Bellini and his son. Tommy would have been much more discreet with his whores. Tonight, when it mattered most that Paul be focused, he was thinking with his little soldier again. Cut a fast and possibly disadvantageous deal so the partying could begin.

Tonight the guests were a couple of Miami drug dealers in Houston for a five-million-dollar score, and behind the smiles Eve decided they were judging how much tattered flesh remained on the bones of the Bellini organization. The night had begun with business when the six of them sat down at the table and Eve put on her best poker face.

'So you've got five million worth of coke to sell,' Paul said. He was making his voice a low growl. On purpose. Eve didn't look at him. Embarrassed.

'Yeah. But we can supply you even more, if our deal works out.' The head Miami guy, Kiko Grace, took a hit off his cigar, blew a stream of Cuban smoke above the table. The cigar fit in with the rest of him: tailored dark Italian suit, black hair trimmed in an expertly stylish cut, shoes polished so you could see your reflection in the calfskin. He had a small, delicate mole near the corner of his mouth, more like a woman's beauty mark, the only softening feature on his hard face.

'We're bringing in sixty-plus kilos this week to see how it goes with you all. We can double it, triple it, no problem.' Kiko's voice was buttery-smooth, satisfied, like the deal was done. 'But we want to be sure you can distribute fast enough for our volume. We can't work with an organization who can't sell it effectively.'

'Our problem is you're asking a premium price for the coke,' Eve said quietly. 'That hurts our margins.' Paul glanced at her, as though he'd forgotten she was in the room.

'Rethink your margins, Eve. You got suppliers lining up to work with you?' Kiko said. He touched the little mole on his cheek. 'No one's eager to have more deals canceled because your organization took a body blow. I know and you know I'm doing you a favor.'

Eve glanced at her boyfriend, Frank, sitting next to her, but he had eyes only for the merlot in his glass.

'Don't misunderstand me. We're sorry about your dad, Paul,' Kiko said.

'Thanks,' Paul said.

'He was a great man,' Kiko said. Eve didn't like the *was*. 'But with him down, a couple of his lieutenants dead, there's not a lot of confidence that you can keep the streets supplied. You don't want to be the Mom-and-Pop store when the dealers prefer mega-store, you see what I'm saying? We're here to help. Give you a chance to really thrive by giving you a steady supply for your dealers.'

'All out of the goodness of your heart,' Eve said. Kiko gave her a crooked smile.

'I like you,' he said. 'You're about as blunt as my mama. No, not out of the goodness of my heart. Out of a desire for profits.'

Eve started to negotiate a point about margins but Paul said, 'Houston's our territory. Just so we're clear.' Accepting the pricing structure, moving on to the next item on the agenda.

'That's all cool,' Kiko said. 'We've got no interest in invasions. Miami keeps us plenty busy.'

'When would you need the money for the first shipment?' Paul said, and Eve bit her bottom lip. Frank gave off a soft wine belch and smiled at José, Kiko's sideman. Eve didn't like José; he said little and watched faces like he was studying a map. He was short and squat, with a plain face and heavy cheeks, but his eyes were in constant motion, watching Eve, then Frank, then the rest of the table. He flicked the nail of his stubby thumb with each of his fingers in turn, like he was ticking off seconds from an internal clock. Playing dumb muscle but smart under the skin. He made Eve nervous.

'Five million even. In cash. By Thursday afternoon,' Kiko said. 'We've got the shipment already here. Hidden in imported pottery that's listed as antique on the manifest.' He laughed. 'It's junk. Break open the bases and there's a half kilo in each one. Stashed near the port. It's safe as a baby.'

'Deal,' Paul said.

Eve took a tiny sip of red wine. Done without discussing it with her in private, and all she could do now was try to protect them in this new alliance. She glanced over at Paul's new right-hand man, the guy who looked like a corporate drone. He was wearing a Brooks Brothers suit, pink Oxford shirt, navy tie. Like he was here to bring a kid to a prep school interview or negotiate a low-level bank deal. Everyone called him Bucks, short for Buckman, his last name, but more because he was supposed to be brilliant about new ways to make money. Eve hadn't seen a single glow of smartness yet.

Bucks gave her a stern look back that said *keep your mouth shut*. Frank, always the host, raised his glass and said, 'Here's to good business,' and they all clinked glasses together.

Kiko smiled at her as her wineglass touched his, like he could smell her disapproval and didn't care.

The deal done, they dipped into the food: the thick steaks brought up from the club's kitchen, salads crisscrossed with blue cheese, two-fisted baked potatoes crowned with cheese and chives. She nibbled at a chef salad, her appetite gone.

Five million. She had five million cleaned and sitting in twenty-two different accounts in the Caymans that she could transfer back to a bank in Houston. The only clean money they had and Paul had spent it all in a minute. The revenue streams were drying up, the muscle not yet loyal to Paul while his dad lay dying, and now their cash reserve was in play with people they'd never worked with before.

'Hey, Frank,' Kiko said. 'Sing a little. Give us a few bars of "Baby, You're My Groove."'

'Please don't,' Paul said. 'We've all heard it about nine million fucking times.'

'That's because it's a timeless classic,' Frank said. He was on his fifth glass of wine.

'Yeah, it gets timeless about every ten years, when disco gets rediscovered,' Bucks said. 'Then it gets un-timeless, real fast. What he won't tell us is how much money he's made off it.'

'I was an artist,' Frank said. 'Money was for agents to worry about. Not my groove.'

'The only groove Frank has,' Eve said, 'is the one his rocking chair's wearing in the floor.'

'Yet you love me still,' Frank said, and she smiled because it was true.

'The folks that make Viagra need to use this for their theme song,' Paul said. 'Pay you a big-ass licensing fee.'

'Silence, please, respect for the artist,' Frank said, and he stood and sang, a capella, the well-known refrain:

> *I'm just saying what's in my heart*
> *Been there from the very start*
> *And it sure 'nough's not some move*
> *'cause baby you're my groove*
> *Baby you're my grooooove . . .*

Eve smiled at Frank as he sat back down and everyone applauded, José whistling through his teeth. Bucks clapped but not like he meant it. The voice was still there, worn, but clear as a bell; a tenor smooth as melting chocolate.

'Voice of an angel, still,' Eve said.

'An old-fart angel,' Frank said, but she could see he was pleased, a tiny stage better than none.

'Man, you ought to do one of those disco reunion tours,' Kiko said.

'Nah,' Frank said. 'Club keeps me too busy. Plus they'd probably make me share a dressing room with the Village People, and ain't no way.'

'But rejuvenating your singing career,' Bucks said. 'That's a worthy goal.'

'Yeah, why don't you draw me up one of your action plans, son,' Frank said. He turned to Kiko. 'Bucks here is a human day planner. Got more goals than a soccer tournament.'

'Does he now,' Kiko said.

'Goals are vital,' Bucks said. 'Goals help us actualize—'

Paul interrupted like he'd heard the words one time too many before. 'Kiko, got a couple of fine girls who can come in and dance for you. There's a worthy goal.'

Bucks shut his mouth, like a switch had been flipped.

Kiko smiled. 'No thanks, man. But I'd like a quick tour of the club, if Frank here would show us around. See who's famous downstairs tonight.'

'You sure you don't want a little private performance?' Paul asked, drawing out *performance* into way more than a hint.

'I got a wife pregnant back in Miami,' Kiko said. 'But appreciate the hospitality.'

'How about you, José?'

José shook his head. 'No, thank you.' Declining because his boss did, Eve thought.

'Sure. That's fine,' Paul said. A little disappointed such a generous offer had been refused, Eve could tell. 'So the money,' he said. 'We'll get it for you, deliver it tomorrow night.' Today was Wednesday.

'Tomorrow afternoon would be better,' Kiko said. 'Why wait?'

'We have to move it from overseas. Tomorrow night,' Paul said, asserting himself too little too late, and Kiko, having won every other point that mattered, gave a slight nod. They stood. Eve rose to go but Paul said, 'Eve, stay a moment, please,' and she sat down, watching Frank, Kiko, and José leave. Bucks stayed at the table.

Paul said, 'Bucks, go downstairs and count boobs, okay? Tell the strippers to wait a minute outside.'

'You're in trouble, queen bee,' Bucks said as he went out the door and Eve felt the blood leave her face.

'What's the matter, Paul?' she said.

'I want to hear your opinion,' he said, ignoring her question.

'They're asking too much for the coke. Our profit's too thin. And they sure as hell want to get their foot in here. Kiko's ambitious. Houston's a workable market for him. The Dominicans here, they've already got ties back to Florida gangs. He could negotiate a separate peace with them. And cut us out. Easy.'

'You thinking everyone's trying to tear us down . . .'

'They are, Paul.' She leaned forward, covered his hand with her own. 'They are, honey. We're vulnerable. Any time there's a power shift, here come the wolves. We need to do several smaller deals, boost our revenues and our profit margins, not cut one big deal with a guy we've never worked with before.'

'You think I can't handle this?'

'You may not realize how weak we are right now. No one gets a second chance with deals like these.'

'This puts us back on top. Get the five million,' he said. 'And Bucks will handle the exchange with Kiko.'

The air in the room felt weighted with smoke, with the world starting to take a left turn. Tommy would have had her handle the exchange. But she said, 'Okay.'

'Change is coming, Eve,' he said. 'Nothing for you or Frank to worry about. I'm gonna take good care of you both. But we're gonna rethink business priorities. My dad, bless him, he wasn't growth-minded. Bogged us down in too many small deals. You're worried about Miami horning in here. They should be worried about me horning in on them.'

'Paul, baby, reality check.'

'How about a reality check on your part, Eve? Who works for who here?'

'I'm trying to give you perspective so you make an informed decision, honey.'

'The decision's made.' Paul Bellini cleared his throat, put on a smile. 'You think I'm such a horse's ass, then you can help Frank with running the club day-to-day.'

To her it wasn't far removed from a job flipping burgers. 'You don't need me and Frank for real work, we'll go back to Detroit. I don't care much for Texas, to be honest.'

'Eve, of course I need you.' He eased back in his chair a little bit. Wriggling his butt into the throne. He was twenty-four and he didn't know his ass from a hole in the ground. Worse, he didn't know what he didn't know. 'As long as you support our new directions.'

She saw she couldn't win. Being put out to pasture, her and Frank both. She had known Paul his entire life and he looked at her with all the interest he'd give yesterday's paper. 'How does Kiko want the cash?'

'Nothing bigger than a fifty,' he said. 'Who you gonna work with?'

'Richard Doyle at Coastal United,' she said. 'He's safe.'

'Yeah, if the doggies ain't running,' Paul said with a laugh. 'Go find Frank, rescue him from Miami Vice. Tell Bucks to take 'em back to their place. And send the girls in, would you? Kiko's shy but I'm sure not.'

What a nice guy he'd turned into since his dad's accident. She stood.

'And Eve. I noticed your body language while I was cutting the deal. Bucks saw it, too. I want your opinion, I'll ask for it. Otherwise, smile and sit still like you're happy.'

If Big Tommy was here and heard him talking to her that way, he'd backhand Paul across the room. But she said, 'Sure, Paul, sure,' and kept her gaze to the floor. She closed the suite door after her.

The two dancers, the tall one they called Red Robin and a stunning black girl named Tasha, chatted in the hall, wearing their stupid theme costumes. Frank wouldn't let the girls simply strip, no, they had to be characters. Red Robin had a leather bikini with cowboy fringe, a holster with little fake pearl-handled revolvers, and a white Stetson. Tasha wore a bra covered with CDs, and a miniature flat fake computer screen mounted in front of her crotch. A computer mouse's cord wound around her throat like a necklace, the mouse resting atop mountainous breasts. Eve wondered how much the gear weighed. She'd heard Paul was hot for this one.

'Y'all can go in now,' Eve said.

Red Robin did, already swaying her hips to the downstairs music, but Tasha stopped. 'Hi, Eve, how are you doing?' Tasha spoke with the clean enunciation of an actress. No street about her.

'Fine, honey,' Eve said with a thin smile.

'I wanted to talk to you . . . you know a lot about money, right?'

'Depends.'

'Well, Paul said you knew how to hide cash. So you don't have to pay taxes on it.'

'Paul's mistaken.' Eve jerked her head toward the door. 'And he's waiting for you.'

'Sure, Eve. No offense meant.' Tasha went inside, shutting the door behind her.

Eve stood alone in the thin light of the hall. Paul deciding deals involving millions – *millions* – and shutting her out. Now an uppity big-titted dancer wanting tips on taxes because Paul mouthed off about cleaning money, a topic his father never would have discussed with a girlfriend.

A little pulse of nausea seeped into her guts. She hadn't wanted to come to Houston, God no, swearing never to set foot in Texas again, but Tommy had insisted she and Frank come to Houston with him when the other mob bosses forced him out of Detroit. Connecting a minor celebrity like Frank to the Topaz had been sheer genius for generating interest and crowds and giving it a more respectable sheen. Then the stroke took out Tommy and now Paul was risking everything they'd built.

Eve walked down the flight of red-carpeted stairs. Club Topaz was in full swing, a cramped city of men. In the dim light a trio of women danced on three different runways, all three of them stunningly beautiful. Throngs of men, and even a few women, were in the crowd. It was big business for a Wednesday night. In one corner a group of young Astros whooped and hollered. In another corner a Houston Rocket and a couple of visiting Dallas Mavericks enjoyed synchronized lap dances by a pair of Swedish twins. Near the main stage, ogling a pole-dancing double-D brunette, was a local actor who'd hit it big in a movie last year and scored an Oscar nomination. And of course, around them, a locust swarm of everyday guys, drawn by knowing that athletes and actors and the famous would be on display as much as the supple thighs and perfected breasts.

Did you all not get enough tit as kids? Eve wondered as she moved through the crowd, looking for Frank. Apparently the tour had slowed to enjoy the attractions. She found Frank, Kiko, and José at a front table, a chesty Latina dancing for Kiko, with a plumage of folded twenties on her thonged ass.

Eve leaned down and said into Frank's ear, 'Paul says give them to Bucks. And I'm ready to go home. Excuse yourself from the table in ten minutes and I'll be in your office.' Frank nodded.

She worked her way back through the crowd and went upstairs, to Frank's spacious office. It was more for meeting and greeting than for reviewing liquor inventory or interviewing staff or talent. Plush chairs, a mahogany table, the inevitable photos of Frank Polo glad-handing every notable who passed through the club doors.

She sat behind his desk, put her face in her hands, and wished that Tommy Bellini wasn't laid up in a bed for the rest of his life. It had been him thirty years ago that she'd met to return the money that James Powell had stolen. For a chance at even greater money, and Tommy had not disappointed. Tommy had liked her, brought her into the organization, given her responsibility, power, and protection. And a life free of cloying attachments.

But Paul was why monarchy fell out of favor. You could have a king with an idiot son and piss away the empire in no time flat and leave the loyal subjects with no jobs. And one did not walk away from the Bellini family with all the information Eve had. You didn't list on your résumé the millions of dollars you laundered or how many hits you knew the Bellinis had ordered. Frank was already relegated to being the club's frontman; God knew what job Paul would give her, probably stuck in a back office counting bar receipts.

If he doesn't kill you.

She had been afraid of Tommy, of course. The fear kept you

alive, the caution of every step you took. He could be kind, generous even, but if you crossed him, you lost money, you lost a finger, you lost your life. He held himself to high standards of performance. Paul wanted respect he couldn't yet command and seemed to have little regard for her or her abilities. Piss him off and she would sink like a stone in the waters of the Ship Channel, sporting concrete sandals and three bullets in her head, one for each decade of service.

The door opened and Bucks stepped inside. He shut the door behind him, gave her a bright, snappy smile.

'Don't you know to knock?' she said.

'This isn't your office.'

'No, it's my boyfriend's office. What do you want?'

'Peace and quiet,' he said. 'This place is too loud. Not conducive to clear contemplation.' Bucks sat down on the leather sofa like he was used to lounging in the office.

'Shouldn't you be guarding Paul?'

'From what? Attack of the killer tits?' Bucks said.

'That tall redhead up there, Robin? I thought you were sweet on her.'

'She's sweet on me. There's a difference. Plus how involved am I really gonna get with a stripper? I can't take her home to mama.'

'I was unaware you had such lofty morals.'

'All this lust, it shows a lack of discipline and self-control.' Bucks leaned back against the leather. 'You handle Paul's money. Makes you important right now. Seems to me I ought to be protecting you more than him.'

'I'm feeling safe, thanks.'

'Chad Channing says you can never feel safe because complacency blocks you from your goals.'

She didn't know who Chad Channing was and didn't care.

'So you giving our friends any money?' he asked.

She let a beat pass. 'No. You are. Paul wants you to handle the exchange, honey.'

'Naturally.'

This guy had Paul's ear, so she decided to try. 'This deal, Bucks,

I have serious reservations about it. These guys are looking for a back door into Houston. They'll crush Paul soon as they get their foot in the door.'

'Paul and I can handle them,' Bucks said. 'Look at Kiko and José. They don't have four neurons between them. Bet neither one of them even got beyond high school.'

'Baby, getting a degree means you spent less time learning the actual business we're in,' Eve said.

'This seems like every other business I studied at Wharton.'

'You won't find an MBA case study on the Bellinis.'

'So what do you recommend?'

'Find out a little more. Why they've approached us. Why aren't they dealing this coke in Florida?'

'Or take a shortcut,' Bucks said. 'Kill them and steal their coke. That'd be one way to sweeten the deal.' He gave her a crooked, half-mad smile.

Eve stared at him.

'You ever seen a frijole popped? They lose all command of their English. Blabbering all this Spanish bullshit, begging for their lives. Doesn't occur to them I don't speak Spanish, so it's not help-ing their cause any.' Bucks leaned forward, put his elbows on his legs.

'Killing people on a whim is what got the Bellinis in trouble before.'

'I might fire your ass on a whim.' Like the power was his.

'Honey,' she said. 'I'd watch how you talk to me. I'm higher up than you in this family, and I'm telling Paul what you said about killing them.' She picked up the phone, dialed the extension for the private suite. Bucks yanked the phone away from her, shoved her back onto the floor. Then he was on top of her, his fingers working into her neck. Not closing around her throat but digging into the flesh.

'I was joking about popping them. I'm not joking now,' Bucks said. Pain exploded from her neck, coursed along her arms, her chest. 'See what I got here? This is all the flesh around the carotid. Now. I start to squeeze, the lights go dim. I shut it off and that's all you wrote. Or I nick it . . . just so . . . and we have a mess on

Frank's nice rug.' He brought his lips close to her ear, the weight of him crushing the breath out of her. 'You. Don't. Fuck. With. Me. You understand?'

'I . . . understand,' she said, large black circles dotting her vision.

He got up, helped her to her feet, eased her into a chair. She watched as he went to the bar and poured a glass of water, brought it to her. 'You'll have a distinctive bruise tomorrow.' Like he was proud. 'Wear a nice scarf. You got one?'

She nodded, stunned. She took the water.

Bucks knelt down before her, put both his hands on her knees. The intimacy of it was worse than hitting her.

'Now let's be friends,' he said.

She nodded, but seething, suddenly more mad than afraid. 'I understand you and Paul,' she said. 'I understand the juice you got in your blood right now. This is exciting. Way more exciting than energy trading, right?'

Bucks gave a slow nod.

'But these guys, they will kill you and Paul without missing a heartbeat. They won't grab your neck and play around. They'll shoot you dead and not think about it again for the rest of their lives.'

'That's why I should kill those guys and get their goods. Now.'

'That would start a war we couldn't win.'

'You've got to start thinking big, Eve.'

She couldn't help it. 'You've got to start thinking, period.'

Bucks frowned at her. His hand moved to his back where she knew he wore his pistol under his jacket. 'You're not being a team player, Eve, and I can't support this negativity. It ends now.'

The office door opened, Frank stumbling inside, the Miami wiseguys in tow.

'Hey,' Frank said. 'They want to see that photo of me singing with Donna Summer.'

Bucks stood and smiled, easing his hand away from his holster, folding his arms across his chest. 'Great. Then you boys ready for a ride back to your condo? Me and Eve are done talking for the night.' He grinned at her. 'This is gonna be our best deal ever, isn't it, Eve?'

She nodded slowly, putting her hand on her throat and hating him.

3

A hundred and seventy miles south of Houston, Whit Mosley couldn't sleep, and he walked from the guest house he lived in at the back of his father's property, past the blue quiet of the pool, up to the main house. His father, Babe, sat at the kitchen table, finishing a chocolate milkshake, eating the sweet slurry with a spoon.

'Hey,' Babe said. 'You want one?'

'No,' Whit said. 'You won't sleep if you eat that.'

'Sleep is a thief of time.'

Whit sat down across from his father. 'Irina asleep?'

'Zonked.' Irina was his father's much younger wife, a year or two younger than Whit, wife number five, a Russian girl Babe had met through a marriage-oriented service and brought to Port Leo from Moscow. 'She's tired all the time. Tired of me being sick.' He shrugged. 'She won't have that much longer to worry about it.'

'Daddy.'

'Whit, it's okay.' No self-pity colored Babe's voice. 'She's too young for death, to be a widow.' He licked chocolate from his spoon, ran a hand over the blondish gray stubble on his head. 'She'll go on. And she'll always love me. But she ain't gonna go back to Russia, and she don't have her citizenship yet, so if she remarries kind of quick, don't hold it against her.' He clinked his spoon back into the glass.

'Can we talk about my mother for a minute?'

'Not with food in my mouth. What brought her up?'

'I want to know if there's anything you never told us about her,' Whit said. 'For example, did she cheat on you?'

29

'What possible difference would any of this make now?'

'Don't shield me. There's no point in it.'

'I believe she did. She got bored with me, frustrated with having so many kids so quick. I never had proof.'

'You ever hear the name James Powell?'

Babe shook his head. 'What you up to, Whitman?'

'Nothing.' Whit picked up his father's ice cream glass, rinsed it out in the sink.

'Who the hell is James Powell?'

'Nobody. You ever think about my mother? Wonder if she's alive?'

'Rarely.' Regret in his voice, as though this admission meant weakness.

Whit didn't look at Babe as he loaded the dishwasher. 'You ever want to see her again?'

A long silence took hold, the kind that carries a weight with it.

Finally Babe said: 'This will sound nuts, but Ellen probably thinks about us more than I think about her, shug.'

'But she left us. She didn't care about us.'

'Whit, you won't remember this, but most of the time she was a real good mother. She held on to you boys tight. Like a life preserver. You all were her chance for normalcy. A life like people are supposed to have. But she liked . . . excitement. Once, right after we were married, I had to go up to the bank in Rockport. We pull up and she said, out of the blue, Babe, what if we robbed it? She had this glittery look in her eye. Like she was hoping to be Bonnie and I was gonna be Clyde. She gave me this sideways glance I'll never forget. We went to Vegas on our honeymoon and she's pregnant, I come back from the bathroom and she's betting a grand – all our gambling money – on a single blackjack hand. She won and I got her the hell away from the table. It scared me. And the years after that I'm filling her up with babies and I guess that wasn't excitement enough.' He shrugged. 'Finally she left. But you can't leave a large family and pretend they never happened. I figure she died a long while back, otherwise she would have called you and your brothers.'

'You said I don't remember her,' Whit said. 'But I remember her scent. I never knew it was gardenia until I was older. I didn't imagine it, did I?'

Babe nodded, smiled. 'Yeah. She used a soap that smelled like gardenia.'

'Why did you marry her?' Whit realized he had never asked before.

'Because we got pregnant with Teddy. But the reason I loved her was . . .' Babe stopped. 'She'd walk into a room crowded with people and read it in an instant, like a map. Know who was mad at who, who was wanting who, hardly without two words being spoken. It was funny to me that she could do that. A little hypnotic, too. And she was smart. Pretty but not bitchy about her looks. After she was pregnant, and we'd only known each other about six months, marrying seemed like a fine idea. I loved her and she would have been a great partner in business. I figured I wasn't gonna do no better.'

'You didn't feel trapped?'

'No.' Babe shook his head. 'Sure, I had money, and she didn't, but Ellen trapped herself. Wanted to be tied down. Forced herself into a structured life. Her mom and her weren't much more than vagabonds, working jobs up and down the coast. She never knew her dad and her mama died right after Teddy was born, you know. I really didn't have anyone else to ask about her. After she left, we all sort of felt we'd been fooled into knowing her.'

'She got tired of normal.'

'She never appreciated normal.' Babe stood. 'Shug, I'm gonna go and sleep next to my beautiful, sweet wife and not talk about Ellen any more.'

'Would you want to see her, Daddy?' Whit asked.

'You mean see her face-to-face?'

'Yeah.'

'Yes,' he said after a moment. 'I would. I don't wish her ill. But I would like to know what was so goddamned more important than you boys. If she wanted to leave me . . . fine. But you boys only got one mama. She stole the most precious thing in the world from you and your brothers, Whit, and you deserve an explanation. An apology.'

'I don't need her apologies,' Whit said. 'Perhaps you do.'

'It's water on the moon to me.' Babe stretched his thin arms above his head. Whit's throat thickened. His father looked the worst he had since his drowning-in-drink days. The healthy glow of long-term sobriety had been replaced by the dimming paleness of the enemy within, chewing through his father's liver.

'You're like your mother,' Babe said. 'I don't mean it bad. But she had to kick over the anthill to see what would happen. You're the same.'

'We could look for her. So you could know what happened to her.'

'Asking if I want to see her and actually trying to track her down are two different things, Whit. I wouldn't waste my limited time on Ellen. I'm invoking the I'm-dying-so-I-get-to-be-an-asshole clause. I forbid you to look for her. In case you're considering it.'

'I never read that clause.'

'Respect my wishes. Please.'

'All right,' Whit said. He could change his father's mind later, if Harry Chyme found his mother. He knew he could. He hadn't heard from Harry in a week. 'It's all hypothetical, anyway.'

'I'll see you in the morning. Love you, shug.' Said more often now, in the sunset of life.

'I love you, too.' Whit watched his father leave the kitchen, in his slow, tired shuffle.

I don't have much time left to find her, Whit thought. Not much at all.

4

Paul Bellini liked to watch the girls dancing in the smoky, thin light. The tall redhead, Robin, was the best technical dancer of all the performers. Bucks liked her but wasn't serious about her, and Paul'd called her up to the private suite to be sure she knew he was top dog. The other was the regal black girl, who danced wearing that custom-fitted computer gear on her body under the name 'Geekgirl.' The audience loved her. She kept her eyes locked on his eyes as she danced, perhaps as excited by the sight of him as he was by her. He took another long swig of Scotch as Red Robin doffed her leather bikini top and dropped it on the floor.

He unzipped his pants, pulled out his penis, hardening in his hand.

'Wait a damn second,' Geekgirl said. She stopped dancing.

'Keep dancing, baby,' Paul said. 'In a minute you can get down on your knees and do your best.'

'Oh, can I?' she said. 'I don't think so.'

'Don't be snooty,' Red Robin said with a good-natured laugh and shimmy. 'Paul's fun.'

'Not me,' Geekgirl said. She crossed her arms over her bikini top. 'I'm not your whore. So fire me. I'm not worried about keeping my job in a place that's getting robbed blind.'

Paul didn't get mad. He grinned, put himself back into his khakis, set his Scotch down on the table. 'Hey, Robin, go outside for a minute. Let me talk to your friend.'

Robin picked up the leather top, tucked her ample breasts back into it, turned and walked out of the room without another word. The black girl stood there, moved her hands onto her wide hips, frowning.

'You know who I am?' Paul said.

'Yeah. You're Paul Bellini.'

He laughed but without humor. 'I own the club. And if I want you to dance for me, then suck me off, sweetheart, that's what you do.'

She sat down, crossed her legs. 'Actually, no, I don't. And if you don't pull your head out of your ass, sweetpea, you won't have a club to play around in. Quit worrying about your dick. I told you you're getting robbed blind and you're worrying about whether or not you get a blow job tonight.'

Paul shook his head and grinned. He'd have her arms broken in about five minutes. 'What's your name?'

'Geekgirl.'

'Your real name.'

'Tasha Strong.'

'You got a smart mouth, Tasha.'

'I only use it for talking,' she said.

'So who's robbing me?' Amusement in his voice.

'Frank Polo.'

'Ah. For how much?'

'Up to ten thousand a week.'

Paul tongued his lip. 'And how do you know this, Miss CPA?'

'Most of the girls dancing in here, they're sweet but not really planning their careers or futures. Like Robin. They're now people. I'm a tomorrow kind of person. I keep my eyes open. I notice details. Like when I'm doing private dances in the suites for a bunch of drunk lawyers, Frank's charging five grand on the credit card. But he's reporting four grand on the books. That other thousand, it's getting funneled into his pocket. That kind of money adds up real quick.'

'You're serious.' Paul's face grew hot.

'I looked on his computer,' she said. 'Compared it to the credit slips I saw after my dances over the past month. I kept a little record in my head.'

'Those files are supposed to be passworded,' he said.

'They are. It didn't stop me.' She shrugged. 'His password is *groove*. That was a real toughie to figure out.' She pointed to the

34

CDs on her breasts. 'I do the Geekgirl gig 'cause I used to work with computers.'

'And now you're a stripper?'

'Job market's better. And you got to follow your dreams.' He couldn't tell if she was being sarcastic. 'Can I have a sip of your Scotch?' she asked.

Paul handed her the glass, watched her take a dainty sip, cradle the crystal in her hands. God, she was stunning. 'You had a stray impulse to look at the books?' he asked.

'Paul – can I call you Paul?'

'Yeah, sure.' He had decided to wait on breaking her arms.

'I figured I could.' Tasha smiled. 'With your daddy in such bad shape, your mind's occupied. You don't realize people around here are jockeying for positions. Seeing where they can take advantage of you. Seeing where they think you're weak.'

'I'm not weak.'

'I didn't say you were. I said where they think you're weak.' She rose, set the Scotch down next to him, eased herself down into his lap. 'And the club is a weak point.' She started to rub his temples slightly. His erection returned, full force, despite the talk of lost money, with this weird-irritating-beautiful woman sitting on his lap.

'The club makes a fortune,' he said.

She squirmed ever so slightly against him. 'Oh, it does. So it's going to attract attention. You got every male celebrity comes through Houston stopping off here. You got thousands being spent every night. You got the best-looking women in Texas dancing on your stage and doing private entertainments in the rooms.' She kissed him once, feathery light, and when she pulled away he leaned a little toward her, wanting more. 'But you got too much money being spent, too much being skimmed, too much sex being sold. It's gonna . . . explode.' She leaned down, kissed him again, let her tongue tease against his.

'I shut the club down, you'll be out of a job.'

'Give me a new job,' Tasha Strong said. 'I'm gonna finish dancing for you. Then I'm gonna screw you good tonight. But because I want to. You try to give me money, I slap you into

35

tomorrow. I like you. I like your smile.' She ran a finger along his lips. He stopped her with his hand.

'You've talked a lot,' he said, and he put an edge in his voice, the way his father used to. He liked, no, *loved* the way she was talking to him but he couldn't let her see that. 'Where's the proof against Frank?'

'In your computers. I copied the files. In case Frank or Eve get wise . . .'

'Eve's in on this?'

'She's got twice the brains Frank does. No way she doesn't know he's skimming.' Tasha Strong unhooked one of the CDs off her top. 'I'm wearing the proof, baby.' Her other hand strayed down to his crotch. 'You want to go home with me and start it up?'

Bucks suddenly realized he was outnumbered.

Chauffeuring the Miami dumbasses wasn't a big deal but he realized, as he pulled out into the thick traffic of Westheimer, he should have brought a buddy to watch his back. It was two against one. But Kiko and José were laughing, a little drunk, rating the dancers as if jiggling were an Olympic event. He decided to take the long way home, wanting to hear what they might say about the deal. He pulled onto Loop 610, taking it toward I-10 East, which would lead toward the glittering towers of downtown Houston. He loved the city, loved its happy chaos, loved the way people drove like maniacs, loved the way the humid air held endless opportunity, even in the bad suck-ass years. Houston made you tough, tough to grab the chances that came your way, tough enough to persevere when the world soured.

Kiko leaned over the dashboard, fiddled with the tape player, and suddenly Chad Channing's confident voice filled the air. 'Make your goals your friends, not your enemies. They are not to be challenged or overcome. They are to be embraced. Love your goals as you love yourself.'

'What's this peace, love, and understanding?' José called from the back seat.

'It's Chad Channing,' Kiko said. 'Don't you ever watch info-mercials, man? He sells thousands of these tapes to' – he paused as though searching for the word that would not insult – 'people who need a little boost.'

'Discover the goals within yourself as you discover your love for yourself,' Chad purred on the tape. 'They're right under the skin, in fact. We're all motivated by goals we haven't even discovered or articulated yet.'

'It's better than coffee for getting me going,' Bucks said, but suddenly he felt a little uncool. He felt Kiko's gaze on him, amused, and he swallowed a thick lump in his throat. He clicked off the tape.

'Oh, man, I wanted to hear more,' José said. 'I haven't had a good arti-cu-lation in a long while.'

'Hey, José, this tape is Bucks' secret weapon,' Kiko said. 'How he stays so cool, so tough, all the time.' Like it was funny.

'That's right.' Bucks kept his voice steady. Greasy little bastards. He hated them both with a blackness that filled his chest. Thought they were clever when they were not worth the grit under his shoe.

As he merged onto I-10 Bucks felt a tickle at the back of his neck. He glanced into the rearview mirror and saw José smiling at him. Kiko, sitting in the passenger's seat, said, 'Because you're so tough and cool, Mr Tight-Ass Executive, I know you aren't going to freak.'

The barrel of a pistol. That was the tickle along his nape. José held the Sig up so Bucks could see it, then put it back at Bucks' throat. 'We ain't gonna hurt you, okay?'

'Man, we're all friends.' Bucks was more surprised than scared. Shooting him while he was doing seventy on a Houston highway wasn't real bright.

'You're right. We're friends. But I wouldn't hit a bump in the road right now,' Kiko said. He carefully eased the Beretta out of Bucks' back holster, Bucks even leaning forward a little to make it easier, deciding to cooperate.

'Houston is pothole city, man, you can't avoid bumps. Jesus, put the gun up,' Bucks said. Suddenly he was watching the highway for ruts that could jar the car, blast his brains across the windshield. 'You don't want to sour your deal with Paul.'

'No, we don't,' Kiko said. 'But we want to have a private chat with you. Because we like you.'

'I like your name,' José said. His voice was low, hard, like it was won in a fight. In the mirror Bucks saw José's peasant face break into a grin. 'Bucks. You're what makes the world go round.'

'Take the next exit,' Kiko ordered.

'This is a bad idea, guys . . .' Bucks started.

' "Delays have dangerous ends," ' José said. 'Willie Shakespeare was right, man. Do what you're told.'

'Take the next exit,' Kiko repeated. Bucks took the Shepherd exit. He had a little .25 caliber gun strapped above his ankle; not a cannon but put it up to Kiko's eye, it'd get the job done. Of course José would blow his head open. While pretending to quote Shakespeare to act like he was smart.

Bucks turned onto Shepherd as Kiko directed. 'Go to that Waffle House,' Kiko said. 'I like 'em better than IHOP, they don't have that fresh 'n' fruity crap.'

'My grandma likes that plate,' José said. 'It's also rooty-tooty.'

'She's their target market,' Kiko agreed.

Bucks turned the Jag into the Waffle House lot. They wouldn't kill him at a busy restaurant, he decided. José moved the pistol away from the back of his head but Kiko pressed Bucks' gun against the flat of Bucks' belly, where it would deliver a nice, crippling gut shot.

He parked at the back of the lot, still calm, weighing how he could get to his ankle gun. Wondering what they wanted. If he would be alive in five minutes.

'Paul's going to be calling for me soon.' Bucks clicked off the engine.

'Not with his eyes full of big boobs,' José said.

'You're new to this line of work, aren't you?' Kiko asked.

'Yes, but I went to business school with Paul,' Bucks said.

'I heard he flunked out,' Kiko said.

'Yeah.' Bucks tried not to look at the gun pressed against his abs. 'But we stayed in touch. I called him when he moved down to Houston with his family.'

'Because a friend whose family is mob might be handy?' José said.

'I like Paul, he's cool,' Bucks said.

Kiko cocked his head. 'You were at Energis.'

Bucks' tongue turned to sandpaper. 'Yeah, I worked there. For a while.'

'As an energy trading exec, right?' Kiko said.

'Man, and people say we're crooks,' José said. 'That company robbed the whole country.'

'You left Energis,' Kiko said. 'Right before the financial meltdown.'

'You sound like a lawyer,' Bucks said. 'Asking questions you already know the answers to.'

'Why'd you leave the company?' Kiko said.

Now Bucks said nothing.

'See, being a businessman,' Kiko said, 'I follow the news. Three Energis energy traders went missing after a night out drinking. Murdered. Bodies and car dumped into Galveston Bay. Looked like a robbery went wrong.'

'That's what it was,' Bucks said. 'I knew those guys.'

'Sure you did. They all worked in your group. Then, six weeks later, your division's at the heart of the Energis multibillion-dollar collapse.'

'Tragedy surrounded me,' Bucks said, 'at that time in my life.'

'Outrageous fortune,' José said. 'Life sucks.'

'There were allegations about you, Mr Buckman. And your friends' deaths. Like they knew about those only-on-paper deals that had boosted Energis stock. And your own wealth,' Kiko said.

'Allegations don't mean much,' Bucks said. 'Proof matters.'

'And now with your business career gone . . .' José said.

'My career's fine.'

'A disgraced energy trader. Mailing out résumés must've been an exercise in humiliation.' Kiko laughed. 'Did you get a single interview?'

'I've never had a stranger so interested in me,' Bucks said. 'You're on the verge of stalkerhood here.'

'Understand,' Kiko said, 'that we own your ass, from this day forward.'

'You want me to come work for you? Forget it. I'm not betraying Paul.'

'Because you got such loyalty to your friends and coworkers, right?' José asked. Coolness in his voice. He looked thick-headed but he sure wasn't, Bucks thought.

'You killed those three guys,' Kiko said, his voice low. 'Because they were gonna talk, were gonna ruin your sweet little setup. You were already getting into Paul's pocket. So he loaned you a private spot for the kill. We were already watching Houston close, man. Watching the Bellinis' every move. See where we could take advantage of them.' Kiko leaned in close. 'Alan Gillespie. Hunter Gibbs. Ricardo Montoya. You brought them to that house the Bellinis own down in Galveston.'

Bucks didn't move. But his blood pounded in his chest, his palms went damp and he hated that. 'You're full of shit.'

'It juices you up good, doesn't it?' Kiko whispered. 'Knowing you have power over another person's life. It's okay. You're among like-minded folks.'

'Part of our surveillance of the Bellini properties included videotape,' José said. 'With Gillespie, Gibbs, and Montoya arriving at the house with you. Time-stamped and everything. You were wearing a nice cashmere jacket, a little warm for the season. Slate-colored shirt, khaki slacks. You were the sober one. It's pretty high-quality stuff.'

'Very nice,' Kiko agreed. 'I'm gonna thank the academy after the world gets to see it.'

'I don't believe you.'

José pulled a portable DVD player from his briefcase. Slid in a disc. Let it run, leaning forward to hold the screen in front of Bucks' face. The house in Galveston. The film image, clearly shot with a telescopic night lens, probably from a vantage point down the street. A car: Bucks' old BMW, followed by a Lexus, pulling up in front. Four men got out of the cars, ambled into the house. Decent shots of their faces, easily identifiable. José fast-forwarded. Then Bucks, carrying out a wrapped body, dumping it in the trunk. Then another. Then another, then driving off in the Lexus.

'Turn it off,' Bucks said.

40

'Your voice has lost its confidence.' José clicked the player off, then sniffed. 'Did you just crap yourself?'

'Here's the deal,' Kiko said. 'We want the five million Paul's paying for our coke. But we'll keep the coke at the same time.'

'You'll start a war,' Bucks said.

'A five-minute war,' Kiko said. 'The Bellinis, they're in a bad jam. Organization's falling apart. Paul-boy needs this deal. We need it to not work. And you're gonna help us.'

'Why me?'

'Because we'll give you a nice cut. And because Paul trusts you. And because we got your balls nailed to the wall,' Kiko said.

'And if I say no?'

'No one ever sees you again,' José said. 'Like Willie S said, "He dies and makes no sign."'

'Excuse José. He's a bit dramatic, got it from his mama.' Kiko's voice was cool as a snake's skin. 'The authorities would be fascinated by that movie.'

'So would *America's Funniest Videos*,' José said.

Bucks glared at Kiko. 'So I get the five mil and just hand it to you?'

'Sure,' Kiko said. 'Just think of stealing the money as a new goal we've articulated for you.'

5

'I've been digging,' Claudia said. 'Into the Bellini family.'

Thursday morning dawned bright and cool on the Texas coast, and Whit and Claudia ran hard along the sand of Port Leo Beach. The beach was a crescent, with a park spooning against it, the water shallow, the bay shielded from the Gulf by the long finger of barrier islands. This was the day of the week they ran together, Whit usually preferring to run in the evening, but now it was a routine with them, starting at the county courthouse, working over the harbor and the beach, then back up through parkland and neighborhoods back to the town square.

'And you found they have a frozen drink named after them?' Whit asked. They hit mile one and the sweet surge of adrenaline, settling into the run, primed his muscles.

'More than that. Harry said that Tommy Bellini was suspected of killing another family boss, right?'

'Yeah.'

'I searched the *Detroit Free Press* on-line archives. The rival – his name was Marino – was whipped to death with a chain. His face was gone. The flesh had been torn from his bones; his organs were in tatters. He'd been beaten long after he was dead.'

'It doesn't seem gangland-efficient,' Whit said. 'I thought they preferred guns.'

'Don't act like that doesn't scare you.' She ran a bit ahead of him, made him catch up with her. 'I made a couple of calls to the Detroit PD. Talked with a detective, pretended that we'd heard that the Bellinis were buying a vacation home here.'

'You lied for me; that's sweet,' Whit said.

'He told me that the police believed that it wasn't Tommy himself. That it had been done by his son, Paul.'

They turned off the beach, heading into parkland, cleanly manicured grass that stretched from the waterfront up to the highway, past wind-bent oaks kneeling almost to the ground.

'Like father, like son,' he said. 'So?'

'So if your mom's alive and Tommy Bellini's out of the picture, his son's a psychopath.' She reached out to touch his chest, slowed him. He stopped running, started walking, not looking at her.

'The detectives in Detroit I talked to said Paul Bellini's one of those kids who's never been told no, doesn't believe people feel the same pain he does. If his family's still involved in criminal activities, he's going to be the new head of the family.'

'If they were criminals, why didn't they do time?'

'People connected to the Bellinis did. Tommy did a brief bit as a kid. But since he became a boss, no, never. Never enough evidence. Or witnesses. Doesn't that tell you about their thoroughness in getting rid of problems?'

'Then they got rid of my mother, probably.'

'You . . . wouldn't try to avenge her, would you? What's the point?'

'Avenge a murder I couldn't prove?' Whit laughed. 'You must think I'm the freaking Lone Ranger, Claud. I get nervous crossing a street.'

'Please. You have a lot more nerve than you've ever gotten credit for, Whit.'

'You and your mom are close, right?' Whit asked.

'Yeah. When she doesn't nag me into downing a pound of Valium, we're tight.'

'I used to lie awake. Wonder if when I was thinking about my mother, if she was thinking about me. If we thought of each other at the exact same time, we'd know the other was still out there. Isn't that stupid?'

'Totally dorky and stupid.' She squeezed his shoulder.

'I'm over that now,' he said, a little too fast.

'I'm sure she must have thought of you. Many, many times.'

'Like in thank God I don't have those kids any more.'

'No,' she said. 'I'm sure not.'

'I won't know,' Whit said, 'unless I ask her.'

'It can't be heroin,' the mother said.

She sat in Whit's courtroom, small-claims court done, the litigants and their families either leaving with stern triumph in their faces or mouthing about the unfairness of life. Now a woman, gutted with grief, stood before his bench. The mother of the young man whose autopsy results Whit had picked up earlier in the week.

He smoothed down his robe and sat back down. 'Mrs Gartner. I'm sorry.' The courtroom was adjourned but still people were filing out, a couple stopping to watch the teary-eyed woman. 'Why don't we go to my office and talk?' He wondered who had told her – probably the police department. Or she had called the ME's office directly. It didn't matter.

'You cannot put heroin as his cause of death, or contributing to his cause of death. Or on anything official. Please.' She did not look old enough to have a son in his early twenties. 'That can't be his legacy.'

'Mrs Gartner, let's go to my office, and I'll get you a cup of coffee.'

She shook her head. 'No, Judge. Out here. You hope you're going to convince me to change my mind behind closed doors. I'm a mother; I have rights. Lance couldn't have been using heroin. He was not a bad boy.'

'I'm sure he was a very fine boy, Mrs Gartner,' Whit said. 'I can tell he was greatly loved. I'm so sorry for your loss, everyone here is.'

Her voice wavered. 'Then do this for me, please.'

'I don't want to cause you a moment's extra pain,' he said. 'I'm sorry. But the drug usage has to be listed as a contributing factor of death. I can't go against the law.'

'Ma'am.' Lloyd Brundrett, the constable, stood close by. 'Please, let's sit down. Get you a glass of water.'

'No!'

'It's okay, Lloyd,' Whit said. He came from behind the bench,

44

took Mrs Gartner's hand, led her to the front row. Lloyd finished clearing the courtroom, closed the doors behind them.

'A word on a document isn't going to change the man your son was,' Whit said. 'You know that.'

'But Lance's grandmother, she heard the rumors about the heroin, she heard my sister talking on the phone. I would like for you to tell her it's not true.'

'I can't falsify a death certificate. I am sorry.'

Mrs Gartner closed her eyes. 'No. Tell her it's not true. Privately. She's outside sitting in my car. Would you talk to her now? She'll believe you. You're a judge.'

'A little white lie.'

'She's in her eighties. She's a hard-shell Baptist. Lance doing drugs will kill her. She has to think he simply drowned. She'll never see a death certificate, I can assure you. If she hears it from you she won't ask any more questions.'

'I'd be happy to talk to her.' Whit stood, smoothed out the somber black robe that covered his jeans, sandals, and pineapple-print shirt. He followed Mrs Gartner and walked out into the bright, hard sunshine.

It had been a difficult conversation, even without the mention of heroin. The old lady was Mrs Gartner forty years into the future, eyes blank with loss and shock. He lied and told her there were no drugs in Lance's system, and he could see the relief embrace her like a wave. She kissed Whit's cheek, thanked him for his kindness. He didn't feel kind. He felt like he had shirked his duty, but what was the harm? An old woman's mind put at peace in the wake of a terrible loss.

The old woman's kiss was still warm on his cheek when his office phone rang while he was shrugging out of his judicial robe.

'Judge Mosley's office.'

'Whit? Hi, this is Harry Chyme.'

'Hey, Harry.' Trying to sound relaxed.

'I've found Eve Michaels. I followed the Bellini trail out of Detroit. She came to Houston with Tommy Bellini.'

Found. His guts knotted. 'I could be there in a couple of hours.'

'Don't come here, Whit. First of all, I don't have confirmation that this woman was once Ellen Mosley.'

'How do we get a confirmation it's my mother? Fingerprints? Pop quiz? Me bring my father there?' He mentally vetoed that last idea as soon as he thought of it.

'I suppose we should do an age progression on a picture of her, see if this woman resembles her enough . . .' But Harry didn't sound encouraging.

'Or walk up to her and ask her if she's Ellen Mosley. I'd do that.'

'Well, that would be blunt,' Harry said. 'Interesting to see what reaction I'd get, but it tips our hand.'

'Where in Houston is she?'

'She's living in a home owned by the Bellini family. She works in finance for a holding company Tommy Bellini owns. Her boy-friend manages a strip club they own.'

'Let's say I come to Houston,' Whit said slowly. 'You could tell me where she's hanging out. I could talk to her. Nothing else for you to do.'

'Except have it on my conscience if the Bellinis decide to use force to keep you from her. She might want nothing to do with you. She might not want to explain to her children where she's been, what she's been doing with her life.'

'I'm coming up there. Tell me where she's at.'

'No.'

'Harry, I'm your client. I pay you for information. You give it to me.'

'I officially waive my fee. You'd be in way over your head, Judge.'

'I've been in tough situations before.'

'But this is your mother. You're not thinking clearly.' Harry paused. 'She could run from you, Whit. She's done nothing to have contact with you all these years. She hasn't wanted to be found. I don't mean to be brutal.'

'I don't care. I can come to Houston immediately, I'll cancel court . . .'

Harry sighed. 'No. I know how much this matters to you. Let me make the initial contact with her, okay?' He paused. 'My dad died ten years ago. What I wouldn't give to see him again. I can't deny you that, if it's her.'

'Tell me where to meet you in Houston.'

'I'll call you back, Judge. When I know. Speak with you soon.' Harry clicked off.

'Harry, please—' Whit was talking to air. Fine. Finish court business, then head to Houston. Take his friend Gooch if he could go, Claudia if she was available and interested.

He picked up the phone, was three punches into her number when he slowly put the receiver down. Not Claudia. A police investigator might not be the first friend to introduce to dear old mom. And Claudia was opposed to this whole enterprise. But Gooch, he was fearless and nuts and inventive in tight situations. Harry might call Claudia, to check up on him, ensure he hadn't come to Houston. So leave sooner rather than later, if Gooch didn't have fishing clients today and could go. Do it before Claudia could stick her well-intentioned nose in and talk him out of going.

Houston. So close. He felt sick and dizzy and happy and afraid, all at once.

'Edith?' He called to his clerk. 'Cancel my appointments for today and tomorrow. I've got a family emergency up in Houston.'

'Military operation,' Gooch said as he finished hosing down his boat. 'That's the way to look at your trip.'

'I was thinking of taking flowers and seeing if she'd talk to me,' Whit said.

'Forget that, Whitman,' Gooch said. He put up the hose, went belowdecks, pulled a duffel bag from a drawer and tossed clothes inside. Then three guns. Gooch was tall and massively muscled, ugly to the bone, the best fishing guide on the coast and the most intensely private man Whit had ever known.

'Slow down, Dirty Harry,' Whit said.

'Families like the Bellinis, they understand a gun. Nothing else. The heartfelt emotion of a family reunion will be wasted on them. Especially if she wants nothing to do with you.'

'She'll want to see me,' Whit said.

'We'll need a base of operations,' Gooch said. 'I got a client up in Houston. Charlie Fulgham. Rich defense lawyer. I'll call and see if he'll put us up.'

'We can stay at a hotel.'

'Naw, Charlie's cool. He's actually given up his law practice. He defended major scuzzballs. Wants to go into entertainment. Bet he knows about the Bellinis.'

'Gooch, I want you to come with me because you're my friend, not because I want to beat them senseless.'

'Be honest with yourself,' Gooch said. 'You're asking me because you know I can handle badasses like these. That's the reason. Quit pretending this is gonna be a cakewalk.'

'If they're mob, yes, I'm scared.'

'You should be,' Gooch said.

'But I think I'm more scared of her. Of what she might say to me. I shouldn't care if she spits in my face and walks away. I shouldn't care.'

'But you do,' Gooch said.

'Don't tell anyone,' Whit said.

6

Thursday morning Eve woke with a start, gasping at the hard dig of Bucks' fingers in her throat. A memory turned to dream. She got up from the bed early, around six. Frank Polo snored next to her. She examined her throat in the mirror. Bruised, but with sickening precision. Bucks had half strangled her, had been going for his gun when Frank and the Miami dealers walked in, and an unforgivable line had been crossed. She could not be treated this way. There was a hierarchy, an order of respect in the organization, and Bucks had ignored it. In Tommy's day, it would not have been tolerated.

But Tommy's day wasn't ever going to dawn again.

One of the monolith-sized bouncers had told her that Paul Bellini had left the club with Tasha Strong. Walking funny and in a big hurry, the bouncer said with a knowing laugh. While she was nearly getting killed by his pet loon, Paul was screwing a stripper. She had half a mind to call Paul's mother, tell her. Save for the last moment that Tasha was black, which would kill Mary Pat Bellini on the spot.

But she didn't; tattling would piss off Paul worse. She washed her face, and when she looked up from the sink Frank was standing behind her. He kissed the top of her head.

'What if Paul sides with Bucks? Did you sleep on that last night?' he asked.

'He's not gonna side with Bucks after I talk to him. Anyway, he needs us now, he needs mentors.'

'Mentors,' he said in disbelief. 'Paul's not a summer intern. He's killed people.'

'Frank, hush, that is not so.'

Frank rolled his eyes.

49

'Anyway, killing a guy is a lot easier than running a business,' she said. 'Paul'll listen to us when he's not drunk and horny. I've got to talk to him before Bucks does. I'm heading down to the club.'

'Leave it alone.'

'What a classy boyfriend you are, really coming to my rescue here, Frank.'

'Because I love you, that's why you need to forget it happened. You're not going to drive a wedge between Paul and Bucks.'

'Hide and watch,' she said. 'Hide and watch.'

'This ain't never been a bad gig, sweetheart. Follow orders and keep your mouth shut.' Frank staggered off to drink coffee.

She showered fast, grabbed toast, and eased her Mercedes down the driveway onto Timber. The house wasn't technically theirs; rather, it belonged in name to Tommy's sister. Eve liked living in River Oaks, perhaps the most exclusive neighborhood in Houston, even though they lived right along its edge. She took an immediate left onto Locke; stately homes lay on her left and the thin ribbon of River Oaks Park on her right. She turned onto Claremont, then onto the major thoroughfare of Westheimer. It was always busy but it was her favorite street in the city, snaking from near downtown out to western Houston. She drove past palm-lined Highland Village with its high-end shops and restaurants, catering to the old oil money and the new tech money, past the sprawling shopping utopia of the Galleria, then into a longer, slightly less tidy stretch of road that included nightclubs, strip shopping centers, and Club Topaz.

Leave it alone, Frank had said. In other words, go ahead and paint a bull's-eye on her back and hand Bucks the gun. Frank grabbed too hard onto the present rather than the long term. Save Paul from a mistake now, earn his undying gratitude. That was the way to solve this problem. Frank couldn't see that. That same stifled vision was why Frank's music career died when disco did. He had a voice suitable for the classiest pop ballads, for music with muscle. Instead, he jumped on a ship doomed to sink and complained no boat ever came to save his ass from the ocean of obscurity.

But Frank had a point. She took a deep breath.

Today, if Paul didn't take her side, she'd act like she'd let it go. Pretend the encounter with Bucks didn't happen. Get the cash for the deal with Kiko, show she could follow orders, show her unquestioned loyalty. And then quietly get ready to disappear again.

Eve waited around the club Thursday morning and into the early afternoon for Paul, wondering why the lunchtime crowd wanted to ogle strippers while chewing on overpriced sandwiches and then head back to work with an unrelieved erection. She went back up to Frank's office shortly after one and Paul was sitting behind Frank's desk, feet propped up on Frank's papers.

'Well, hi,' she said. 'Been looking for you, honey.'

'Where's Frank?'

'At lunch. With a liquor rep. I've been trying to reach you.'

'So you and Bucks,' Paul said, 'had a little spat.'

'You got my messages.'

'Yes. I talked with him this morning.'

'And?'

'He says you misinterpreted his actions.'

'I misinterpreted him going for his gun,' Eve said. 'What, he wanted to show me a monogrammed clip?' She pulled the scarf from her throat. 'You see the bruise. He tried to cut off the blood to my brain. He's nuts.'

'You know, I'm under a lot of pressure,' Paul said, although he looked as relaxed as a cat fresh from a dinner bowl. 'You and Bucks, being the people in the world I trust the most, don't need to be snarling at each other.'

She didn't like the smile on his face, not at all. Too calm. Too sure of himself. And this *trust the most* crap, she didn't believe it. 'If I misinterpreted him, then I'm sorry, but do you think what he did was right?'

He ignored her question. 'Have you got the cash ready for the transfer to Kiko?'

'Yes. Richard Doyle from Coastal United Bank is meeting us at the Alvarez office, over by the port this afternoon.'

'Fine. You can go with Bucks.'

'Okay,' she said.

'It's amazing how much disapproval you can pack into one word, Eve.'

'Kiko Grace will gut you from stem to stern if he gets a chance and you're dead if you forget it.'

'He's afraid of me.'

'You got the transfer set up with Kiko, or is he too scared of you to meet?' she asked.

'Bucks and a couple of boys will take the money to wherever Kiko's got the stash and we do the exchange. The dust is hidden in decorative pottery. They'll truck it out to a safe place east of town. Have a little pot-smashing party later.'

At least Paul had the sense not to go to the exchange himself, he'd learned that much from his father. 'When?'

'Tonight. I want to get that coke on the street.' He laughed. 'Lots of depression in Houston these days, everybody needs a little pick-me-up. Even you and Frank. Hey, sit down for a minute,' he said.

She sat.

'Frank,' Paul said. 'How's he doing?'

'Fine.'

'He spending a lot of money lately?'

'Not that I know of.'

'Because,' Paul said, 'we're missing serious funds from Club Topaz.'

She let five seconds pass. 'Frank's not a skimmer.' A little panicky thrum quickened between her ribs. Surely Frank wasn't that stupid.

'Because he doesn't have the brains for it?'

'Frank's not dumb.'

'Be honest with me, Eve.'

'I don't know anything about him skimming money,' she said.

'A little here and there's okay. A perk of the job. At least my dad viewed it that way.' Paul leaned back in his chair, laced his fingers together on the flat of his silk shirt. 'What I don't like is the idea of

Frank taking advantage of my dad being stuck at death's door and helping himself because it's easier.'

'Frank's not a thief.'

'I spent the evening checking the books against the receipts, and Frank's had his hand, no, Eve, his fucking *arm,* deep in the till.' He'd gone from easygoing calm to screaming, his face red, spit flying from his lips.

This was why Paul didn't give a crap what Bucks had done to her. Her heart filled her throat, her mouth.

'You want me to talk to Frank for you?' She prayed he'd say yes, let her handle it, get the money back, not send the muscle pounding down on Frank. 'You know Frank, he doesn't know numbers, he probably entered a few figures wrong in a spreadsheet. He's not the brightest star in the sky.'

Paul dragged his sleeve across his lips. 'Yeah. You talk to Frank. Because I don't want to smash Frank's face in. He brings in the celebs. Without Frank's touch we're just another high-end titty bar. The staying power of minor celebrity never fails to amaze.' He smiled, a cold one like his father used. 'If he's having money problems, he should let me know; I'll take care of him.' Paul's voice was now gentle, steady. It scared Eve.

'Of course, Paul. There's a reasonable explanation . . .'

'I have to be able to trust him, Eve. If I can't trust him . . . if I can't trust you . . .' He let the words fade into the quiet. 'Then I have to take corrective measures, regardless of my affection for you or Frank.'

Corrective measures. Tommy's old code words for a hit. Dizziness spun through her head at the idea of Paul ordering her and Frank killed. She thought of Ricky Marino, his body thrashed into shreds by a chain. She didn't know for sure that Paul had done it. But people had whispered: Yeah he sure had, whooping and screaming and making a tantrum into a gut-wrenching kill that ended up discrediting his father and destroying their organization in Detroit.

'I'll make good on anything Frank's done,' she said in a rush. 'And if I pay it back and you're still mad at him, then let us go back to Detroit.'

'Wow.' Paul gave a soft laugh. 'I haven't even shown you proof of Frank's skimming. You sure seem ready to believe he'd do it.'

After a moment she said, 'Well, you wouldn't accuse him without good reason.'

'Finally you show faith in me,' he said.

'Of course I have faith in you, honey. Always.'

'You want to see the proof?'

'Yes.'

He handed her a CD. 'Destroy it when you're done,' he said. 'One file shows the charges actually made on client cards. The other shows the nightly revenues. There's a big shortfall.'

'I'll check it carefully. If it's him you'll get your money back and an apology. And he'll work for free, no salary, for six months. He'll show you respect, Paul, I promise.'

'Frank's stealing from me, from my dying father, and you, you want to lecture me on how Bucks behaves and what deals I enter into.'

'I'm not lecturing you,' she said. 'God forbid. So who found out Frank was skimming?'

'Doesn't matter.'

He got up from behind Frank's desk and she stayed still as he walked behind her chair. After a moment he put his hands, thick-fingered, on her shoulders. 'I know you returned money to my dad years ago. A big load of cash he otherwise would have lost. So I'm giving you fair warning. You clean Frank's nose. You get the money back he stole. And you and Frank keep breathing. Understand?'

'Yes,' she said. The pressure from his hands tightened on her shoulders, her collarbone. His thumbs rubbed the sides of her neck, tickled them slightly. Avoiding the bruise Bucks had left.

'I forgive once, Eve. Not twice.'

'Thank you, Paul,' she said. 'I'll fix it. How much does he owe you?'

'About ninety thousand,' he said. The pressure on her throat increased.

She said nothing. It could be worse. She could call Detroit, talk to a couple of old friends, get a loan. Frank, the idiot, what had possessed him? 'I'll fix it,' she said again. 'Please, let me talk to him first? I'll straighten this out.'

Paul Bellini eased the pressure of his hands, slowly turned the chair so she faced him. Leaned down close to her. 'Frank steals from me or my father again, I'm gonna take him to a doctor I own in Arizona. I'll have his tongue removed. No anesthetic. Then his mouth surgically sewn shut. I'll let him starve like that for weeks and then I'll take a chain to him and put him out of his misery.'

'I understand,' she said. She fought down a wave of nausea.

He leaned back. 'Now. You and Bucks go get that money for me. I'll see you when you get back, all right?'

Eve stood, fought to keep from trembling. 'All right.'

'Drive careful,' Paul said. 'That traffic's a bitch.'

7

Eve sat at Frank's desk, peering at the computer screen. Frank still hadn't returned from lunch, which he considered a marathon event, and he'd forgotten his cell phone on his desk. She was reviewing the files on the CD Paul had given her and gritting her teeth. The discrepancies between large credit charges and the books had started small but widened in the past two weeks. In one case, a private party of ten in a suite had incurred charges of nearly ten thousand dollars. Only five appeared on the spreadsheet for the same charge, the other money diverted and never making it into the Bellini pockets. A little, yes. A perk. This much was unforgivable.

The slow crooked twist of a headache sprouted in her temples and she craved a hot bath, a cold glass of wine, and silence.

Her cell phone beeped and she clicked it on, hoping it was Frank.

'Eve? It's Bucks. I'll meet you at the exchange,' Bucks said. 'I'm running a little late on other business for Paul. Sorry.' The barest hint of conciliation in his tone.

'He wanted us to go there together,' she said.

'Sorry, can't. I'll meet you there.' He took a breath. 'Hey, Eve. About last night. I apologize. I was out of line. Too much wine. I was kidding around with you, okay?'

'It's forgotten, honey,' she said, trying to sound relaxed.

'Eve, I do respect you. The great work you've done for Tommy all these years.'

She didn't believe him, not for a moment. But she needed him on her side now, with Paul furious, and said, 'It's okay. We need to work together well, for Paul's sake. Let's have a drink after the errand today.'

'Drown the hatchet,' he said with a little laugh. 'But not at the club. I'll take you to a classy place with a really stellar wine list. I'm sure you're tired of looking at tits in strobe lights.'

'That sounds good.'

'I'll see you shortly,' Bucks said, and hung up.

Odd. She would have thought that Bucks would have ridden with her, been her shadow in getting the money. Especially if he knew about Paul's accusation against Frank. But fine, whatever. She closed the accounting files and headed down into the nearly deserted club. A few men still sat at tables, watching a dancer. An air of failure hovered about them, guys alone in the afternoon who didn't have desks to return to, and she wondered if most of them were salesmen having off days, blowing commissions they hadn't earned.

She walked out into the bright, hard Houston winter light, headed for her Mercedes.

Frank. That idiot. She wondered why he'd skimmed. He didn't do drugs beyond a rare and purely social toot of coke. He had no gambling problem. Their finances were fine, not grand, but then they didn't need much. Tommy provided fairly. Paul seemed far less inclined to share the wealth. Ninety thousand. It was a long slow bleed that she couldn't afford. She was in her late fifties now; she couldn't launder and courier money forever.

She had already taken a few precautions over the years, in case she needed to run. Credit cards under an assumed name, cash hidden in secret deposit boxes. She could drive right now to Houston Intercontinental, get on a plane. To Detroit. Or where no one knew her, find the Montana of the next stage of her life, begin again.

And what then? She could not conceive of landing a normal job. What on earth would she put on a résumé? Her history of the past thirty years might as well be a blank tablet, a life run on empty. And she couldn't leave Frank behind.

If Paul wanted you dead, she told herself, you'd be dead already. He's mad but he's not killing mad.

So who told him about the skim? Not Bucks, because Bucks would have grilled her about it himself. So someone else.

57

She drove onto the 610 Loop that encircled Houston, gliding the Mercedes around slower cars. Midafternoon traffic moved like a European Grand Prix, cars weaving, brakes used often and not wisely. She headed past acres of industrial buildings, the newly refurbished Gulfgate shopping center, the dazzle of Reliant Stadium and the forlorn quiet of the Astrodome.

She headed north, over the Sidney Sherman bridge that arched over the vast Port, watching the road but taking in the view of Houston and the Ship Channel below. The Port of Houston was huge, the major artery for shipping from the Deep South down to Mexico, Central America and South America. Massive storage facilities lay to her left, acres full of just-unloaded Volkswagens and Audis to her right, freighters and tankers idling at the docks. The Port made her nervous; it seemed a door where a person could be seized, taken anywhere in the world, and never found again, all in a matter of days.

The next exit past the Port was Clinton Drive, and she took it. The rest of the traffic on the road were eighteen-wheelers. She headed away from the highway and on her right was an array of rail lines and gates where heavy trucks rumbled out with cargo. On her left were weedy lots, a prosperous-looking lumberyard, a tire reseller, brick bars with signs offering ICE COLD BEER and BEBIDAS COMPUESTAS, a Chinese restaurant, a tiny walk-up taco stand.

She turned her Mercedes right onto McCarty, and a block down turned again into a little parking lot. A bar stood at the end, Rosita's, with a hand-painted sign above the door, a woman with a snake entwining both her arms, unlit neon signs for *cervezas* in the window, and next to it a small office built of cinder block, painted white. The world headquarters, as she always called it, of Alvarez Insurance. Interested parties who called the number on the door got a heavily accented voice on the answering machine, basically apologizing that Mr Alvarez could not accept any additional clients. The glass door announced BY APPOINTMENT ONLY in both English and Spanish, and what could be seen of the office looked empty, drab, uninviting to thieves since it was rarely occupied. Tommy had used it for meetings and exchanges, and cleaned money through it as a business. Mr Alvarez was nominally retired but sold a lot of life insurance policies overseas that were cashed in within a year of purchase, moving money back into the country. Last year he had moved nearly four million of Bellini money, all propelled by Eve's finding a new loophole in insurance law.

No cars were parked nearby. Richard Doyle drove a Cadillac and he wasn't here yet. She hoped he hadn't succumbed to his ongoing, deep addiction and swung by the horse track on the way over. Five million in cash could be a temptation. She'd have to count it, brick by brick, twice, before she'd sign off.

Eve got out of the car, wrinkling her nose at the distant smell of the Port. She was fumbling for the office keys in her purse when the man turned the brick corner of Rosita's, not twenty feet away, and hurried toward her. 'Excuse me, ma'am?'

Eve glanced up at him, her hand still deep in her purse. She didn't know the man: attractive, balding, fortyish, khaki slacks and a navy blazer.

'Yes?' Eve said.

And the man brought up a small camera, one small enough to hide in his hand, and snapped three pictures. He lowered the camera as Eve ducked her head and he said, 'I didn't have a high-quality close-up to use. You're Ellen Mosley, aren't you?'

Eve froze. Then her feet moved and she hurried back to her car.

'If you're not Ellen Mosley, why are you running from me?' the man asked.

Eve didn't look at him again, fumbling for keys. Her skin felt like ice. She forgot entirely about the car's remote entry. 'Taking my picture like that, what kind of freak are you?'

'One of your sons wanted me to find you.' The man didn't come closer. 'Let me help you.'

'Help me?' Doyle and Bucks would be here any minute. Jesus, who the hell are you? she wanted to scream at the man.

'Do you ever think about your sons, Ellen?'

'That's not my name and I don't know what you're talking about.' She jammed the car key into the lock, turned it, yanked the door open.

'Would you like to see one of your sons?'

'I don't have children,' Eve said. She felt like a fist had smashed through her skin, her muscle and chest bones to seize her heart and squeeze it into gel. She sat in the car, slammed the door, thumbed the lock switch. The man hurried to her car window, calling to her through the glass. Calling her Ellen, unbelievable.

'If you want to see your son, I can arrange it. No one has to know. Please. Forgiveness isn't impossible . . .'

Eve powered up the car, threw it into reverse, peeled out from the lot. She watched the man standing in her rearview mirror, not giving chase. Of course not. He probably already knew Eve's license plate, knew where she lived. But she knew nothing about him.

She gunned the car down McCarty, back onto Clinton, toward the highway.

Harry Chyme watched the gray Mercedes tear away from the parking lot. The woman had glanced at Harry when he'd yelled through the window that he could help her, that no one had to know if she saw her son, the unexpected words about forgiveness. He'd nearly had her. Harry tucked the camera back into his pocket. This wasn't going to be easy for Whit to hear. Certain dogs should be left sleeping, even better left to die in their sleep. He had wrestled with taking this direct approach, but he had waited until she was alone, far from Bellini colleagues, and it had gotten him the answer he needed before Whit decided to charge up here: not interested.

Whit could stay home and Harry could go back to doing divorces.

Harry walked around to the back of the bar, where he'd parked after following her to the Port from the club. Go back to his hotel, call Whit, tell him the woman wasn't Ellen Mosley. Perhaps that would be best. See if . . .

A voice sounded behind him. 'Hey, buddy. You bothering Eve?'

He called you Ellen Mosley.

Eve got four blocks down Clinton before she pulled over in

front of an abandoned warehouse and vomited into a ditch. She hadn't eaten much today and she spat a long ropy strand that tasted of orange juice into the chopped tops of the roughly mown grass. She wiped a tissue across her lips, looked back down the road as if the man in the navy blazer would be leading an avenging charge of Mosleys, Babe in the lead, six angry sons marching behind.

But the road was empty.

She got back into her car. She drove along Clinton, past the highway, into blue-collar Galena Park, past a little motel that catered to truckers, fast food spots, an old-style barber shop. She pulled into a McDonald's parking lot several blocks down. She put her lipstick back on, keeping her hand steady. What if the man was still there in a few minutes when Bucks or Doyle showed? Would he watch them, follow them? She should have said, *Sorry, you have the wrong person, I don't know who you're talking about*. Bluffed her way out and gotten into the office. But she was already rattled by Paul telling her about Frank; she wasn't using her brain, her best weapon.

She went inside, bought herself a Coke. Drank it, further washing the hot-yuck taste from her mouth, ate a mint. Tried to call Bucks on her cell phone. No answer. Tried to call Richard Doyle at his office. No answer. She didn't leave a message with either.

She called Paul and he answered. 'I can't get in touch with Bucks. Tell him the meeting with Doyle's off.'

'Why?'

'There's a heating problem in the building.' Their code for police are watching. The man wasn't police, but Eve couldn't give the real reason to call off the exchange.

'I'll let him know.'

'Tell him to call me. I'm down Clinton at the McDonald's.'

Paul hung up without another word.

Eve sat down at a booth with her Coke and three booths over a mother fussed over her trio of small children, all with ketchup-smeared lips, vrooming the little plastic roadsters that came with their lunches and letting their hamburgers cool on the trays. The mother was cajoling them in Spanish to eat their burgers, not fill up on their fries. The boys ate the drooping fries like birds devouring worms. Three little boys. She watched the children.

Your boys probably ate a lot of meals at McDonald's. God knows Babe never knew how to cook.

She waited, now that the shock was subsiding, for regret to fill her heart. Sadness. Her children had not been mentioned to her since that long-ago day in that small wreck of a motel room in Bozeman. James Powell, threatening her kids, her broken ties to them raw and fresh, her nestling the little gun in his snoring mouth.

But instead she felt scared and confused. Her kids couldn't be looking for her, they couldn't. She watched the clock tick its minutes. Fifteen passed. She drank a second Coke, tried again to call Doyle and Bucks.

Eve got back in her car, studied the wheel. She didn't want to leave the plastic womb of the McDonald's, didn't want to go back to the Alvarez office. But Doyle would be there by now, and Bucks would still show if Paul hadn't reached him. She couldn't screw up this job, no, not after Frank had put them on the firing line. She started up the car, turned out into the lot, headed back to the office.

A car she recognized as Richard Doyle's Cadillac sat parked near the Alvarez front door. No sign of the man in the navy blazer. She pulled up next to Doyle's car; he wasn't sitting behind the wheel. She got out, went up to the door, her key ready this time. But the door was unlocked and she pushed it open.

She smelled the crisp stink of gunfire as soon as she stepped through the doorway.

Eve froze. There was no sound but the quiet hum of the air-conditioning. The office had a small reception area, with two offices and a tiny kitchen in the back. Silk flowers that needed dusting stood on the bare receptionist's desk. She took her gun from her purse, held it in a firing stance. She moved forward, into the main office she used for her exchanges.

Richard Doyle lay on his back. He was a florid-faced good old boy, but the rosy, full cheeks paled in death. Two bullet holes marred his forehead, dark and wet. Blood splattered his shirt and tie; another bullet had found his chest. The man in the navy blazer lay next to him, two bullets in his forehead, blood on his eye-glasses, eyes wide, mouth slack. His hand was on his chest, three of his fingers ripped by a bullet.

Eve knelt by the man supposedly sent by her son. Felt his pockets. Empty. No camera with her pictures inside, no wallet, no ID. She stood, her legs wobbly. Her foot stepped on Richard Doyle's hand and she jumped back quickly.

There was no sign of the five million in cash Doyle was bringing to her. No duffel bag, no suitcase, nothing.

She moved through the rest of the office. There were few hiding places. Empty. The back door to the office was unlocked as well. She pushed it open, looked back into an alleyway. Empty except for a pickup truck she knew belonged to the bar owner in the neighboring building. And a car that looked like a rental, a non-descript Taurus. She took two steps toward it.

And heard sirens begin their cry on the moist breeze.

She shut the door, ran back through the office, back out the front. Got in her Mercedes, revved it away from the storefront. She pulled onto McCarty, back toward Clinton, and when she was a block away she saw in her rearview mirror a Houston police car wheel into the lot, pulling up near the bar. Someone must have heard shots and called the cops.

A car pulled out after her onto the road, from across the street, a silver Jag she recognized as Bucks'.

He revved up close behind her. In the rearview he gestured to her to stop. She slammed her foot down on the gas, accelerating toward a red light that would put her back on Clinton.

Her cell phone beeped. Bucks' name was on the readout. She scooped the phone up.

'What's the hell's going on?' Bucks said.

'What?' she screamed.

'Why are you hauling ass out? . . . Why are there cops . . .'

'They're dead!' she screamed.

'They?'

'Doyle and some guy. And the money's gone.'

'What? What guy? Pull over and let's talk. Right now.'

Her heart felt like it suddenly exploded. Who knew about the meeting? She knew, Paul knew, Bucks knew, Doyle knew. 'You killed them,' she said. 'You shit, you took the money.'

'No. Pull over, Eve,' he said. The Jag drew closer; she floored her car, zoomed through another light shifting from yellow to red, went left onto Clinton, headed for the highway. Bucks stayed with her, leaving a chorus of honking cars in his path. 'Where's the goddamn money?'

'I don't have it,' she said. 'You killed them, you took the money.'

His voice was quiet as death. 'Pull over right now, Eve,' he said. She sped on and he rammed the Jag's bumper into her rear. She tore the Mercedes around a pickup truck and a semi heavy with goods from the Port. The Jag wheeled around the trucks, started to pull even with her. A sharp ping sounded, of metal hitting metal. He was shooting at her.

She veered across the lines, into oncoming traffic, accelerating toward a truck that laid heavy on its horn. The truck roared off the road, plowing into a lumberyard's wire fencing and a parked pickup. She glanced over, saw Bucks closing on her, rounding a station wagon, edging past a braking semi.

Eve tore back into the northbound lane as another truck thundered past, missing her by inches, and cut off Bucks. She aimed left, onto the entrance ramp for 610. A scream of metal sounded behind her. In the rearview she saw the Jag swerve around the back end of another service truck, piping and a ladder flying free from the truck, Bucks peeling away, the left side of his Jag damaged. But still coming.

Now on the ramp, she jammed the accelerator to the floor, hurtling into midafternoon Houston traffic, pounding on the wheel, going up the immediate rise of the bridge.

He came up fast after her, nearly clipping another semi carrying Hondas in a zigzag stack, ripping across lanes, leaving a wake of slamming brakes and screeching horns. Firing at her. Two bullets hit the edge of her rear windshield, ricocheting off. She swerved to the left, nearly colliding with a frightened woman in a pickup truck, a child in the passenger seat, screaming at Eve in terror, and Eve tore back to the right, away from them, thinking, that's it, he'll hit me.

But as they rushed down the incline of the bridge, Bucks went left, getting the pickup between him and her, and as he sheered back to follow her she darted into the speed lane, flooring the pedal, moving in and out of the array of trucks, cars now trying to get out of their way. A cloverleaf exchange came up; Eve went toward the exit that would put her on 610 E and watched him try to follow, and then she wrenched the wheel, bolted across every lane and hit the ramp for I-45 to Galveston. He couldn't get over, nearly spun out trying, and two cars behind him rammed into each other. Brakes squealed. She couldn't see him then, merging into traffic now. But he didn't come up in her rearview. She drove toward the coast, finally taking an exit after ten minutes. She'd lost him. She waited for another fifteen minutes, then ventured back onto I-45. When she reached the 610 interchange traffic was backed up, two wrecked cars being cleared. No one looked hurt but there was no sign of the Jag in the few seconds she had to scan the stalled cars. She took 610 to Kirby, a major thoroughfare that threaded back into the heart of Houston.

The coldness in his voice played over again in her head, ordering her to stop. Shooting at her, determined to kill her. Sure. She was the last witness.

Bucks had killed Doyle and the other guy, taken the five million. And now he was going to accuse her of taking it. He said, she said, and who would Paul believe?

She knew the answer.

She pulled into a bagel shop parking lot. She fumbled for the phone, called Paul. Tell him. No answer except for Paul's voice mail. She said, 'I don't have the money, I didn't take it, and if Bucks says different he's a goddamned liar. He took it, he's trying to kill me. Don't believe him. Call me, please, Paul. Please.'

Paul had to believe her. He had to know she was telling the truth. But, oh God, Frank had helped himself to money, Paul had threatened them both, he would believe she was ripe to run, the five million fueling her engines.

She steadied her hands on the wheel. She needed a place to go, a way to talk to Paul that didn't put her at risk. Not face-to-face right now, that would be suicide if she'd been set up. And Frank. If they thought she'd taken the money they'd go after dumb sweet Frank. *I'll have his tongue cut out*, he had said.

She dialed Frank's phone. No answer.

Run, she thought. Run like hell. She tore out of the parking lot.

8

'What is the difference between a tick and a lawyer?' Charlie Fulgham asked.

Whit and his friend Gooch waited.

'The tick falls off you when you die. What do you call a lawyer who doesn't chase ambulances?' Charlie shifted his balance, brightened his smile.

'Retired,' Whit said, praying this ended the routine.

'Man, but you're a judge,' Charlie said. 'You've heard them all.' He shook his head, leaned against the doorway, stuck his hands in his pockets.

'Look,' Whit said, 'a lawyer with his hands in his own pockets.'

'That's even older,' Charlie said.

'And lamer,' Gooch said in his throaty, low rumble.

'My problem is, I don't got a good comedy routine if I tell jokes. I have to tell stories, but if I tell stories on my former clients, I get sued. Vicious circle.'

'Aren't most of them in jail?' Gooch asked.

'Only the guilty ones,' Charlie said.

'Thanks again, Charlie, for putting us up on such short notice,' Whit said. 'This sure beats Holiday Inn.' Whit walked to the guest bedroom's window. Charlie's house was in the tony West University Place section of Houston, near the Texas Medical Center and Rice University, old homes full of old money and new money and well-scrubbed families.

Charlie Fulgham didn't look like a sharkish lawyer. He was boyishly heavy and apple-cheeked, with thick blond hair, wearing a summer Lilly Pulitzer shirt in the winter and rumpled khakis.

'You're welcome,' Charlie said. 'Yours to use. I'm heading out of town tomorrow. Got a gig in San Antonio. At an actual comedy club.'

'Is it amateur night?' Gooch stretched his massive arms above his head, gave a jaw-cracking yawn.

'So I'm not very good yet,' Charlie said, 'but I'm totally fearless. A club's just a courtroom with drinks.'

'Except everyone is sitting in judgment of you,' Whit said.

'Go back to practicing law, Charlie,' Gooch said. 'I'm horrified that wealthy scum of Houston may be lacking representation.'

'I need a good society murder,' Charlie said. 'People have way too much self-control these days.'

Gooch said, 'Talk about being engaged three times but never married. That's a hell of a lot funnier.'

'Yes, but that rips my heart open,' Charlie said.

'Comedy is pain, bubba,' Gooch said.

'Especially mine. I got to go work on my act. I got good lines about mold lawsuits. Y'all stay as long as you need to.'

'I don't expect we'll be here long, Charlie. Thank you again,' Whit said.

'Sure.' Charlie closed the door behind him and they heard the tread of his step going down the wooden stairs.

'Nice guy,' Whit said. 'That audience is in for a laugh-a-minute treat.'

'That boy'd rather humiliate himself in front of an audience that's gonna boo him off stage than take another case and a big fat retainer. I hope he makes it. I can't afford for him to get poor and stop his sport fishing.'

Whit dialed Harry Chyme's cell phone. He left a message: 'Harry, it's Whit. Call me.'

Gooch cracked his knuckles. 'Let's talk about the Bellinis. About a plan of action.' Gooch bent over his duffel bag, pulled out a gleaming Sig Sauer, handed it to Whit. 'Know your world and get the right spear for it, grasshopper. This is for you. Like I said, this is the only thing the Bellinis will respect.'

Whit held the gun. Beautiful, he thought, although he had never been one much for guns. He knew how to shoot, but it felt awkward and heavy in his hand. 'This won't be necessary.'

68

'Shows what you know about mob families.'

'Harry said my mother's boyfriend runs a high-end strip joint for the Bellinis.'

Gooch took the gun from Whit's hands. 'Charlie says Paul Bellini owns Club Topaz. Let's start there.'

'I don't think my mother's working there, Gooch.'

'Why don't you go to the strip club? See what you can see. I got another angle I'd like to work.'

'I'm calling the shots, Gooch. You understand? I know you're treating this like a secret mission, but it's my family problem. I want to handle it my way.'

'Yes, Your Honor.'

'Tell me I heard sincerity,' Whit said.

'I'm deceit-free right this minute.'

'What's this other angle?'

Gooch watched the tree limbs rocking near the window as the wind stirred them. 'You can try to find your mother at a Bellini hangout. Present yourself as Whit Mosley, nothing to hide, a guy trying to find his mom. Or you can convince Harry that now you're here, he needs to tell you what he knows and not shield you from the big bad truth. Or . . . take a more aggressive approach.'

'Aggressive.'

'Let's say you find her, Whit. And she has no interest in seeing you or in a sweet little reunion with your dad before he dies. I'd say toss her over your shoulder and haul her to Port Leo. That's kidnapping, although I can't imagine a jury would convict you and she wouldn't have a lot of sympathy if she pressed charges.' Gooch let a crooked smile creep across his ugly, kind face. 'The problem is the Bellinis. They probably don't take kindly to a guy coming in and hijacking key members of their family. So let me kidnap her; you keep your hands clean.'

Whit paced to the bed. 'Thanks, but no, Gooch. She'll come with me.'

'Why? There's nothing in her interest to make her do so.'

'She'll come,' he said again.

'Whit,' Gooch said, his voice going quiet. 'Man, I do not want to screw with your head. The bitch—'

'Don't call her that.'

'St Ellen has had thirty years to make amends. She wouldn't know you if she walked past you on the street. What, she sees you, she suddenly cares? A heart grows where there was stone?'

'Did you read that in a bad poem?'

'I wrote that in a bad poem.'

'So your backup plan is to kidnap her and keep the Bellinis at bay?' Whit said. 'You're a freaking strategic genius.'

'I'm trying to save you time.' Gooch shook his head. 'So what's it gonna be?'

'I'm going to see if my new Plan A works first.'

'What's Plan A?'

'Find her,' Whit said. 'And get her away from these people. If I can talk to her, really have a conversation with her . . . that's all I need to do.'

'You have an unrelenting and hopelessly naive belief in the goodness of people, Whit. Why should she talk to you?'

'I'm not so good, Gooch. There's a man she knew in Montana,' Whit said. 'I mention his name, I'll get her undivided attention.'

9

Night had begun its fall, and the mercury lights pooled over the lot of Club Topaz. Paul Bellini stood at the window of Frank Polo's office, watching the valets park cars, the blood hammering in his head, in his chest. He took a calming breath. He liked to play a game with himself, look at the cars, figure out how much money each driver would spend. A Porsche would be a guy who would drop a couple of hundred, because it was himself and a friend. Your Lexuses, BMWs, Mercedes, often four to five guys together, up to a thousand easy. Best of all would be a little fleet of cabs and limos arriving: those meant groups, bachelor parties, sports teams, packs of young wolves ready to lay out serious cash. The lot was half full; it was still early for a Thursday, but the empty parking slots pissed him off.

Paul closed the heavy shades of the office with a flick of a button. The little whir of the device was the only sound in the room, except for the labored breathing and soft crying of Frank Polo.

'Where is she, Frank?' Paul asked. His voice was kind, a quiet murmur of buddyhood. A whisper between friends.

'Oh, Christ, I don't know,' Frank Polo sobbed. He sat in his office, curled up on the chair. Paul had punched him twice in the ribs, backhanded him. Frank's lip was swelling, would purple before long.

'You hear from her?'

'She left two messages on my cell phone. Crazy ones. They don't make sense.'

'Nothing makes sense right now, Frank,' Paul said, his voice an ooze of concern. 'I got five million in cash missing. I got two people who could've took it, Bucks and Eve. Bucks comes running straight to me, tells me what happened. Eve runs.'

Bucks sat in the corner, pouting, bleeding from his own mouth where Paul had punched him, staring at Frank.

'Bucks could've taken it . . .' Frank started.

'But you know, he isn't already stealing from me,' Paul said. He sat down next to Frank, touched his jaw gently. 'Frank. This is going to get real ugly, real fast. And I don't want that. You're family. Help me understand this.'

'I really, truly don't know where she is,' Frank said. 'I haven't talked to her.'

'You don't help me, then I got to put a hit on her. That's gonna tear my heart open, Frank.'

'Well, don't,' Frank said.

'You love Eve. Help her now. Tell me where she is, so we can talk to her.'

'I don't love her if she stole five fucking million from you,' Frank said. 'It's over between her and me if she's turned traitor.' He wet his lips with his tongue, looked up at Paul, like a dog looking shyly to nuzzle a stranger's hand.

'Now. Eve called you.'

'Yeah. I forgot my cell phone, left it here. Stayed a long time at lunch. Then ran errands. I came back here, got to glad-handing with an early group, a bunch of Japanese businessmen. I didn't come back up to my office until an hour ago.'

'Play me the messages on your phone,' Paul said.

'I erased them, I wasn't thinking straight.'

Paul frowned. 'What did she say in the messages? And don't you lie to me. I start snapping fingers if you do.' And he took Frank's hand, ran a fingertip along the finger and palm, and positioned the middle finger between his own, bent it back, ready to break.

Frank gasped. 'She said Doyle and another dink had gotten shot at the exchange point, the money was gone, Bucks had tried to kill her and for me not to go home.'

'Where did she want you to go?'

'She wanted to meet me at the Neiman's at the Galleria. At five.' It was already past seven.

'Where you been this afternoon? What the hell were these errands?'

'I went over to the Platinum Club. They got new dancers, girls we ought to have.'

'You spent the afternoon ogling tits while your girlfriend stole five million from me,' Paul said, giving the finger a little twist. Wondering if the snapping bone would sound like a twig or louder, like a pencil.

'Uhhh,' Frank moaned. 'Jason, the bartender at Platinum . . . he'll tell you I was there. And I talked to two of the girls that we want to recruit for Topaz. Ginger and Anita. They'll vouch for me.'

Paul let go of his hand, turned to a muscular man with dyed-blond hair standing near the door. 'Gary, call the Platinum. See if his story checks out.' Gary stepped out of the office.

'I need that cash, Frank,' Paul said. 'We got a deal going down late tonight, and now I got to call them and postpone. How do you think that looks to a man like Kiko?' He glanced over at Bucks. 'Get a couple of guys over to Neiman's, have them walk the Galleria. And keep a guy watching Eve and Frank's place.'

'I'll take care of that,' Bucks said. 'Personally.'

Paul cocked his head. 'Frank here could be right and you're lying to me.'

Bucks blinked. 'I'm not. I'm here, Eve isn't. This isn't compli-cated.'

'You tried to strangle her and nearly pulled a gun on her last night,' Frank said. 'She's given her life to this family and you dare to touch her . . .'

'She tried to call off the exchange, Frank,' Bucks said. 'Told Paul there were cops watching. Well, that was a lie. There weren't any cops there.'

Frank swallowed. Bucks gave him a thin trap of a smile.

'Where else would she go, Frank?' Paul went to the wall of Frank's office. He ran a finger along the three platinum records: 'Baby, You're My Groove'; 'Boogie City'; 'When You Walk Away.' He took down 'Baby' and shattered the framed record on the corner of Frank's desk.

'Oh, God, not my disks!' Frank stood in horror.

Paul picked up a jagged shard and turned back to Frank. 'Tell me where she is, Frank.'

'Jesus, Paul!' Frank screamed. 'This is me, please!'

'This is you between me and five million,' Paul said. 'Where would she go?'

Frank swallowed. 'Not to our house. She won't come to the club or any of our hangouts.'

'She got a place she goes when she's stressed?'

'What, you think she went for a spa treatment?' Bucks said. Paul shot him a look and he went silent.

'If she took the money,' Frank said slowly, 'she won't be staying in town. If he's framed her' – he nodded toward Bucks – 'she's probably gonna go back to Detroit. Where people have sense.'

'Be very careful, old man,' Bucks said.

'Paul. Get real. You think Eve took that money? Seriously?' Frank pleaded.

'You been skimming club money from me, way more than's acceptable. I know you have.'

Bucks said, 'Hasn't there been a big outbreak of initiative around here?'

'So,' Paul said, 'it's not a big jump to Eve deciding to take a lump payment and retire.'

'She would have taken me with her. She didn't,' Frank said.

'So you say. She's been bitching about the way I fart ever since Dad got hurt. She doesn't like how I'm running things. She knows she's gonna be retired. You've screwed the pooch big time, Frank. So she takes the money and runs.' Paul leaned down close to his face, ran the tip of the jagged vinyl along Frank's eyebrows. 'Where's the money you took?'

'I stashed it in an account in a bank in Katy,' Frank said. Katy was a distant suburb west of Houston, a nice quiet town, known for good schools, football, and big malls.

'All ninety thousand?'

'I haven't spent it. It was a loan I was gonna pay back in a few months. With interest.'

Paul shook his head. 'Loan? Do I look like an ATM, Frank? You see any fucking buttons on my front?'

'No.'

'Why did you want a loan?'

Frank worked his mouth. 'I wanted to cut a new record . . .'

Bucks laughed, short and sharp.

'I'm gonna cut you a new record,' Paul said. 'Right after I cut off your fingers and your balls and your ears.'

'Please, Paul . . .' Frank's voice broke. 'I'll do whatever you want to make it right . . .'

Paul let go of Frank's shirt, took a step back. 'That ninety thousand, it's not so bad. Not nearly as bad as what Eve did to me. I tell you what. You get her and the five mil for me, you can keep the ninety thou.'

'Paul, you're gonna let him get away with that?' Bucks said.

'You shut up,' Paul said. 'You find Eve, Bucks, you can have the ninety thou.'

Bucks shut up.

'I'm not trusting either of you too much at the moment,' Paul said. 'That's why you both got to prove your loyalty. Bring her to me. Think of it as a modified contract. You two boys are the only bidders.' He glared at Frank. 'You give me your Katy account info and I'm moving that money back where it belongs.'

'Sure, Paul,' Frank said.

'You steal one more cent from this club, and I'm going to kill you. With this broken record. An inch at a time.'

'I understand, Paul.'

'Not an inch. I'm going fucking metric. A centimeter at a time.'

'I understand, Paul.'

'I don't think you do, Frank,' Paul said, and he reached out, grabbed Frank's hand, turned the palm skyward, and with one swipe of the shard laid the flesh open. Blood spurted. Frank screamed. Paul shoved him to the floor. Frank clutched the torn hand to his chest.

'Next time, I'm slicing your dick,' Paul said. 'Now call Doc Brewer and get yourself sewed up.'

Frank staggered toward the phone. 'You go downstairs and call the doctor. Get out of my sight. You get blood on the carpet I'm cutting the other hand,' Paul said.

Frank tucked his hand inside his suit jacket and fled from the room.

'He's lying,' Bucks said. 'He knows where she is.'

'Nah,' Paul said. 'No way he'd come back here if he knew.' Paul gave him a smirk. 'He's an old guy and a has-been. He was stupid. You're not stupid, are you, Bucks?'

'No.'

'Good. Because I got a couple of soldiers searching your crib right now. They're not going to find five mil in cash there, are they?'

'No. I told you I don't have it. Thanks for the vote of confidence, man.' Bucks stood, squared his shoulders. 'You brought me into this business, Paul. I owe you everything. I'm not going to betray you. We both know that.'

'You had the same opportunity as Eve.'

'You hired me,' Bucks said. 'But you inherited her.'

'Tell me again what you saw.'

Bucks took a breath. 'I was running late getting to the exchange . . .'

'Why?'

'Fender bender on I-10. Two lanes closed for about fifteen minutes, traffic sucked.' Bucks shrugged.

'Then what?'

'I get to Alvarez. Door's open. I go in, find Doyle and this guy dead. Bodies still warm. No sign of the money.' He paused. 'I check Doyle's pockets. His wallet, his ID's gone. The man doesn't have ID on him. The smell of gunfire is still fresh. There's even a casing on the floor. I pick it up, pocket it. Then I get the hell out, being sure I'm not leaving prints.' He tented his fingers. 'I pull the Jag across the street, start to call you, and then here I see Eve tearing back into the lot. She goes inside. I wait to see what happens, then she comes tearing out before the cops show.'

'If she had killed them and taken the money while you were stuck in traffic, why the hell would she come back?'

Bucks held up the casing. 'She found she was missing one and came back for it.'

'Eve would be thorough if she planned a heist like this.'

'She's not a hit man, Paul. She could have missed a casing in a panic. Or she was coming back for another reason.' Bucks put the casing on the desk.

'Her coming back was a huge risk.' Doubt in his voice.

'I'm telling you what I saw. Even a lady sharp as Eve isn't going to think straight all the time.'

'I don't like not knowing who the man was with Doyle.' Paul sat down. 'I want you to find out. The cops are going to be looking closely at a banker getting killed down at the Port. They'll come after us if they make the connection between my dad and Alvarez Insurance.'

'First they have to make the connection,' Bucks said.

Paul shook his head. 'This is like finding out your favorite aunt is a two-dollar whore. It's depressing.'

'People often disappoint.'

'You better not,' Paul said. 'I'm trusting you, man. Find her. Find the money. See if we can push back the deal with Kiko until Saturday night. But he can't know we don't have the green. He knows that, we're dead in the water. No one will supply us. That money's the starting point for us.'

'Starting point,' Bucks said.

'The reason I wanted you working with me,' Paul said, 'is that I'm going to be bigger than my dad ever was. I need your expertise a lot more than I need muscle with guns. We're gonna run Houston, Bucks. And when we've got that base to work from, I'm going after the men that humiliated my father, that drove him out of Detroit. Barici. Vasco. Antonelli. They're dried-up old men now. The racketeering laws have broken most of them. They worry so much about the Feds, they won't see me coming, but I'm going to annihilate them and they won't be able to touch me.' He jabbed a finger at Bucks, his face reddening. 'But I need this deal to jump-start us. To build a stronger power base with an ally like Kiko.'

'You're not mob anymore,' Bucks said quietly. 'With all due respect, Paul, leave it alone. They're old men. They don't have nearly the power they once did. What's to be gained from it?'

'Eve knows those guys. She could run to them with the money, if she wanted. They'd give her sanctuary, shelter. She's old school. She and them, they'd understand each other. She knows how I work. So you got to find her and the money. I'm not gonna let my family be humiliated again.'

'If I can't find her—' Bucks started.

'Hey, Bucks,' Paul said. 'If you don't find her, nobody's ever gonna find you.'

10

Whit passed under the eagle eye of the bouncer, who looked carved from a redwood, paid the twenty-dollar cover, walked into the thump of the music, the strobe lights blinking against his skin.

Club Topaz was dark as a dimly lit closet, a happy-hour crowd thinning out and a well-heeled, post-dinner crowd settling in. The only fully lit areas were the stages, awash with white glows from both ceiling and floor. The crowd was mostly men, with the exception of a few women who wore uncomfortable smiles, as if here under mild protest. The decor was heavy on gold and chrome, a strange mix of Roman antiquity (perhaps to suggest an impending orgy) and contemporary sleekness. The club had retro-guido written all over it, probably part of the cheese-factor appeal, but it was spotlessly clean, the waitresses moving among the tables with precise energy, the cogs of the club all warming up to produce a night of longing and money.

A woman was dancing solo on the stage, and her moves were not of the simple shake-the-tits variety. She was tall, redheaded, and she moved with easy grace and wry suggestion, performing to David Byrne's cover of Cole Porter's 'Don't Fence Me In' as opposed to a generic dance-club beat. She was dressed as a skimpily clad cowgirl, a Stetson perfectly angled on her head, topless but wearing a thin bandolier that divided her high and mighty breasts, leather chaps over a sparkly G-string, and a holster. She drew her guns and sprayed a couple of heavy-jowled men with water. They hooted and clapped. She blew imaginary smoke from the gun's barrel and the men howled in appreciation. She moved with the confidence and style of a Broadway dancer who happened to be showing her breasts, a funkier Fosse girl.

Removing her gunslinger gloves, she dropped them on the balding head of a delighted patron.

Whit moved to the bar, looking for Gooch. They'd decided to come in separately. Gooch had been in for ten minutes already. He saw Gooch, sitting alone at a corner table, nursing a beer, watching the stage. He selected another corner table and sat down.

His stomach dropped as he realized his mother was possibly less than a hundred yards away from him. He could come face-to-face with the shadow that had always loomed over his life. While surrounded by strippers and men waving crisp dollar bills. It was not the reunion he had envisioned as a child. Little flowers of sweat blossomed under his arms, along his ribs, on his back.

A waitress, dressed immaculately in a white shirt, red leather vest, black bow tie and a black leather miniskirt, snug over supple hips, appeared almost instantly. 'Sir? What may I get you?'

'A Corona, please.'

The frosty beer, with the requisite lime slice perched in the bottle's opening, quickly materialized on a napkin before him. He paid with cash and watched the tall redhead finish her show to wild applause while the announcer's voice said, 'Give it up for Red Robin! She's heading back to the plains to' – a pause hung in the air – 'rope her dogies, and she'll be back in a while. Now coming onto our main stage is Desire O'Malley, she's got a pot of gold at the end of her rainbow!' And in a burst of Celtic drums and fiddles, a bosomy colleen with a jaunty green hat and suit jacket river-danced onto the stage, clogging with a surprising degree of expertise, barely restrained breasts jiggling. She wore a little fake leprechaun's beard that she tossed into the crowd amid laughter and clapping.

It was horndog-ridiculous, but the women were extraordinarily pretty. None of them – and Whit watched a few working the room, offering lap dances or sitting and chatting with customers – had a weary, worn look to them from eking out a living in an exploitative field. *Playboy* could come through with a camera crew and do shots to fill a year's worth of magazines in ten minutes.

He glanced past the stage. He saw two doors that looked like they led to restrooms and a darkened alcove, lit with a thin, red gleam. Offices, he guessed. On the left side, away from the stage, stood a curving staircase, with burnished cypress rails. A small velvet rope closed the staircase off, with a PRIVATE sign hung discreetly on the rope. At the top of the staircase stood another door, shut.

He took a sip of his beer and a voice next to him said, 'Would you like a dance, sir?'

Whit glanced up to see one of the most beautiful women he'd ever laid eyes on. She was movie-star gorgeous; skin the color of lightly milked coffee, hair cut short because the hair could never be more than a frame for that stunning face. Full mouth, cheekbones high, delicate jaw, brown eyes you could drown in. A brief bra of CDs covered her top; a thin, fake computer screen, shaped to fit, covered her loins over tearaway hot pants.

'I got Ds in computer science,' he said.

She laughed. Politely. Like the line wasn't new.

'I'd die of happiness if you danced with me,' Whit said.

'Not with you,' she said. Letting him have his joke. 'For you.'

'A lap dance?'

'Sure.'

'How about just sitting and talking to me for a minute?'

She hesitated. He supposed there was actually more intimacy in talking than in dancing; she could gyrate, give a little hip sway, expose her breasts and it would be less revealing than a conversation, where they would have to scope out each other as actual human beings.

He asked, 'How much is it for a dance?'

'A hundred.'

'Well, you put a hundred on my tab but sit here and chat with me for a minute,' Whit said. 'No dance. I'm recovering from heart surgery.'

She signaled the waitress with a twirl of her finger. Whit realized he'd have to give a credit card; he didn't have that much cash on him. A risk. But he had to talk to people, and there was no reason to believe if his mother worked here she would see one out of dozens of credit receipts. He gave the waitress his card and the

81

black girl sat down next to Whit at the little table. 'What's your name?' he asked.

'Geekgirl,' she said.

'No, really.'

'Tasha.'

'Hi, Tasha, I'm Whit.'

'I've heard a lot of lines in this place but heart surgery is a new one.' She fixed him with an intelligent, amused gaze.

'I'm a weak man, like every other man here.'

'You in town on business like every other man here?'

'Yeah. I'm a location scout for a film company.' He'd considered several ploys to get him into the offices of the club and in an instant decided on this one.

She raised one perfectly styled eyebrow. 'A film company.'

'Sorry. I'm not in casting,' he said. 'I assume this place is thick with aspiring actresses.'

'Yeah, we got girls here hungry to do Shakespeare. Hoping to bring deep new angles to Ophelia.' Sarcasm in her tone. 'Not me.'

'What are you aspiring to?'

'World peace,' she said.

He swallowed a thick gulp of beer. The waitress came and brought Tasha a club soda, slice of lime bobbing among the ice cubes. 'Blessed are the peacemakers.'

'Don't take anything I say,' she said, 'seriously.'

'You strike me as a woman of refinement and intelligence.'

Her smile got tight. 'I'm a naturally friendly person.'

'What's upstairs?'

'I'm not that friendly,' she said.

'I didn't mean to imply that, Tasha,' Whit said.

'Private suites. We get a lot of famous people here, like to have their food and drinks and dances out of the glare. So are you trying to impress me with your Hollywood connections or are you really looking for a place to shoot your movie?'

'I suspect I can't impress you very easily. You seem too smart for that.' And too smart for this place. He watched as Desire O'Malley finished her number, wearing a glittery shamrock-shaped G-string over her clover as she bounded off the stage. 'And yes, I'm scouting

82

for a thriller. Hero is a spy trying to capture a rogue agent who's stolen a deadly virus. His romantic interest goes undercover as a stripper in three scenes to get close to an informant. So we need a club.'

'Why aren't you shooting in LA?'

'Texas is cheaper. So who would I talk to here about filming?'

'Frank. But be warned, he'll want to be in the movie.'

'Frank.'

'Frank Polo. He's the manager. But kind of a figurehead.'

'I know that name.'

'Sweetpea, if you know his name you don't have good taste in music.' Tasha leaned forward, started to sing in a clear alto that cut through the humping music of the performer on stage. '*Baby you're my groove . . . baby you're my groove.*'

'I know that song.'

'Frank never recovered from his Saturday night fever.' She shrugged. 'He had gold records then and now he's managing this place. How far can you fall?'

'This is a very nice club, Tasha.'

'Absolute paradise. I hope to retire here one day.'

'So how could I get a meeting with Frank Polo?'

She studied him. 'If you're not legit, honey, I won't waste Frank's time with you. No offense. You got a business card?'

He didn't of course, but he made a show of searching his wallet and his shirt pocket. He'd dressed in khakis and a loose shirt, and now he thought he didn't look Hollywood enough. No mousse in his hair, no way-cool sunglasses. 'I don't have one on me. I must've given out the last one at Club Yes.' This was another fancy strip club; he'd seen a billboard for it on the highway.

'You must've,' Tasha said, polite and unconvinced.

'I'll give Frank a call,' Whit said. 'Or does he have an assistant I should talk with?' He patted his pockets again, as though gathering his thoughts. 'See . . . you don't want to commit to people that you have an interest in filming at their business. Get their hopes up if it's not right. That's why they call it scouting.'

'Sure,' Tasha said. He realized he was overexplaining, talking too fast for much credibility. 'My assistant did call club man-

83

agement earlier, though. She spoke with Eve? Eve Michaels?' He made it a question.

'Yeah. I know Eve,' Tasha said. 'But she's not . . .'

'Tasha,' a voice rumbled behind Whit. 'Your presence is requested upstairs.' A wiry guy who looked rather corporate-drone for a strip club employee walked past Whit's chair, leaned down on the other side of Tasha, whispered to her. She nodded once, gave Whit her indulgent but professionally distant smile.

'Excuse me. It was very nice meeting you, scout. Enjoy your evening at Club Topaz.'

'Thank you, Tasha.' She rose and walked past the wiry guy, who turned to leave.

Whit said, 'Excuse me.'

The guy turned back to him and gave him a smile cold as ice. 'Yes?'

'I'd paid for her to sit with me for a bit,' Whit said. 'I believe I'm due a partial refund since you've whisked her away.'

'Whisked,' Cold Smile said. His bad-mood scowl deepened. 'Sorry. No refunds.'

'How about a favor instead?' Whit said. 'Where could I find Eve Michaels?'

Cold Smile sat down across from him.

'I understand she's involved in the management of the club,' Whit said.

'Not really. Why were you looking for her?' Cold Smile did not have the look of a club thug. Nice suit, conservative haircut, a rep tie over a pale blue shirt. But a freshly swelling lip, like he'd taken a punch in the past hour.

'What are you, her receptionist?' Whit asked.

Now Cold Smile didn't smile. 'What's your name? I'll tell her you're looking for her.'

'Never mind my name. My business with her is private.'

Cold Smile looked at Whit as though trying to fit him into an odd equation. 'Well, come with me, buddy. I'll take you to her.'

Whit glanced through the strobing lights over at Gooch. Desire O'Malley, the wild Irish rose, shimmied out a lap dance for Gooch.

'You want to go or not?' Cold Smile said.

This was happening too fast. Being taken before his mother. But he thought of his dad and he stood up. His stomach felt like it was left behind in the chair.

'This way,' Cold Smile said and Whit followed him, moving past the velvet rope and upstairs toward the suites. Whit glanced back at Gooch, couldn't see his friend's face, obscured by Desire's smooth back.

The second floor had the reddest, richest carpet that Whit had ever seen, and they made no noise as they went along a row of doors with gold numbers gleaming on them. Cold Smile knocked on number five, opened it, peered in.

Here we go, Whit thought, *Hi, Mom.* He followed Cold Smile inside.

But the room was empty.

Cold Smile grabbed the back of Whit's neck in a pincer hold, working the nerves and carotid like dough with his other hand. Whit gasped, the air in his lungs thickening into jelly. One arm went around his throat. Then he felt the unwelcome jab of a gun into the small of his back.

'I pull the trigger,' Cold Smile said, 'and you're riding a wheel-chair for the rest of your life.'

Whit held his breath. Not hard; he barely had any air left.

'It's not been a good day at the office,' Cold Smile said in a low growl. 'I want to know why you're looking for Eve, and I want to know in the next five seconds. Five. Four. Three—'

'She owes me money,' Whit said. It was the first thing that came to his mind, a blast of lightning through his brain.

The gun didn't waver from nestling against his spine. 'For what?'

Whit's mouth dried. 'I had money I needed moved offshore, cleaned up.' Harry had said his mother worked in mob finance, this was a possibility. 'But she didn't return my money.'

'That bitch is freelancing now?' Cold Smile said. 'Turn around.'

Whit did and Cold Smile socked him dead-on in the face and Whit staggered back. He closed his hand into a fist and lurched forward but the gun's cool barrel abruptly pressed against his forehead.

'How much money?' Cold Smile said.

'What does it matter to you?' Whit said. The guy was being too artful, too fancy in his handling of the gun, in his stance right now, like he held a sword's tip at Whit's throat. Enjoying it now, not being brisk and businesslike.

The door eased open behind him.

'Room's taken,' Cold Smile called, not glancing back. 'Try one down, please.' Spicing his voice with a little friendliness.

'But I like this room.' Gooch slammed the door behind him. Locked it. A knock immediately followed, a young woman's voice barely audible on the other side of the door. 'It's the dorks-with-guns room.'

'Get out, man.' Cold Smile darted a glance back at Gooch but pushed the barrel's point deeper into Whit's forehead.

'I will. And I'm gonna go straight back to Detroit and have a little talk with Joe Vasco. You know him. The guy who ran the Bellinis out of Detroit.'

'Who the hell are you?'

'Your better half,' Gooch said. 'You shoot my friend, Vasco's guys fly down from Detroit, take your stringy ass out to the bayous, and feed you to the gators a pound at a time. Shouldn't take more than three or four days for you to die.'

'Vasco,' Cold Smile repeated.

'Yeah,' Gooch said. Cold Smile lowered the gun. Whit didn't move. The gun wasn't screwed into his skull now. He started breathing again.

'What's your name?' Cold Smile asked.

'What's yours?' Gooch said.

'They call me Bucks,' the guy said.

'Bucks?' Gooch asked, a smile on his face for the first time. 'As in money, or as in rhymes with fucks and sucks, like you're a prison bitch?'

'As in money,' Bucks said in a dead cold voice.

'I'm Leonard.' It was Gooch's real first name, rarely used. 'The guy you're threatening is Michael.' It was Whit's middle name, never used.

'And you're from Vasco?'

'You're catching on quick. Is calculus your hobby?' Gooch asked.

'I'll go get Paul.'

Gooch shook his head. 'No need to rush to Paul and tell him we're here.'

'He doesn't know?'

'That's the way Mr Vasco wants it. Ever since Tommy's in the hospital, Vasco's wanting to see what Paul does. Wants to make sure he's sticking by the agreement. Staying out of Detroit. Staying out of the business. No drug dealing, no money cleaning, no illegal activities.'

Bucks frowned. 'Whatever we're doing in Houston is frankly none of Mr Vasco's concern.'

'Pull your head out of your Brooks Brothers ass, son. If we tell Mr Vasco that Paul is stepping out of bounds, getting into lines of work that aren't his to go into, then he'll send a few ill-tempered gentlemen to straighten you dinks out and you'll be one unhappy, mostly dead wanna-be,' Gooch said.

'That's assuming you get back to Detroit,' Bucks said, and Whit saw the momentary fear leave the man's face, replaced by brittle anger. Gooch had gone too far.

'Man, cool it,' Whit said. He glanced at Gooch. 'You cool it, too. Let's talk, all right?' His face ached and the skin under his eye was already beginning to throb. He was going to have a shiner, and a sudden rage boiled at him. This guy knew his mother, saw her, knew her business. He wanted to pound his fist into Bucks' mouth.

'Why'd you lie about the money? Why didn't you say you were from Vasco?' This thought, moments late, made Bucks' voice rise and he turned back to face Whit. Gooch's fist slammed into the back of Bucks' head, drove him down to the floor.

'Because you're nothing but an ass wiper.' Gooch made his voice more growl than talk. 'Because we don't owe you an explanation. You understand me?'

Whit knelt, took Bucks' gun from him. Now pounding rocked the door, a key fumbled in the lock. Whit placed the gun on the table, his hand near it.

Two thick-necked guys came into the room, staring at Gooch, at

Whit with his clearly just-punched face, at Bucks now sitting on the floor.

'What's going on, Bucks?' one asked.

'Friends of mine,' Bucks said, 'playing a joke on me. Everything's fine.' He gave a nervous little laugh.

The two muscles looked at Gooch and Whit again.

'Sorry I had to keep Miss O'Malley out of the room after she brought me up,' Gooch said. 'Part of the joke.'

The two muscles looked at Bucks.

'Nicky, it's fine. It's cool. Tell Desire we'll give her a big tip for her trouble,' Bucks said, standing.

'Yeah, I got a big tip for her,' Gooch said, and now the men laughed.

'It's all cool. We'll be down in a minute,' Bucks said, and the two men backed out and shut the door behind them.

'You see how it is?' Bucks said. 'I give the order, they'd kill you.'

'I see they'd try. Detroit's watching,' Gooch said. 'You remember that.'

'So what happens if Detroit doesn't like what they see?' Bucks asked.

'I wouldn't be too loyal to Paul,' Whit said. Bucks looked over at him again, as if for the first time. 'We want to talk to Eve Michaels.'

Bucks tented his cheek with his tongue, made a clicking sound in his mouth. 'She's not around the club often.'

'Give us a home number then. An address,' Gooch said.

Bucks didn't say anything for several seconds, as though chewing over his choices. 'She's out of town for a day or so.'

'Do you have a cell phone number for her?' Gooch asked.

'No, sure don't,' Bucks said. 'Call me later.' He took a pen from his pocket; Whit could see the bulge of a cell phone inside. As Bucks jotted the number on a napkin, Whit took a step to one side.

'One question,' Whit said and as Bucks turned toward him Whit popped him with a right jab, below the eye, left of the nose. Then another. Hard. Bucks staggered back, fell on the floor.

'Now we match,' Whit said. He grabbed the gun from the table, pointed it at Bucks, and reached into the man's coat pocket for the cell phone.

'Hey . . .' Bucks said.

'Shut up or I'll dig this in your forehead like you did me.' Whit turned on the phone, found the address book, clicked through the numbers listed inside. EVE CELL was one. He committed the number to memory and dropped the phone on Bucks' chest.

'You did have her number,' Whit said. 'That's one lie you've told us. You don't get two, asshole.'

11

Bucks found Tasha in the dancers' changing room, buds nestled in her ears, swaying to music in front of the mirror. He yanked out an ear bud, heard the thin thump of her song. 'Where the hell is Paul?'

'Up in a private room. Alone.' She glared at him over her shoulder.

'No time for you anymore?' he said. In the mirror he was watching her chest, covered by thin white Lycra. She'd taken off all the computer crap; it lay in a jumble on her makeup table, like a system undergoing repair.

She took out the other earphone. 'He's watching a basketball game. He's in a real sour mood.'

'Word is you're his new girl.'

'Word is.'

'That blond guy you were talking with.'

'Yeah?'

'What'd you talk about?'

'He's a scout for a movie production company. Looking to film a few scenes here.' She examined her lipstick in the mirror.

Bucks was silent. 'He run a tab?'

'Yeah. Why?' Now she watched his face in the mirror.

'No reason. A movie here, that'd be cool.'

She said nothing, watching him with a wry smile.

'What's your problem?' he said.

'Did you get punched in the eye? It's starting to swell,' Tasha said. 'Paul isn't going to like that.'

'Why would he care?'

'A black eye, that's a good advertisement for a bad-ass. Really shows you command respect.'

'I fell on the stairs, hit the railing,' he said, and as soon as the words were out he regretted them, saw she knew he was lying. Little Miss Smart Mouth, uppity and acting like her brain was as big as her tits. He wanted to reach out, grab those perfect breasts, and twist them in a fierce squeeze until she screamed. But she was Paul's now. If Kiko Grace or these Detroit dinks had their way, Paul would go for a long swim in Galveston Bay. And Miss Smart Mouth could join Paul, when Bucks was through with her.

'You should be more careful on that thick carpet,' she said. 'Watch your step.'

'Don't you need to go shake your tits for the slack-jawed masses?' he said.

'I doubt Paul wants you talking to me that way,' she said, and left as Red Robin, sweaty from a lap dance, came in to towel off.

'Hey, sugar,' Bucks said. He had decided being real sweet was a good idea right now.

Robin gave him a quick kiss. 'Hi. What happened to your eye, baby?'

'Fell and hit the staircase, like a dumbass.'

Robin kissed the mark by his eye. 'Angel baby. I'll go to the kitchen, get you an ice bag.'

'In a minute. I want you to do me a favor. Keep an eye on Tasha. Tell me what she's up to.' Bucks put his arms around her, gave her another short little kiss.

'Up to? She's shaking her ass, just like me. Not up to anything.'

'I want to be sure she's not screwing over Paul.'

'Um, okay,' Robin said. 'I'll keep an eye on her. We staying at your place tonight?'

'It's gonna be a late night, sweetie. Deals and all. You go on home. I'll see you tomorrow night.'

'Let me get you that ice pack.'

'Get it to go. I got things to do.' He gave her an affectionate swat on her thonged rear as she went out the door.

Bucks went back into the club, found the waitress who'd waited on the table in question. The charge card was to Whitman Mosley. The ugly jerk who had come up to the room with Desire O'Malley hadn't used a credit card, had paid strictly cash.

Whitman Mosley. The name did not ring a bell. Maybe the guy was using a pseudonym that would not be recognized as a Vasco loyalist from Detroit. But the guys' story . . . well, he didn't quite believe it. Because they were too interested in Eve. Didn't ask about the other players in the Houston organization. And the blond guy had a too-weird, nervous-sad look on his face when Bucks talked about Eve. None of it sounded right to him.

He dialed his cell phone, calling Nicky, one of the guys who'd interrupted his discussion with the two men.

'Yeah?' Nicky said.

'You following them?'

'Yeah. About six cars back. Now we're on Buffalo Speedway. They're driving aimlessly. Like they're deciding where to go.'

'Don't lose them,' he said. 'I will kill you if you lose them.' He clicked off the phone, stepped back out into the thrum of the club.

He should call Kiko. He didn't want to.

He took a calming breath. Go deep, he thought. Be centered. Keep your focus on the goal. Many will seek to pull the goal away from you. Destroy them. But never lose sight of the goal.

Bucks walked upstairs to Frank Polo's office. Frank was there, sitting on the couch, his hand now neatly stitched. A glass of pinot grigio sat on the side table, beaded with cold. The Bellinis had a doctor on call who liked discounted cocaine, didn't mind house calls, and thought discreetness a saintly virtue. The doctor was leaving now, and he nodded politely at Bucks, then looked again at him.

'You want a compress for your eye? It's gonna go shiner,' Doc Brewer said.

'No, thank you.'

The doctor left.

Bucks sat down next to Frank. Handed him the cold glass of wine. Put a hand on Frank's shoulder.

'Let's be realistic. I can't compete with you on landing the ninety thousand.' Bucks shrugged. 'Eve's gonna contact you. You know it. I know it.'

Frank swallowed a gulp of the wine. Then another, watching Bucks. Waiting.

92

'We're on Paul's shit list. But he still has faith in both of us. Or we'd be heading for the bay right now.'

'He's pretty goddamned mad.'

'He's mad, yes. But Frank, you and I are all he has left to make a go of this deal with Kiko. He needs you and me to be his team to help make it happen.' Bucks slid into his business-meeting voice, smooth, ready to rally the troops. 'You help us find Eve and I guarantee I can get him to forgive your stealing. You can even keep the ninety thou.'

'A team.' Frank considered the idea, tenting his cheek with his tongue. 'Fine, Bucks, we're a team. So don't lord over me that I made a mistake, okay? It was a loan.'

'I understand,' Bucks said. 'I do, man. I know what tough times are like. I wish you'd asked us for the money up front.'

'Paul might have said no.'

'To you? Never. You're the closest thing to a dad he's got.'

Frank held up his bandaged hand.

'Okay, an uncle, then.'

'Sucking up isn't you,' Frank said. 'You don't have to bother trying with me, Bucks.'

Bucks gave him a crooked smile. 'Fine. Are we supposed to believe you manipulated credit cards and book entries on your own to the tune of ninety grand? You're a singer. You're not an accountant. Eve set it up, didn't she?'

Now Frank stared into the yellow of his wine.

'Didn't she, Frank?' Bucks said quietly.

'She might've,' Frank said after a moment.

'Ah. A breakthrough,' Bucks said. 'But your girlfriend took off, left you holding the bag. You can pick 'em, Frank.'

'I've not been lucky with women,' Frank said. 'Most singers aren't.'

'Artistic temperament,' Bucks said. 'Joe Vasco.'

Frank made the sign of the evil eye.

'Am I supposed to know what that means?' Bucks said.

'I can't stand Joe Vasco.'

'You been in touch with him, huh? Wanting old friends to take over Tommy's ops now that Paul's pissing you off?'

'Joe Vasco isn't my friend,' Frank said. 'He's not a friend to any friend of Tommy Bellini.'

'Let's be sure of that, Frank. You and Eve, you're not on a new payroll?'

'If I was, then I wouldn't need to borrow ninety grand, would I?'

'Point taken,' Bucks said.

Frank's Valiumed smile faded. 'I'm going home.'

Bucks grabbed Frank's bandaged hand, dug his nails into the stitches. Frank yelled. Wine sloshed onto the carpet. 'You're gonna let me know if you hear from her, right, Frank?'

'Yes. Yes.'

'And to build our team spirit, I'm going home with you. In case Eve calls you. Now. Go downstairs and wait for me.'

Frank set down the wineglass and staggered out, his palm cradled to his chest.

Bucks dialed a number. Listened for an answer. He had to buy precious time, and now. 'Bad news. There's a delay about the money,' he said.

'Not what I'm wanting to hear, Bucksy,' José said.

'They had a problem at the bank. Nothing serious. Eve couldn't wire the full amounts back into the country. A temporary delay. Until Saturday.'

'Be kidding.'

'I'm not.'

'Kiko's going to be upset,' José said. 'Highly upset.'

'That's your problem.'

'Man,' José said, 'that's your problem. You just don't know it.' He was quiet a moment. 'You not turning on us, are you, Bucksy? Because if you're messing with us, we send the police that film and some buttered popcorn.'

'You got me, I know it, okay?' God, he hated José. And calling him *Bucksy,* like he didn't know what he was doing, like he was a child. It made his skin crawl. 'You're going to get your money, I promise.'

'Call us. Tomorrow morning.' José paused. 'With good news only.'

'Good night,' Bucks said. He hung up the phone. Not much

time. He had to get every gun from Paul and Kiko's sides aimed at Eve Michaels. Make sure all the blame stayed firmly on her. Point it at Eve and these two dinks that were looking for her. It didn't matter why they really wanted to find her; he could paint them as her partners in crime.

The dinks. Why would Frank or Eve, who hated Vasco – he knew that part of the Bellini family history was true – call Vasco for help? They wouldn't. So who were these two jerks? Guys from Kiko, testing him? Or plants from Paul? Hopefully not, hopefully just two dumbasses that Eve screwed over. But he could screw them over big time now, make them the target instead of himself, if he played out the game right. Planned his work and worked his plan, like *Chad Channing's Goal Winners!* tape 3 advised.

He took a deep breath, closed his eyes, envisioned a to-do list with clean little checkmarks, the beauty of completion.

Next angle to work, go reassure Paul. Bucks roamed back to the party suites. He found Paul in one, leaning back from a worked-over plate of enchiladas and a couple of empty Shiner bottles. Hiding in beer and comfort food while Bucks did the heavy lifting. In the corner a basketball game was on, the Rockets overpowering the Jazz.

'What happened to your eye?' Paul asked. 'Squeeze the wrong ass?'

'Accident. It doesn't hurt,' he said. He'd break that jackass Michael/Whitman's fingers the next time he saw him.

'You're not bringing me Eve's head on a platter, or my five million,' Paul said. 'I'm not sure why you're here.'

'No, Paul, I don't have her yet,' Bucks said. 'But I got an extension with Kiko. Said it was a bank problem.'

'Good.'

'New problem,' Bucks said. 'I found a couple of guys who seem extremely interested in Eve. They might be a help to us.'

'Who?'

'Guys were here looking for her, gave me a line about her cleaning money for them. Wanting to find her real bad.' Bucks didn't mention their supposed Vasco connection or that they didn't seem to know Eve's cell phone number because it didn't fit into the theory he wanted to feed Paul. 'These two, they're her partners, they can lead us to her,' Bucks said. 'But—'

'Bucks.' Paul stood, turned off the television, shrugged into his jacket. 'If these guys know where she or the money's at, rip it out of 'em. Then kill them. Do your job, man. Now.'

12

'I had no idea you were a mafioso from Detroit,' Whit said.

Gooch turned his van into a diner parking lot. Pie Shack, off Kirby, the lot half-full of cars. 'Lots you don't know, hoss.'

Whit traced his finger along the phone number he'd written on a napkin downstairs in the club before heading for the doors, suddenly afraid he'd forget it in the rushing thrill. Eve Michaels' phone number. The combination of numbers that could open a long-confounding lock. What if this woman wasn't his mother? What if she was?

'Bucks can figure out we're not real mobsters with a couple of phone calls,' Gooch said.

'Yes. He's strange. Bucks looks more like he's a corporate lackey than gang muscle,' Whit said. 'You pushed him too far. I saw it in his face.'

'Because we hit a very raw nerve. He's scared, and he's willing to switch sides to someone who could outgun his boss. Maybe Bucks is on precarious footing. Something's rotten in Bellini-land.'

'Or he's an opportunist,' Whit said. 'This is one great ally you pick for us, Gooch.'

'Fate picked him, not me. Surprised you punched him.'

'He's between me and my mother, and he would have shot me if we hadn't been in a busy club.'

'He would have shot you anyway. Those rooms are sound-proofed. No one would have heard over the bump-and-grind. And they'd carry you out after the club closed.' Gooch kept his eyes on the parking lot, on cars coming in and out. 'We weren't followed. That means he doesn't want the rest of Paul's crew knowing about our chat.'

'You spoke with authority back there, Gooch.'

'Marine Corps. You learn how to speak properly. Hoo-rah.'

'I don't think so,' Whit said. 'You know this world, don't you? These men. Organized crime.'

'I watch a lot of movies.'

'Which bear no resemblance to the real world,' Whit said.

'You hitting him was a smart move,' Gooch said. 'Act afraid of him, you're dead. This is social Darwinism at its next-to-most advanced. Only prison is more brutal.' Gooch glanced over at him. 'This is a side of you I didn't quite expect, Your Honor.'

'This is me . . .' Whit stopped.

'What?'

'This is me finding my mom. It's like training your whole life for a single event, like the Olympics or the Super Bowl or the World Series, and now you can't make a single misstep. If I screw this up . . .' He could roll down the window, wad up the napkin, toss the number into the street. Go home to his dad, take care of him. Walk away from clearly serious trouble.

'Call her,' Gooch said quietly. 'Tell her you'd like to see her.'

'What if she's not my mother, then won't I be a fool?' Whit said. 'I can think of one threat to get her here, and it's not how I want to start a new relationship.'

'Let me talk to her,' Gooch said. 'I'm much more charming and refined.'

For now, she was Emily Smith.

Insurance came in many different forms, and for Eve, protection lay in a safe-deposit box at a branch bank on Kirby, west of the Rice University campus and the sprawl of the Texas Medical Center. Inside the box, a black purse held an Illinois driver's license, a mint Visa credit card, a passport in the name of Emily Smith and five hundred in tidy bricks of cash. She retrieved the purse after listening to news radio in her car to hear if there was breaking news about a double homicide near the Port. There wasn't. But it wouldn't be long and she'd know how much of a description, if any, whoever called the police had given of her.

At least the police won't kill you. Why should Paul believe you after Frank's skimming?

And the answer to that question made her blood race.

She'd seen what happened to thieves in Detroit. Pliers, blow-torches, broom handles were the toys of choice of the men charged with finding where missing money lay. If they believed Paul and Bucks over her – and given Frank's recent pilfering, it was more than likely – they would torture her for days before putting a bullet in her head, even if she couldn't reveal where the money was hidden.

If she ran, she looked guilty and they would never give up. She had saved herself once before, taking his stolen cash back to Tommy, and she figured it was the way to save herself again. Find the money, prove Bucks took it, get the money back to Paul.

She needed a hiding place to wait out the crisis and hatch a plan. Paul might not be watching the airports yet; he would be soon enough. He could pull Kiko into the search as well. Kiko would have a vested interest in getting hold of the cash. She could drive anywhere in the country. But then that would leave Frank alone, and she was afraid of his bearing the brunt of her supposed guilt.

She decided to stay in Houston, at least for the moment.

Hiding out at a dive motel was out of the question; her car wouldn't fit in. So late that afternoon she headed west on I-10, out into suburbia, took the Addicks exit on the edge of Houston, and got herself a room at a nondescript Hilton. She used the Emily Smith card to pay, believing that paying in cash would attract undue attention at a nicer hotel, holding her breath while the card was processed. She'd paid a lot of money for the Emily cards and documents, getting them from an old friend in Detroit who specialized in false identities, and when the desk clerk handed her back the card along with a slip to sign she nearly collapsed in relief.

She tried Frank on the phone. No answer. She showered. Put her clothes back on. Ordered room service, soup and salad, and ate. She needed basics but she didn't want to go to the nearby sprawling malls. She'd found her rock, her comfort zone, and she wasn't eager to get out of it.

Would you like to see one of your sons?

She poured a soda from the minibar, drank half of it down, wiped at the tears that chugging the fizz brought to her eyes. Maybe the man wasn't from one of her kids. Maybe it was a trick of Bucks'. He might have found out about her background. A way to shock her into leaving the exchange.

But there were much easier ways. The guy who took her picture had to be legit.

Her sons. She did not think of them every day but she did on their birthdays, at Christmas, when classes started, although they were all grown now and long past anxious first days of school. She had pictures of them, hidden in the house in Houston; not even Frank knew about them. The thought of losing those photos, never seeing them again, made her ribs hurt.

Eve turned on the news at ten. It was the lead story: two people found shot in an office near the Port. The glossy-lipped anchor faked a frown of personal concern. 'The two bodies have not been conclusively identified.'

Her cell phone rang. She looked at the caller ID: Frank. She clicked it on.

'Frank?'

'They're going to kill me because of you,' Frank said. His voice was low, aching. 'Paul sliced my hand open. You happy?'

'I didn't do it.'

'I told them that. They don't believe me.'

'Bucks did it,' she said.

'I knew it, that bastard.'

'He's got the money.'

'Can't you prove he did it?' Frank said.

'No.'

'He's sticking to me like a horny fan,' Frank said. 'I'm calling from the men's room on the second floor at the club. Hiding in the toilet.'

'Frank . . .' she started, then stopped.

'They gave me a Valium shot; I'm a little fuzzed. I do love you, babe. Even if you did this. I'm having to act, though, like I hate you. Or they'll kill me dead. I told 'em you'd called me, wanted to meet at the Galleria. So don't go there. Where are you?' he asked.

'It's better for you if you don't know. I need to get that money back, Frank. Or prove I didn't take it.' She suddenly didn't feel tough or smart, she simply wanted to be at home in bed with him, watching an old movie, snuggled under the covers.

'Make a deal with the cops. They'll protect you.'

'I'm not doing that.'

'Eve. Baby. Then come in. Talk with me, with Paul.'

'If he doesn't already believe me, I'm dead. Or Bucks will shoot me dead to protect himself before I get two words out.'

'You stay away, Paul believes even more that you stole it,' Frank said.

Her anger at Frank boiled suddenly. 'Your damn skimming. You're half the reason I'm in this trouble. Why on earth did you take money from the club?'

'Everybody pinches,' Frank said. He sounded as mournful as a schoolboy called before a growling teacher. 'But this guy in LA, he said if I could front the money, he could get me recorded and we could sell the CDs on eBay. Or get me guest backup gigs. I still got a name, Eve. It would have worked. Then I would have fed the money back into the club, no one had to know. I figured you'd help me do it.'

'Frank. My God.'

'I'm sorry. I'm sorry.' But she heard resolve in his voice. 'I messed up, so I'm gonna save your ass.'

'How?'

'I can find where Bucks put the money,' he said.

'Frank, you can't find your dick most days.'

'Jesus, you're good to me. What a sweetheart.'

'I'm scared. For once, I'm scared, all right?' Her voice shook. 'I don't have a way out of this. I can't even come home, Frank.'

'I'll meet you. Anywhere.'

'No,' she said.

'What, you don't trust me now?'

She didn't, but she wanted to trust him so badly her need was a sour taste in her mouth. The fact he'd stolen money and Paul hadn't beaten him to a pulp . . . Paul wanted him healthy. To help find her. Frank might be bait.

'You don't love me,' she said. 'This ends it, doesn't it?'

'Sweetheart, I do. But I need you to tell me where you're at,' Frank said.

'Frank . . .' she began, then stopped. 'It's not a good idea.'

'You protecting me or yourself?'

'Both. I'll call you tomorrow.'

'Evie,' he said, and his voice broke slightly. 'I love you. Whatever happens . . . I love you.' Like he expected to see her next in a coffin, to set a rose in her cold, folded hands. She felt a distance begin to widen, a gap between them that hurt her chest.

'Has anyone . . . else been looking for me?' she asked.

'What do you mean?'

'I . . .' She couldn't say it. Frank didn't know about the husband and sons she'd walked away from; at the least she never told him. Port Leo seemed now like a story that had happened in another woman's life. 'Never mind. I'll talk to you tomorrow. Good-bye.'

He started to protest but she clicked off the phone.

She believed that, with all his faults and vanities, Frank did love her. But love didn't bind every heart as tightly. She loved her children, in a way, more as little playmates than as treasured responsibilities, but she had walked away from them. Love was a condition you could get over, and maybe Frank had recovered. Fear could make him leave. She couldn't trust him. And she couldn't put him in further danger.

She lay down on the bed. Her Beretta was at her side. Probably by tomorrow Richard Doyle would be identified, and the police would naturally scrutinize his dealings at the bank. She and Doyle had been very careful. But if Houston Police Department brought in the Feds, and Doyle had left any traces in moving money that she didn't know about, it was probably over. HPD was a smart force, very capable, and of course so were the Feds. She might have to run from the mob and from the FBI. She could try and cut a deal for the Witness program, but she'd known of people who went into WitSec and still got killed.

Her cell phone rang again. No caller ID. She clicked it on.

'Ms Michaels?' A man's voice she didn't know, low.

She said nothing.

'Silent treatment, and you don't even know me yet.'

'Who is this?' Eve sat up on the bed.

'My friends call me Gooch. I met a gentleman tonight named Bucks who is very protective of you. We had to beat him up to get your phone number.'

'I don't know you.'

'Bucks seemed rather desperate to know why I wanted to find you. I got the impression you'd caused him to have a bad day.'

'What do you care?'

'I don't like this Bucks guy at all. He's got a black eye right now and he doesn't like me either,' Gooch said. 'He's a common enemy to you and me.'

'And why do you want to find me?'

'I can explain,' Gooch said. 'Meet me tonight.'

'I'm not meeting anyone I don't know . . .'

'You know the Pie Shack restaurant over on Kirby?'

She did. Pie Shack was an all-night eatery famous for delectable pies and big-plated breakfasts, an eclectic favorite with the late-night bar crowd, Rice University students, night-shift workers. It was always crowded, presumably safe. If this was a trick and Bucks was planning an ambush, it was hardly a good choice.

'Go there. To the rear booth. We can talk. Tons of people around, no need to be afraid. Because you sound kind of nervous and upset.'

'I'm not meeting anyone I don't know who calls me out of the blue.'

'James Powell. Bozeman, Montana,' Gooch said.

She let ten seconds of silence pass, her tongue drying into sand. 'I don't know that name and I don't intend to continue this discussion.'

'The police in Montana would be interested in talking to you even after almost thirty years.'

She finally gave a coarse laugh of disbelief. 'If you're a black-mailer, buddy, you've picked the worst day possible.'

'You have something I want,' Gooch said, 'but it's not money. Skip meeting with me and I'll happily give every bit of information I have on you to the Feds and to the police back in Bozeman. I'll see you at Pie Shack in thirty minutes. Come alone. No gun.' He hung up.

She was scared, but she calmly checked the clip in her Beretta and put it in her purse. The leather of the bag was thin. She could fire right through it. She had closed the curtains but now she opened them slightly, looking out across the coastal plain, covered with strip centers and housing developments and chain restaurants that made this part of Houston practically indistinguishable from any other major city. She could burrow deeper down in the sprawl, hiding in the anonymity of sameness. Rain, starting, turned the lights of suburbia into smears.

She sat back down on the bed. James Powell. She had not thought of him in weeks. You could not kill a person and wipe them from your mind, but James Powell did not haunt her every day.

James Powell. Her sons. The past rising up out of nowhere, this phone call and the strange man today, it could not be coincidence.

Eve got up and dug her car keys out of her purse.

She headed out the door.

13

'I have a surprise for you.' Tasha was a little breathless after the sex. The first night with Paul, him wine-drunk, had been nothing to savor. But tonight, nervous and seeking release, he had been a smarter lover, conscious of her pleasure, taking an interest in it first with his fingers and mouth. The good, leisurely lovemaking done, she smoothed out a raised lock of his brown hair. 'It might make your night,' she whispered, getting up from the bed.

'Baby, my night was already made.'

She went to her computer, checked her e-mail, keyed a button. Papers peeled out from the printer. She picked them up, read them, tossed them on his naked stomach.

'What's this?' he said.

'Credit reports.'

He picked up the pages. She waited for him to speak. He blinked at the data, but it was clear his mind was fuzzed so she sat down next to him.

'About your problem with Eve,' she said. 'I know a guy who's a black hat.'

'A what?'

'A hacker. Gets through computer systems. He worked with me at Houston PrimeNet as a security consultant. We both lost our jobs at the same time. Energis was our big client. They went under, we went under.'

'Yeah,' he said.

'So my friend Ralph, he's what you call socially maladjusted.' She ran a finger along Paul's leg, watched the flesh goose-bump. 'He started hacking because he couldn't find a job for the longest time. He hid himself a Trojan inside the Visa and MasterCard authentication systems.'

'A what?'

'A Trojan.'

Paul still gave her a blank look. 'It's not a condom, baby,' she said. 'It's hidden computer code that does what you want. Get you account information, for example. He uses it now and then to steal an account. He's been asking me business advice, ways we could make the most money off of this little private access. He doesn't want to get caught before he can make serious profit.' Tasha patted the papers. 'I can solve your Eve problem.'

'You could get me five million?'

Tasha took a very subtle, calming breath and locked her smile in place. 'No, sweetpea. He can't get you five million in cash. But let's say Eve planned to run. And let's say she took the precaution of getting new credit cards under new names.'

Paul's eyes widened.

'When a credit card is used for the first time, it creates an initial entry in the account file. So I asked him to find all first-time credit charges in Houston and Galveston for today. For planes, trains, rental cars. Hotels if she's hiding out. And to key it to women's names or cards with the same initials as the name.'

'Holy shit.' Paul stood up and scanned the pages. 'Her name's not here.'

'No. And this only works if she hasn't used the card before. But there's twelve women who bought plane tickets, one named Margaret Scott to Detroit. That could be Eve. Or if she's hiding in town, she might've rented a room. Three rented hotel rooms as initial charges as of eight tonight. Alice Masters at the Doubletree over on Post Oak. Deanna Lopez at Moody Gardens, down in Galveston. Emily Smith at the Hilton out by Addicks, out on the edge of town.'

'My God, baby, you are amazing.' Paul kissed her, hard, slow, grateful, and she felt him rise in her hands. She tickled him with her fingertips.

'There'll be time for that later,' she said. 'See how I can help you?'

'Tasha, what a team we could make.' He tongued her ear.

'Sweetpea.' She cupped his chin with her hands. 'If I give you Eve Michaels, what are you going to give me?'

He smiled, put her hands back on his erection.

'That's a given,' she said. 'I'm asking for a bonus.'

'Okay.' He kissed her. 'But I need to make a call, get guys out to those hotels.' He started to scoot off the bed.

She gave him a little squeeze and he stopped, one leg on the floor. 'Let's move beyond bonus to an actual cut.' She curled her feet up under her rear.

'You're cute when you're smart,' he said.

'I'm never not cute, then,' she said.

'How big of a cut?' A tease touched his voice, one she liked. He ought to shove her out of the way, make those phone calls. But he was giving her time to listen. He was passing her test. She slid her fingernail down his strong Roman nose, along his cheekbones, as though she was mapping out a course.

'Call your guys first. See if they can find her.'

He hurried to the phone, made the calls while she watched. Two guys each, dispatched to each hotel. When he was done, he came to her, gave her another kiss.

'Now you,' he said.

'My cut should be about a half million.'

He laughed, looked blank, laughed again. 'Don't we aim high?'

'I'm serious. Ten percent, finder's fee. I got to pay Ralph for his help. And I want to quit stripping and get a new job.'

'What job?'

'Eve's,' she said. 'Let me be your money minder from now on.' She moved her fingertip along his mouth, stuck the fingertip between his lips. He flicked his tongue across the nail, kissed the flesh.

His voice thickened as her finger roamed down across his stomach, tickled at his navel. 'Think you're qualified?' he said.

Okay, he had flunked. 'Qualified?' Tasha pointed at the papers. 'I handed you Eve and your five million. You lose her this time, she gets away, maybe I don't ask Ralph for his help again. We can let her walk off if you aren't interested in playing nice.'

'How about I give you and Ralph fifty K? It's a lot for a few minutes work.'

'Not if it saves your ass.' She got up from the bed, knelt down, searched under the bed for her panties. 'I'm sorry I bothered.'

Tasha didn't hear him rise from the bed as she stood. His fist closed in her hair and he yanked her head back, bared her throat, gave her flesh a little nip. He eased her onto the mattress, his grip still tight. It didn't hurt, much, but a hot boil of anger rose in her chest.

'You're not going. We're not done,' Paul said.

'Let go. Please.'

'You don't threaten not to help me. You got that, Tasha?' He pushed her face down into the sheets. 'Now. What are you going to do?'

'Help you.'

The pressure on her head eased slightly and his voice softened. 'Besides that, baby.'

'Paul,' she said, 'I can do a lot more for you than be good in bed.'

'Clearly. You're the smartest person I know right now, Tasha. But I don't like it when you make me get rough with you.' He let go of her hair.

Like his ill temper was her fault. She crafted a careful smile, made it rise on her face, looked up at him with a mix of patience, desire, and calmness. She reminded herself that right now, she needed him. That wouldn't always be the case. And she filed this nasty minute of roughness away, to remember, to use later. 'So. I help you, you're gonna help me, right?'

He kissed the top of her head. 'You usually deliver the goods before collecting the reward. But I'll give you and Ralph a hundred thou, final offer.'

'Okay,' she said. She didn't believe him.

Now he smiled, kissed her lips. She stayed still. 'Cool, baby, and you've given me an idea with Ralph. I want to know everything Frank Polo's been charging on his accounts. Eve, too. And Bucks.'

'Bucks?'

'Tasha, he's my friend. But that doesn't mean I trust him right now.'

'Do you trust me?' she asked.

'Sure I do,' he said. 'Sure I do. And that's why I've got a real special job for you to do.' He leaned down, gave her a slow, gentle kiss, and this time she kissed back.

14

Gooch slipped the hostess a ten-dollar bill and nabbed a large booth in the back of the Pie Shack. Whit sat across from him. The place had the treasured atmosphere of an old neighborhood café: mirrored walls, neon art of thick slices of pie on plates, coffee steaming up from a mug at every booth. The huge window by the booth that faced out into the lot was smeared with rain. Thunder sounded far off, a brief rumble.

'Now we wait,' Gooch said.

Whit glanced back at the doorway. 'I shouldn't sit here, by the window. She could see me. Run.'

'I doubt she'll know who you are after thirty years, Whit.'

'I don't know.' He fidgeted in the booth, checked his watch. 'She's late.'

'She's going to be. At least fifteen minutes. If she's survived this long working for a crime ring she's going to be cautious. She'll put us on the defensive.'

'She's not going to talk to me in a busy place.' The Pie Shack was full. The two closest booths – there were no tables – were both occupied, one by three gay guys rehashing their evening at a local club, the other by a wine-happy quartet of women, laughing at themselves and digging through thick slabs of meringued pies, attempting to sober up with pots of black coffee. Both groups seemed wholly captivated by their own conversations. A riser of plants separated the booths from each other, obscuring views and dulling sounds.

Whit watched a Lincoln Navigator with tinted windows drive through the lot, mist rising from its tires. Then a pickup truck, then a Lexus.

'Easy, boy,' Gooch said. 'She'll talk to you. She has a nice-sounding voice.'

'She's probably more nervous than I am.'

'She has reason to be. Sit at the counter and keep your back turned to the front door,' Gooch said. 'You won't scare her off that way when she walks in.' Gooch cocked a finger at him. 'It's gonna be okay, buddy.'

'Thanks.' Whit took a seat at the long, curving counter. Turned his back to the front door. He ordered a cup of decaf, dosed it with milk, and hunched his shoulders over the curl of steam. On his right a woman in a security guard uniform plowed through an omelette doused in chili and cheese; she gave him a glance that showed she noticed his bruised face but said nothing. On his left a young man with three earrings ate butter-soaked waffles and read *Sports Illustrated*.

Whit stirred the milky swirl of his coffee. No mirror was mounted above the bar to let him watch arrivals and departures. But he heard the jingle of the door as it opened and closed, and each time the little bell tinkled he tightened his grip on his coffee cup. He tried not to care. He glanced over at Gooch's booth; he could barely see the top of Gooch's crewcutted head over the divider of fake ivy.

He had played out in his mind a thousand times what he would say to his mother. Why did you do it? What did we do wrong? How could you? I hate you. I forgive you.

The day she had left, his four oldest brothers had gone with family friends to see a movie in Corpus Christi. He and Mark, the littlest boys at two and three, had played in the backyard, worn themselves out playing chase while his mother sat and watched. She'd put them down for naps and, while they slept, she put her bags in her car, placed signed divorce papers on the dinette, and left Port Leo forever. He imagined that before she walked out the door she kissed him good-bye, cuddled him, told him she was sorry. She probably had done none of those things.

Sweat tickled the undersides of his arms, the backs of his legs.

The door jingled.

He waited, watched the hostess leading a young couple to a

front booth. He relaxed a moment. Then he saw an older woman, her back to him, dressed in a rumpled suit and no raincoat, heading right for Gooch's back booth.

'I don't know you.' Eve Michaels slid into the booth. She clutched her purse close to her right side. My God, she thought, the guy was a bruiser. Built big and broken-mirror ugly. Hands as big as hubcaps.

'I'm Gooch.' He didn't rise from the booth, wisely not making any move to scare her, but he did offer one of the plus-sized hands. She didn't shake it. She had her hand on the Beretta, pointed at him inside the purse. She flicked her gaze to her left; the kitchen door was right there. In case she had to shoot and run.

'That's a very nice purse, by the way,' Gooch said.

'Thank you.'

'What are you aiming at me? A .357 Magnum?' Gooch asked.

The waitress approached, took her order for coffee and lemon pie, and left.

'Most women put their purse on the side that isn't by the aisle,' Gooch said. 'You've got it right next to you, on the aisle, and your hand went in it as soon as you sat down.'

'Like I said, Mr Gooch, I don't know you.'

The waitress returned with the coffee, poured Eve a steam-kissed cup, refreshed Gooch's mug, walked away. The booth of drunken women brayed loud and long at one of their own jokes.

'Coffee doesn't make you jittery, right?' Gooch said. 'I don't want you jittery with a gun pointing at me.' He sounded unconcerned. 'I'd prefer you put both hands on the table.'

She didn't. 'James Powell?'

'We can talk about him later,' Gooch said. 'Why does the mention of your name send Bucks into a tantrum?'

She decided he wasn't a cop or a Fed. This wasn't the place they'd pick. Not the words they'd use. 'He's a thief and he's framed me.'

'What did he steal?'

'Tell me who you are before I say another word.'

Gooch glanced up and past her shoulder. 'I'm not from your

friends. Paul Bellini can lose every dime he's got and I won't care.'

She tightened her grip on the gun. 'You're not here about the money?'

'Money. No. Love,' Gooch said.

'I don't . . .' she began and then a young man with a face much like hers slid into the booth next to Gooch.

'Hi, Ellen,' he said. His voice was steady. A little husky. Not cold but not exactly friendly.

She didn't move. Didn't speak.

'Still pointing the gun? At him or me?' Gooch asked. 'Really, Mrs Mosley, it's time to let it go.'

Eve stared at the young man. Then, slowly, she put both hands on the table.

15

Ten seconds passed and Whit said, 'Are you trying to figure out which one I am?'

'You're Whitman,' she said. Her voice was a low, gravelly alto, roughened. She coughed once, cleared her throat. Put a hand up to her mouth as if stifling a hiccup, then back down again. Staring at him. Her mouth was open slightly, a little wet. 'You're Whit-man.'

'I'm impressed,' Whit said.

'I'll sit up at the counter,' Gooch said. 'Let y'all talk.' Whit rose, Gooch scooted out, Whit sat back down and the whole time she never took her eyes from Whit.

Whit folded his hands on the table.

'You've got a nasty bruise on your face.' Her voice was flat, not motherly.

'Got one and gave one back. To your buddy Bucks.'

'Good for you.' She swallowed. Outside the rain pelted down harder, a cloudburst flowering, water puddling by the curbs, a laughing trio of Rice students running and screaming through the rain toward their car.

'I figured,' Whit said, 'that when you saw me you were either going to run in shame, tell me you never want to see me or my brothers again, or say you're sorry.'

She rubbed at her temples. 'I'm sorry.'

'You didn't even deny who you are. I guess that was the other option.'

She sipped at her coffee, set the mug down carefully. Her hand shook; she covered it with her other hand. 'Denial would be pointless. You've found me. Congratulations.'

The waitress stopped across from their table, grabbing a fresh pot from the coffee stand, filled a carafe, set it on their table.

'Don't you want to know how? Or why?' Whit asked. He kept his voice quiet.

'Not right now, Whitman. I'm trying to collect my thoughts. Catch my breath.' She tried to smile.

'I go by Whit.'

'Whit. Sure. Your father was never that crazy about the name Whitman, even though it was from his family.'

'He grew to like it.'

'May I touch your hand?' she asked unexpectedly.

He hesitated. He had not imagined physical contact, but shock and rejection and angry words hitting like missiles. 'Why?'

'I would just like to touch you.'

Heat surged in the back of his eyes, in his throat, in his stomach. 'Okay.'

She put her hand on top of his. Not holding. Touching. Her hands were worn, but her nails were freshly manicured, painted a mild red, and a good-sized diamond glittered on her left hand.

'Are you glad I found you?' he asked.

'I have mixed emotions about it. But not because of you.'

He didn't understand her comment, so he let it pass, his long-considered game plan of what to say evaporating in the heat of the moment's reality. 'I always figured this would happen on *Oprah*. Unexpected reunions.'

'We're more *Jerry Springer*,' she said and it made him laugh for a moment.

Her lemon pie arrived; the waitress set it down by their joined hands; Whit said he didn't need anything, thank you, as she took out her order pad. She left them alone.

'How is your father?' Eve asked. 'Your brothers?'

'Wow, a sudden bout of caring.' He knew the words sounded ugly but he couldn't help himself.

'What else am I supposed to ask you, Whit?' she said. 'Your opinion on the Middle East? Your favorite TV show? Whether you prefer wine or beer?'

'I'm not much for drinking,' Whit said. 'Daddy drank himself sick for years after you left.'

'Is he still drinking?'

'No. But he's dying. Cancer. He has four months, max. That's why I wanted to find you.'

She digested this news in silence. 'You sent a man looking for me.'

'Yes. A private investigator.'

She released a long, wobbly breath. She put her other hand over her eyes but now she took his hand, squeezed his fingers. 'Fortyish? Dark hair, a little rumpled, looked like a schoolteacher?'

'Yes. You saw him?'

'Yes.' Now she looked at him. 'I saw him once.' She reached for her coffee, drank it down. When he said nothing more, she said, 'I'm truly sorry about your father. And to see you . . . I'm happy to see you. More than you could ever know, baby. But this is a bad time.'

'There's no good time, is there? In your line of work.'

'Whit.' Her voice shook. 'What do you know about me?'

'You work for Tommy Bellini.'

'I'm in trouble. I may need to leave town very quickly.'

'You're not going to do that.' He clutched her hand. 'You're coming back with me to Port Leo. See my father. Apologize to him before he dies. See my brothers. They're all well. Happy.'

'I can't. I can't.'

'You have grandchildren,' Whit said. 'Beautiful grandchildren. Four of them. Teddy has three girls, Joe has a little boy.'

Her lips thinned; her eyes filled. 'I can't, please don't ask this of me.'

'You can. Please.' Suddenly a truth pierced his heart, a certainty he hadn't known before. 'They'll forgive you. In time. If you get to know them, let them know you.'

'I would put your family in danger, Whit. People want me dead.'

'All the more reason to come with me then.'

'You have no idea of the trouble I'm in.'

'What if I helped you?'

'You don't know what you're saying.' She reached for his cheek

116

but then put her hand back atop his. 'Seeing you means everything to me. But you don't want this trouble, baby. You can't handle it.'

'Don't call me baby. And I can.'

'Oh, tough guy because you survived a black eye? These people will cut off your dick. Shove it down your throat. Rape you with a broomstick.' Eve let the ugly words hang between them. 'I don't want you stepping one foot in this world.'

'I'm not walking away from you. We could call the police, get you protection.'

'No,' she said, her voice a strained whisper. 'It never works well enough. They'd find me, kill me.' She withdrew her hand. 'Go have a good life, Whit. Tell your brothers I'm glad they're happy. I'm sorry for Babe, I truly am.' She put her purse in her lap, glanced out the window. The showers had lessened in the last minute, the storm taking a breath, and a Lincoln Navigator eased past the restaurant, slowing for a car about to pull out from a parking slot.

'You changed soaps,' Whit said. 'You don't smell of gardenia any more.'

She froze. 'What?'

'That's really my best memory of you. Gardenia. Your neck always smelled of it.'

She wiped tears from her eyes, her mouth trembled.

'I need more from you than the smell of soap. I really don't want you to leave,' Whit said. 'If I ask Gooch, he'll toss you over his shoulder, throw you in his van, and drive you all the way to Port Leo, Ellen.'

'Eve. No one calls me Ellen.'

'Eve,' he said, as though tasting the word. 'Look at me. I want to know exactly what's happening. Exactly. Otherwise I'm going to go to the police and—'

The window exploded.

Whit hit the floor in front of the booth, airborne chunks of pie and a gush of hot coffee flying around him, shards of glass bursting in from the barrage of gunfire. His mother screamed. She was cut or shot, trying to get down into the well of the booth, blood streaking her face. Whit grabbed her shoulders and dragged her below the window line into the mess of gunshot pie and pooling coffee and water.

The gunfire stopped.

Screams wailed around them, ranging from full-out shrieks to hiccuping moans of terror. The party girls were facedown on the floor or huddled in the leather womb of their booth, the window by them cracked and webbed. The waitress lay sprawled by Whit, a shattered plate still in her hand, eyes open and still, gray hair dislodged from a bun, her throat a wet wound.

'Back door,' Eve said. 'Run . . .'

He clutched her head to him, searching for the wound. 'You're shot.'

'No, oh no,' she said. Her eyes went wide.

Then people started running, a mad stampede out of the restaurant, toward the front doors.

Whit pulled Eve toward the swinging doors of the kitchen and his mind registered Gooch, his gun drawn from a back holster under his jacket, jumping from booth top to booth top, heading for them, and a man, swarthy, rushing the window, jabbing the remaining cracked glass out of his way, swinging the eye of a semiautomatic toward him and Eve.

The gunman paused to smile – a smile that said *you're so fucked* – and the gesture cost him because the next bullet fired came from Gooch's Sig Sauer and the gunman fell back.

'Back door,' Eve said again, crawling past the dead waitress, pushing Whit along. He grabbed her, rammed through the swinging doors as the gunman, either hit or not, blasted off another round. Whit, Eve, and Gooch landed on the cool tile of the kitchen, the cooks and bakers mostly gone, one girl babbling into a wall phone. Whit got Eve to her feet, followed two terrified dishwashers barreling toward a fire exit.

As he reached the door, the dense, staccato thrum of gunfire hit pots and pans and countertops. A hard gong sounded, a bullet striking the exit door north of his head. Gooch returned fire and Whit shoved Eve out the door. The kitchen staff scrambled through the parking lot, running, yelling in Spanish.

Gooch's van was parked near the rear of the lot and Whit

steered Eve toward it. He glanced back. Gooch had taken cover near a Dumpster, gun leveled at the back door. Waiting.

More shooting inside. Whit pushed Eve through a line of cars, putting vehicles between them and the door. 'Gooch!' he screamed. 'Get out, come on . . .'

The gunman came out the door, holding the young woman who'd been on the wall phone as a human shield. Gooch didn't lower his gun.

'The cops will be here in thirty seconds,' Gooch called. 'Let her go.'

'We want Eve!'

Eve and Whit ducked down by a red pickup truck. Her hand tightened on his.

'You hit Eve, man,' Gooch called, 'and she's bleeding bad.' From his vantage point the gunman couldn't see if Eve was with him or not. In the distance police sirens began to shriek in their approach.

Then a Lincoln Navigator wheeled around the restaurant. The gunman shoved the young woman to the pavement and dashed toward the car.

He made it three steps and Gooch gave him a bullet for each. He skittered a little dance, collapsing before the open door of the Navigator. The SUV sped onto Kirby, door still open, rumbled into a shopping center parking lot and hard-turned onto a side street.

The girl ran back into the restaurant, and Gooch sprinted from the Dumpster toward them.

'Go,' he yelled. 'Now.'

'The guy . . .'

'He's dead, Whit. We got to get out of here.'

'We can't leave,' Whit started. 'This is a crime scene . . . that waitress is dead . . .'

'We have to.'

'But . . .' Whit almost said *I'm a judge, I can't do this,* but if his mother heard that, she'd take off running herself.

'You want the cops to take in your mom? Because they will when they find out her connection to this,' Gooch said. 'Find her, lose her, all in short order.'

Whit pulled Eve into the back of the van with him and Gooch powered up the engine, tore out the back of the parking lot onto a feeder street that ran parallel to Kirby, vanishing with a right into a residential neighborhood, and was two blocks away by the time the police cars and ambulances tore into the lot, red and blue lights making the broken windows glitter like diamonds.

16

'Hospital,' Whit ordered Gooch. 'Now.'

'No,' Eve said. 'I'm not hurt, Whit. I'm okay.'

'No hospital,' Gooch said. 'At least for now.'

They headed back to Charlie Fulgham's house, ten minutes away from the restaurant; back down lower Kirby, cutting through the quiet of the big old houses of West University Place, taking a winding route along tree-shaded roads with names like Tulane and Rutgers and Loyola. Gooch drove at the speed limit and came to a complete stop at every sign. West University Place police were notorious for ticketing for the smallest traffic infraction.

Eve lay on her back in the van. Whit pulled off his blue shirt, mopped her head free of blood. The wound in her scalp wasn't too big, probably from flying glass, but had bled with the flooding tendency of head wounds.

They hurried her inside, Gooch parking the van at the rear of Charlie Fulgham's driveway, out of sight of the street. Charlie sat in his kitchen, drinking a beer and flipping through a copy of *Texas Bar Journal*, marking stories with a red pen, when they staggered in.

'What the hell happened?' Charlie stared at Eve and Whit's bloodied shirt.

'First-aid kit?' Gooch asked.

'Yeah. Here.' Charlie rummaged in the back of the kitchen pantry, pulled out a little plastic case that seemed wholly inadequate to stitch up the carnage of the past fifteen minutes. 'You want me to call 911?'

'No,' Gooch said. 'We'll tend to her.'

'This is my mother,' Whit said. Weird, the words of introduction coming from his mouth, never spoken before. 'Eve, this is Charlie Fulgham. Our host.'

'Hi,' Eve said.

'Uh, hi,' Charlie said. Eve gave him a weak smile, her shoulders still shaking. Now, in clear light, Whit saw she had a score of small cuts and abrasions on her hands, her arms. His hands, too, and a sharp sting lashed his forehead.

'They didn't follow us,' Gooch said to Whit. 'The guys or the cops.'

'Gooch,' Charlie said. 'Let's talk, you and me, in the living room, as in right now.'

'Sure,' Gooch said. Calm. Like he hadn't shot another person to death a few minutes before.

Whit swabbed at Eve's wound with a wet washcloth, took scissors from the kit and clipped away the graying hair close to her cut. The wound was not bad, but it needed closing. He sprayed disinfectant on it and she winced. He cleaned and taped the wound shut, covering it with a strip of gauze.

'You need a stitch or two.' He shook two ibuprofen painkillers into her open palm. 'We could make up a story, take you to an emergency room. You should see a doctor.'

'No,' she said. 'Paul will have those watched closely now.'

'He can't watch every hospital in Houston.'

'Sure he can,' Eve said. Gooch returned to the kitchen, without Charlie, still holding his gun. 'He tracked you two to the Pie Shack.'

'Or he tracked you,' Gooch said.

'Not hardly,' she said. 'Nicky and his driver wouldn't have let me reach you if they were tailing me. They would have taken me at first sight. I'm surprised they didn't grab me in the lot . . . I must've come in on the other side of them circling around the diner.'

'Bucks must've ordered us followed,' Whit said.

'No,' Gooch said, 'I would have spotted the tail.'

There was a silence in the room, except for the distant sound of a television sparking to life in the living room. 'Or not,' Eve said. 'Are you infallible?'

'Practically,' he said in a cool voice.

'Practically isn't going to be good enough. Paul and Bucks can hire as much muscle as they want to get me. They simply have to offer a cut of the five million and I've got an instant megabounty on my head.' She shook her head at Gooch. 'I hope you have an army to back you up, Gooch. Paul will hunt you down like a dog for killing Nicky.'

'You're welcome,' Gooch said. 'I hope I get to save your sorry ass again tomorrow.'

'Stop.' Whit sat down, closed his eyes. 'Is Charlie upset?' he asked Gooch.

'No. I gave him three dollars. Retainer. All three of us are his clients as of this moment. Commit all the crimes you want.'

'Clients?' Eve asked.

'He's a top defense lawyer, Eve,' Gooch said.

She stood. 'No. Nobody else knows anything about me, all right? I don't want a lawyer.'

'Sit down, please,' Whit said and after a moment she did. 'Gooch, what did you tell him?'

'That there are bad guys after Eve, but for him not to worry. He's cool,' Gooch said.

'He's going to kick us out.'

'I said, he's cool. Come here a second, Whit.'

Whit followed Gooch into Charlie's den. In the corner was a gun vault, with an array of rifles, pistols, and knives. Several weapons were shining with fresh polish, others looked antique and unusable. Charlie glanced at Whit and Gooch. He had been looking out the back window, not watching the TV.

'Good God,' Whit said.

'The people I used to defend were scum,' Charlie said. 'This was my security blanket if they got mad at me.'

'Charlie, I'm sorry. We don't want to drag you into trouble,' Whit said.

'Whatever Gooch needs,' Charlie said, 'Gooch gets.'

'I once did a big favor for Charlie. Private business,' Gooch said.

Whit started to ask and Charlie shook his head. 'Go to your mother, Whit. We'll talk when you're done.'

Gooch followed Whit back to the kitchen. Whit wadded up his bloodied shirt. Eve watched him. 'Sorry about your shirt,' she said.

'It's okay.'

Now she stood, came to his chair, knelt by him. 'Your eye, it needs ice. And you're cut—'

Gooch, with a slight smile, aimed his gun at Eve. She didn't move, didn't blink. 'Very touching, Florence Nightingale.'

'Gooch,' Whit said. 'Stop.'

'Tell all, Eve,' Gooch said. 'How will they come after us? Why are they shooting at you, if you're so high and mighty in the organization? What's this about five million you owe them?'

'Gooch, put that down!' Whit said.

'Honey, you don't scare me,' Eve said. 'If you were going to shoot me, you could have shot me back at the diner.' She closed her hands around Whit's knees.

'Listen closely,' Gooch said. 'I'm not your son. I'm not emotionally shredded about you the way Whit is.'

'Psychoanalysis from you? That's like a surgical lecture from Jack the Ripper,' Whit said. 'You are way out of line, Leonard. Sit your ass down over there and take that gun off her.'

'Whit,' Gooch said softly. 'You don't see what I see.'

'I see you putting down that gun and sitting your butt down. Now.'

Gooch lowered the gun.

Eve watched him. 'I like you, Gooch. You don't mess around, do you?'

'No, I don't.'

'I'd like a glass of water, Whit,' Eve said. 'It's a long story.'

'Story, then drink,' Gooch said.

'She bled, Gooch, she's thirsty.' Whit went to the counter, filled a glass with ice and water, set it down in front of her.

'You forgot the lemon slice,' Gooch said. 'And the lace doily.'

'Turn it down, please,' Whit said, thinking, *You killed a man, Gooch, and you don't seem remotely bothered by it.* The depth to which he still did not know or understand his best friend gave him a tremble along his ribs.

'I see we've already picked teams,' Gooch said.

'You're not helping,' Whit said.

'Helping. Who saved your ass tonight and who put it in danger? Do I need to draw flash cards for you?'

'Thank you,' Whit said.

'Thank you, Gooch,' Eve said. 'Not so much for me. For Whit.'

'Sell it to Hallmark,' Gooch said.

'I'll answer your questions,' Eve said. 'Since you've asked so nicely. And because you can take Whit and get out of this mess, right now.' She took a long sip of cold water. She told the story in its entirety: from Paul's determination to cut a big deal to keep his throne and make the Bellinis more powerful, her assignment to get five million in clean cash to pay off Kiko, Frank's skimming and Paul's warning to her, the stranger's unexpected arrival at the exchange site, Eve fleeing then returning and finding the men dead and the five million in cash gone, and Bucks' subsequent chase of her.

'He was your PI, wasn't he, honey? I'm so sorry. So, so sorry.'

At the mention of Harry's death, Whit put his face in his hands. The kitchen was quiet. From the den came the hushed voices of the TV, Charlie flipping through the local stations to see if there were any reports about the Pie Shack shooting. Lazy rain pittered against the darkened windows.

'I shouldn't have had Harry try to contact you,' Whit said. 'Holy God, what have I done?' He thought of Claudia, back in Port Leo, her friend now dead, trying to imagine a way to tell her, wanting to tell her before anyone else did but not knowing how he would explain it.

'This isn't your fault, Whit,' Eve said. 'It was the wrong place at the wrong time. Harry must have followed me there.' She reached out, touched his leg. Gooch made a snorting sound. Whit put his hands down.

'You say Bucks killed Harry and Doyle. And has the money,' Whit said.

'Yes,' Eve said. 'Bucks either wants it for himself or wants Paul to fail so he can take over.'

'So what happens to the deal now?' Whit said.

'It doesn't happen,' Eve said. 'Without that money.'

125

Whit refilled his mother's glass with ice cubes and water, set it down in front of her. 'Before we were attacked, you told me you wouldn't go to the police. Now innocent people are dead. We have to call the police. Or have Charlie call them.'

'Nicky killed the waitress, Gooch killed Nicky. Isn't that justice?' Eve said. 'Of course, Gooch here might not want to deal with courts.' Her voice almost sounded hopeful.

'Not a worry,' Whit said. 'It was self-defense.'

'Not how the court of Paul Bellini will view it,' she said. 'You kill one of his guys, you die. There's no plea bargaining.'

'So I kill Paul Bellini if I have to,' Gooch said.

'You don't kill anyone else, Gooch,' Whit said. 'And Eve, you and me go to the police and you tell them everything you know. They get you into the witness protection program . . .'

She laughed. 'No, no, no. That's worthless. I'm not getting a new name, a bad hairdo, and a nice split-level in Boise to spend the rest of my life looking over my shoulder. I testify, I'm dead. They find you.'

'What makes you think you have a choice?' Whit said.

'Ah. So this is the revenge on me for being a bad mother?' She shrugged. 'You can call the police, Whit, but you do and I'm not saying another word. Your testimony about the money is hearsay.'

'Harry Chyme was a man I liked,' Whit said. 'I liked him more than I like you. And he died because I wanted to find you.'

'It's not my fault.'

'But it's your problem, Eve. Don't threaten me with what you will and won't do. I'm telling you what you'll do.'

'There's my boy,' Gooch said.

'You gonna tell the cops Gooch killed a guy and fled the scene? Stops sounding like self-defense then,' she said.

'Still a bigger risk for you, sweetheart,' Gooch said.

'Why save me then put the screws to me?' Eve turned to Whit. 'I don't understand.'

'I'm not letting Bucks get away with Harry's murder. You may be more casual in your attitude.' And he thought again of the man she had possibly left Port Leo for those long years ago, the dead man in Montana. The so-called suicide. He tried to imagine her killing a man, sitting hunched in her rumpled, wet suit, with a bandage awkwardly taped to her head, her makeup smeared by the rain and him having wiped up her blood.

'You wanted to meet me, right? That's the reason you came looking for me. Or was it to bully me? Blackmail me?'

'I don't understand.'

She glanced at Gooch. 'Gooch mentioned James Powell when he called me, said you would put the Montana police on me.'

'Yeah. It was my idea,' Whit said.

She looked at him with disappointment. 'Oh, Whit. I didn't kill James Powell,' Eve said. 'He killed himself.'

'And you got custody of the money?' Gooch said.

'What money?' she asked.

'I don't give a rat's ass about James Powell,' Whit said. 'I wanted to find you so I could bring you back to Port Leo. To see my father before he dies. I'm not trying to screw you over.'

She crossed her arms. 'Fine. I'll go. You and Babe and the rest of the boys can tell me, to my face, what a sorry mother I was and I'll take it without blinking. But I only go on my own terms.'

'Don't negotiate with her, Whit,' Gooch said.

'Let's hear these terms,' Whit said.

'I have to get my name cleared with Paul. He has to know I didn't take the money. That means either proving Bucks took it or finding the money and returning it to Paul. Otherwise, I'm dead. And I'm not spending the rest of my life on the run, Whit.'

'Because you're a homebody now,' Gooch said.

'Leave us alone for a moment, Gooch. Please,' Whit said.

Gooch, without a word, got up and left.

'I need a friend like him,' Eve said. 'He's your personal pit bull. You're lucky.'

'So you want our help.'

She wiped the traces of lipstick away from her mouth. 'I don't want you in danger, Whit. But I have nowhere to turn. Frank is not going to stick out his neck to help me. Bucks has framed me, beautifully. And no one believes me. I can't do this on my own.'

'Fine. Then we call the police.' He had to try it again.

'In which case I say nothing, I don't go back to Port Leo with you, and Gooch takes his chances with the Harris County legal system.' She shrugged and opened the first-aid kit. 'Let me tend your cuts.' He let her, his back stiffening at her touch as she dabbed ointment on his skin.

'You didn't cry much when you got skinned as a kid. Not like Mark,' she said. 'He screamed like a cut banshee.'

'Don't go down Memory Lane with me. You don't have a ticket.'

'Look, I'm not going to be June Cleaver.' She got up, filled a baggie with ice, wrapped a towel around it. She handed him the ice pack, sat back down across from him.

'So how do we help you, Eve?' Whit asked.

'Your friend seems more than competent under fire.'

'His brain got baked by the sun a long time ago; he doesn't know any better.'

'He was smart tonight,' she said. 'What do you do, Whit?'

He hesitated, at first thinking she was asking him what choice he was going to make but realizing she was asking what his job was. If she knew he was a judge she'd run, vanish again. He was an officer of the court. What he was contemplating, what he had done, would result in his immediate dismissal from office if it were known. He loved his job, but sitting across from his mother he thought: *it's a job. Nothing more.* 'I don't want to talk about me.'

'If you help me find the money, and clear my name,' she said, 'I'll go to Port Leo with you.'

'We should go to Port Leo now.'

'I've given you the deal, Whit. Help me or let me go.' She paused and, when he gave no answer, she stood. 'Fine. Go ahead. Let them kill me.'

'Now you sound like a mother.'

'I know I was nothing as a mother. I know.' Her voice grew hoarse.

'Actually, my dad said you were a good one before you took off. I wouldn't remember.'

She studied the warm wood of the kitchen table.

'Were you bored? Decided kids were no fun?' He kept his voice calm. 'What was so wrong with us?'

'You thought it was your fault.' She passed her hand over her eyes. She went to the sink, ran fresh water in her glass. 'Oh, God,' she said, her back still to him. 'I'm sorry. There was absolutely nothing wrong with you, Whit. Or your brothers or even your father. Nothing. It's me. I'm the one that's bent, I'm the one that's broken.'

'You broke everyone else by leaving.'

She drank her water, watched him over her shoulder. 'You seem well-adjusted.'

'I'm tough.'

'But you came looking for me. You got a hole I'm supposed to fill?'

'So you do have a nerve to hit,' Whit said. 'Now you're sounding downright bitchy.'

'Baby, I am downright bitchy.'

'That probably served you well in your new life.' He shook his head. 'The mob. You traded your kids in for the mob.'

'I hope you never have to make a really terrible decision, Whit. Most people don't. They amble through life and they whine about moments of inconsequence.' She finished her water. 'I hope you get to amble.'

'Don't ask for pity. You made your choice. I doubt you've had years of sleepless nights worrying over us.'

'I don't expect you to understand,' Eve said, 'and I'm not going to explain to you. They're going to kill me in the worst possible way to make me tell them where the money is.' She steadied her voice. 'I've never been more scared in my life, except on the day when I left you.'

'You were scared.'

'Very much so. You think it was easy? It wasn't . . .' She stopped. 'I'm not going to try and explain it.'

'You couldn't.'

'Then I won't waste my breath.' Eve went to the back door, opened it. The brisk, wet night lay outside, black under the arches of the live oaks. Rain dripped from the branches. 'You won't see me again. Thank you and thank Gooch for saving my ass tonight. I appreciate you delaying the inevitable. Bye, Whit.'

He got up, slammed the door shut. He didn't want her to go. Found and lost, all in the matter of an hour. Her face was still, blank. Waiting.

'Do you have a plan?' he asked. 'On how to get the money?'

'I have a couple of ideas on how to nail Bucks, prove he's betrayed Paul. Get evidence that Paul will believe. But I can't do it alone.'

'Here's the deal, Mom.' He let the little odd word settle between them. 'We nail Bucks for Harry's murder. Then you come with me to Port Leo to see my father and my brothers. And if you trick me or run out on me again, I'll give you to the Feds myself in two fricking seconds and you can fry in hell for all I care.'

'Deal,' she said.

17

Friday morning in Port Leo was gorgeous, the air clear and the sky the color of pearl. When the light filtered in through her window and awoke her, it didn't bother Claudia Salazar that she had gotten barely five hours of sleep. Last night the Port Leo police department, working with the sheriff's departments in Encina and Aransas counties, had busted a burglary and fencing ring. Arrests and interviews had kept Claudia up until 2 a.m.

But the sun, even in winter, beckoned.

Claudia went for a leisurely run on the smooth flat of beach along St Leo Bay, the sand wet beneath her sneakers. The fishing boats already sailed the horizon, out past the thin barrier islands that guarded the Texas coast. The morning air was February-cool but she pulled off the windbreaker she'd worn down to the beach, tied it around her waist, turned around and ran back the length of the beach and the park, letting the warmth sift through her body. Her sweat was light and she felt good.

She walked back to her small apartment, stopping for a bottle of grapefruit juice and an egg-and-potato breakfast taco at a small convenience store up from the harbor. She sipped at the juice and ate her taco as she headed past Port Leo's shopping and arts district and the courthouse square, watching the tourist birders heading out with the cameras and binoculars from the bed-and-breakfasts near the square, eager to spot the coast's famed, precious whooping cranes. At home she stood under the shower's hot spray, then turned the water icy cold for a deliciously long minute, then hot again. When she got out and toweled off, she went into her bedroom to dress. The message light on her answering machine was blinking and she frowned, hoping it wasn't work calling since she'd put in well over sixty hours this week.

She listened to the message. 'Ms Salazar? This is Barbara Zachary at Chyme Investigations. Please call me as soon as you get this message. Please.' The voice was shaky.

Claudia dressed in jeans and a T-shirt, and dialed the phone. She knew Barbara Zachary slightly, a single mother who did occasional support work for Harry. If there was a break in Whit's case, she couldn't imagine why Harry would call her with that news first instead of Whit.

'Chyme Investigations.'

'Barbara Zachary, please.'

'This is she.' The woman's voice sounded wooden.

'Hi, this is Claudia Salazar. You had left a message for me?'

'Yes.' Then silence. 'Harry is dead.'

Claudia's nice warm muscles turned to jelly. She sat on the edge of her unmade bed. Her breath seemed frozen in her chest. 'Oh, my God.'

'He was shot in Houston. Down near the port. Yesterday afternoon. It took them a while to ID him. He didn't have any ID on him, but his rental car was parked nearby. The license plates were taken off. That slowed them down until they traced the VIN number.' Barbara's voice broke again. 'I cannot believe Harry is gone.'

'My God.'

'I know he had a case in Houston he was working,' Barbara said. 'For Whitman Mosley, and Harry told me you were the referral.' The barest hint of accusation tinged her voice, as though Claudia bore a terrible share of responsibility. 'There's no answer at Judge Mosley's house. Can you contact him for me? The Houston police will want to talk to him.'

'I'll hunt him down right now. Who's the investigating officer in Houston?' Claudia grabbed for a pad.

'His name is Arturo Gomez.' Now Barbara broke into sobs. 'I'm sorry. This is . . . difficult. He was so sweet to me.'

'I'm so sorry.'

'I'd worked for him from the beginning,' Barbara said. 'He never took any dangerous cases.'

'I want you to tell me,' Claudia said. 'Everything you know.'

'They found Harry in an insurance office near the Port of Houston with some man, I don't know his name. I don't know anything about him.'

Five minutes later, Claudia was at the door of the guest house where Whit lived, behind the main Mosley house. No answer at the door, but Whit's Ford Explorer sat in the driveway. She hurried back up to the main house, rapped on the door, rang the doorbell.

Irina Mosley answered the door in a cotton robe, hair looking disheveled, like she'd had a long night. She was a beautiful woman but the sudden weight of Babe's illness had thinned her already waifish face. Claudia didn't particularly like Irina, thought of her as the trophy wife who'd seen a rich old man as a passport out of Russian poverty, but the thought that her husband was dying softened Claudia's heart.

'Claudia, hello,' Irina said. She always spoke so quietly, as though an eavesdropper lurked nearby. She looked exhausted, dark blotches under her eyes.

'I'm sorry to disturb you so early. Where's Whit?'

'Off to Houston.' Her voice hardened.

'Why?' *Some man*, Barbara had said. *They found Harry with some man.* Claudia's skin prickled beneath her windbreaker. Oh, Jesus, Whit.

'He didn't tell me,' Irina said. 'He left right after court yesterday.'

'Did he fly? His car's still here.'

'No,' Irina said. 'He went with that Gooch person.' She frowned in distaste.

Claudia thanked Irina. She went back to her car, tried Whit on her cell phone. No answer on his. Please, not Whit, too.

She drove home and called Barbara Zachary. 'Apparently Whit's in Houston.'

'Oh, my God. What if Judge Mosley's the man with Harry?'

'I'm sure Whit's okay,' Claudia said. She thanked Barbara, gave her sympathies again, and hung up. Then she called Whit's cell phone again. Got his bright drawl on his voice mail, asking her to leave a message. She did, asking him to call her. Hung up and lay back down on the bed, a sick twist in her heart, her back, her throat.

She called her police chief, said she was going to Houston for the weekend. He wasn't happy but she was quietly insistent and told him that a friend had been murdered. She did not say that possibly two friends had been murdered. Then she left a message for Arturo Gomez at HPD headquarters, explaining that she had information on the Harry Chyme case and asking him to call her as soon as possible. Then she packed her gun, her permit, two extra clips, her badge – although, of course, she had no jurisdiction in Houston, but she felt she needed it – and her clothes, called her mother to tell her she was going out of town for a couple of days, and headed for her Honda.

Whit is okay, she told herself. *He is okay.* Repeat as needed.

Claudia drove fast, a steady twenty miles above the speed limit.

18

'Don't bother talking to the hit men,' Bucks said. 'Let me. Best that you don't know who's doing what in case the police ask questions.'

'Wrong,' Paul said. 'That's been part of the problem.' He stood at the window, watching the sun start its slow peek above the oaks. Early morning haze lay on the grounds of the Bellini estate, off Lazy Lane, and Paul had awoken Bucks with a 6 a.m. phone call, demanding he get to the family house. Bucks had been sleeping on Frank's sofa in the faint hope Eve would return to the house. Not likely, but he couldn't take the risk of not putting forth a clear and visible effort.

'Chad Channing says it's really important to delegate, and you do that beautifully,' Bucks said.

'Delegate your ass,' Paul said. 'Don't lecture me this morning. I'm not in the mood.'

'The money being lost is a matter of trust, not delegation,' Bucks said. 'You trusted the wrong woman.'

'I don't trust anyone, Bucks. Except my mom.'

Bucks, nervous, no coffee yet, lit a cigarette, blew smoke away from the comatose figure of Tommy Bellini.

'Don't smoke in here around my dad, for God's sakes.'

'He doesn't have a lung problem,' Bucks said, but he inched open a window and thumbed the cig out into the garden.

'If the trellis catches fire, I'm kicking your ass.'

'Paul. Has it occurred to you I'm pretty much all you've got right now?' Bucks said. 'If you and I don't stick together, we're sunk. Frank's useless. Eve's gone. Kiko's gonna go nuclear if we can't deliver the money. You've got Nicky dead after the moron shoots up a diner. I'm the one who's standing by you, man, and you treat me like I'm a leper.' He narrowed his eyes. 'Gratitude lightens the heart.'

'Did Chad Channing say that, too?'

'No, Sister Mary Clarence.'

'That was Whoopi Goldberg in those nun movies.'

'And my algebra teacher back in school.' Bucks shut the window. 'Fine. You want to talk with the hit guys, that's fine. They get caught, they sing, they finger you instead of me. It's really no skin off my back. All I want is this thieving bitch caught and punished for the hell she's put us through.' Bucks forced himself not to glance over his shoulder at Paul to watch for a nervous tic of reaction.

He knew it was Paul's hot button. Paul would either trust him or not. The silence stretched to ten seconds, and Bucks thought *I've played the wrong card*. But then Paul said, 'Fine. You handle it. But I'm picking who you work with. MacKay. The Wart. Jerry Smacks. You got it? And I expect detailed progress reports from each of them. I want to know exactly what's going down. At all times.' He jabbed a finger toward Bucks' face. 'Don't mess up.'

'Yes, Paul,' Bucks said. Now he could capture Eve entirely on his own terms. He kept his smile inside. It was important, Chad Channing stressed, to keep certain victories private.

The *tacqueria* on Mandell, not far from the heart of the artsy Montrose district, was a faded jewel. The door flaked once-bright paint like shredded lettuce. The young cook who had taken over for the gifted old woman who had run the kitchen for four decades inevitably scorched the beans and served runny eggs. Therefore the restaurant was empty in the early haze of Saturday morning, when Bucks slid into the back booth. The waitress brought him coffee and he drank half of it down in a long, steady gulp.

If the new owner had half a brain she'd torch the place for the insurance. He'd suggest that to her, burn the building with the beans, take a cut. Say eighty percent. The place looked starved for goals and resolve.

Bucks had summoned three of them and they arrived within five minutes of each other. For an odd reason he thought of the Magi, the Wise Men in loud garb. MacKay was a tall, dark fellow, a Jamaican with dreadlocks that had once hung to his waist but had now been trimmed to a more modest shoulder length. An ugly scar bisected his upper lip and he wore a plain white shirt, untucked, loose green pants and sneakers. He smelled like sandalwood; too much scent in the close air of the *tacqueria*.

'Hey.' MacKay slid into the booth. 'Who else you taking bids from?'

'Wart and Jerry.'

'Aw, man. Wart is a sick one,' MacKay said. He lowered his voice to a whisper. 'He killed a family, you know that? A family, man, there are lim-its.' He gave the last two syllables the emphasis of disgust.

'Not if he got paid.'

'Jerry can't shoot his pee in the bowl,' MacKay said. 'How 'bout you give me the deal and we close it right now. Save you from dealing with an ass like the Wart.'

'I'm opening it to all three of you. Competition is good for the soul,' Bucks said.

MacKay lit a cigarette. 'Man, do you keep plaques in your jacket so you always got advice to offer?'

'Yes, and they're bulletproof.'

MacKay laughed. 'Bucks, I set you up with Bob Marley, Ziggy, Miles Davis, instead of that self-improvement tripe. Too much prepackaged advice, it'll soften your head.' He looked at Bucks' face. 'Man, order yourself a raw steak for that eye.'

'I fell and hit a stair railing.' No one was believing that lie. Bucks fought the urge to put a bullet through MacKay's skull and instead sipped at his bad coffee.

The other two men arrived at the same time. Darrell Branson, called the Wart, was fortyish, balding, with the carefully cultivated look of a CPA. He wore a summer suit five years out of fashion, no tie. The third man was called Jerry Smacks, and Bucks hated the habit of marathon gum chewing that had earned Jerry his nickname. He was thirtyish, always sunburned because whatever money he made got spent down in Cancun. He rearmed his mouth with a fresh stick of spearmint as he sat down, folding the foil into a perfect square and tucking it into his shirt pocket.

The waitress brought them coffee and then Bucks said, 'Maria, why don't you and the cook go for a walk. Get yourself doughnuts down at the 7-Eleven.' He slid her a twenty.

The woman vanished into the kitchen and after a moment, she and the cook left, turning the OPEN sign to read CLOSED, shutting the morning cool out behind them, all without a word or a change in their poker faces.

'Gentlemen,' Bucks said. 'The deal is simple. We're looking for a woman named Eve Michaels. She's stolen cash. A large amount. She stole it practically right under my nose, so the pressure's on me to get it back. Fast.' He cleared his throat, fixed each man in turn with the kind of forceful gaze corporate VPs blasted at hopeless underlings. They waited, blank-faced, unimpressed. 'I've got to have the cash back; I believe she'll keep it on her or close at hand. She has two men who are working with her. One of them is a killer. He's ugly as a baboon, about six-six, big, broad-shouldered, goes by the name Leonard. He killed one of our men. The other is smaller, around six-foot, normal build, hair blondish and a little long, looks like a surfer type. His name may be Michael or Whitman Mosley, or he may be using a credit card in that name. Him I want hurt badly.'

'Man, I'd pick a cooler alias,' said MacKay. 'Whitman sounds like a school principal.'

The Wart said, 'They local?' He had a voice as soft as just-washed baby clothes, little more than a whisper.

'Eve we know.' Bucks pushed a picture of her he'd taken from Frank's house to each of them. 'The men, we've never seen them before.' He pushed pictures of Gooch and Whit, slightly grainy images recorded on a Club Topaz security camera when they had paid at the door and entered.

'You said the deal was a single hit,' Jerry Smacks said. 'Now you're talking three-for-one. This ain't coupon day, kiddo.'

'I sure don't mind a multiple job,' the Wart said and dosed his coffee with milk. 'Assuming multiple job, multiple paycheck.'

'Getting Eve is priority one. I want her dead. The other two guys, box 'em if you want. I'll pay a bonus of ten biggies for each of them. Mosley hurt as much as you want before you're done.'

The three mulled this. MacKay finished his cigarette, lit another, sipped at his coffee, gave Bucks an odd little smile.

'You got any idea where they at?' the Wart asked.

'We believe Eve is using a credit card under the name Emily Smith. She used it last night at a Hilton at the Addicks exit on I-10 but she abandoned the room. She matches the description of the woman who checked in. Try there; she doesn't know we're wise to her and if she returns to the hotel you get an easy mark. She uses the card again, all three of you get the call on where she's at. Her shelter's got to be coming from these two guys. We got her cell phone number. We're gonna offer them a meeting time tomorrow, trap them, maybe offer Eve's boyfriend to them alive for a share of the money. If you haven't boxed them by then, you're invited to the meeting to wrap 'em up and you can split the pot or you can bow out.'

'What if they leave Houston?' the Wart asked.

'The deal's still open,' Bucks said. 'You find them outside the city, wherever, we'll cover expenses and increase the bonus to twenty apples.' They all knew whatever noun he used was meaningless. Apples, biggies, shirts, cars: it all meant dollars, in the thousands.

'How many apples Eve steal from the garden?' MacKay asked. Laughing.

'That's not a concern. You find the apples, we'll share a good bite with you. But it would be a mistake to take any apples for yourself. A big mistake, gentlemen.'

'I'm a professional,' the Wart said. 'I'm not a thief and I resent the implication.' Jerry Smacks and MacKay said nothing, apparently being free of resentment.

'What if we find her and there ain't no apples?' Jerry Smacks asked. He shifted his wad to the other side of his mouth.

'Don't be stupid,' Bucks said. 'There's no question about her having the money.' He swallowed past the sudden thickness in his throat.

MacKay raised an eyebrow; Jerry smacked his gum; the Wart studied his knuckles. 'You sure Eve dead is what your boss wants?' MacKay asked.

'I'm sure,' Bucks said. 'I got your numbers. We'll call as soon as we get a lead on her. If you hear of three people who recently bought new ID papers, flashing around big cash, or putting a cross-hit out on Paul or me, you call us.' They nodded, except for MacKay, who watched Bucks with a new amusement.

'Questions?'

They had none.

'Good,' Bucks said. 'And I'll hope you'll work as a team. Together we can get this project done and done quickly. Be win-win for everybody.'

The Wart took his three pictures of Eve, Gooch, and Whit, scrutinized them, then folded the prints into a square and ate them like he was in an old spy movie. Jerry Smacks pushed the picante bowl toward him. 'You want salsa with that?'

'The two witnesses who saw us all,' the Wart said around the paper in his mouth.

'Who?'

The Wart jerked his head toward the front door. 'Waitress and cook.'

'Wart,' Bucks said. 'They think I'm a bookie. Harmless.'

The Wart looked unconvinced.

'Do you kill everyone you pass on the street, Wart? In case they actually looked at you?' MacKay asked.

'It's a business precaution,' the Wart said.

'No. That would attract more attention.' Bucks thought of the Wart not as a psycho for hire but as a single step toward a goal. The Wart gave Bucks a flat look as he got out of the booth with Jerry.

'Stay a second,' Bucks said to MacKay, who was getting to his feet. 'I'm going to Jamaica on vacation when all this is done and I want restaurant recommendations.'

MacKay sat back down in the booth. The Wart and Jerry Smacks gave each other a glance but left.

'I really see you exploring island cuisine, Bucks,' MacKay said.

'I know you're better and sharper than those guys,' Bucks said. 'And I need your help.'

'Wow, smarter than a dumbass and a sociopath. You make me feel extra special, but I'm afraid to ask the question on my mind,' MacKay said.

'What?'

'That this lady didn't steal the money, but that you want her blamed and killed for it.'

'Jesus, what put that in your head?' Bucks said. 'I want this bitch dead for what she's done to me.'

'You seem a shade more interested in her being dead,' MacKay said, but with a smile, 'than in getting the money back.' The weight of an unspoken accusation hung in the quiet air.

Bucks considered his options, then put on his best negotiator's smile. 'MacKay, think what you want. But I got an extra job for you. Worth a lot of money. As long as it stays private between you and me.'

19

Whit awoke on the floor of the guest bedroom. He'd crashed on a sleeping bag, a blanket over him. He had thought at first he wouldn't sleep at all, but the exhaustion zapped him hard until he awoke with a start. Looked up to see Eve watching him from the bed, her arms wrapped around a pillow. She was sleeping in an oversized T-shirt of Charlie's that announced LAWYERS HAVE BETTER BRIEFS and a pair of plaid pajama bottoms dug from the bottom of a bureau.

'I haven't watched you sleep in a very long time,' she said. 'Traces of your face, they're the same as when you were a baby. It's weird.'

'When did you ever watch me sleep, with five other kids vying for your attention?' He rubbed his face. His whole body hurt: his eye, his jaw, his arms, his back.

'I always watched you, Whit, you were always special to me.'

He wished he could believe it, but he didn't. He couldn't. 'Did you sleep okay?'

'Enough to function.' She handed him a shopping list. 'We need the stuff on here for our project. And I need clothes.'

'Now you'll make me feel like a son,' he said. 'Running your errands.' He put his head back down on the pillow.

'A step at a time. I'm not cooking you breakfast. Gooch is already up and I can smell bacon.' She rose from the bed and he saw she was small, a little bent, and there didn't seem to be enough of her for her absence to have left such a hole in his life.

Eve prodded him with her foot, leaned down and kissed the top of his head before he could protest or stop her. 'Get up, honey. We've got a real busy day.'

After a moment, he did.

Friday midmorning meant the maintenance crews hit the mani-cured turfs of River Oaks, and Frank Polo, fuzzy from wine and painkillers, pulled a pillow over his head to ward off the invading buzz of lawn equipment. He was vaguely aware of his hand throbbing, a belch of cheap pinot grigio souring his mouth, the absence of Eve from the bed, then he remembered everything.

Morning light slanted through the windows. Frank heard a soft voice from the den, regular, even, quiet. He padded downstairs, scratching his balls under his boxers and his half-open robe, stumbled through the living room, and flicked on the kitchen lights. The room was spotless; Eve liked a clean house. Her de-votion to tidiness and detail was part of the calm precision that attracted him to her. Nothing like him, all disarray and clothes jumbled on the floor.

He noticed before he clicked on the lights that the coffee machine was already on, a pot full.

'A setback is an opportunity,' the soft voice said. 'A setback is a time to reevaluate our goals, our aims, and our methods in actualizing our achievements.' The tape player was at Bucks' elbow and Bucks sat at the kitchen table, a cup of coffee in his hands.

'Sleeping beauty,' Bucks said. 'Good morning. I had an unplea-sant night.' He turned off the tape, more of that self-help oatmeal he swallowed day and night.

'I bet you're gonna have a shitty day, too.' Frank poured coffee into his mug. 'So how'd you sleep?'

'The situation has changed, Frank.'

'Changed.'

'Nicky Lott and Terry Verdine followed two smart-asses who came by the club last night looking for Eve. They tailed the guys to the Pie Shack on Kirby. Eve shows up. She met with both of the guys, then one. Nicky, being a fucking idiot, decided the fastest way to nail Eve and make Paul happy was to blaze guns. He opened fire on Eve and the guy through the restaurant window.'

'Jesus Christ.' Frank felt his heart drop to his feet.

'The guys fired back, they got away with Eve. Killed Nicky. Shootout's all over the news.' Bucks ran his hand through his hair. 'The cops will ID Nicky fast. He has a tiny possession record but nothing but hearsay to tie him to Paul. A woman got killed, people got hurt. This was exactly what we don't need.'

'My God.'

'I got Max watching the Pie Shack. Her car is still parked there. The police are all over the lot, and they'll be running a license check on every car. They'll ask questions. So your penance starts right now, Frank. I want you to go pick up Eve's car.'

'Okay.' Frank sat. 'How do I explain leaving it behind?'

'Tell 'em you were at the shooting, panicked, walked home, now you're coming back to get it.'

'That's a bit of a walk,' Frank said.

'Frank.' Bucks remembered *Chad Channing's ThinkIt, LiveIt!* rule 23: *Patience never wears thin, it's always in style.* 'You got the keys that fit the car, they're not gonna question you. Tell them you heard shots, didn't see anything, ran. Tell them you were meeting a secret girlfriend there and you didn't want your regular woman to know about it. I don't care. Go get the car back. And try not to steal it.'

Frank ignored the jab. 'Fine.'

'Have you talked to her?' Bucks asked. 'Truth please.'

'I tried to call her again. I couldn't reach her.' Frank set down his coffee, inspected the bandage on his hand.

'Who are these new friends of hers, Frank? She had partners in stealing this money.'

'I have no idea.'

'Get one.'

'If she was planning this and cutting me out, she's not gonna use people I can point to in five seconds,' Frank said. 'Does MBA stand for Moron Boy Association, Bucks?'

Bucks threw the coffee from his cup into Frank's face.

A cry caught and died in Frank's throat. The coffee was cool, milky, sweet. Not hot. He blinked at Bucks, who smiled and went to the counter and refilled his cup. Steam rose around his fingers.

'Chad Channing says you should contemplate before you speak.

Very sound advice, Frank. Now contemplate harder. Eve has partners. Who could they be?'

Frank went to the sink, wet a paper towel, mopped his face. 'Anyone who wants to take us down. The other drug rings in town. Jamaicans. East Coasters. A few people connected to the New Orleans cartels. Or even our buddy Kiko.'

Bucks' mouth twitched. 'Does the name Whitman Mosley mean anything to you?'

Frank frowned. 'Whitman Mosley. No. Sounds like an ad agency or a law firm.'

'You ever hear Eve mention guys named Michael or Leonard?'

'No.' Frank gave Bucks a crooked smile. 'If it's another crime ring that's working with Eve and they've stolen Paul's investment, you're cooked. You don't have the men, the resources to fight.'

'I got every guy here in Houston to fight for Paul.'

'Didn't they teach you economics?' Frank said. 'Paul has lost five million. So no money, no cocaine deal. How exactly is Paul gonna keep the cash flowing? The club doesn't make enough for the large-scale drug purchases he wants. How's he gonna keep the muscle for enforcement, the money to grease the necessary palms?' Frank shook his head again. 'You like your balls in a meat grinder?'

Bucks clicked his tongue. 'You know, my niece, she loves your records. She has those seventies-themed parties now and then. Of course to her it's ancient history.'

'That's cool,' Frank said.

'She's thirteen. That age of complete cluelessness. They dress in bell-bottoms, ugly shirts, gold chains. All that junk you used to wear trying to look like a bad-ass when you looked like a clown. They call the parties trash disco.'

'Yeah,' Frank said. Waiting.

'You see, to her, it's funny,' Bucks said. 'How stupid the clothes were. How bad the music was. Your whole life, it's a joke to people, Frank.'

'And you're what? A supernoble Bob Dylan fan, one of those "lyrics matter" music Nazis?'

'I don't like any music,' Bucks said.

'That's what makes you a freak,' Frank said.

'I'm going to offer you important advice,' Bucks said. 'Ditch the negativity.'

'You got that from a self-help tape, didn't you?'

Bucks' eyes narrowed, and Frank saw the man's eyes shift, the ugliness gather.

'Every time I've killed,' Bucks said, 'I've used a gun. But Chad Channing says you need to expand your skill range, to meet new challenges. So if I kill you, Frank, I'm not using a gun. I'm beating you to death. First your kidneys, your major organs. Then your arms, your legs. Your throat. I'll save your face for last.' Bucks took a calming breath. 'Her computer. Where is it?'

'Upstairs.' Frank's voice was weak.

Bucks' cell phone rang. 'Yeah?' he said. A pause, then naked shock on Bucks' face.

'All right,' Bucks said. 'Follow him if they let him have the car. Call me right back.' He made his hand into a revolver, snapped fingers at Frank. 'You got one minute to get your pants on and be out in my car. Some dink's picking up Eve's Mercedes.'

Frank ran. Bucks hurried out to his Jaguar and in thirty seconds Frank ran back out, pulling a shirt on, the pants not even zipped up all the way before he jumped in the car. Bucks backed the Jag out of the driveway, went past River Oaks Park, headed toward Kirby.

'Who's the guy? One of her partners?' Frank asked, breathless.

'Better be that son of a bitch that punched me,' Bucks said under his breath.

'I thought you fell into a railing,' Frank said.

20

From a van idling on the other side of the thin strip of River Oaks Park, Whit watched the Jag speed away. Then he drove around to the side of the park that faced onto Locke, parked a block away, got out of the van. He jogged down the street, Eve's house key in his hand, a backpack over his shoulder. He walked up to his mother's house like it was exactly where he belonged.

Whit slid the key home, turned the lock, waited for the warning *br-reep* of the alarm Eve had mentioned. But it wasn't armed, and there was only the soft chirp the alarm made when he opened the door. Bucks and Frank Polo hadn't set the alarm when they rushed out. He closed the door behind him and locked it.

His mother's house. He took two steps into the marbled foyer. A scent of coffee touched the air. The house was French Provincial in design on the exterior and the inside was simple but tastefully decorated. The Bellinis owned the house and it was a disco king's castle, so Whit expected gold-necklace thug decor. But the antiques looked authentic, the dirty plates in the sink were actually fine china, and when he peered into the acreage of den beyond the kitchen he saw a TV as big as a giant's eye and leather-upholstered furniture to seat twelve.

He took the knapsack off his shoulder, scooted on his butt underneath the huge oak kitchen table, and pulled the knapsack under the table with him. It was heavy; he had gone at ten this morning, when a Radio Shack off Kirby opened, and bought out the supply of small digital voice recorders. They needed to know what Bucks knew, and since Bucks' Jag was parked in front of Eve's house at 7 a.m. when Gooch drove by, Eve decided that Bucks was still sticking close to Frank Polo.

Whit unrolled a hunk of black duct tape with his teeth, checked the settings on the voice-activated recorder, and carefully attached the small device to the bottom of the kitchen table. He tore another chunk of tape loose, affixed it to the bottom part of the recorder, being exact so he didn't cover the microphone. He tugged on his eavesdropping device; it didn't give.

Illegally taped conversations would never stand up in court. But right now court didn't matter, and he wasn't trying to get evidence of actual crimes. He wanted to know what they were planning against his mother. Eve wanted to hear what Bucks said if he incriminated himself, so she would have evidence for Paul. Transmitters would be better, since he wouldn't have to come back in a day to see if they'd gotten any results, but time had been short and he simply went with what was most expedient.

Whit slid out from under the kitchen table, headed into the huge den. A wall of old leather-bound books bought by the decorative yard rather than for their literary value lined one side of the mammoth TV. A thin layer of dust lay atop the gilded pages. He checked another recorder, stuck it behind the thick editions of *Moby Dick* and *War and Peace*, deciding they were safe from Frank, or Bucks' interest.

He hurried upstairs, his feet quiet on the soft plush of the carpets. Down an upstairs hall he found the master bedroom. A mess, as though it had been searched. Probably by Bucks. A suit of clothes, stained with blood on the lapels and front, lay on the floor in a heap. He hoped he wouldn't find a corpse in the tub. There wasn't one.

One of the side tables was draped in silk, and he slid under its tenting to attach a digital recorder on its underside. There. Whit stood. The final request Eve had made was to copy the hard drive on her home computer.

I've got enough info there to put Paul away. If the worst happens to me, Whit, you need it for protection, she'd said over the morning coffee. Assuming Paul or Bucks hadn't already moved it or erased it.

He found the office down the hall from the bedroom. Clean, tidy, no files, no papers out for the casual observer. He sat down in front of the PC and powered on the machine. It began its start-up whir.

Downstairs, the front door opened, the alarm system gave a little ping. Then the door shut.

He got up, went to the top of the stairs, moving silently.

Behind him the PC played its quiet but annoying start-up fanfare. In a bedroom across the hall he peered out past a drape to the front driveway; a Honda that hadn't been there before sat parked across the street. Whit moved quietly back into Eve's office, thinking: *I am so screwed.*

He heard movement downstairs, heels on tile, then silence. Then the soft pad of feet on the carpeted stairs.

Whit drew the pistol Gooch had given him from the knapsack. He stepped back into the room's small closet and eased the door shut. Most of the way. He could see the PC's start-up screen completed, icons against a black background.

'Frank?' a voice called out. A woman's voice, a little throaty. He listened for more than one tread. Footsteps went by the office door, down toward the master bedroom. 'Frank? Bucks? You here?'

Then the quiet again. He heard movement centering around the bedroom. The intruder checking out the room. He concentrated on breathing without sound. He squatted in the closet, a fur coat tickling his right cheek and throat, a long tweed coat itchy on the other side of his face. Clothes you could wear for five whole minutes in a Houston winter. He pointed the barrel of the gun toward the closet door.

You going to shoot another person? In cold blood?

He counted. Frank and Bucks could return at any second. He didn't have forever to get out of this house.

Now footsteps approached from down the hall. On the PC screen, the desktop blanked into a colorful array of bubbles bouncing around the monitor. He figured whoever the other intruder was, she hadn't heard the PC's annoying trill.

A figure passed before the crack in the closet. Then took a seat at the system, pulled the office chair close to the desk.

149

He could see her back. A young woman, dressed in a dark blouse, black leather slacks. She turned, he saw her profile.

Tasha. The beautiful stripper with the computer equipment as her gimmick.

He watched her fingers dance on the keyboard, saw slivers of screens appear on the monitor. She took a CD out of her purse, popped it in the tray, moused around the screen. He heard the whir of the hard drive, the whine of processing.

Tasha sat back.

She was working on the computer. What? Copying files? Deleting them by reformatting the hard drive? Sweat inched along his ribs. She could be destroying the evidence Eve needed to dangle over Paul's head. His teeth bit into his bottom lip. But if he showed himself, what would he have to do to her? He wasn't going to hurt her and she could tell Frank and Bucks that he'd been in the house. If they had half a brain they'd search it then, find the voice recorders.

But why was she here when they were gone? She'd called their names, parked in the driveway, must've had a key to open the door.

He heard the click of keys being pressed.

'Baby, they're not here.' She was talking on a cell phone. 'Yeah. Yeah. I'm getting it done. We're good to go.' A pause. Whit was suddenly conscious of every inch of his body itching, of sweat that felt like it was pooling in his shoes. 'You ordered the hit yet?'

Whit closed his eyes. There was a long pause.

'I don't want details,' she said. 'Don't go there. We ought to go down to the Caribbean for a few days, have a holiday.' Another pause. 'Don't get all pissy-ass on me.' Pause. 'That's right, that's right.'

Screw the recorders. She knows what's going down and I need to know.

Tasha said, 'I'll call you back,' and he saw, in the crack of the door, her drop the phone back into her purse, zip it shut. He counted to three and kicked open the closet.

She spun toward him but he had his pistol at her jaw line before she could turn entirely around.

'Don't move. Don't scream,' he said.

'Please don't.'

'We never did get to finish our chat last night,' Whit said. 'Did we?'

21

'Is there a problem, Officer?' Gooch said. 'I just want to get my car and go to my meeting.'

'Tell me again why you waited so long to come back,' the officer said.

'I ran from the restaurant when the shooting started. Headed to a friend's house off of Westheimer. Drank a bunch. Slept real late.' Gooch put a shake in his voice. 'I haven't touched a drop in five years. Last night knocked me off the wagon. But I'm okay now. Had two pots of black coffee.' He wiped at his lip. 'I got AA over at St Anne's in twenty minutes, I really need to make it.'

The officer examined the license Gooch offered. It was in the name of Jim O'Connor, a license Gooch had acquired a couple of years ago for emergencies.

Gooch stood at the back of Eve's car and rattled the Mercedes keys in his pocket. Eve had told him that the car, owned by Paul, was actually registered in the name of a company fronted by an investment broker who was in Paul's pocket. The broker liked gambling over in Bossier City and Biloxi a great deal on long weekends, and he liked the hidden lines of credit Paul provided him even more.

The cop said, 'One minute, Mr O'Connor,' and headed to the patrol car.

Gooch sucked air through his teeth. He hoped that in the dives for cover and the mad run for the exits no one had seen him return fire or shoot the hostage-taker. The second gamble was that the in-the-Bellini-pocket broker would simply say, yes, Mr O'Connor is using my car, there's no problem. Thinking that O'Connor worked for Paul and was using the car. But that broker would for sure be calling Paul as soon as he got off with the police. The Bellinis would know someone had grabbed Eve's car from the scene. He was surprised they hadn't yet, but they were allergic to cops, and there were several cars remaining in the lot.

The officer was taking a long time on the radio. There would be no criminal record for the policeman to access on Jim O'Connor. Gooch smiled. Finally the patrolman signed off, came back, asked Gooch for a statement of what he'd seen last night. Gooch said he'd seen the window shatter, and had run like hell with everyone else into the parking lot. He had not seen the shooters; they'd taken off.

'And you left this really nice car sitting here?' the cop said.

'I thought more of saving my ass than saving the car.' Gooch bit his lip, put on that anxious face that Whit seemed to wear so often lately. 'It was nuts. I got to my friend's house, started drinking, and lost myself in the bottle.'

'Your car's got what looks like a couple of bullet nicks in it.'

Gooch said, 'Well, there was a lot of shooting going on. Y'all gonna get the guy who did it?'

'He's dead. It was on the news.'

'I don't watch TV much,' Gooch said.

The policeman made a production of reinspecting his license, frowning again at the Port Leo address. He tapped it. 'You're a ways from home.'

'I moved here this week to work for a company called Third Coastal Investments.' He knew that was the name of the broker's company. 'I'm sure considering going back to small-town living.'

'If you stay in Houston, you need to update your license. In thirty days.'

'Yes, sir, I will.'

'Fine. All right. Thanks, Mr O'Connor. We'll be in touch if we need more information.' The policeman nodded and his voice softened. 'Good luck at your meeting. I've been clean eight years. You don't want to slide.'

'I know. One day at a time.' He shrugged. 'I'm gonna go to St Anne's now. Thanks.'

Gooch drove the Mercedes past the police barricades and turned right onto Kirby. He headed away from River Oaks, toward the Southwest Freeway, toward West University Place. He watched the rearview mirror. Within four blocks, as he came to the intersection of Richmond and Kirby, a Mustang, inadequate-penis red, hovered up behind him.

'Hello, goombah,' Gooch said. He got out of the car, ignoring the braying honks from the cars stacked behind him. Went to the Mustang's window, the driver behind it wide-eyed. Possibly reaching for a gun under the seat.

'Hey,' Gooch leaned down and yelled through the window. 'You tell Paul and Bucks to back off, all right? And you're gonna get the special served up last night at the Pie Shack if you follow me through this light.'

Fuck you, Mr Mustang mouthed through the window, but Gooch saw in the crinkle of his eyes that he understood. He was thirtyish, thick-armed, going gray early. Not bright-looking.

Gooch tapped on the window with one finger. 'You I'll deal with first. The guy last night? Once through the throat, once through the heart, once through the balls. I like the symmetry of it.'

The Mustang's window started to go down.

'Listen carefully, dick,' Gooch said, 'you shoot me, you got me dead next to a car that's attached to Paul. Police gonna remember it for sure. They're already asking me about Paul Bellini when I'm picking up the car. So they know. They know last night's dead guy's connected to him.' The police had said nothing of the sort, but Mr Mustang couldn't know. Let them sweat.

The Kirby light turned green. The honking behind the Mustang doubled, a big-haired brunette in a convertible Lexus leaning on her horn like the blare alone could make traffic disappear.

'You understand the message?' Gooch said, unfazed by the other drivers.

Mr Mustang, a molten glare in his eyes, nodded.

'Good,' Gooch said. Cars began to pass him, five inches away, in the other lane, a symphony of blaring horns. He reached down to his calf, hefted up his jeans cuff, pulled from a leg holster a stainless-steel knife with a wicked blade, and rammed it into the side of the Mustang's front left tire. The air whooshed from the sidewall. Gooch got back into the Mercedes and drove through the light.

He reached for his cell phone, dialed Charlie's house.

'Hello?' Eve.

'I have your car,' he said.

'Good.'

'Call Whit. I'm not being followed at the moment. I took care of the tail, but your old friends will spot him stuck in traffic soon enough, will collect him, and head back to your house. Whit should be done by now.'

'Are you coming straight back here?'

'Yes,' Gooch lied. 'I don't normally do fetching. Getting this car back was a big risk.'

'It got them out of the house.'

Gooch clicked off without a good-bye. Instead of continuing south he cut over on Bissonet to Shepherd, headed back toward Westheimer. Toward Eve's house. He didn't like the idea of Whit alone there.

22

Tasha closed her eyes, the gun nuzzling along her jaw, and thought: *It can't end like this, not now, not when I'm so close.*

'I figure you owe me about sixty dollars' worth of talk still.' Whitman Mosley stepped back from Tasha, the gun off her jaw now, but still trained on her.

'Sixty dollars' worth,' she said. She kept her voice steady. 'That's cool.' When he took the step back she sighed out a held breath although she still sat ramrod-straight in the chair. 'Odd spot for a movie location, scout.'

'Why you playing with the computer?' He glanced over at the screen. A status bar, burning files to a CD, showed it was halfway filled.

'My friend owns this house and everything in it,' Tasha said. The thought of Paul gave her confidence. 'He gave me a key. I come and go as I please.' She ventured a smile. 'You're the burglar, scout. Or did you have a key, too?'

Whit said nothing. Watched her.

'Eve,' Tasha said, putting a little creak of fear in her voice. 'You found her.'

Whit shrugged.

'She hiding in here, too, Whit?' See what that got her.

'No, she's not.'

'Whitman Mosley was the name on the credit card you used to charge my time last night. I Googled your ass this morning, scout. Whitman Mosley's a justice of the peace down on the coast in Port Leo. Feature stories written about you in the Corpus Christi paper. A bad-ass judge. Took down a senator, busted up an illegal archaeology dig. Haven't you been busy.' Tasha squinted. 'They didn't

156

include a picture though.' She'd played the one card she had; she knew who he was. If he was going to hurt her, he'd do it now.

Whit shrugged. 'A name to use.'

'Let's say it's you. Why does a small-town judge care about a woman like Eve Michaels?'

'Why does a smart woman like you hang with thugs?'

'Job market's tough,' she said. 'Might be tougher for you real quick. Makes me wonder what the Texas Board of Judicial Review would have to say about a JP smacking people around and pulling guns on them and harboring felons.'

'I wonder,' Whit said, 'what the FBI would make of you discussing a hit.'

'I didn't say hit. I said *it*. I have that urban accent thing happening.' What else had he heard? Her throat tightened.

'Who's the hit on, Tasha? Eve? Me or my friend? All of us?'

The laptop stopped its whirring. 'I'll take that CD, please,' Whit said.

Wordlessly, she ejected the CD and handed it to him. She thought: *this is not good.*

'Copying files instead of taking the laptop,' Whit said. 'Makes sense if you didn't want Frank or Bucks to know you had all these files. What's the data about?'

She raised an eyebrow. 'We're playing twenty questions until Bucks and Frank come back?'

'Answer me. What are these files?'

'Stuff Paul wanted,' she said. 'Everybody in this is cheating and stealing from him now, he wanted to know if there was any record of it.' She shook her head. 'Eve's a dead woman walking, you know that?'

'I want you to deliver a message for me, please.'

'I love your manners,' she said.

'You tell Paul that Eve doesn't have the money. She didn't take it.'

'She accused Bucks.'

'He's a solid bet. And now you're all at each other's throats, and Bucks could benefit. Or Kiko. Or someone else.'

Tasha crossed her arms. 'Yeah. Eve.'

'You're wrong. I don't give a rat's ass about the money,' Whit said. 'I want whoever killed the men at the office, all right? And I want Paul – and his people – to leave Eve alone. Forever. Guarantee her safety.'

Tasha shook her head. 'Better ask for nuclear disarmament. More likely to get it, scout.'

He held up the CD. 'This buys me a treaty, Tasha. FBI would love records relating to the Bellini family.'

She didn't want him to leave with that CD. A cell phone lay on the desk by her purse, a bigger, old model, and she slowly took it, turned it toward him. 'Fine. You win. Call Paul yourself.' She turned the antenna toward him, her finger sidling to the side button, and thought *you don't want to kill him but girl, you better.*

He started to reach for the phone but then he shoved her hand and the phone went off, a shot popping from the little snub antenna, and the window that faced out onto the backyard shattered. He yanked her up from the chair, smashed her wrist against his knee. The phone gun dropped and she screamed. He kicked it under the desk.

'Bad girl,' he said. 'I read about those in the papers. Big with gangs in DC and Miami. And I saw the antenna was open-ended. Handy if you don't want anyone to know you're armed.'

'You're hurting me.'

'You just tried to shoot me, so you lost all room to complain,' Whit said, but he let her go, pushed her back into the chair. He steadied the barrel of his gun at her face. 'Give me a reason why I shouldn't shoot you right now.'

'I aimed at your shoulder,' she said. 'I wasn't gonna kill you.'

'Let's be friendly and clear. I'll shoot you in the knee if you do one more single thing to piss me off.'

She was silent.

'Now. Who's the hit on, who's carrying it out?'

Tasha bit her lip. 'The hit's on Eve,' she said. 'Paul could get any of a dozen people locally to carry it out.'

'Give me names.'

'Well, Bucks.'

'How about fresh new names?'

158

'There's a guy, real vicious bastard, named the Wart. He used to have a bad one on his face, but he got it taken care of. The name stuck.'

'Who else?'

'I don't know. Truly. I don't. Probably more. Five million is a lot of money to lose.' She squinted at him. 'Simplify, scout. Tell Eve to give back the money. Leave it in an airport locker, call us, leave the key where we can get it. Tell her to walk away and I can chill Paul down.'

'She doesn't have it. Bucks framed her.'

'Or she's got it and she's sharing it with you, and you're blowing smoke,' Tasha said.

'If we had it, and we intended to keep it, we wouldn't be sticking around Houston. She wants to prove to Paul she didn't take it. Tell him for us.'

'Since you have the gun,' Tasha said. 'You didn't do it. Not at all, scout. Let's all go have a latte.'

'If we get into a fight with Paul,' Whit said, 'this will end badly. For everyone. I assume you don't want Paul or his business hurt.'

'Useless to negotiate with me. I'm merely the girlfriend.'

'Behind every great man,' Whit said. 'You're smart and you can help me. And help yourself and Paul.'

'I'll tell him you're trying to find the real thief,' she said. The cold look that had come into Whit's eyes scared her a little now. He meant business as much as Paul did. She suddenly envisioned him taking her with him, forcing a deal with Paul, and that would ruin everything. Like Paul would pay to get her back. He wouldn't.

'I already gave you the message he needs to hear,' Whit said. 'But I want information. Has the deal with Kiko Grace been called off?'

'If Eve didn't have a death sentence on her for stealing the money, she'd have one for telling you about the deal.'

'Answer me, please.'

'You don't have to say please when you have the gun,' she said. 'As far as I know the deal's still on.'

'So what's Paul going to tell Kiko if he can't get the money back?'

'Call off the deal, I suppose.'

'And what? Ask Kiko not to sell to Paul's rivals?'

'Call Paul and ask him. What do I look like, Robert Duvall in *The Godfather*? I'm not his *consigliere*. I'm just a dancer.'

He held up the CD. 'Tell Paul to cancel the hit on Eve. Look hard at everyone else who has a motive to bring him down, because she didn't do it. If he doesn't want the Feds to get a detailed phone call from Eve about the Bellinis over the past thirty years, with these files, he needs to back off. Am I making myself crystal clear?'

'Like Waterford, scout.'

Downstairs, the front door opened, the alarm giving off its little soft bleep of announcing entry.

23

Paul Bellini watched the slow, slow rise and fall of his father's chest. His mother had converted a spare bedroom into a miniature hospital ward, and Paul wondered exactly how much money it was costing a day to keep the old guy going. His mother wouldn't tell him, and once he'd shoved her about it, pissing mad, and Mary Pat Bellini said, 'Every cent is for your father, not another word,' and a deep welling shame overcame him. But last week, he'd sat by his father, calculating each breath in terms of dollars spent, and before he'd had two thoughts he'd wrapped the ventilator's electric cord around his ankle, wondering how many shakes of the foot would pull the plug. Literally. How long his dad would breathe on his own, or if he'd go with a merciful snap of the fingers. It would, after all, save money. A lot of money. And yeah, give his dad his dignity, too. That was a bonus.

He took his father's hand, felt the faint warmth in his fingers. Kissed the fingers, tucked them back under the sheet.

'I need you to wake up, Dad. Now.'

No answer.

'I'm in trouble, Daddy. Wake up.' Keeping his voice lower than the hum of the machines.

Of course nothing again.

'Two guys got killed at the Alvarez place. And the cops are gonna be on the Alvarezes like white on rice, Dad.' When he used a Southern expression his father had always affectionately tapped him on the jaw, telling him *don't talk like your mom* but not meaning it bad.

He brought up his father's hand, brushed it against his jaw in a little limp slap.

'Do I pay the Alvarezes to keep quiet? Do I kill them? I don't want to fuck up again, Dad.'

He could hear his father's voice inside his head: *Nothing to connect you to Alvarez. And one thing to connect you to Eve. Doyle, and he was a screwup who probably owed money to any number of lowlifes. Pray the cops focus on him. Pray the old lawsuit that we won against the cops slows them down enough if they start looking at you, Paulie.*

Paul got up, went to the window. The window was taller than he was, facing onto the lush green yards and live oaks that led to the stone walls and gate at the front of the house. No reporters yet. What if Eve goes to the press? The thought was impossible to swallow; she'd incriminate herself. But if she got immunity, hell, she might end up giving interviews to *People*. Get a book deal. Appear on Oprah. Nausea wrenched his guts, and he put his forehead against the windowpane.

The paper said the guy with Doyle was a Corpus Christi PI named Harry Chyme. But why was he there? What did he know about Doyle or the Bellini operations? The loose end of Harry Chyme, entirely unexpected, worried Paul sick. He'd asked Tasha to check up on the name Harry Chyme using her and her friend's computer knowledge, see what they could dig up.

He went back to his father's bed, kissed his cheek, squeezed his hand, waiting for an answering tightening of fingers. Nothing.

It was time to go. Kiko had phoned ten minutes ago, asked for an early lunch meeting, just the two of them. Paul went to the garage, popped open the back of his Porsche. A long length of heavy-gauge chain lay there in a burlap bag, the same chain he'd used to kill Ricky Marino back in Detroit. He'd boiled it repeatedly, sure that would eliminate any usable trace DNA evidence. The chain was not an item he could throw away. It felt a part of him, seared into his hand and head with every lash he'd laid on Marino's flesh.

He thought of using it on Eve. She'd scream, beg for mercy within five seconds. On Frank. The thieving, stupid little bastard, hit him in the throat with it, stop the singing forever. On Kiko, his perfect clothes shredded by the links, his perfect confidence torn away like flesh from bone.

The Porsche purred as Paul pulled out of the driveway, past the ornate iron gates his dad had bought in Italy. He headed west on Westheimer, threading through the molasses traffic of Uptown and the Galleria, past the glass citadel of the Transco Tower, one of the tallest buildings in the world outside of a downtown area. He passed high-rise hotels, Neiman Marcus, ultratrendy eateries. He headed west and the trendiness began to fade as surely as if he had crossed a border. Now there were Persian rug shops, cellular stores in strip malls, neon written in languages other than English. He drove past Club Topaz; the lot was almost empty, although a noontime crowd would start to materialize soon.

Seven blocks down on one corner was a small Greek deli; Paul parked the Porsche, went inside. Kiko Grace sat in a back corner. No José this time, which seemed odd. Paul glanced around the room, trying to make Kiko's backup. Two older men sat at the counter, a couple of younger guys in another booth, not watching Paul walk by. He decided it was them and wondered exactly how many soldiers Kiko had brought to Houston. Or had already recruited here. Cash worked wonders. When you had it.

Kiko offered a hand as Paul slid into the quiet hush of the booth. 'Hey.'

'Hey. I asked the waitress to give us a few minutes,' Kiko said. 'Because I'm not sure I want to eat with you.'

'What's the problem?' Paul asked, knowing the answer.

'Do you or do you not have the green cleaned yet and ready at hand?' Kiko said. Not sounding mad yet.

'I'm greener than a golf course, man.' Paul laughed.

'Then why am I hearing you don't have it?'

'Who said so?'

'I got a phone call saying so,' Kiko said.

'From who?'

'An anonymous but concerned citizen.'

'Don't yank me,' Paul said. 'Was it a woman?' That bitch Eve, she was trying to sour the deal for him. Or cut her own deal, buy the coke herself with his and his father's money. It would be

163

brilliant, a quick way to cut his throat and cut him out in one swift move.

'The caller was a man. Told me to read in the *Chronicle* about a banker getting whacked down at the port. I'm gonna ask again, and you better not be fucking lying to me. Because if you don't have the green,' Kiko said, 'we got to negotiate a new deal.'

'We've had a small delay. You'll have your money this weekend.'

Kiko sipped at his ice water. 'I hate surprises. They make me uneasy. I get uneasy, you get unhappy.' He gestured at the waitress. Kiko ordered sandwiches for them both and beers, not even asking Paul what he wanted. It was an insult, Paul decided, but he had no leverage at the moment. So he gave no reaction. But he thought of that chain, coiled in his car, and wondered how many of Kiko's teeth he could shatter with the first blow.

'So who killed your banker?' Kiko said. Not letting it go yet. Not reassured.

'I don't know any dead bankers,' Paul said. 'It has nothing to do with our deal.'

'Our deal is dead at the moment,' Kiko said. 'That fries my ass, a fucking dink I don't know calling me, knowing my business. Right now my anonymous caller has more credibility with me than you do. Because he *knows*.'

Paul tried not to swallow, show he had a tense lump in his throat. Kiko fell silent as the waitress brought them cold beers.

'Everything is fine on my side,' Paul said. 'If you don't want to do business with me, don't do business with me. I can focus on lots of other projects, and you can try to find another single buyer for your goods.' Man, he didn't want to bluff now, but he couldn't sit still and endure a lecture from this Miami greaseball.

'I hope it's fine, man. I sincerely hope. Because let's share a moment of clarity. If you're trying to score without paying me, if you're trying to screw me over, I'm going to have your whole family killed.' Now Kiko gave a smile that offered real warmth to it. 'We clear?'

Paul wanted to say, don't threaten me you greaser son of a bitch, do you know who I am, but he kept quiet. There was no point, nothing to be gained, and he would be patient until he had his money and the coke. He needed the deal, so for now, he would take the disrespect. But never forget it. Kiko Grace had made a serious error.

He made himself say, 'We clear. Absolutely. The deal is on. You will have your money.' Wondering who had called Kiko. A man's voice. Frank, trying to find maneuvering room? One of Nicky's friends, upset about his death at the Pie Shack, looking to switch sides? Or Bucks, thinking that Paul was fading and Kiko was the new power in town?

The sandwiches came, in thick pita bread, rich dressing leaking out the side, homemade potato chips mounded around the sandwich. Paul picked up his sandwich, bit, chewed, couldn't taste the food.

Kiko watched him. 'Good, isn't it?'

Paul made himself smile.

24

Scream, Tasha thought. *He won't shoot you. Scream your head off.*

'Not a word,' Whit whispered to Tasha. He kept the gun steady on her but his scalp sweated, the skin along the back of his legs prickled.

He heard the downstairs voices rising in anger, Bucks saying, 'How hard is it to follow a goddamned car? Isn't he a high school graduate?' Then a pause.

'Call Paul,' Frank Polo said. 'Right now. Or I will. You're the one who messed up, Bucks.'

Whit moved to the broken window, saw that the roof sloped down to the covered walk between the house and the garage. Thumbed the latches, pushed it open. Heard footsteps treading up the stairs, Frank's voice, rich like chocolate, still arguing with Bucks to get Paul on the phone.

Whit lowered the gun and went out the window, stepping onto the shingled roof. Tasha ran out of the room and screamed *'Bucks!'*

He skidded down the shingles, glancing up to see a man's startled face at the busted window. Whit jumped onto the walkway's roof then dropped down on the wet patch of cool green lawn. In the backyard a brick path snaked through the grass. The back windows were curtained, no Bucks yanking open the drapes to fire on him.

The yard was fenced; with another house on each side, close up against each property line. He ran to the fence on his right and a big dog barked angrily. He cussed and ran to the other fence. A back door opened behind him. He didn't look back.

Whit jumped onto a trellis dense with ivy. A *thweet* popped on his left and the ivy shredded as a silenced bullet pocked the fence. Whit hauled himself over the fence with a huge pull. Another *thweet* and the passing bullet yanked his windbreaker's back; he smelled a puff of burnt nylon as he dropped down into the neighbor's driveway.

Not shot. He sprinted past a parked BMW, pulled himself over the black iron fleurs-de-lis that topped the driveway gate. Frank's house was on his left now, and he ran at full steam toward the L intersection where Timber Lane met Locke Lane and the narrow green of River Oaks Park lay.

He heard the *thock* of tennis balls against damp courts at the near end of the park but he couldn't see the players, and screaming for help was no good. Gooch's van was another thirty feet away and Whit measured out his life in those steps, his sneakered feet slamming against the street, thinking *he'll have to chase me down the street but how far can his gun reach?* He ran and as he turned onto Timber Road a gray Mercedes barreled down the street at him.

He risked a glance behind him and saw a young man with white-blond hair – not Bucks – chasing him onto Locke, gun in hand.

Whit angled to get the van between him and the man and he heard the crack of the gun, the silencer off, sure, to let the bullet fly farther. He was ten feet from the van . . . five . . . the gun fired again and heat passed his throat like an angel's wing.

He thought he was hit. He rounded the corner of the van as the Mercedes accelerated, revving in sweet German force, and thundered past Whit.

Whit glanced back, saw the Mercedes aiming at Blondie. Saw Blondie turn and run and the Mercedes clip him. Blondie went over the windshield. The Mercedes spun out, its front crashing into a modest little Honda parked at the intersection of Locke and Timber, and Blondie fell, went down on the other side of the car.

Gooch. In Eve's car.

Whit scrambled to his feet. Felt his back, his arm. No wound although a sting lay across his neck; there was no gush of blood.

Gooch yelled through an open window. 'Go!'

Whit ran, got the key into the van, started the engine. He watched in the rearview.

The Mercedes was gone. Blondie stood, staggering past the street corner, gun still in hand.

Whit floored the van. Shots fired in River Oaks; the police would be here in ninety freaking seconds. He headed fast down Locke Lane, squealed onto Claremont, then ran a red light and drove past Westheimer. He stayed straight, heading all the way back to the quiet of West University Place.

They could stop Paul Bellini dead in his tracks now. Get Eve to review the CD, identify the most incriminating files. They could be sent, anonymously, to the DA's office or the FBI or whoever would descend on Paul like a pack of wolves fastest. He'd have to check evidentiary law, decide who would be best to approach. But the win was in their grasp. A negotiated safety for his mother, and they could be in Port Leo by tonight or tomorrow. At the light at Bissonnet he turned left, checking his neck in the rearview mirror while he waited for the arrow to go green. A graze, nothing worse. A millimeter the other way and his carotid artery would be sprayed all over the manicured green of River Oaks Park. He breathed hard but steadied his hands.

He took a circuitous route through the quiet, narrow streets of West U, driving past the fancy blue street signs, but there was no sign he was being followed. After ten minutes of driving and watching his rearview he pulled the van into Charlie's garage. Charlie was gone; he had left this morning for his stand-up gig in San Antonio, with them promising him to lie low and do nothing untoward or illegal. As soon as Whit parked, Eve was at the back door, opening it, worried.

He ran in, she slammed the door behind him.

'They shot at me, nearly hit me. Gooch saved my ass.'

'Whit, oh no, baby, here, sit down.'

It did not even bother him that she called him baby. He collapsed on the couch. She examined his neck, got a damp cloth. He told her about Tasha, their discussion, her attempt to shoot him, the blond guy's chase of him.

'I hope Gooch broke the son of a bitch's legs,' Eve said. 'That's Gary, one of Paul's thugs. Not bright, but a good shot.'

'Gary wasn't with Frank and Bucks when they left,' Whit said. 'He must've followed them back.'

Eve ran the washcloth along his face. 'This stops now,' she said in a hoarse voice. 'I don't want you hurt.'

'It does stop now. I got the CD Tasha was burning of your laptop's files. Files Paul wanted. If it's got the goods on Paul we can tell him we'll show it to the police unless he leaves you alone. And then we'll show it anyway.'

Eve stopped wiping. 'Let me see this CD.'

For an instant Whit didn't want to give her the disc. In case she didn't want to show it to the cops, didn't want to implicate herself.

'We'll wait for Gooch. I want him to see the data, too.'

'Don't you trust me, Whit?'

'Yeah,' he said, not knowing if it was true. 'But we'll wait a minute for Gooch, okay?'

She sat next to him, doctoring his graze. They waited. But Gooch didn't come back.

25

Bucks watched the tall, ugly punk on the bed. The man's eyes were closed, and he was tied down with sailboat rope Frank stored in the garage. Tasha had draped a cold washcloth across his bruised face, but the man hadn't stirred.

From the upstairs window Bucks watched Frank Polo and Tasha Strong in the driveway. The damaged Mercedes was tucked into the garage; still driveable, at least enough to limp into the driveway and then behind the closed doors. The bullet Gary had put through the Mercedes' back windshield couldn't be seen. A police car had arrived minutes after Tasha and Bucks got the punk and Gary into the house, and the Mercedes into the garage. Frank stood out in the driveway and he had chatted with the cops, explaining another car crunched into his friend's Honda then veered into their yard before taking off. He had no idea why a neighbor would have reported shots fired. The sound of the accident perhaps? Or kids running around in the winter sunshine with BB guns? Youngsters in the park last week shot grackles out of the oaks. Frank, with a smile, asked the officers if they heard his songs on the oldies stations, and would they like an autograph for their wives? The police had asked their questions of him and Tasha; she said she owned the Honda, didn't see the other car hit it. The police left. Tasha swept up the broken glass in the street.

Frank could be awesomely cool when he had to be.

'How's the guy I hit?' a gravelly voice behind Bucks said. The punk – he had said last night at the club his name was Leonard – had one eye open. 'Did I kill him?'

'You're shot, buddy, and you're wondering if you killed some-one?' Bucks said.

'I'm shot?' Leonard seemed surprised. But his eyes were un-focused.

'Bullets are funny things. He shot at you but it went through the rear windshield and an edge of the headrest and hit you in the back of the head. Broke the skin but it bounced off your skull, I think. You pulled up hard into our yard, I leaned in and belted you twice with the butt of my gun. Your head must be made of granite, partner.'

'I'm shot,' the man said. He rubbed at the back of his head, as though he expected a bullet fragment to be protruding like a bump. 'Gonna be a long wait for the second bullet.'

Bucks sat down by him. 'Why should I want to kill you, partner?'

'I've messed up your plans,' Leonard said.

'But I'm highly adaptable,' Bucks said. 'You need to be adaptable, too. So answer a few questions for me, and I don't stick my gun in your pants and shoot your dick off.' He tossed Gooch's wallet on the bed. 'Who are you, Mr O'Connor, and why do you have such a grudge against me?'

'You're nothing to me,' Gooch said.

'What's the real name? I'm thinking it's not O'Connor.'

'Guchinski. My friends call me Gooch. You can call me sir. Mr Vasco's not gonna be happy about—'

'Drop it. You're not from Detroit. Or from Joe Vasco. I made a couple of calls this morning. No one there ever heard of you.'

Gooch closed his eyes for a moment, shrugged. 'That's correct.'

'So who are you and what do you want with Eve?'

Silence.

'See, Gooch, I don't think you were her partners and she double-crossed you. I heard you were all cozy last night at the Pie Shack. So why were you looking for her last night?'

'She's the long-lost mother of my friend.'

'Don't give me lines.' Bucks stood. 'Where is Eve and your buddy? Mosley, is that his name?'

'I don't know where they're at now. They're moving. Don't want to get caught.'

'Gooch,' Bucks said. 'Consider your situation. You should have a goal. To continue breathing in the next five minutes. Do what you need to accomplish that goal.'

'They wanted Eve's car, I said I'd get it for them,' Gooch said.

'Where's the five million?'

'In my wallet.'

'Seriously.' Bucks sat back down again.

'It's just you and me here,' Gooch said. 'So bag the act. You've got the money and you're blaming Eve. It's a smart move. You've played well off the situation. I'd applaud if I could.'

'I don't have the money, asswipe.' Bucks grabbed Gooch by his shirt, shook him hard. 'I don't have the goddamned money!' He forced his voice to calm, forced his breathing to go steady.

'I think you do—'

Bucks hoisted Gooch's head up by the hair, whispered hard in his ear. 'I don't have it and I never did, you idiot asshole. Eve has it. If she says I've got it, she's lying, she's playing you for a fool.' He let go of Gooch's hair, stalked around the room. 'Jesus, I've hired three hit men to find her. I'm spending a fortune I don't have to find this woman. If I had all that money, I would have left town, dumped it in a Swiss banking account, gotten the hell out of Houston immediately. I wouldn't bother with a frame. I don't want a job with Paul that bad. You think he's ever going to give me five million? You think this is my dream job? I used to be somebody.' Bucks steadied his voice. The panic he'd been fighting down felt like it might surge, blacken his heart, short-circuit his brain. 'I am somebody. I don't have it, Gooch.'

'I,' Gooch said, 'don't care.'

'You better care. Who shot Nicky? You? Your friend?'

'Does it matter?'

'It will to Paul. I can tell him it wasn't you. If you help me.'

Gooch said nothing.

'Y'all have the money. I need the money.' He got his voice low, put his mouth close to Gooch's ear. 'Paul will kill you if he thinks you can't help him, okay? But I'll cut a separate deal with you and your friends. And you get to live.'

Gooch considered. 'What's the deal?'

'We could split the money and I can make sure Paul never

bothers any of us again. But I have to have that cash. Listen, Paul can cut a new deal with his buyers. Just buy half the coke tonight, not the whole shipment. It's not ideal but it would preserve the deal, at least for a few more days. And you would still get half the money, and you get to live.'

'Let's say you and I cut a deal. What's to keep Paul from coming in and shooting me at any second? While I'm your captive I don't have a single guarantee,' Gooch said. 'And even if you get half the money, you just let me go?'

'You're right,' Bucks said. 'You don't have a guarantee. Except my word that I'll keep Paul from killing you because I can't afford to have your death sour a deal with Eve and Mosley. But I need you to tell Mosley and Eve to give me half the money. Or Paul will come at you like that guy in Detroit he chain-whipped to death. Man, I saw pictures. You don't want to end like that.'

Gooch said nothing, watched the ceiling. 'They don't have the money. They can't cut the deal you want.' Gooch closed his eyes. 'It's really painful to watch a mind work at such a slow pace.'

'Painful,' Bucks said. 'Friend, you're gonna learn nine new meanings of the word.' He patted Gooch's cheek. 'If you won't deal, you'll just have to take what comes. I have an idea on how to keep you on the table as a bargaining chip.' He went to the top of the stairs. 'Dr Brewer, come up here, please.' Chad Channing stressed the importance of keeping all your bases covered.

Twenty minutes later, Bucks went back downstairs. Tasha Strong was on the phone. She nodded, hung up, and Bucks sat down across from her. Frank Polo sat at the kitchen table, sipping a glass of red wine, rubbing his face. The blond kid, Gary, was on the sofa, frowning, while Doc Brewer, who had tended to Frank's injury last night, returned to his interrupted work of stitching up a cut on Gary's head. The muscle assigned to watch the Pie Shack lot, Max, with the spare tire now on his Mustang, was out in the garage surveying the damage to Eve's car.

'That was Paul,' Tasha said. 'Wants the guy brought to his house. Easier to keep him hid.'

'The guy still hasn't regained consciousness,' Bucks said. Forced himself not to look over at Doc Brewer. 'I mean, a head injury like that, he may be out for a while.'

'Long while,' Doc Brewer chimed in.

'So he can't give us information yet on Eve.' Bucks crossed his arms, looked hard at Tasha Strong. 'Tell me again what happened.'

'Paul wanted to see if there were any incriminating files on Eve's computer. I didn't think there would be, because she would have taken the whole laptop, but she didn't.'

'Why you?'

'I used to be a Web designer, I'm comfortable with computers,' Tasha said. 'He said go check it out, so I did.'

'Why didn't he ask me?' Bucks said.

'Ask him,' Tasha said.

'Sounds like a matter of trust to me.' Frank sipped at his wine.

'Shut the hell up,' Bucks said.

'So I come inside with the key Paul gave me, and I hear a noise. I go up to check the computer, but before I can do anything, Mosley surprises me with the gun. And then he starts asking questions. About you, Bucks.'

'What about me?'

'Where you live. Where you eat. How often you got muscle with you. Are you even a decent shot. Stuff like that.' Tasha gave him a thin smile. 'They must be planning to come after you. Tit for tat, since you put a hit on them.'

Bucks commanded himself not to flinch. 'And what did you say?'

'I told him I didn't know you well. Didn't know where you lived, anyplace you hung out other than the Topaz. He fired a shot, through the window, to scare me. I told him I didn't know. Then he told me to stay quiet when y'all came in, and he went out the window.' She folded her arms.

'You find anything interesting on Eve's computer?' Bucks asked.

'I didn't have time to look. I'll do that now.' She stood.

'We'll take the computer with us when we move Guchinski over to Paul's house,' Bucks said. 'All have a look together.'

'Whatever,' Tasha said.

174

Frank set down his wineglass. 'If there was anything valuable on the computer, Mosley would have taken it.'

'Shut up,' Bucks said again, and Frank laughed against the rim of his wineglass.

'Mosley might have copied the information instead,' Tasha said. 'If I hadn't caught him, no one would know he was here. And they'd have information we didn't know they had.'

'Major strategic advantage,' Bucks said.

'Baby, You're My Moron,' Frank sang.

Doc Brewer stood in the kitchen alcove. He was a short, gray little man with a face the color of faded concrete, and his voice was always soft, as though he preferred to sidle through life unnoticed. 'Usually I don't volunteer my opinions,' he said, 'but look at the other side of the coin. If he wasn't here taking something, he was leaving something behind.' Tapped his ear.

Everyone shut up. Bucks stood on a chair, inspecting the ornate light fixtures. He looked along the windowpanes. He pulled the phone off the wall, checked its back. He ducked his head under the kitchen table.

'Well, hello there.' Bucks reached for the digital voice recorder.

26

Friday evening, darkness settled over Houston, the sun painting the clouding sky the orange of joy, the gray of sadness. Whit wanted to drive back to the house on Timber; Eve forbade him and he decided it was a bad idea, an ambush waiting to happen. Or maybe they'd chased Gooch and he'd had to lose them and was taking his time getting home, ensuring he wasn't followed back to Charlie's house. The news came on; there was no report of a shooting along the quiet of a River Oaks street. No report of a man matching Gooch's description turning up dead.

Whit sat with Eve at Charlie's PC, studying the data on Tasha's disc.

'This isn't exactly a backup of the hard drive, Whit,' she said.

He leaned down, looked at the spreadsheets before him. Columns of numbers with annotations and footnotes inserted beneath that made no sense to him.

'So what is it?'

'These spreadsheets show operations from the legit Bellini businesses. And then these are the semilegit businesses, like Alvarez Insurance. We use them to clean the money from the drug deals, by making it look like the funds are coming from legit accounts from various holding companies. But these files' – she pointed to an array of spreadsheet icons – 'I've never seen before.'

'But she was copying from your drive.'

'You sure she wasn't copying from this CD onto my hard drive? You were tense. Maybe it was the other way around.'

'I should have taken the whole laptop,' he said.

'Then they'd know someone had been in the house.'

'They'd know anyway once Tasha talked.'

She shook her head. 'Honey, you think I kept records so a Fed with a search warrant could walk in, seize a system, and indict us? No. I switched out hard drives every few weeks and destroyed the old ones. But I kept the files that made the drug money look legitimate.'

'So how would Tommy Bellini know if his books balanced?'

'He and I would review them together before I destroyed the drug files. Of course that stopped after his stroke.' She glanced at him. 'The idea was to park a certain amount of real money in his legit interests. So you go ahead and pay the taxes on those. The rest went into his pocket, backed by the money-cleaning books. Out of that he paid salaries, expenses, and so on.'

'And supplies. Like the coke.'

She nodded.

'Why would Tasha have these other files and want to put them on your laptop?' he said. 'Unless she's part of the frame. She's in with Bucks.'

Eve scrolled down through the spreadsheets. 'This looks more like an extra set of cooked books.' She began to click open files, studying them. 'Hey. These are files for businesses Paul doesn't own. With lots of money parked in them. Look at these revenue figures.'

'So why does a stripper at his club have an additional set of cooked books on a CD? Why?'

Eve frowned. 'Let's say Paul gives her the CD, asks her to back up the data on the laptop. Then these are extra files already on the CD – data he was keeping secret from me. I didn't think he had operations I didn't know about but now anything's possible with Paul.'

'Again, why not simply take the laptop? It's his.'

'Because he doesn't want Bucks or Frank to know it's gone.'

'Because he suspects Bucks but doesn't want to tip his hand,' Whit said. 'Or Frank. You said he embezzled from Paul.' Whit leaned over her, watched the screen. 'Let's consider another possibility. She has these files on the disc. But did she also copy these files to the hard drive in return?'

'Why?'

'Part of the frame-up on you,' he said. 'Bucks could say you were incorrectly cooking the books with this data.'

'Those files would have a date stamp for when they were placed on the hard drive.' She clicked the mouse, expanded a view. 'See. They're showing as transferred today.'

'But it could be edited once they were on the machine. Assuming Tasha has the computer know-how, and I'll bet she does. Bucks didn't want Frank around when the files were added. So he asks Tasha to do it when they're gone.'

'I prefer simplicity,' Eve said. 'She's in bed with Paul, he wanted to know what was on that system without alerting Bucks and Frank. He's a sneaky ass.'

'She's sneakier,' he said. 'She had that little gun hidden in a cell phone. Have you ever seen that used?'

'No, but I've heard of them. Paul might've given it to her.' She pointed again at the spreadsheet icons. 'This bothers me. This data makes the Bellinis look like they've got way more income that is being cleaned than they actually do, in lots of places that don't exist. I don't believe Tommy or Paul truly has this money. So what would be the point of putting it on my computer or tying it to other Bellini financial records?'

'What would the Feds do if they got this information?'

'Start auditing each and every company. Start tracing the money trail. Start shutting down operations, making arrests.' She pointed at the cooked-book files. 'This would make them pee in excitement.'

'Then we have a negotiating point, right? We could put Paul in jail.'

'And me in jail, Whit.' She touched the back of his hand. 'Is that what you want?'

'I didn't do the crime,' Whit said.

'No, you didn't. I told you, I go to prison, they'll still kill me. I have no doubt.' She stood, walked to the window. 'There has to be another way to use this to get Paul to back off on having me whacked.'

Whit said nothing for a few moments. He tried Gooch's cell phone again, calling on his own cell, not wanting to call on Charlie's home number. No answer. 'This isn't right,' he said.

'We have to assume they got him,' Eve said. 'You said he was pulling away but they may have shot him.'

'In the middle of River Oaks?'

'He's not here, is he?'

'I messed up,' Whit said.

'No. Gooch shouldn't have shown up there. He told me he was coming straight back here. He didn't stick to the plan, Whit. It's not your fault.'

'He saved me from getting shot, and I left him.'

'You did what he wanted.' She touched his face.

'Where would they take him?'

'The Bellinis own two houses in River Oaks. The one Frank and I were in, and another, much bigger house on Lazy Lane.' She crossed her arms. 'Lazy Lane's a street where practically every house has a guard station. Dogs roaming property. Heavy protection. If they take Gooch there we'll never get in.'

'We're not abandoning him.'

'Paul owns a house down in Galveston, too, but it's for sale. I doubt they would head down there.'

'I can't risk Gooch's life. I'm calling the police,' Whit said.

'And tell them what?' Eve asked.

'Everything,' he said.

'Will that help your dad, Whit?' she asked. 'You want him to see you in jail before he dies?'

'Your concern for my dad is a little late,' Whit said. 'Like thirty years.'

'I'm more concerned for you.'

'And your own hide.'

'Sure,' she said. 'You have me pegged, anyway. What I did to you defines every aspect of me as a person, right?'

'Yes,' Whit said. 'Would anyone ignore abandoning your family in estimating your character?'

'I suppose not.' She sat down on the couch. 'Call them, then. They'll arrest the both of us. Me for the felonies I've committed, you for the knowledge of them. That's at least three years in prison, Whit. You already turned your back on law and order, baby.'

He sat down on the couch, put his face in his hands.

'Whit? What are you going to do?' she asked quietly.

His cell phone buzzed. He answered it, praying it was Gooch. 'Hello?'

'Whit? It's Claudia.'

'Hey,' he said, his stomach sinking at the sound of her voice.

'Thank God,' she said. 'You're okay?'

'Sure,' he said.

'I'm in Houston. Did you know about Harry Chyme?'

'Yes,' he said. 'It was on the news. I'm so sorry, Claudia.'

'Had Harry found your mom, Whit? Tell me.' A crackle marred Claudia's voice on the line. 'Whit? Did you hear me?'

'No, he hadn't found her,' Whit said. Seeing how the lie tasted in his mouth. 'I talked with him briefly, he said he thought Eve Michaels was in Houston, but I didn't hear anything more from him.'

'Are you still in Houston?' she asked.

'Yes.'

'Where? I want to see you. Now.'

'This is a bad time, Claudia. Really. I can't talk right now.'

'I'm staying at a Hampton Inn near the Galleria. I came to Houston to find you, find out what happened to Harry. And you are going to tell me what the hell's going on. When I heard Harry was found dead with a man, and you had gone to Houston . . . I've been scared to death. I've left you messages, why haven't you called?'

'I'm sorry, Claudia. I'm sorry. Go back to Port Leo, okay? I'm okay and I'll talk with you later.'

'Whit, for God's sakes, this is me!'

'You're one of my best friends, Claudia, and I love you and I don't want you involved in this. I'm sorry. Go home.' And he clicked off the phone.

'Girlfriend?' Eve asked.

'No. Good friend.'

'I didn't even ask if you were married. Or had been.'

'I haven't been. But I won't be bringing a girl home to meet you.'

'You shouldn't. I would probably scare a nice girl.'

He said nothing.

Eve sat next to him on the couch. 'They will torture Gooch if they have to, Whit. They'll blow the fingers off his hand one by one. Cut off his balls. Cut him so he bleeds to death an inch at a time. Strangle him until he's nearly dead then give him the gift of breath back. Then strangle him. Again and again, till he's begging to die. He'll tell them where we are. We've got to find a new place to hide.'

'They'll never break Gooch,' Whit said. 'If he's dead and beyond our help, we're too late. If he's not, he'll never turn on us.'

'Whit. He's an incredible person. I can tell that. But these people will break him.'

'Tell me. Have you seen them hurt people before?'

'Yes,' she said after a moment.

'And did nothing.'

'Stop judging me, Whitman.' Her voice was as low as a whisper.

'If I were judging you, I would be walking out the door. I would never have even tried to find you. Because I did, Harry is dead. Gooch may be dead. I don't blame you. I blame me.'

'Whit . . .' Her voice softened.

'My choices,' he said. 'So I got to fix it. I'm calling the cops. But you, take Gooch's van and go. You're good at hiding, they'll never find you. You leave. I'll stay to get Gooch.'

'Absolutely not. I'm not leaving you to face this alone.'

'You have to, because if I call the cops you'll be arrested.'

She put her face in her hands, shook her head.

'And I lose you all over again,' Whit said. 'But I can't let them hurt Gooch.'

She looked up at him. 'What if there's another option?'

He got up, walked to the window, let the drape drop down. 'I don't know how to beat these people.'

She followed him to the window. Slowly, awkwardly, she hugged him. His arms tensed under hers. She rested her head against his chest and he let his breath loose.

'I don't have a right to hug you, son,' she said. 'But pretend I do, okay?'

He stood there in the fading light, his mother holding him and his heart fractured along a thousand fissure lines, a thousand hurts, a thousand wishes. The house was quiet and he listened to the hush of her breath. Slowly he hugged her back.

'I'll make it all right, son,' she said.

Her cell phone, tucked in her purse, rang. She broke the hug and went to the purse, dug it out, clicked it on. 'Yes?'

She listened for a moment, then handed Whit the phone. 'Bucks. He wants to speak to you.'

'Hello?'

'Your friend is made of stern stuff,' Bucks said. 'I'm impressed.'

'Is he alive?'

'For now.'

'Prove it to me.'

'He's unconscious. Not in good shape.'

'How do I know you have him?'

'Hmmm,' Bucks said. 'His name is Gooch but his ID says Jim O'Connor.'

Whit closed his eyes 'I assume you're not just calling to gloat.'

'Of course not. I'm calling to discuss Gooch's future.'

'I'm listening.'

'I'll guarantee Gooch's safety. You give me half of the five million. You keep the other half.'

'We don't have the money,' Whit said.

'I think it would hurt poor Gooch's feelings to know you don't value his life.'

'I do. But we don't have the money,' Whit said again, but then thinking: *maybe Gooch told them we do to keep them from killing him, so play along to buy time, dumbass. But if Bucks has the money, this is nothing but a trap.*

He had to choose. Now.

'There are people hunting you right now, asshole. People who make me look like an Eagle Scout, okay? This is really your best option. And I've got a 9-millimeter aimed right between Gooch's eyes at the moment. He's asleep and he'll never know what hit him. I suppose that's a mercy. Oh, wait, I feel a hand spasm coming on—'

'Okay,' Whit said. 'Okay. I'll deal.' Eve stared at him, shook her head.

'You have until tomorrow at six p.m.,' Bucks said. 'I'll call you back with details. Call the police, the Feds, your friend dies. In a fashion that won't be pleasant. And then we'll come after you and Eve anyway.'

'Since we're negotiating,' Whit said. 'There's a little matter of way cool data we have. Computer records about Paul Bellini's accounts. The paper trail that leads to fat federal indictments. Release Gooch. Tell Paul to cancel the hit on Eve. Right away.'

There was silence for a moment, then a soft laugh. 'I admire the ballsitude, man. Truly. You're a focused individual. But I know what was on that computer, and it was crap that doesn't matter. That laptop's got nothing. You think I wouldn't check her files as soon as Eve went running? Whatever you got, it's nothing to me. Six o'clock tomorrow, man. I'll call you back with details.' He hung up.

'Jesus,' Whit said. 'Is he a moron?' He told Eve what had been said.

'Bucks has the money,' she said. 'It's a trap.'

'I don't think he does.' But then Whit stopped, thought it through. 'Unless Paul was listening in on that call and it's all for show. And Bucks knows we'll say we have the money just to save Gooch.'

'That's a distinct possibility,' she said.

'But then, why not spring the trap immediately? Why give us until tomorrow to deliver the money?'

Eve shook her head. 'The money's got to be due to Kiko in the next day or so. If they have it earlier, they can close the deal earlier. Bucks doesn't want that deal closed now.'

Whit rubbed his face, paced. 'I don't think Paul was on that call. More likely Bucks wants Paul and Kiko both badly off-balance. He could have taped that call, play it for insurance if he needs it. It makes him look better than us, even when he said he'd deal for half the money. The question is who has the money, and I've just admitted to it. Shit!' He punched hard at the sofa cushions.

She hugged him. 'It's okay, you did it for Gooch. But let's keep our thinking simple and clear, Whit,' Eve said. 'I still think Bucks has the money right now. He needs as many fingers pointing away from him as possible. So he keeps Gooch as a tool to keep us in line but also as a means to delay the deal – he can say he's in negotiations with us that only stay open as long as Gooch is alive. He's got our hands tied and Paul's hands tied. Either until he can vanish with the money or cut a separate deal with Kiko that shuts out Paul and leaves him on top.'

'And he's not afraid of the cooked-book computer records. That doesn't make sense. He should be scared to death—'

'But he's not,' Eve said. 'Because he's not staying with the Bellinis, so he's not worried about getting caught with them. He's playing every side against the other because he's flying.'

'I played right into his hands,' Whit said. 'He—'

Eve put a finger to his lips. 'Someone just came in the back door,' she whispered.

27

'I blew off a third date for you,' Vernetta Westbrook said.

'I appreciate your sacrifice,' Claudia said.

'I suspect he has back-hair issues,' Vernetta said in her rasp. 'But a sweet guy. I'm on the fence in that petty, should-I-date-him-again way.'

The two women sat under the not-moving ceiling fans of the Goode Company barbecue restaurant on Kirby, the air heavy with winter damp and the wood-scent of ribs and brisket. Their plates held shreds of stray meat and onion and pickle chunks mired in barbecue sauce. The benches under the fans were mostly empty; it was too cool for outside dining but Vernetta smoked.

They had eaten their way past the awkwardness of old school friends who have not spoken in too long. They covered Claudia's failed marriage, the embarrassing level of coverage she'd gotten in capturing a serial killer on the coast, Vernetta's move from defense lawyer to working at the Harris County DA's Special Crimes bureau, her endless parade of wrong guys, mutual college friends' misfortunes and triumphs.

The meal done, Vernetta opened a fresh Shiner Bock, lit a cigarette, and took a relaxed puff. Claudia edged toward the subject she'd wanted to touch. 'So for real, how are you liking working for the DA's office?'

'Now we're getting to the favor,' Vernetta said. 'Work-related. Color me surprised.'

'I have a friend who was murdered here a couple of days ago. Harry Chyme.'

'God, I'm sorry.' Vernetta bit at her lip, tapped ashes into her plate.

'Does his name ring a bell, Vernetta?'

'You mean has the special crimes division gotten involved in the case?' Vernetta poked at a dollop of cole slaw on her plate. 'I'm not sure.'

Claudia could smell a blow-off coming. 'Arturo Gomez is the investigating officer. You know him? He hasn't returned my calls yet.'

'Gomez is very capable. Very ambitious. I imagine he sees police chief ahead of his name one day.' Vernetta blew out a stream of smoke. 'You have information on the case or are you wanting to dig around?'

'Before I go barreling in as the rural cop and make myself look stupid I'd like to know the players. Obviously Harris County has a much more elaborate setup than what I'm used to in Encina County. So can you give me the lay of the land?'

Vernetta raised an eyebrow. 'Well, from my side of the map, the DA's Special Crimes Division, we're involved in crimes where the police department needs the input of lawyers. We focus on gangs, narcotics, major and consumer fraud, major offender and theft rings, asset forfeiture.'

'You reacted like you'd heard Harry's name.'

'I have.' But then she sipped her beer again, and Claudia waited. She had to be careful. She wanted to give the Houston authorities whatever help she could in Harry's case, but she didn't want to get Whit in trouble. Something was terribly wrong, when Whit would not talk to her, when he would warn her off and tell her to go back to Port Leo.

Maybe he had information, and he hadn't contacted the authorities. He might be breaking the law in this crazy search for his mother.

Claudia waited, sipped tea. Finally Vernetta stubbed out the cigarette.

'Tell me why you're meeting with me instead of Gomez if you've got info.'

'I need to know details of the case before I go in and talk to him,' Claudia said.

'Why?'

'I just do, and I know we haven't talked in a while, because life gets in the way, but I wouldn't ask if it wasn't important. Please. I can tell you know more than you're saying.'

Vernetta lit a fresh cigarette. 'Harry Chyme and a senior VP from Coastal United Bank named Richard Doyle were found shot to death in an insurance office on McCarty, one exit up from the Port of Houston. The office is owned by an eighty-three-year-old insurance agent named Joe Alvarez. We're not sure who all his insurance clients are, but his family lives rather well. Since yesterday, the Alvarezes have their lawyers talking for them, which means they're saying nothing.' She shrugged. 'I suspect our office will serve a grand jury subpoena on Mr Alvarez by Monday morning if he's not more forthcoming.'

'What if he doesn't talk or takes the Fifth?'

'Then we give him a grant of immunity. That way, he can't take the Fifth. He refuses to answer then, he's in contempt of the grand jury.'

'So Alvarez is covering for someone.'

'McCarty Street's not exactly a hotbed of high-dollar insurance clients,' she said. 'I bet Alvarez Insurance is a front. We'll find a connection between Doyle and Alvarez as we subpoena Alvarez client records and records from the insurance companies.' She took a sip of beer. 'Doyle was known as a high-roller, heavy gambler. We've started going through his finances, and he seemed to have very heavy debt. But he had clean hands at the bank.'

'So far.'

'So far. Divorced a few years ago, alienated from his teenage kids, the kind of guy who'd bet on paint drying.' She paused. 'Most likely Doyle owed money and didn't pay. What we haven't known is Harry Chyme's connection. Do you know?'

Claudia took a deep breath. 'Harry was investigating a case with a loose connection to the Bellini family. I take it you're familiar with them?'

Vernetta let nearly ten seconds pass before she answered. 'Oh, sure. They were being watched from the moment they arrived in Houston. But they've stayed clean. Mrs Bellini is old Houston money, a debutante who never outgrew the gown. Her husband's set himself up as an art importer. They haven't gotten into trouble.'

'Are you sure?'

Vernetta tapped her nails on the worn wood of the picnic table. 'Trouble that could be proved, let me say. There was a little dust-up a few years ago. Anonymous tip that they were dealing drugs, not anything you could get a warrant on, but a hotshot investigator decided to chat with Tommy Bellini, went to his house. Mr Bellini and hotshot got into an argument. Hotshot shoved Bellini down in a marble foyer, Bellini got a fractured hip. He sued HPD. Big mess. Almost funny, a guy who was certainly ex-mob suing the cops for brutality. HPD paid through the nose, people lost careers over it. They've left the Bellinis alone, but in fairness, they've had no serious reason to look at them again. Don't expect the police to rush at the Bellinis without hard evidence. They don't want another killer lawsuit.'

Claudia considered. 'Say Doyle had a connection to the Bellinis, and Harry was trying to get information from him. The Bellinis didn't want Doyle talking to Harry.'

'Or Harry got caught with Doyle at the wrong time. Or these gamblers, Claudia, they get in deep real fast. The level of debt can quickly rise into six figures, and they get desperate and scared. Maybe Doyle was trying to sell info on the Bellinis to Harry.' Vernetta tapped fingernails on the table. 'I'd like to know about this case Harry was working.'

'A friend of mine . . . his mother had not been in touch with him for many years. Harry thought a woman working for the Bellinis was my friend's mom.'

'Gomez is attacking this case from every angle Doyle brings to it, not from anything to do with the Bellini family. You better talk to him.'

'Yes,' Claudia said, her stomach twisting, the smell of the barbecue suddenly making her queasy. 'I think I better.'

'The Bellinis?' Arturo Gomez said. 'You got any proof?' They stood on the lawn of Richard Doyle's ex-wife's house, where

Gomez had been questioning her about Doyle's acquaintances and where he agreed to meet Claudia and Vernetta.

'No,' Claudia said. Gomez was immaculately groomed in a gray suit, haircut no older than two days and still styled as though he'd just left the salon. Fortyish, ready to make the career leapfrog from investigator to executive and a shade impatient.

'Maybe the Bellinis lent him money,' Vernetta said.

'I've got two detectives and an accountant going through Doyle's finances. So far we've found he owes money to at least three small-scale loan sharks who hang at the racetracks and at the Biloxi casinos. But no one we can connect to the Bellini family.' He laughed. 'It hasn't exactly occurred to anyone. They keep their noses clean.'

'Perhaps Doyle used the small sharks for his gambling loans, and the Bellinis for bigger amounts,' Claudia said.

'How big is Port Leo?' Gomez said, not unkindly. 'You deal with a lot of loan sharking down there between the shrimpers and the retirees?'

'Claudia bagged a serial killer,' Vernetta said. 'You got one on your wall, Art?'

Gomez cleared his throat.

'Vernetta, don't,' Claudia said. 'Harry was looking for Eve Michaels, and he ended up with Richard Doyle. There has to be a connection.'

'True enough,' Gomez said. 'This friend of yours. I want to talk to him. Now.'

28

They heard the slow click of the back door shutting.

Whit moved through the den to the window that faced onto the backyard. No sign of Charlie's car in the little curve of driveway. Whit glanced at his mother; she pulled her Beretta from her purse, leveled it at the den's opening. She shook her head and mouthed the words *get down*, jerked her head at the couch. Telling him to take cover. He stayed right where he was.

No way that anyone had followed him, not with the chaos of Gooch rescuing him. Unless Gooch broke. Unless he talked.

'Eve?' a voice called. 'Are you here?' Not Charlie's voice. Velvety.

She aimed the gun at the door. Whit moved quietly next to her.

'It's Frank. I'm alone. Paul, Bucks, nobody knows I'm here.'

Eve glanced at Whit. The gun shook slightly in her hand.

'I'm coming in. My hands are up. I'm unarmed. I've got news about your friend.' And with that a man stepped into the opening of the den, arms up, fingers spread in high five, open palms, one hand bandaged. He was pale and frowning.

It was the man who had watched Whit from the upstairs window when he jumped from the roof.

'Eve, baby.' He glanced over at Whit, then back at Eve. 'Hi, sweetheart.'

'How did you find us?' Eve asked. Her voice was jagged. Not happy.

'Your friend's cell phone. I took it without Bucks knowing. It had a call to this number in the call log section. I got a reverse directory on the Internet, I found the address.' He stared at Whit. 'Hi. I'm Frank Polo. I'm Eve's boyfriend.' He wiggled fingers in a wave.

'That's up for discussion,' Eve said.

'I'm here to help you, sweetheart. What would Bucks and Paul do to me if I knew where you were and didn't tell them?'

'Shut up, Frank. Check him for a gun,' Eve said. Whit patted Frank down. No gun, no knife, just the paunch of soft flesh under the silky shirt and black slacks.

'Nothing,' Whit said.

She lowered the gun. Frank stepped forward. She brought the gun back up.

'Baby, baby,' he said quietly and she put the gun down. Frank embraced her, and she stiffened, then sagged against him. She started to cry, then shook her head and wiped the tears away. Frank kissed her forehead, held her, murmured, 'I'm sorry, I'm sorry,' again and again. He looked at Whit.

'Is your name Whitman Mosley?' Frank asked.

'You don't need to worry about his name,' Eve said. She stepped away from Frank, wiping at her nose, her eyes.

Frank glanced at Eve's face, then Whit's, then Eve's again. 'Okay, whatever.'

'Where's Gooch?' Eve said. 'Our friend.'

'Bucks has him. They've moved him to the house on Lazy Lane. It's the most secure.'

'Is he hurt?' Whit asked.

'He got a real bad whack on the head. Unconscious but they had our doctor look at him. Bucks wanted to get Gooch moved and get Paul's mom out of the house. Paul's sending her to Vegas for the weekend with a friend before they start rough on Gooch to get him to talk.' Frank paused. 'Everyone's believing that Eve stole the money.'

She hit his shoulder, once, twice. 'Sure they are, thanks to your damned skimming. How could you, Frank, and how could you be so dumb?'

'I messed up, so I'm here to help you out of this,' Frank said. He held up his bandaged hand. 'They've already been at me. I can tell you exactly what they're doing, what they're planning, so you can get away.' He took her hand and Whit saw her fingers close around his.

'What's your plan?' Whit said.

'Before I start sharing my brilliance,' Frank said, 'I'd like to know exactly what role you play.'

'I'm helping Eve,' Whit said. 'That's all you need to know.'

'You're the problem,' Frank said. 'Bucks and Paul know you got new friends, Eve. That doesn't mesh well with the money being gone.'

'You must care about her,' Whit said, 'since you're here at considerable risk.'

'Considerable ain't the half of it,' Frank said. 'Eve. You're never gonna convince them you didn't take the money. So you got to turn. Go into Witness Security. Call the FBI, offer them Bucks and Paul.'

Eve shook her head. 'You know what happened to Gene O'Brien. And Lydia Mancini. They went into WitSec and they still made the hit parade.'

'They also were stupid as mules, calling friends in old neighborhoods,' Frank said. 'They let a trail be created back to them. You won't. What else you gonna do?'

'If I had that five million, I could vanish on my own terms. Anywhere in the world,' Eve said. Whit shook his head.

'Bucks ain't leaving it around to be found or mouthing off about how smart he is,' Frank said. 'Was this the idea behind hiding the voice recorders? We found one in the kitchen. But they're tearing the house apart. Max already found three.'

Three was all Whit had hidden. He wanted to sit down badly.

Frank looked again at Whit. 'This is bugging me. You look like Eve. What the hell's going on here?'

'He doesn't look like me, don't be an idiot,' Eve said.

Frank sat down on the ottoman in front of a heavy leather chair, put his face in his hands. 'Okay, if you won't cut a deal with the cops, my idea is tell Kiko that Bucks stole the money, that Paul is breaking the deal. It's supposed to close tomorrow night. Kiko then comes after Bucks and Paul, guns blazing.'

'Or Kiko finds another buyer?' Whit said.

'Sure. That's gonna dry up revenue for Paul, gonna hurt him bad. Real bad.'

'Why should Kiko talk to me?' Eve said.

Frank cleared his throat. 'Because if they all think you're gonna turn to the Feds, you're as much a threat to Kiko as you are to Paul. You can finger him as having been in on the deal. That's real leverage.' He tapped at his forehead, gave Whit a crooked smile. 'No one thinks I have one of these. But I do. Eve wouldn't have given me the time of day if I was dumb as a stump.'

'So we tell Kiko,' Whit said, 'and what if Kiko doesn't believe us and comes after us?'

'Then we're screwed. But what if,' Eve said slowly, 'Kiko already knows the money's gone. This kind of news, it gets out on the street fast.'

'He's Miami,' Frank said. 'He don't have ears on the street here. But if they war, they take each other out and you're safe.'

'I wish,' Eve said.

'None of this rescues Gooch,' Whit said. He told Frank about Bucks' offer, keeping the story simple and not adding in all of his and Eve's theories as to Bucks' true loyalties.

'Your friend, consider him dead,' Frank said. 'Sorry. They have three sick bastards hunting you. You have your hands full without an impossible rescue, kid. As for Bucks, he's following Paul's orders to the letter so far as I can see.'

Whit went to the phone. 'All I have to do is call the police, say a man is being held against his will at that address. End of story.' He wanted to see Frank's reaction to his suggestion.

He got a shrug from Frank. 'And the cops got their asses taken to the cleaners the last time they set foot on Bellini property. They'd have to have reasonable cause for a warrant,' Frank said. 'They're not in a hurry to get rid of Gooch, not while he could tell them where you or the money's at, and for sure not while Paul's mom is around. Paul's not gonna let his mom hear him kill a man.'

'Then you help us get Gooch,' Whit said. He turned to Eve. 'His safety is nonnegotiable. We're getting him out.'

Eve nodded. 'I agree.'

'Who is this Gooch guy to you? Why you running around with these younger guys, Eve?' Frank sounded hurt. 'Who are you?'

Whit nearly laughed. 'It's so not what you think.'

'Gooch saved my life, Frank,' Eve said. 'He and Whit saved me, okay, and they've helped me out. I owe them.' She gave Whit a glance, almost embarrassed, freighted with guilt.

'Yeah, babe, you've always been so debt-conscious.' Frank cleared his throat.

Whit said, 'I sure don't trust a scum-ass drug dealer any more than I trust Bucks or Paul. But Frank's right, if we can make Kiko believe the Bellinis are trying to screw him on the deal, the heat goes up on them.' He paused. 'I'm going to call Kiko and set up a come-to-Jesus meeting.'

'No. I should go,' Eve said.

'No. Me.' Whit turned to Frank. 'I'd like to know what your plans are, Frank.'

'My plans?' Frank asked with a blank look.

'Are you leaving town?'

'No. I'm not leaving Eve. Ever.' He took her hand.

'Your concern is touching,' Whit said.

'It's the most he's ever shown,' Eve said, but not unkindly.

'I'm here, at total risk of my life,' Frank said. 'That counts for more than roses that wilt in a day and poems nobody can remember.'

'Go to where they have Gooch,' Whit said, 'and do everything you can to keep them from harming or killing him in case they change their minds. We turn Bucks' timetable around to our advantage, use Frank's idea. Kiko's going to miss his cartoons tomorrow morning. We'll tell him there's no money, but not until he has much less time to plan or react, less than twenty-four hours before he's supposed to get his payment. Make him escalate the pressure on the Bellinis in exactly the way we want. Eve. We're spending tonight at a motel. Not here. You better go, Frank. It's best you don't know where we're at.'

Frank gave Whit a measured look. 'I'm trusting you to take care of the woman I love.'

Someone loved her. He watched his mother touch Frank's shoulder, Frank's defiant frown.

'I'll take good care of her,' Whit said. 'You take care of Gooch for me. Tomorrow morning I call Kiko, and we let the shit hit the fan.'

29

'You don't know me,' the young man said, 'but I have an important business proposition for you.' He sat down next to Kiko on the cool granite of the bench, not looking at him, watching the college students amble by, drinking their Saturday-morning coffee.

'Propose away,' Kiko Grace said. He had been lying on the bed in his rented condo, watching a rerun of a boxing match on ESPN with the TV set to mute, listening to his pregnant wife gripe on the phone about her morning sickness. He was about to switch over to A&E and see who was on *Biography* when call waiting clicked. He thumbed the button and a voice said, 'If you want the five million in cash that's due to you and you want to know why Paul Bellini's screwing you over, be at Rice University in thirty minutes. Near the statue of the man sitting in a chair in the main academic quad. Come alone. I see anyone with you, I call the police and your ass is in jail in five seconds.'

'How did you get this number?' Kiko had asked.

'I'll see you in thirty minutes,' the voice said. 'Dress like a student. But no backpack. No weapons. We're giving you critical information. Do what we ask or you won't be seeing your five million any time soon.' The caller hung up.

Kiko clicked over to his wife and said in Spanish, 'Baby, I'll call you back. Go shopping, it'll pick you up.' Spending money seemed to cure every other ailment she had, but he couldn't deny her a thing.

Kiko, walking toward the rendezvous point, decided whoever called him had made a brilliant move. The quad at Rice University was beautiful, a manicured expanse of lawn and walkways, the statue at the middle of the grounds, a few students milling around the front of the library. It was Saturday, so there wasn't a heavy traffic of people going to and from classes. Not an easy place for him to bring José and tuck him away. He felt himself not fitting in, even though he wasn't much older than these kids. He wore jeans and a Miami Hurricanes sweatshirt, looking too old to be in college and knowing it. He sat at the granite block under the sculpture of William Rice sitting, open book in hand.

José lingered in the archways near the art gallery at the quad's corner, wearing a T-shirt and baggy khaki work pants, pretending to be maintenance even without a uniform, poking at a shrub as though it were diseased, his pistol on a calf holster under his trousers.

But Kiko couldn't see him now. He risked a glance at the guy who had sat next to him. Blondish, thirtyish, dressed more like a grad student than a professor.

'Paul Bellini is screwing you over,' the man said.

'I don't know any Paul Bellini.'

'You had dinner with him Wednesday night. You ate a salad with way too much blue cheese dressing, most of a ribeye, caramel cheesecake. The wine was an Australian merlot, you drank one glass. You didn't stay to watch the strippers dance in the private room.'

'Who are you?'

'A friend, because we have a common enemy,' the man said. 'Paul Bellini is setting you up, Mr Grace, because he's desperate. He has no intention of paying you your money. He's going to take the candy you brought into town and then he's going to whack you.'

'And why should I believe you?'

'You don't have to,' the man said. 'Wait for the bullets, then make up your mind.'

'I'll be gone from Houston by late tomorrow night,' Kiko said.

'They fly caskets out late? I thought that was more of a morning operation,' the man said.

'You got any proof or you just moving your lips?'

'I can't prove that he's ordered a hit on you. That's entirely your gamble if you choose to believe me or not. But he doesn't have your money. He had it ready for you, but it got stolen. You know Bucks? Bucks stole it.'

Kiko gave a smile. 'Did he now.'

'Has Paul confirmed with you the money's missing? Or is he feeding you a steady diet of "just a minor delay"? Promised you the money tonight, and he still doesn't have it. Because Bucks has found his fool, and it's Paul.'

Kiko didn't answer the question. 'Why you telling me this? What's in it for you?'

The man didn't look at him, watched two young women walk by, their laughter floating on the air. Waited until they were well past. 'Paul thinks Eve Michaels stole the money. If you want your money, force Paul to cancel a hit he's put on Eve.'

Kiko waited. 'Why shouldn't I let Paul deal with his own internal problems? I hate interfering with other folks' staffing issues.'

'We have financial information that could bring Paul down. We give it to the Feds, they're gonna know you were dealing with him.'

'No money's changed hands,' Kiko said. But he felt a sick little sinking of fear in his ribs, his gut.

'We'll tell the Feds, the police. They'll watch your ass under a microscope, Mr Grace. You don't want that.' He shrugged. 'Bucks turns over the money to either you or Paul, I don't care, as long as they know Eve didn't take it, we're off safe, we'll give up our financial data to you and Paul. You see? We don't want the money, we don't want the drugs. We want the hits called off, we want Bucks brought down.'

'To do all you ask,' Kiko said, 'I have to kill both Bucks and Paul.'

'Your call.' The man stood, handed Kiko a slip of paper. 'Here's a phone number where you can reach me, day or night. You do your part and I'll do mine and then your name is safe.'

'How do I know you're not playing me against Paul?'

'I guess you don't. But Paul Bellini's lying to you, and I'm not.' The man smiled. 'I'm going to walk away now. Good luck.'

'I'm not done talking to you.' Because he decided when meetings were done, not this nobody.

'Yes, we are done,' the man said. 'And if you don't take any action, you go down with the Bellinis. We want to be left alone. You want your money. We have a mutual enemy. Take care of him. Please.' He turned to walk away.

Kiko stood. Started to follow him, watching to see if José could see him now, glancing to the left. José was talking with a man in a university maintenance uniform, pretending not to speak English, starting to back away from the college worker.

The man turned, held up a hand. 'There's a lot of windows in that building to the left. The classrooms are empty today. I've got a friend up there with a high-powered rifle. He'll take your arm off if you take another step or follow me until I've left the campus.'

'Don't you threaten me.'

'Not threatening. Promising,' the man said.

Kiko watched him vanish around a corner. Stood there, hating that he couldn't move, watching José turn and walk away from the maintenance guy. Finally taking a step, walking, no shot coming.

No sign of the man in the parking lot. Gone. He got in his rented Lexus, José already sitting in the driver's seat. Kiko got in the back and didn't say a word until he was on Main Street, driving on the edge of Hermann Park. His furnished condo was on Fannin, in the heart of a trendy real estate area for those who favored convenience to downtown.

'Well, this dink says there's no delay in getting the money. He says there's no money, period.' He relayed the conversation with the man.

'You believe him? Think Bucks has got the money and is holding out on us?'

Kiko tongued his cheek, clicked his teeth. 'I don't believe Bucks would risk that film coming to light. So no, I don't believe our new friend regarding Bucks.' He drummed fingers on the dashboard. 'Now Paul-boy, Paul might be working a new angle and not clueing Bucks in. Telling Bucks there's a delay and Bucks don't know better. That's a serious worry.'

'So now what?'

'I don't like complications. We're gonna have an A-1 serious talk with Bucks, right now. If he's lied, he's dead, too. I'm thinking this guy and Eve Michaels have the money and want me and Paul shooting at each other.'

'You're dead-on right,' José said. 'Like Willie S said. "*Be able for thine enemy rather in power than use . . .*" '

'What the hell does that mean?' He liked José but didn't like José acting too smart.

'Means that you have to be competent to deal with those who piss you off. No holds barred, Kiko.'

'Fine. So when we get what we want,' Kiko said, turning on the radio, fiddling to find a salsa beat, not wanting to hear another word of Willie S, 'we be able for our enemies on a big scale. We kill everybody.'

30

'Not another roach motel tonight,' Eve said to Whit as they drove away from Rice. They'd spent Friday night in a cheap dive out on I-45 north of downtown. 'We can find one that's laid out better for defense.' The open lot of the motel made her nervous; she'd been standing by the window when Whit fell into restless sleep, and when he awoke this morning.

The Greystoke was a quiet, elegant hotel, owned by an old oil family, at the edge of the Galleria shopping district. Eve liked it because anyone following them or trying to find them could not park on Westheimer to watch the flow of traffic in and out of the hotel's doors. All the hotel's parking was handled by valets, so you couldn't be watched from the hotel lot. Across from the Greystoke a gas station had been razed, and construction was under way on yet another needless upscale restaurant and shopping plaza. Security constantly guarded the construction site, so it could not be used for surveillance.

'This feels relatively safe,' she told Whit.

Safe. It wasn't necessarily the condition he worried most about as he went about life, but life wasn't life any more. Frank had called this morning, said, 'Gooch sedated, okay, roughed up a little' and hung up. And now Whit had hopefully unleashed Kiko against the Bellinis. While Whit waited in the quietly tasteful hotel lobby, Eve – wearing dark glasses and a blondish wig – got them adjoining rooms with her Emily Smith Visa card. Within five minutes they were in their rooms.

'I'm not sure Kiko believed me,' Whit said. 'I got the distinct impression he knew more than I did. He seemed overconfident. Could he be behind this? The theft of the money?'

Eve looked blank. 'I don't see how. He couldn't have known where the exchange point was.'

'Harry followed you. Why couldn't Kiko have? In a way, it would be brilliant. He'd have the money and the Bellinis are turning on each other, self-destructing without him lifting a finger. Then he steps into the vacuum, with their money, and still with his five million in coke to sell. He's doubled his profits in a day.'

He saw that the thought had not occurred to Eve, with her unrelenting focus on Bucks, and her face went ashen. 'Whit. Let's just run,' she said.

'And leave Gooch? Absolutely not.'

'He matters a great deal to you, doesn't he?'

'Yes.'

'Sort of odd, considering you have five brothers. You hardly needed another one, honey. Aren't you close to your brothers?'

'I'm close to Mark. Not so much to the others. I love them all. But we don't all see each other much, I'm the last one still in Port Leo. I've seen them more since Daddy got sick.'

Eve knotted her fingers together in her lap. 'I would have thought me leaving brought you all close together.'

'The wounded crawl off to their own corners,' Whit said. 'We all died a little then. In certain ways it toughened us, did make us close. But it screwed up how we got close to people.'

'I'm sorry.'

'No, you're not,' Whit said. 'You know, I don't hate you. Clearly I don't, considering what I'm risking to save you. But an "I'm sorry" won't cut it. Because I don't believe you'd change a thing about what you did. You've had the life you wanted, Mom.'

'How do you know that, Whit?'

'Because you chose never to come home.'

She sat next to him. 'I'd change one thing,' she said quietly. 'I'd have taken you with me. I nearly did. But Babe would have never let you go.'

'You're right. He loved his children.'

She winced. 'I loved you, too.'

'Abandonment is a strange form of affection.'

'I was a strange mother.'

'So, really, why'd you do it?'

'Does it matter?' She got up from the bed, went into the bathroom, washed her face, washed her hands. She came back into the room, mopping at her face, wiping it clean.

'Does it matter why me and my friend might die trying to save you?'

'In your heart, you've either forgiven me or you still love me. The human heart is capable of a lot more than it gets credit for.' She folded the towel. 'I'm not sure I still loved you a few days ago, Whit. You and your brothers were abstractions to me. I didn't know you as men. I didn't know the people you've turned into. I had no years of memories to tie you to me. Although God knows I've imagined. And I sacrificed more for you, years ago, than you'll ever know.'

'Like what?'

She pursed her mouth, like she had said too much. 'It doesn't really matter. If I tell you, I sound like I'm pleading a case for you to understand me. Or to love me. You either do or you don't,' Eve said.

'Love doesn't leave. It doesn't die. People walk away from love. I love you because at the least you gave life to me and I loved you when you were with me. And I loved you when you were gone, because I wanted you back, more than anything in the world, I wanted a mother. Maybe this time I'll be the one who walks.'

'You haven't walked away yet,' she said and he heard the little tremble of fear in her voice, and he felt ashamed for what he had said, the pointless hurt of it. Nothing he said to her was going to hurt her the way she had hurt him. Words could not equal years of indifferent silence and for a moment he hated what she had done to his family with a depth that made his stomach turn.

'I'm trying to save you, not change you,' he said. 'What happens if we make it through this? You run again? Or you suddenly decide you're my mom for real.'

'I'm never, ever going to let you go again, Whit. Not after what you did for me.' She came, sat next to him, put her arm around him and for a moment her touch was like a memory, and he could see her cradling him against her arm and shoulder, sitting on their back porch, reading him a book, his brothers nowhere around. He wanted to believe her, with a thrum in his chest as hard and real as sudden pain.

'Let's order room service,' she said. 'You used to love pizza, I remember. Pepperoni with mushrooms, thin crust.'

'It's still my favorite,' he said. His voice was hoarse but she didn't seem to notice.

She called room service. He went back into his room, shut the door, showered fast, tried not to imagine Gooch with his nails being pulled out or a bullet tearing through brain matter or his penis stuffed into a blender or whatever bit of deranged sickness Paul and Bucks might inflict on him if all went wrong. He dressed and went back to her room. Eve sat on her bed watching the local news.

'Nothing new about the murders or the shooting at the Pie Shack,' she said.

'We've clearly made the decision to trust Frank up to a point. Can we?' Whit said.

She switched off the TV but kept her gaze fixed on the blank screen. 'He loves me.'

'That's not always an indicator of loyalty.'

Now she looked at him. 'Stop swiping at me. For a while, so we can function as a team.'

He gave her a smile. 'I wasn't jerking your chain. Besides, you've had an almost thirty-year break from Mosley-family sarcasm.'

She laughed. 'Yes, that's true. God, you boys had mouths.'

Her cell phone rang. Frank calling. Whit answered.

Frank's voice was as hushed as if he were in church. 'Paul's getting his mother, kicking and screaming, off to Vegas now. If Paul's working over Gooch, it will be soon.' And clicked off, no good-bye.

Whit turned to Eve. 'I want Frank sticking close to where they have Gooch. We need someone else to stick on Bucks.'

'I don't have a traitor in mind,' she said.

'Actually, I have an idea,' Whit said. 'But it's really risky. More to me than you.'

'Who?'

'Her name is Claudia,' he said. 'And I'm going to ask her to go against her grain in helping us. But I need Bucks' address.'

Eve wrote it down for him and he went into his room. God, this could be a mistake. If Claudia found out he'd left the scene of a crime, failed to report Gooch's kidnapping, and harbored a fugitive – even if it was his own mother – she would lose all respect for him. Their friendship would fracture. Permanently. Claudia believed in rules, fiercely. He was breaking them right and left, caring that they were broken, knowing the pain of leaving a little of himself behind each time, but he was making the choice. She was his friend. She would help. If she could focus on Bucks, it could save Gooch without calling the police and having to turn over his mother.

He paced for a minute, deciding, and then called Claudia's cell phone before he talked himself out of it. She answered on the second ring.

'Are you speaking to me?' he said.

'Depends. I want you to answer my questions.'

'All right.'

'Are you really okay?' she said.

'Yes.'

'Do you know who killed Harry?' Surprising him with the bluntness of her question.

'I have a suspicion but no proof.'

'Who?'

He swallowed. 'A man named Greg Buckman, also called Bucks. He's a former energy exec involved in a crime ring here. Doyle was delivering money for a drug deal. Bucks killed the banker for the money and Harry was at the wrong place at the wrong time.'

'Why was Harry anywhere around these people?'

'Bucks is connected to the Bellinis.'

'Where is your mom, Whit?'

'I haven't found her. Yet.' The lie felt fine in his mouth and he closed his eyes.

'So you rushed to Houston, on what, impulse?'

'I wanted to be here if Harry found my mom. I couldn't sit around waiting in Port Leo.'

'The Houston police want to talk to you, Whit.'

'Fine. When?'

'As soon as possible. Why, are you booked today?' Losing patience.

'Not today. Tomorrow or Monday.' When this had played out and he had Eve safely hidden. Where she couldn't be taken away from him.

'I'm sorry that your calendar is so full.'

'If you want to help me, truly, Claudia, turn the police onto Greg Buckman. But he's very dangerous.'

'No. You should talk to the police with me. Or the DA's office. I have a friend who works in Special Crimes; she can help us.'

'I don't want to talk to anyone but you right now.'

Claudia said nothing for several seconds then said, 'I'm listening.'

'Buckman lives at 3478 Alabama, number 12. It's a fancy townhouse. He's about six-one, maybe one sixty, thinning blond/brown hair, dresses very conservatively, like a Brooks Brothers poster boy. He drives a silver Jaguar, late model. Vanity license plate of B-L-E-E-V.'

'Believe?'

'He's a big fan of Chad Channing, the self-help guy.' Frank had given him this information.

'He sounds very frightening.'

'I believe he has killed at least two people,' Whit said.

'There's no mention of him in Harry's records. His assistant gave those to the Houston police. She faxed me a copy this afternoon.'

That meant the police now knew the name Eve Michaels. 'Harry mentioned Bucks in a phone conversation.'

'Whit, you tell me the truth right this second. Have you found your mom or this Eve Michaels? Are you protecting her?'

'Claudia, please.'

'You have found her. Where are you?'

'I can't tell you. Please don't ask me.'

'Whit. Do you want the police actively looking for you or your mother as material witnesses? They are insistent on talking to you.'

'I'm asking for your understanding.'

'You're asking me to suppress information related to two homicides. To Harry's murder! I can't. I'm a peace officer. You're an officer of the court. You've sworn an oath, Whit. You—'

'I'm asking you to get information. To follow Buckman, watch him. He killed Harry for this money, he's got to have it hidden close to him. But no police, Claudia, please.'

'You have freaking lost your mind,' Claudia said.

'Meet me,' he said. 'Meet me and I'll explain. But no police. Just you and me.'

'Of course I'll meet you. Where?'

'There's a little Mexican restaurant off Montrose, on Richmond. Chapultepec's. It's in an old house. I'll meet you there in thirty minutes.'

'Fine,' she said.

'Claudia?'

'Yes?'

'I've really messed up,' he said. 'I thought I did the right thing and now, I know I've really messed up.'

'We'll fix it,' she said, and he wanted to believe her. 'I'll see you in thirty.'

Claudia clicked off the phone. She wrote down the address and description for Greg Buckman. This morning she had driven to the murder site, drawn by a need to be close to where Harry died. But it was still roped off, under police tape. She didn't get out of her car, drove by twice before heading back to her hotel. But now. Now she could do something. She picked up the phone.

'Vernetta? I heard from my friend that was Harry Chyme's client. I need you to come to a meeting with me.' She sighed. 'He won't be happy about it but I need you to help me talk sense into him.'

Thirty minutes later, Claudia sat in a booth at Chapultepec's, sipping water, nibbling from a mound of nachos. Vernetta sat four booths over, waiting for Whit to arrive and sit so she could join them. Claudia traced the beer rings on the worn wooden table with her fingertips, waiting for Whit, waiting to see if he was still the man she knew, afraid of what she had heard in his voice.

The nachos grew cold. Whit never showed.

31

Two Louis Vuitton bags, one for makeup and hair, one for clothes, were all his mother was taking to Vegas but to Paul her packing process was slower than moving mountains. He was ready to shove his mother out the door when Tasha pulled up in the circular driveway, ten minutes too early, in her little Honda.

Not what I need, Paul thought, but he smiled and gave Tasha a too-quick, just-friends hug, knowing his mother was watching from a window.

Tasha leaned back from him. 'I stink now?'

'No. I'm tense. Bad, bad day. Getting my mother out of town.'

'Introduce me. I bet I make her want to stick around.'

He took her into the hallway. Frank Polo and Mary Pat Bellini were already in the foyer, Frank wheezing, with Mary Pat's two packed-to-the-brim bags.

'Mom,' Paul said, 'this is Tasha. She's a friend of mine.'

'How nice to meet you,' Mary Pat Bellini said and her smile seemed to rise like a fence as she shook Tasha's hand. 'What a lovely sweater.'

'What a lovely home,' Tasha said. 'Paul has told me all about you. For hours on end.'

'You're catching me heading out the door.' Mary Pat glanced at Paul. 'Practically being pushed. My son thinks I need a little vacation. He doesn't give a lady much choice.'

'He can be real pushy,' Tasha said. 'But in the sweetest way.'

'Mom, Frank'll drive you to the airport. Have a great time. Don't go crazy at the baccarat tables, okay?' Frank looked surprised at the announcement of his assignment but he picked up Mary Pat's luggage and carried it out to her Mercedes' trunk.

'Paul, darling,' Mary Pat said. 'You look like you're considering a coronary.'

'I'll see you on Tuesday, Mom. Unless we got developments here and you need to stay in Vegas.'

'I'm not being gone from your daddy that long, Paul. Forget it.'

'Or away from Paul, either, right?' Tasha said.

Mary Pat snapped a quick smile at Tasha. 'Nice to meet you, dear.'

'It's great to meet the woman who raised Paul. The source of his brains and good manners.'

Mary Pat's smile brightened but it was aimed at her son. 'I'll call you when I get to my hotel, Paul.'

Paul kissed his mother, shut the door, watched Frank pull out past the extra guards at the gate. 'Thank Christ she's gone.'

'The color went out of her face because of the color of mine,' Tasha said.

'That's a terrible thing to say,' Paul said. 'She treats all my girlfriends bad. She was very accepting of you. I have lots of black friends.'

'Business associates, yeah,' she said, 'but I doubt you have many black friends. Or friends, period.'

'What's that mean?' Paul sounded hurt.

'Friends are a luxury for a guy like you.' Tasha ran a finger along his jawline, made her voice husky.

'But I have you.' He pulled her close, gave her a quick kiss. She allowed it, kissed him back, teased his mouth for a moment with her tongue. She broke the kiss. 'Ralph did that credit check you asked for on Bucks and Frank and Eve.'

'Great.'

'I need five thou to give Ralph, sweetie. For this and finding Eve's credit card. I got to throw him a bone.'

'If he can wait, I can pay him and you more when we get the money.'

Tasha considered his offer with a frown. 'They're all clean. Nothing unusual. I don't know if that helps you or not.'

He looked a little deflated. 'Okay. Come inside. I need a favor.'

She followed him into the grand living room, her eyes checking each piece of furniture, noticing the rich silk of the draperies, the marble on the floors, the fresh flowers in every vase. She had imagined a former mob wife would lean toward zebra stripes and magenta, bad taste run amok. Instead the house was simple and elegant, all at once, and a twinge sounded in her heart. A lot of pain and death had bought this beauty and Tasha Strong fought an urge to smash it all, set it afire.

'Dad moved his eyes a bunch more today.' He led her upstairs and into a front bedroom. The room was dark, lit by the greenish goblin glow of medical equipment. Tommy Bellini lay in the bed, eyes at half-mast. Tasha expected a nurse but instead Doc Brewer was there, checking Tommy's eyes.

'How is he?' Paul asked. 'I think he's more alert.'

'He's the same, Paul,' Doc Brewer said.

'Our guest upstairs still unconscious?'

'The same,' Doc Brewer said. He patted Tommy's hand and excused himself.

'Brewer's an idiot. Dad knows what's going on,' Paul said. 'Knows I'm in trouble. He's fighting up toward consciousness.' He lowered his voice. 'I was changing his diaper earlier and he was sporting wood. That's a good sign, right?'

'Sure, Paul.' It surprised her he would tend to his dad.

'Maybe he needs additional stimulants to regain consciousness.'

'That's not how comas work, sweetpea,' Tasha said.

'Well, Mom's been reading to him. Or leaving books on tape playing next to his bed. All his favorite books. Robert Ludlum, Louis L'Amour. He loves those. And I run Mel Brooks movies on the DVD player for him.'

'So read to him.'

'What about a direct approach?' Paul said. 'You could do a lap dance for him.'

She blinked. 'A lap dance.'

'It couldn't hurt. And he had a woody earlier, so he's still got some juice in his brain.'

'Do you ever hear yourself talk, Paul?' A lap dance for a guy two seconds from choking on his own drool.

'What's that supposed to mean?'

'I admire your concern for your dad. Really. But you have millions missing, Kiko isn't waiting forever for his money, you've got a guy half-dead upstairs you're going to start torturing, you've got Eve and this Whit man gunning for you. The police could descend on you any second. And you want me to lap dance for your comatose daddy.'

Paul slapped her.

She fell back against the withered legs under the covers. His legs felt like sticks under the sheets.

'Don't mouth off at me. Especially in front of my dad.' Like Tommy Bellini was going to open his eyes, shoot them a disapproving look.

'You hit me, Paul.' She slowly got up from the bed. 'After all I've done for you . . .'

'I hit you because I want you to realize the seriousness of my request. I didn't ask you to do him, that would be gross.' He took a step toward her. 'Just rub against him. If it works, it works. I'm sorry, baby, please.'

'And we could all get written up in a medical journal.' She moved to the other side of the bed, keeping it between her and Paul. 'Charming. He can wake up and slip the tip in my G-string.'

'Tasha. I need my dad. I need him bad now because I don't know what to do.' He started to cry. More than cry. Blubber.

'Paul, don't.' She was still spitting mad and the sight of tears on his face made her even madder. She hated to see a man cry; it turned her stomach.

'Kiko's gonna put my balls in a grinder. I got to have that money.'

If he had cried for his father, her heart would have softened toward him. But he was crying because he was afraid for himself. It wasn't tears for his dad or for anyone else. She wanted to slap him.

'Hush now,' she said quietly. 'Be strong, Paul.'

'I need my dad. We've spent all this money to take care of him, he sure ought to get better.'

Tasha counted to ten silently. 'Paul. Your father's not going to recover. Ever. That's clear to everyone but you. You've got to take charge, take responsibility.' She touched his shoulder. 'Let me help you.'

Her pager beeped. She glanced at the readout. Ralph, her computer hacker friend. She pulled a cell phone – a real one, not the clever little gun she carried that no one knew about except, now, Whit Mosley – out of her purse and dialed his number.

'Tasha.' Ralph sounded excited. 'Emily Smith is using her Visa again. At Greystoke Hotel. The charge is for two rooms.'

'Which rooms?'

'Charge doesn't say.'

'Ralph, you are a god.' She clicked off and turned to Paul, told him what Ralph reported. 'You got 'em in your sights, sugar. Call Bucks, call your dogs in for the kill and act like a man.' She lowered her voice, came to him, put a hand on his chest. 'I done the work for you. I got a lock on Eve and her buddy. Now go make your daddy proud.'

32

'You lied to me,' Kiko said.

'I told you exactly what I was told,' Bucks said. 'That there was a delay in getting the money.' He rock-steadied his voice. 'Paul lied to us both because Eve robbed him blind. She's gutted him. He has very little left he can quickly convert to cash with that money gone.'

'Why should I believe you now?' Kiko said.

'Eve stole the loot, I swear. Kiko, you know I wouldn't screw you over, I've got too much to lose. I'm about five minutes from capturing her ass. I got a team working to grab her for Paul.'

'There's been a change in plan,' Kiko said.

Bucks listened to what Kiko said, closed his eyes. 'I understand.' He clicked off the phone, waited for the horrible *thumping* in his chest to subside.

Adapt. Adapt. He could still come out on top. The phone rang in his hand and he answered it, heard Paul telling him where they thought Eve was now, and truly thanked God and Chad Channing together for the strength they were giving him.

Bucks waited in his Jag with MacKay. They were parked a half block from the Greystoke Hotel in the shadow of a new real estate development, in a parking lot where a restaurant was closed and shuttered. They could sce most of the porte cochere for the Greystoke. Cars arrived in a steady stream; the hotel had an up-scale martini bar that attracted locals. Valets scrambled around the vehicles. But what pissed Bucks off was a car pulling in next to them, a Cadillac with Jerry Smacks driving and the Wart in the passenger seat.

Bucks sipped from a water bottle. The next hour would deter-
mine how he played his next card. He felt warm and calm,
confident for the first time in a day.

'They gonna wonder why you're here with me,' MacKay said.
Now both men were looking over into Bucks' Jag. Jerry Smacks
gave a friendly little wave with his hand. The Wart didn't smile.

'Why are they together?' Bucks asked.

'More likely to make the hit, working together,' MacKay
said. 'Better to split the fee rather than none at all. Cut me out,
too.'

'So why are we here together? In case they ask.'

'My car broke down, you giving me a ride,' MacKay said. 'Quit
worrying, you're the boss.' He eased down the window; Jerry did
the same.

'Gentlemen,' MacKay said. He didn't volunteer why he was in
Bucks' car and Jerry Smacks didn't ask.

'So you boys sitting here jerking or what?' the Wart said. 'We
gonna go in?'

'Need to know,' MacKay said, 'which of the fifteen-odd floors
they're on, for starters. The registration desk isn't gonna give that
up.'

'I'm not inclined to walk through a front door,' Jerry Smacks
said.

'Yeah, you struck me as a back door kind of guy,' MacKay said.

Jerry folded a rectangle of gum into his mouth, muttered to the
Wart. Then he looked past MacKay to Bucks. 'How you want us
to handle it, Mr Buckman?'

'I pay the bounty, gum boy,' Bucks said. 'I don't do the job for
you.'

'Fine,' the Wart said. He started to get out of the car. 'Then I'm
gonna—'

'Whoa,' MacKay said. 'Target number two.'

A tall blondish man stood at the valet spot. He gave the
attendant a dollar and hurried to a slightly decrepit Volkswagen
van that had been brought up to the curb.

'That's our boy,' Bucks said. His bruised eye throbbed at the
sight of Whit. 'Eve's alone in the hotel. MacKay, you and Jerry go

in. You know what I need. I'll follow our boy. Wart, you come with me.'

'Why me?' the Wart yelled.

'He's part of the contract,' Bucks said. 'Kill him, you still get paid.'

MacKay was out of the car already, buttoning a leather jacket, lifting his dreadlocks free from the collar, hurrying across the pell-mell rush of Westheimer. Jerry Smacks followed. The Wart huffed into the Jag and before his door was shut Bucks wheeled into traffic, earning a blare of horns. He cussed. Honking might attract Mosley's attention. But the van, four cars ahead, stayed in the left lane, didn't slow, didn't turn.

A charge of electricity played along Bucks' skin. Man, this was a rush like cutting a deal with California power buyers, seeing how far he could shove the rates down their desperate little throats, calculating his enormous commissions in his head. He jammed in a Chad Channing tape, upped the volume. Chad's reassuring baritone filled the car. 'It's important to remember,' Chad Channing said, 'that goals are as real as the air we breathe. They surround us. They permeate us, like oxygen. They sustain us. The life lived without goals is life without breath.'

'I heard this about you,' the Wart said. 'But I didn't want to believe it.'

'Listen and learn.' Bucks drummed his fingers on the steering wheel, as though the tape had a pelvis-grinding backbeat.

'Yeah, a tape's gonna tell me how to live.'

'Do you have goals, Wart?' Bucks asked.

'Yeah. Pop this guy, collect my money, and spend the evening with good Thai pad noodles, a bottle of Glenfiddich, and a couple of hours with a nice little whore I know.' The Wart checked his gun again, keeping it low, below the line of the windows. 'Loser's got to get off Westheimer first. Too many people around.'

'Those are powerful goals you got, Wart. You've got a rich life.'

'I'm content,' the Wart said. 'You didn't say if you prefer head shots.'

'Let's get him alone first,' Bucks said. 'Make him hurt. Make him talk. And if he doesn't tell me what I want to hear, you can take as few or as many shots as you want, buddy.'

'Nice-looking guy,' the Wart said, 'Reminds me of the jocks who treated me like a nothing in high school. Guy like him, I usually take special care of the face. Dead or not. You ever see what's left of a face after you hook a gun along the gumline and fire through the lip?'

'See? You've got a goal.'

'So embrace your goals. Say them, each morning, like a prayer,' Chad Channing intoned from the tape. 'Make meeting your goals not simply your challenge, but your bliss.'

'Turn that crap off,' the Wart said. 'It's working my last nerve.'

Bucks could smell the five million, feel it in his hands. Not just money. Sudden power. Now. So close. Eve and this bastard had hidden it and if his luck was sweet the guy was driving to get it right now. That thought, that thought was golden. This was his reprieve.

'Oh, please, yes,' he said as Whit turned onto Richmond. 'Yes, buddy, take me right to bliss.'

MacKay and Jerry Smacks walked into the handsome lobby of the Greystoke, Jerry muttering about taking the front door. The valets nodded but gave them no special notice as a crowd of departing guests came out at the same moment. MacKay made a beeline for the lobby phones. He didn't even glance at Jerry as he picked up a phone.

'You want to tell me the plan, friend?' Jerry said.

'Just play along.'

'You aren't cutting me out of the action, bud.'

'Emily Smith's room, please,' MacKay said into the phone.

'Very direct approach,' Jerry said.

'Ms Smith,' MacKay said after a moment. 'Hello. Paul sent me. The tall young man who just left? He's here with us now. We have him. You understand me?'

There was a pause.

'You have two minutes to come down to the lobby. We've taken him away in a car.' MacKay kept his voice low and friendly. 'You are not to make a scene. You are not to scream or do anything other than what I tell you to do. Or your young man pays the price. Do you understand me? You have a minute and fifty seconds now. I'll see you momentarily.' He hung up.

'Cool,' said Jerry Smacks. 'I like your efficiency.'

'Follow my lead and don't get in the way,' MacKay said.

Jerry pasted a smile on like MacKay's, quiet and friendly, and the two men went to the elevator bank. There were five elevators. MacKay studied the numbers. Two young Asian women pushed the up button, an elevator arrived empty, they boarded and held the door for MacKay and Jerry.

'Thanks. Waiting for a friend,' Jerry said.

The elevator shut.

'A minute left,' MacKay said. 'We'll see how much this guy matters to her.'

Eve replaced the phone in the cradle. How? How could they have found her, how could they have grabbed Whit? They called her Ms Smith. They knew about the credit card. They had her son.

She dialed Whit's cell phone, her fingers shaking, expecting there to be no answer or worse, the cool steel of Bucks' voice.

'Yeah?' Whit answered after two rings. Calm.

She nearly collapsed in relief. 'A man just called, said they snatched you.'

'No one has me. I'm driving.'

'I have two minutes to get to the lobby or they say they'll kill you.'

'Get out. Get out now.'

'How? They're in the lobby.' Eve tried to keep her voice calm but the urge to run surged in her bones.

'Find another way, I'm heading back to the hotel,' Whit said.

'No. It's a trap. Don't risk it.'

'Get the hell out, Mom. Come to the back of the hotel. I'll pick you up there.'

'Don't risk it. I'll call you where to come get me. Don't come back here.'

'Stay calm. I'm coming, head for the back,' he said.

She hung up the phone. She left the small bag she'd packed, grabbed her purse, checked her gun inside. Closed her hand around it. The CD with Paul's files on it was in there, too. Whit had left nothing valuable in the room. She put on the wig, hat, and glasses she'd used checking in. She opened the door, peered down the hall. Nothing but empty hallway, with an abandoned room service tray a couple of doors down. The soft buzz of a basketball game played on a television a room away. She ran for the elevators, pressed a down button.

MacKay said. 'Her two minutes are up.'

'Give her one more,' Jerry Smacks said.

'Hardly, man,' MacKay said. 'Go get the car, bring it around fast. We're leaving in a hurry.'

Jerry left, and MacKay watched the lights above the elevator, watching for each elevator to make its inevitable drop to the lobby, letting out couples, an elderly woman, a teenage girl. Then one car stopped at two.

MacKay headed for the middle of the lobby, watching the stairs exit. Waiting to see if she'd come out, gambling to herself he wouldn't grab her with other witnesses in the lobby.

Another minute passed. MacKay bolted for the front door.

On the second floor, Eve ran past the hotel's conference center, past a spa and an exercise room, past a set of meeting rooms named after famous Texas artists, dead and living. The Ney. The Umlauf. The Kohler. Laughter bubbled behind doors, people who didn't have a life-or-death care in the world. A stairway led to the pool and she hurried down it.

She called Whit on her cell. 'I'm heading to the back of the hotel.'

'I'm on my way,' he said.

'Stay on the phone,' she said.

The pool was empty, but in the Saturday afternoon sun a couple of women in their forties sat at a table, sipping coffee and chatting quietly. A waiter set a two-tiered tray of cakes between the women. Eve walked past them. There was no gate opening to the back of the hotel but she spotted a service entrance, leading to the kitchen. Dinner prep work was under way, a couple of men in chef's clothes glancing up at her as she rushed past their chopping and dicing.

'Excuse me, ma'am . . .' one started and she ignored him, heading for the red glow of an exit sign.

'Hey!' the chef yelled again, petulant as a toddler. 'You can't barge in here . . .'

She turned back to the chef, put the phone down for a second. 'My ex is in the lobby. I have a restraining order against him. Excuse me.'

The chef started to apologize, conciliation in his voice, but she didn't wait. She hit the door. A hallway, another exit sign at the end. She ran through that door into the cloud-broken light of Houston winter, the narrow lot behind the hotel empty except for valet slots lining the back lot, the hum of traffic from 610 like a ghost whispering in her ear. Next to the lot sat an office building, a squat crystal of green glass, ten stories high, and beyond it a concrete parking garage. Deserted on a Saturday. Then an Italian restaurant with a gargantuan neon sign, then a steakhouse, both lots a third full.

And then the Cadillac wheeled around the back of the lot, thundering for her.

Eve turned and ran, skimming the back of the hotel, aiming for a loading bay at the far corner of the hotel. She jammed her hand deep in her purse, closed her fingers around her Beretta. She turned to fire but the car was now seven feet behind her, slamming brakes, and she went across the hood, the windshield, the air in her lungs whooshing out. With a gasp she fell off the Caddy, the asphalt biting into her face and palms.

A car door creaked open by her head.

'Nice braking, man,' a voice above her said. Jamaican accent. She scrabbled to her feet; her ribs, her legs thrummed as if on fire. Her gun and phone were gone. Dropped.

'Eve Michaels,' the Jamaican said. He smashed a pistol across her head. She hit the pavement again, blood trickling along her cheek. The Jamaican picked her up, handcuffed her, shoved her in the car.

'What the hell are you doing?' A gravelly male voice, not Jamaican, yelled. 'Waste her and let's—'

Then the distinctive double pop of a silencer. Eve waited to draw breath, wondering if the passing from life to death was truly so instant and painless that you didn't realize it had happened. But she still needed to breathe. She did. A car door popped open, and she heard the dull thud of dead weight hitting the pavement. Then the car started.

She risked a glance upward. The Jamaican, in the driver's seat, leveled her own gun at her.

'Eve,' he said. 'You see how it is? That guy wanted to hurt you. I killed him. Makes me your friend.'

She put her head down on the backseat.

If she raised her head, Whit might see her. He would be heading back to the hotel. He'd chase them, get himself killed. Stupid kid.

Just let him go. Stay down and keep him out of it. Do the right thing for once in your life, Ellie. She thought of him as a baby, her easiest because he was the last and she was too tired to worry about every little cough or scrape. She sure hadn't wanted another but here he came, her best. The only person ever in her life to truly come looking for her. Like she mattered.

'Here are the rules,' the Jamaican said as he made two sharp turns to the right, ignoring car horns pealing behind him, heading onto Westheimer, then onto the frontage road of Loop 610. 'You stay down. You get up, I shoot off a finger. Get up again, I shoot off a tit. Clear?'

'Clear,' she said thickly. Her head hurt like it'd been cut open and the brains rearranged. 'I won't make trouble.'

'Good call. Hey, you want a stick of gum? Lots of spare spearmint up here.' The Jamaican gave a little laugh.

Eve closed her eyes. *Let me go, Whit. Let me go, baby.*

33

Whit spun Gooch's van in a screeching U-turn back toward the hotel. A Ford truck, a Lexus, a Blazer, and a Jag passed him, and in his rearview the Jag spun, following him again, and he spotted the license plate. BLEEV.

Bucks. So much for a separate peace.

Whit floored the van down Westheimer, dodging around slower-moving cars. Cars honked at him and in the rearview mirror the Jag closed on him. Two men in it. Bucks driving. A guy he didn't know, who looked like an accountant, balding, glasses.

Caught between the wolves hunting his mother at the hotel and Bucks. Lose them first, tell Eve where to meet him, or grab Eve then try and lose them? The wrong choice could mean death. In less than a minute.

On the phone he heard his mother scream.

He headed for the hotel, the steering wheel in a death grip. Ten seconds. Twenty. Thirty, veering hard around a truck.

Whit tore into the porte cochere at the Greystoke Hotel at thirty miles an hour. He sent one valet diving for safety. Whit nearly clipped a Porsche roadster, smashed an ornate potted fern, spraying the fragments across the flagstones. Screams and angry yells echoed behind him. He sped around the hotel's corner, then around it again into the back lot. The Jag hadn't pulled in after him. Waiting for him to pull out. Or blocking the exit around the other side of the hotel. A body lay before him in the parking lot.

Oh, God, no, he thought. But it was a man, not his mother, and he pulled up and leaned out to look. A man he didn't know, two daubs of blood on his forehead, eyes wide and staring, mouth open, a grayish wad of gum on the lips like a withered tongue.

His mother's red phone a foot from the guy, the screen broken and battered. The hat she'd worn atop her wig next to it. He opened his door, scooped up her phone and hat, stood by the car for a tense eternity.

'Eve!' he yelled. 'Eve!' Then, 'Mom!'

Nothing. Him parked by a dead man, anyone could come around in a minute and see him with the corpse. He got back in the van and waited. Thirty seconds passed. She wasn't here.

The Jag edged around the building, now behind him. No choice. He floored the van, swerved onto the narrow alley feeder that led back onto Westheimer, nearly side-swiping a parked truck, driving past the turn-in for the valet parking, the Jag revving hard, now near enough to ram him.

Pings sounded against the van's back door and his driver's side mirror broke. Shooting at him. He couldn't outrun them, not in the van.

Whit ripped through a red light, barely missing an old Chevy pickup, and rocketed up the entrance ramp onto Loop 610, the vast highway that circled the heart of Houston. In the rearview mirror a man, the bookish one, leaned out of the Jag's passenger window and emptied a rifle toward Whit, the cars around him braking and peeling away, drivers suddenly caught in a war zone. Whit jerked, as though he were hit, and the Jag slowed. A pickup truck and a Lexus SUV arced away from him, slamming into each other, spinning, barely holding onto the road, a Cavalier's driver standing on his brakes, rear-ending the Lexus. Cars stopped, trying to pull over out of harm's way, other drivers scrambling past them, not knowing about the battle in the lanes ahead.

Then Whit saw a patch of empty lane, spun the wheel with all his strength, prayed the van wouldn't roll. The van turned 180 degrees, the burnt smell of smoking rubber and strained engine thickening the air.

He was now facing against traffic on a Houston highway, a suicide drive, and he slammed his foot on the accelerator. Straight at the Jag, stopped by the other collisions.

He saw Bucks' face, the mouth working in shock, saying *you crazy motherfucker*.

The bookish guy opened his mouth in a scream, ducked back into the car, struggling to pull the rifle through the window. Whit stopped by the driver's side, had his gun out and aimed at Bucks' head.

'Where is she?' he screamed. 'Tell me or I'll kill you!'

Bucks wriggled, trying to get out of the line of fire and Whit thought *shoot him*. But he didn't. A car missed the van by inches and he would die if he sat here, more traffic coming over the rise from 610 out of Bellaire.

A bullet tore into the trim above Whit's head, Bucks firing wild at the bad angle through the open window, emptying the clip. Whit floored the van, vrooming into sparse oncoming traffic that hadn't slowed, horns wailing. He yanked the wheel and suddenly he was on the grassy slide down to the frontage road at seventy miles an hour, hurtling downward into traffic, his head slamming against the roof, the van barely holding its wheels to the grass.

He swerved to move in the direction of traffic, roared down the frontage. He tapped his brakes at the red light at San Felipe, barreled over the curb, smacked through ornamental oleanders trimming the parking lot at a small shopping center, and drove back into the tree-lined quiet of River Oaks. No sign of the Jag in pursuit. He slowed his speed to the limit, checked the rearview mirror again and again and again.

Perhaps he'd been lucky and an eighteen-wheeler loaded with explosives had plowed into them, sitting on the highway, like a scene out of an overwrought action movie.

Or maybe Whit didn't matter now. They had Eve. So they thought they would soon have the cash. They had Gooch. And odds were Bucks had the money.

Whit had nothing, nothing at all. He could go home. He felt dead. It was over. Insane. Insane of him to try and help her. He should have simply taken her to the police, turned her over. Talked her into it. Now he had nearly killed a man, put innocent lives at risk.

He picked up his cell phone, forced himself to take a steadying breath. Blinked, dialed.

'Hello?'

'Frank. Can you talk?' Whit said.

'Not at the moment. I'll call you back in ten minutes.' And he hung up.

Whit drove back to Charlie's house, sticking to side roads, hoping that the shot-out mirror and any bullet holes in the van weren't attracting attention. He pulled into Charlie's empty driveway. Sat and waited.

The phone rang.

'Yes?' Whit said.

'It's Frank. Sorry, I was dropping Mary Pat off at the airport for Paul.'

'Meet me at Charlie's house.'

'What's wrong?'

'Get here.' He clicked off the phone, put his head down on the steering wheel.

Frank arrived about twenty minutes later, pulling up in the driveway behind Whit. Whit got out, thinking *what do you know, have they called you, have I made a terrible mistake in trusting you?*

'They got Eve.' He told Frank what happened. 'They knew where we were, the hotel we hid at.'

'Oh, God, no.' Frank put a hand over his mouth.

'They knew where we were.'

Frank heard the accusation in his voice. 'I didn't know where you were.'

Whit grabbed Frank's shirt, pushed him against the van. 'Eve didn't tell you?'

'I swear to God, no. If I'd betrayed you, Whit, I sure as hell wouldn't show up to help you now.'

That was true. The Bellinis must have picked up their trail in another way. 'Where will they take her?'

'Probably the house here on Lazy Lane, with Gooch.' His voice shook. 'I can't believe they haven't called me to tell me they got her.'

'You sure they haven't?' Whit said.

'They haven't. I'm on your side, Whit.'

Frank was his best hope, this glorified lounge singer. 'Go back to the Bellinis. See if they bring her there. Then call me.'

'Calling you may be difficult. If she's alive, they'll want me to talk with her, to reason with her. I can't leave her to their mercies. Me being there might keep them from torturing her worse or killing her.' Frank went ashen.

'Frank, help me. Please.'

'You're her kid, aren't you?' Frank held Whit's shoulders. 'You're not a regular wiseguy or hired thug.'

'Yes. I'm her son.'

'I knew it. I knew I saw a strong resemblance. Man, I didn't even know she had a kid.' Frank shook his head, looked at Whit like he'd never seen him before. Gave him a hard hug.

'We hadn't seen each other in thirty years,' Whit said into Frank's shoulder.

'Oh, God, I never knew.'

Whit stepped back from Frank. 'What about Gooch?'

'Now that Paul has her, his value is nothing. They don't need him.'

'No. No.'

'Whit, they're gonna kill her, it's practically guaranteed. Your friend, too. Leave town.'

Whit said nothing.

'Did you hear me? There's nothing you can do. Go home and pray they don't come looking for you. They can be animals.'

Whit's eyes felt hot. No. There had to be a way. He slowed his breathing, tried to imagine a way through the maze. He needed a bargaining chip. Or a weapon.

'Go back to the house,' Whit said.

'I'll call you as soon as I can.' And Frank turned and hurried back to his BMW, as though relieved suddenly to be on his way back to the Bellini fold. He hadn't asked if Whit would call the police; he had to be afraid of that. But he got a bonus point for not asking. Whit watched him drive away.

Whit stumbled into the house, reached for his cell phone. The police. Call them, tell them everything. Claudia would help him.

The phone rang in his hand. Frank probably calling back, now really worried Whit was calling the cops. He said 'Yes?'

'You drive better than you bluff.' Kiko Grace's voice.

How would Kiko know . . . Whit closed his eyes. 'What, you got Bucks to switch sides?'

'I'm a persuasive man,' Kiko said.

'You have Eve.'

'Yes.'

'Like I told you, we don't have the money. She can't help you. Please don't hurt her.'

'I'm not interested in your sob story,' Kiko said. 'I'm interested in the money. Now. We can deal. Her for the money. And don't tell me again you don't have it. I don't believe you. You say those words again, I jam a gun up her old ass and pump a couple of rounds. Better than fiber.'

Say anything, to buy time. 'Fine. I'll bring you the money. Don't hurt her.'

'Now we're cooking. Now we're smoking.'

'It will take me time to get it. We didn't hide it all in one place.'

'Wise of you.'

'You tell Bucks to call off any more killers he has. Working for you or for Paul.'

'Paul's plans are none of my business,' Kiko said. 'He got more problems than plans anyway.'

'So Paul's out of it? It's just between you and me now?'

'Far as I'm concerned.'

'I'll bring you the money,' Whit said, panic rising in his throat. 'Tomorrow.' Bargaining for more time, anything he could get.

'No. Tonight.'

He knew he couldn't back up further. 'Fine. Be five million poorer.'

'You're not in a situation to make demands,' Kiko said.

'I have what you want.'

'And so do I,' Kiko said. 'But I'm not an unreasonable man.'

'Tomorrow at sunset,' Whit said. 'At the Mecom Fountain on Main Street. You come alone. You bring Eve, I'll bring the money.' Mecom Fountain was about as public a spot as you could get in Houston, on Main Street in a traffic circle that was constantly busy, between the Montrose arts district and Hermann Park.

'No. Pick another place.'

227

'Then I'll count the money myself,' Whit said. 'I'll buy Eve nice flowers for her funeral. But I'll have the money, not you.'

Kiko was silent. 'All right.' Whit could hear the tinge of greed in his voice. 'I'll send my associate José with Eve. I'm not doing any more public appearances.'

'Mr Grace?'

'Yeah?'

'Watch out for Bucks. He turned on Paul, he'll turn on you.'

'I appreciate the concern,' Kiko said. 'Don't get cute and call the police. I have friends on the force. Any word from them that my name's been mentioned to anyone, and Eve dies. You got it?'

Probably a bluff but he couldn't risk it. 'I got it,' Whit said. Kiko hung up without another word.

Whit sat down at the kitchen table. Bluster. He had nothing left but bluster. This mess was of his making and he had nothing left but the kind of bluster he used to whip kids in juvie court into shape.

But bluster made the world go round some days.

Whit went to Charlie's gun cabinet, the source of one of Charlie's jokes ('When you've got clients like mine . . .'), but the guns looked deadly serious. Rifles, pistols, an antique German gun from the turn of the nineteenth century. Wicked knives in hand-stitched leather sheaths. Whit opened the cabinet, staring for a moment, letting the life he knew slip away like a mere shadow swallowed in greater darkness. He would be dead or different by sunset tomorrow. The thought left him cold but suddenly less afraid. He reached for the first gun.

Whit wondered if this was what it felt like for his mother, years ago, abandoning one life for another.

34

'He doesn't show for a meeting,' Arturo Gomez said. He had a pleasant voice, one that rang in his chest, an actor's tone. 'He doesn't sound particularly cooperative. Does he need the serious encouragement an arrest warrant offers?'

'You're jumping the gun. I'm concerned for Judge Mosley's safety,' Claudia said. 'I'm afraid he's in danger.'

'Or he's blowing smoke up your butt.' Gomez shuffled through a file. Claudia and Vernetta Westbrook sat on the other side of his desk at HPD headquarters.

'Frankly, sir, I don't like the tone you're taking,' Claudia said. 'Whit's not hiding anything. He made an allegation to me, one he said he couldn't prove. But he wouldn't accuse another person lightly. And it's entirely unlike him to miss a meeting with me. He's a professional.'

Gomez locked his gaze on her, raised an eyebrow, as if asking *what more do you know, never mind your friend?*

'Art, you got Advil? I don't even know this friend of Claudia's and he's given me a bad-ass headache,' Vernetta said. Trying to defuse the attention.

He pulled a bottle of aspirin from his desk, pushed it to Vernetta.

'Given what Judge Mosley told me,' Claudia said, 'will you question Greg Buckman?'

'On what grounds? Your tipster, who can't make a simple meeting? I need cause. I need a boatload of cause before I approach anyone connected to the Bellini family.'

'You have enough cause to question him,' Claudia said. He'd taken a tone of speaking down to her, and she suspected it wasn't

229

his usual way of dealing with officers from other jurisdictions; he wanted her on the defensive, giving in to a rise. 'And Whit is a respected judge, not a sleazy back-alley informant.'

Gomez studied her. 'Chyme's looking for Mosley's mom, right? Mosley won't come talk to you and instead points the finger at an Energis exec, which is synonymous with leper in Houston. So where's the mom? Why hasn't your friend brought you around to meet this mother?'

'He said he hasn't found her.'

'Yet he can find all these people who are supposedly connected to her. Like this Greg Buckman,' Gomez said. 'Doesn't ring true, and if you weren't friends with this guy, you'd see that clearly.'

'Perhaps the mom,' Vernetta said, 'doesn't want to be found.'

Gomez nodded. 'Because she's committed a double homicide. Say she didn't want to be found by her kid real bad. We've acted like Chyme was in the wrong place at the wrong time. But it could have been he was the target and Doyle got in the way.'

'Harry was looking for Eve Michaels,' Claudia said. 'We don't know that she is Whit's mother.'

'Sure, I can bring in Buckman. Or Eve Michaels. They're in with the Bellinis, they promptly shut up, get a lawyer who starts prepping for another harassment lawsuit against HPD, and we get nowhere.'

'So you do nothing? Surely not.'

'That's not what Art is saying,' Vernetta said, diplomacy warming her words. 'Art, checking into any connection between Greg Buckman and the Alvarez family, or with Buckman or Doyle and Chyme, might bear fruit.'

'Or the Bellini family,' Claudia said. 'Or Ms Michaels. I think it's time to start looking hard for her, since Whit isn't having luck.'

'Fine. We'll start making inquiries,' Gomez said. 'Get your friend in here. Or I'm going to tell the TV stations that I'm looking for a judge who may be withholding information on this case. What do you think that will do to his career?'

'You'd ruin him but tiptoe around the Bellinis. Are you so afraid of another lawsuit?' Claudia asked.

Gomez shrugged. 'Afraid? No. Aware? Yes. If Buckman killed

Doyle and Chyme, or if he knows who did, we will absolutely bring him to justice. But I'm a realist, Ms Salazar. I have to be. That means anything connected to the Bellinis is handled carefully and with thought, so our asses are armored.' He glanced at Vernetta. 'We have found it very difficult to break into any information about the Bellinis. Tommy Bellini learned from his past. We don't catch them committing crimes. We don't find people willing to roll over on them. If they're still breaking the law, they have been extremely careful. It's frustrating when we can't find a crack in the door to get a search warrant.'

'I don't envy you your job under these circumstances,' Claudia said. 'Thank you.'

'If Judge Mosley doesn't feel safe,' Gomez said, 'we could provide him with protection if he'll come in.'

'I don't know that he's in any danger, but this behavior isn't like him.'

'Is there another aspect to this case you're not telling me?' Gomez said.

He found his mother and is protecting her. It would be easy to admit what she believed to be true. But she forced herself to be silent. Gomez and Vernetta might believe a man would do anything to protect his mother. Lie. Kill. They didn't know Whit. She did.

'No,' she said.

'Detective Salazar, don't get a cute idea or two. You have no jurisdiction here.'

'I'm absolutely aware of that,' she said.

'Absolutely is good,' Gomez said. 'Remember it and live it.'

They left, and she drove Vernetta home.

'Claudia,' Vernetta said, 'go home. And I don't mean back to the luxury of the Hampton Inn.'

'Whit's in trouble. I'm not leaving.'

'Your friend's not worth you getting involved in his extreme mess. You could be a police chief one day. Not a hint of improper procedural behavior, even as a private citizen, can hang over your head,' Vernetta said. 'Don't screw with your career. You can always get a new friend.' She paused. 'Are you sleeping with this guy?'

'No,' Claudia said. 'We've been through a lot together. He's a good guy.'

'The good ones are worth a certain amount of grief,' Vernetta said. 'But not beyond a certain amount.' She started to get out, then shut the door again. 'I can promise nothing to you. Understand that. But the DA would love to get the Bellinis if he could. If your friend has information but isn't coming forward because he's broken the law himself . . .'

'Whit never would,' Claudia said.

'I'm just saying,' Vernetta said. 'We could talk immunity. It's not granted often, and it's solely the DA's decision. No guarantees. But it could be a starting point. Think about it.'

Vernetta got out, shut the door, and went to her house, and Claudia watched her go inside, envying her certainty in always knowing what was exact and right.

Greg Buckman. If Gomez was reluctant to act, she wasn't. Life was a series of choices, and the best choices you made were to help the people you cared about. Claudia made her choice. She pulled out into traffic, the beginnings of a plan forming in her mind.

35

'What do you mean, you don't have them?' Paul screamed into his phone.

'I mean we don't have them. They got away.' Bucks paused. 'And Eve shot Jerry Smacks. Left him dead in the hotel's back lot.' Bucks let the lie settle in, let Paul sweat under the weight of everything crashing and burning for a change. 'Gonna bring big heat if the cops connect Jerry to us. Not to mention we barely got off the highway alive.'

'How could you not have them?' Paul demanded.

Bucks wondered for a second: why did I pick you for a friend? Then he decided he hadn't picked Paul, Paul had picked him, because the weak were drawn to the strong. That's what made leaders great. Chad Channing had a whole tape about strength.

'This isn't acceptable, Bucks,' Paul said.

'Paul, I'm real open to suggestions. They're gone. It's over. They've got you over a barrel.' *You.* Not *we.* He wondered if Paul would notice. 'Chad Channing says you got to recognize destructive behaviors and cut your losses . . .'

'You know, Bucks, fuck Chad Channing,' Paul said. 'Fuck him and every tape he ever made. Call Kiko. I want a summit meeting. We're gonna strike a new deal.'

'You don't have a negotiating chip,' Bucks said.

'I have guns that can be placed at heads.' Paul's voice rose, at the edge of a scream. 'Call Kiko. Get him here. He can bring José, but that's all. Tell them I've got the money now.'

'You aren't going to whack him?'

'I am. I am. It's what Dad would've done.'

'This is an extremely bad idea,' Bucks said.

'We kill José to show we mean business, we torture Kiko, he tells us where the coke's at. Then we kill his greaser ass.'

'And you bring his associates down on you like a nuclear bomb,' Bucks said.

'They're in Florida. That's tomorrow's problem.'

'All right,' Bucks said. 'I'll set up a meeting with Kiko.'

'At the club, he won't be suspicious coming there. We'll bring him back to the house. And do it right, Bucks, because right now you're the biggest single dumbass on the planet.' He hung up.

Gooch was laid out on the bed in front of Paul. Unconscious. He roused slightly and Paul turned up the Frank Polo tape somebody had left in the bedroom stereo, letting 'Baby, You're My Groove' thunder down the hallway as he worked Gooch over as though he were a punching bag. Face, ribs, stomach, arms. His knuckles hurt, but that pop of flesh against flesh made him happy, let out his tensions. Gooch seemed unconscious again. Doc Brewer came in and very gently shook his head at Paul.

'He needs to wake up, I got to talk to him,' Paul said.

'He's taken a bullet in the back of the head.'

'There ain't no hole, how bad hurt could he be?'

Brewer gave Gooch another injection. Checked the man's eyes, breathing. 'You want him to give you information. Then let him recover enough to talk. Beating him is making things worse.'

'What'd you give him?'

'My own home brew of cool-you-downs. Do you need a little shot, Paul?'

'Smack. Give him some smack or something to hype him up hard. A big dose. I want him talking. I want his fucking mouth running away from him.'

'Leave him alone, Paul. Please, for a minute, let him recover—'

Paul's fists hurt but he still popped Doc Brewer a hard one. The doctor fell to the floor. 'Stimulants. Get him conscious and talking. Now. Or I just start mixing shit in your bag and jabbing a needle in your old ass.'

'Paul?' Tasha said behind him. She turned down the Frank tape that was playing, helped Doc Brewer to his feet. 'Let the doctor do his work. Gooch can't tell you anything valuable right now. Come

234

downstairs with me. Let me calm you with a little massage, sweetpea.'

Bucks clicked off the phone. He stayed still on the couch, watching Kiko and José's amused expressions, hating them as much as he hated Paul. 'He's having a bad day,' Bucks said. 'He wants to kill you at a meeting.'

'His day's gonna get way worse,' José said.

'Tell him the deal's off.' Kiko jerked his head at José. 'Go get that bitch talking.' José got up without a word, headed back to the bedroom.

Bucks didn't like to hear screams or begging. It made him remember his friends, briefly pleading for their lives in the little house in Galveston. Unpleasant.

'I got to settle with MacKay,' Bucks said. 'Give a bonus to the Wart, too, so he'll keep his mouth shut and won't go work for Paul.'

'Smart move you made,' Kiko said. 'Can this MacKay be trusted?'

'He could have run to Paul when I told him I wanted his help to grab Eve, not kill her or turn her over to Paul. He didn't. I didn't cut a deal with the Wart, but he seems cool. As long as he gets paid for his efforts.'

Kiko slid him a thin brick of cash. 'We'll give 'em a bonus when she spills about the money. They did good work. Another thousand for each.'

Bucks reached for the money; Kiko covered it with his hand. 'Bucks. You picked sides. Ours. Don't forget that.'

'I won't. If she talks . . .'

'You want to know where the money is, don't you?' Kiko said. 'Yes.'

'That money,' Kiko said, 'really isn't your concern any more. Don't worry. You're gonna get a nice little cut.'

'Great, Kiko, thank you.' Bucks cleared his throat. 'The film of me and my – friends, um, I've done what you asked. Give me the film. You promised. Please.' He hated himself for adding on that desperate word, but he did.

'After we have the money. That was the deal.' Kiko gave a little smile, waved Bucks away with his fingers. 'You don't want to change the deal, do you? That wouldn't be fair.'

Bucks nodded, fighting the red rising in his cheeks. He wasn't quite out the door when Eve let out her first scream, and he closed it fast behind him.

'You sure you want to hit Kiko?' Tasha asked.

'Yeah.' Paul rose from the bed, paced around the room, worked his shoulders loose. 'Yeah. Forget this peaceful-coexistence crap.'

She curled her legs under her rear. 'Paul?'

'Yeah?'

'I'm proud of you,' Tasha said. 'Now you're big and bad. Come here.' She shrugged out of her top, unfastened her bra. His breath caught, his lips parted at the sight of her breasts. 'Come be big and bad with me.'

He joined her on the bed, eased her out of the rest of her clothes. She let him take her, savored the vigorous, calculated pistoning of him inside her. Made a memory. All else aside, he was an awesome lay and those were rare in this crowd, and she knew it would probably be the last time between them. She came with surprising intensity, crying out against his throat. He didn't relent, full of testosterone and blustering confidence, this morning's tears forgotten. She came again a few minutes later and then he did, with an eager gasp, and lay down next to her, his head nuzzling her breasts, his hand cupped over the firmness of her belly. Groaning the usual about how hot she was, how good she felt.

'Paul, Paul,' she murmured. He kissed her, with real tenderness, on her throat, her eyelids.

'Love you,' Paul said.

'Oh, don't,' she said. Teasing him. Plus, she knew he didn't really. He was saying what he thought she wanted to hear because he didn't know her. And because he was scared and frightened, more than he would admit, and he needed to feel loved. The word was a bribe, shyly offered. She ran a finger alongside his jaw, tickle-gentle, like she really cared about him. 'You love too quick, babe.'

'I know,' he said.

She sighed, curled into his chest. 'Loving fast can be a curse.'

They lay together, breathing each other's breath, and then he got up and started the shower. She knew he liked them long and hot, with a blast of skin-prickling cold at the end. She pretended to drowse and counted to twenty, then pulled on her panties and T-shirt and snuck downstairs. Terry Verdine, one of Paul's men, stood guard out in the yard, Max and Gary sat in the kitchen watching cable and sipping coffee. She ducked into the room where Tommy Bellini lay in his stupor. A camouflaging hum of the monitoring equipment thrummed and Tasha hunkered down behind the bed. She pulled her cell phone out of her pocket and dialed.

'It needs to be tonight,' she said when the phone was answered. She listened for a moment, laughed softly. Then stood up, clicked off the phone.

Tasha Strong patted Tommy Bellini's wasted legs. 'No dances for you, sugar pot. Sorry.'

She hurried back upstairs. Paul was still wasting hot water in the shower. She stretched out on the bed, waiting for him to be done.

Paul was out of the shower and toweling when his cell phone rang. Tasha handed it to him. He didn't say thank you.

'Yeah?' he said.

'Hello, Paul. This is Whit. Eve's friend. I want Gooch ready to travel. At ten this evening, you will drive him to Lancey's Grille on Buffalo. You'll let him off in the lot and then drive away.'

'Really.' Paul toweled off his arms, his waist, tossed the towel on the floor, glanced at Tasha like he expected her to pick it up. 'Where's my money, asshole?'

'Kiko has it,' Whit said. 'He took it from us.'

'You're lying.'

'He grabbed the money from our room at the Greystoke Hotel. Eve and I got away.'

'No. He would have killed you.'

'Clearly he didn't. So he's got the drugs and the cash, and he doesn't need you.'

'You're lying. Why the hell would you warn me?'

237

'Because I want my friend back. I'll give you Eve in exchange for Gooch.'

Paul stopped dead. 'Say what?'

'You're such a dumbass,' Whit said. 'Kiko has the drugs. He has the money. He doesn't need you at all. But Eve, she originally stole the money for Kiko. She was working for him. She turned on him, went on the run. I didn't know it, she double-crossed me. But she doesn't know I know. So I'll trade you her for Gooch. I want out of this war, man, okay? I don't want you coming after me. I give her to you, then we're settled, you understand?'

'I'll settle it now. Do you want to hear your friend die?' Paul yelled. 'Because I'm getting my gun right now—'

'Eve can help you get your money back – and more. She knows plenty on Kiko. She could put his ass in jail if you treat her right.'

'Trust a traitor? How do I know any of this is true?'

'Decide for yourself. This is a limited-time offer.'

A beat passed. 'I'll be there.'

'One more thing,' Whit said. 'We have your financial data on a CD I got when I ran into your girlfriend Tasha at Eve's house. Data that could slice and dice you, that can show just how your legit operations tidy up the money from your drug deals. Kiko didn't get the CD when he got the cash.' A pause. 'But if you don't show up, or you've killed Gooch, then Kiko gets a copy. The DA's office gets a copy. Kiko and the DA, knowing all your secrets. Either way, you're deeply, soundly, thoroughly laid open for everyone to see. Do we understand each other?'

Paul stared at Tasha. 'I understand.'

'You come alone. You come unarmed. We make the exchange and we both leave. Any deviation from that, and the data goes to the DA. Lancey's Grille. You and Gooch, no one else. I'll have hardass backup, man, so don't screw with me.' Whit hung up.

Paul clicked off the phone. He grabbed Tasha's arm, hard. 'Explain yourself. Right now.'

'What, sweetpea?'

'Eve's partner, Whit. He says he got computer files from you, stuff you took off Eve's laptop. He wants to trade them for Gooch, alive, or he sends the files to the police.'

She shook her head. 'No, sweetie, he was there to bug the place with voice recorders. We told you that, Bucks and Max found where he'd bugged the rooms. I didn't see him take anything off her computer. Bucks and I looked at her computer together. Wasn't anything off or on that shouldn't be there. And Bucks cleaned the system. Whit's bluffing, he's got to be.'

'You're lying to me, Tasha.' He gave a broken little laugh.

'No, I'm not, Paul. These people are trying to hurt you. I'm on your side. He's trying to get you riled. Force you into a mistake.'

Paul pushed her toward the door. 'Get Max and Gary. Tell them to bring Gooch. And a high-powered rifle. You're coming, too. We all gonna have a long chat with Eve and her buddy. I'm gonna get the chain out. Kill this guy and Gooch once I get Eve. Then I'm gonna have a real, real long chat with Bucks.'

Tasha nodded. 'Whatever you say, sweetpea. Whatever you say.'

The parking lot was dark. The shopping center, a fancy one that had skidded on hard times, was L-shaped. Lancey's Grille, closed now, was a café that served breakfast and lunch, nestled at the lonely end of the L with a long service road to its left. Traffic from Buffalo Speedway, a busier road, didn't have a clear view of the front of the café. The rest of the stores were closed and quiet, the glow from the light poles giving off soft pools against the oily asphalt. At the opposite corner stood a small stone church with a wide, dark parking lot, and across from it a new townhouse development was under construction, earth turned open like a grave around newly poured foundations.

In the shadows of the serviceway behind the restaurant, Whit waited. Four minutes and then Paul was due, and Whit expected he would arrive on time. He had told the lie he thought most likely to convince Paul, trying to knit together the facts that he knew with an informed guess that Bucks must have made some explanation to Paul as to why the capture of Eve failed. His gun, one of Charlie's, weighed like a tire-iron in his hand. He had never shot a person before, had not particularly enjoyed deer or quail hunting with his brothers, didn't thrill at the pull of the trigger and the bark of the bullet.

But he was going to shoot Paul Bellini.

Whit would shoot Paul in the knees when he had to – as soon as Paul knew there was no Eve to trade. Knees were small targets. Chests were so much bigger. The thought made him sick and he shook it off. Talking tough on the phone had felt like play-acting, but this was real. He had to do it. For Gooch.

Headlights turned into the parking lot. A Porsche. Slowly moving toward the restaurant's front. Parking at the edge of the glow thrown off by the mercury lights. Two cars went by on Buffalo and then the streets were empty for a moment.

Whit tucked the gun into the back of his pants.

The door opened. Paul Bellini stepped out from the driver's side. Left the door open. Kept his hands down by his side. He wore a heavy leather jacket, thick-armed.

'Put your hands on your head,' Whit called.

Paul didn't raise his hands. 'This is an exchange. Not a surrender.'

Whit stepped out from the dark. 'Where's Gooch?'

'He's in the trunk.'

'Open the trunk and bring him out.'

'Slow down. Where's Eve?'

'In my van.'

'Get her out here.' Paul took a step forward.

They stood ten feet away from each other, the dim light flat against the asphalt, Paul more in the light, Whit on the edge of the dark.

'This is how it works,' Whit said. 'I give you the keys to the van. Eve is inside. You give me the keys to the Porsche. I drive off, you drive off.'

'I'm not trading a Porsche for your shit-ass van,' Paul said.

'You're a real long-term-vision guy, aren't you? I'll get Gooch out, dump the car, and call you to tell you where your car's at, okay?' The weight of the gun pressed against the back of his pants. Sure that Paul had a gun under that leather coat, wondering *am I fast enough to fire before he can?* Figuring the math of death, dizzy but not exactly afraid.

Paul surprised him with a little laugh. Too calm for this. 'Sure you will.'

'I don't want your car, you dumbass.'

'Fine. Bring me the keys, then, buddy.' Paul gestured at Whit with his fingertips. Whit took one step forward, walking into the light.

'By the way,' Whit said. 'The same files I got from Tasha after she copied Eve's hard drive, they're attached to an e-mail message outlining your activities. Addressed to the DA's office and to the police. It's scheduled to go out in an hour with all those files attached. If I'm not there to delete that message, it mails. So you kill me, you're still screwed. Do you understand me?'

'Perfectly,' Paul said. 'You're a clever bastard. You want a job?'

'We've got different work styles.'

'How do I know you won't send the files anyway?'

'Trust me.'

'Trust you.'

'I'm trusting that Gooch isn't dead in that trunk,' Whit said.

'I'm trusting the same about Eve.'

Across the street, in the darkened church lot, a gentle little pop sounded. Like a door clicking shut. Then another. Paul started to glance over his shoulder, then didn't.

'What was that?' Whit said.

'The sound of me trusting you. Here are the keys,' Paul said. He tossed them carefully to Whit, who caught them one-handed. 'Go.'

Whit tossed the van keys to Paul. 'Now we each turn around and walk away.' Deciding he could open the trunk with the remote, be sure Gooch was okay, then drive off fast. He wouldn't have to shoot Paul, he could outrun him in the Porsche. Whit stepped into the cool pool of the light.

He heard clinking, saw a glint in Paul's hand. An end of a chain was there, thick-linked, Paul pulling it free from his jacket's sleeve and running forward, Whit reaching for his gun. The heavy end of the chain was already swinging toward his face and Whit fell back onto pavement, his gun under him. The chain whirled, arcing above Whit, the light showing Paul's face twisted in triumph. Whit raised his arms to shield himself.

Paul Bellini's head blossomed in red. The crack of the rifle shot echoed against the brick walls and Paul fell, the strings of life cut.

Then silence except for the chain falling across Whit, clanking against the concrete.

Whit scrabbled to his feet. He couldn't risk leaving Gooch in that Porsche trunk. He had to know. He ran to the sports car. He still had Paul's keys in his hand.

A shot roared again, the bullet whistling behind his head. He hunkered low on the concrete, crab-crawled into the Porsche.

A bullet slammed against the car's side. He was aware he was driving off in a murdered man's car, leaving a van behind that was registered in Gooch's name. The night had taken a horrible left turn.

He started the car, blasted out of the lot, the Porsche's wheel cool and clean and responsive under his hand. God, please let Gooch be inside.

He didn't hear the sound of another shot.

Whit tore down the service road, back around the building, barreling out onto Buffalo. He turned at the service road that ran parallel to Highway 59, shot down to Shepherd, finally pulling into a closed Catholic school, clicking open the trunk door.

Gooch lay inside, his face a collage of purple, sluggish, tied up. But breathing.

He had Gooch, but the situation had gotten a thousand times worse.

Tasha watched the Porsche rocket away. Gary lay dead at her feet, the scorch hole in his temple from the cell-phone gun black like a burn. Max was next to him, a similar little gap in the back of his neck still smoking. She left the rifle on the asphalt, straightened the latex gloves she'd hidden in her purse earlier, got in the Mustang Max had driven them over in, and started up the engine.

She could see Paul's body on the pavement, face down, as she drove past. Too bad, really. Born in the wrong family. Born in a decent family, he might've made his looks, his ambition work for him. She'd miss the sex; he'd been good at that, but that punching and crying crap worked her nerves. Thank God that was over.

No need to go check Whit's van. She knew Eve Michaels wasn't in there anyway. Whit Mosley was a liar.

Tasha Strong drove off into the night, humming a little, smiling at her dream unfolding.

36

You're screwing up, Claudia told herself. She waited in her car outside the gated compound at Greg Buckman's address at 3478 Alabama. It was shortly after eleven on Saturday night, and she heard the soft strains of a party: laughter, a thumping bass beat, the clink of bottles. *Because you go down this route, you're putting your career at stake.*

The file in her lap told her all she could learn in short order about Greg Buckman. His credit history (excellent), his income (over two hundred thousand a year or so ago, but less than thirty thousand reported to the IRS last year), his family (two parents who lived in Little Rock, one sister). All delivered courtesy of Barbara Zachary, Harry Chyme's assistant, who didn't need to be asked twice when Claudia said, 'I got a lead on a guy who may have info about Harry's death but needs pressuring to make him talk. Can you dig on him?' and Barbara, dialing and typing like an avenging angel, working the keyboards, Internet databases, and phones with a singular purpose, faxed pages to Claudia's motel with rapid-fire response.

She scanned through the credit pages again. No charges to his Visa or his AmEx for anything other than restaurants, bars, and a surprising wave of charges to bookstores, both brick and on-line. He must be a voracious reader. Most criminals weren't, but then maybe he wasn't what Whit thought he was.

The grabber, of course, was his drop in income. He'd made a fortune at Energis. But that money, and the chance to earn a high salary in the corporate world, had evaporated in the wave of shareholder lawsuits. He claimed, on his last tax return, to run a consulting company, but she wondered how eager companies were to hire an exec tarred with the filth of the Energis brush. The company, nationally, had been reduced to a joke, a catchphrase for greed and malfeasance. No matter that thousands of honest workers had toiled there with good intentions.

Newspaper clipping next, and her mouth went dry. Three Energis employees vanished a few weeks before the story broke about the company's shady accounting and deals. Greg Buckman, named as their supervisor and friend, was quoted in the story. 'We're deeply concerned. These are terrific, goal-oriented individuals, and they and their families are in our prayers. Our candle-light vigil for their safe return will be held in our headquarters lobby at seven this evening.'

Goal-oriented. Odd praise.

A follow-up clipping on the case didn't quote Buckman but relayed that the three bodies and their car had been found, driven into a remote part of Galveston Bay. More clippings on Energis. Buckman was senior management in an energy-trading division that was part of the massive accounting scandal. No criminal charges filed against him, but his name was mentioned frequently enough that a long shade of suspicion settled on him and he'd lost a fortune in the civil lawsuits.

This past crime, his reputation smeared at Energis, was a doorway to him.

She had known Whit Mosley most of her life, had gotten much closer to him when he became justice of the peace and they started working together, but she had never heard him speak in the strained voice with which he had spoken to her. He was clearly involved beyond the scope of the law – in over his head, she guessed – and he had wanted her help earlier but not now. Either because he had crossed a line he shouldn't have or he wanted to keep her out of danger. She hoped it was the latter.

Claudia closed her eyes. Say Whit found his mother. She works with a crime ring. She wanted nothing to do with Whit and the crime ring came after Whit to scare him off. But why wouldn't he call the police, then? Because he didn't want his mother implicated? Whit wouldn't stand there and take abuse. So, a different angle. Say his mother wanted to be with Whit, aimed to leave her life of crime. Her colleagues in the ring didn't want her walking away. She knew too much. Or they found out Whit was a judge and it made them nervous, this new family connection to law and order. So they came after Whit and his mom. But again, why wouldn't Whit simply call the police? Because he *did* want to protect his mother – but from prosecution. Bust the crime ring, bust his mother. It could be one and the same.

She dug in her purse for an aspirin, dry-swallowed it, ignoring the bitter taste.

Or worse, Whit and his mom knew who the killers were and were hiding. But still in Houston. Why? What was to be gained by staying here? The anchor had to be timely, large, and powerful. Information on the Bellinis. Evidence to be retrieved. Money.

So what do I do now? Operating out of her jurisdiction was an entirely foreign concept to her, a violation of common sense and professionalism she'd never considered. But Whit changed everything. He'd always had that effect in her life, the one friend who always made life seem a little edgy and funky and ever-new. The kind of friend you'd keep a secret for, to protect him. If you had to.

Claudia got out of her ancient Honda Accord, walked along the gated entryway. A car pulled up to her left and she stepped to where she could see the driver's fingers enter a code on the keypad. It looked like 2249. She stood, arms crossed, like she was waiting for a friend to pick her up, studying the far end of the street. She waited until the car had driven in, noticed that the crossbar fell almost immediately.

She got in her Honda and drove up. Tried the code of 2249. Didn't work. She tried 2248. This time the cross bar creaked up and she quickly drove inside. She nosed into a visitor parking space near the community pool. She tucked her service revolver into her purse. Number twelve was Buckman's. A single dim light glowed, a light left on in the kitchen. She pressed an ear to the door.

The soft fuzzy murmur of television. She rang the doorbell.

After a moment, the door swung open. A tall redheaded woman, pretty, wearing a T-shirt that said TOPAZ in glittery cursive, the T-shirt one size too tight. Loose jeans. And a loose look in her eyes, wine or beer or pot working its easy magic.

'Hi,' Claudia said. 'My name is Claudia Salazar. I'm sorry to bother you so late in the evening, but I'm a freelance writer doing a book on Energis and I'm trying to get an appointment with Greg Buckman. His number's unlisted, but a friend of his told me he lived here.'

'He's not here and he doesn't talk about Energis,' the tall redhead said. 'Sorry.' She started to close the door.

'He's been treated like garbage in the press. I want to fix that,' Claudia said. The door stopped, the redhead watching her. 'People at certain levels at Energis, their reputations have been savaged. They can't get real work again. But they couldn't have all known about the accounting abuses, because folks would have blown the whistle earlier, right? People like Mr Buckman were following orders. He didn't really do anything wrong.'

The redhead gave a slight nod, surprised at this heartfelt monologue.

Claudia let a beat pass. 'I want to tell that story. Defend the people who got their reputations assassinated, even though they never faced a criminal charge. That's not the American way. They need a forum to clear their names.'

'Out of the goodness of your heart?' Now the gaze wasn't so vacant, a little smarter.

'Out of an interest in fair reporting.'

The redhead studied her. 'I'll see if he's willing to call you.'

'Are you his wife?'

'Girlfriend,' she said with a smile. 'I'm Robin Melvin. Don't misspell it in your book. Can you mention me in it? My mama would absolutely die.'

'I'm sure you want Greg to have options in his life again, Robin. Go to work for another energy company, right? Command the respect and salary he had before.'

'Yeah.' Robin bit her lip. 'That'd be nice.' A stab of guilt touched Claudia's heart for misleading Robin, but this seemed the shortest distance to the end.

'Could you and I talk now? I'd like your insight on this; how it's affected you. I can meet Greg face-to-face when he gets back. Make my case in person to him. I know talking about Energis is

247

painful. But my book might be a big help to him. Let me fire a shot in his defense.'

Robin considered. 'Well. Okay. You and I can wait for him. He should be home soon. You want a glass of wine?'

Claudia nodded and stepped inside.

The townhome was high-end, one of the nicest Claudia had ever seen, but Buckman's furnishings were sparse. Clean. Minimal but expensive. A leather couch, an entertainment system with more controls than a flight simulator. A stack of DVDs. She glanced at the titles while Robin Melvin fetched the wine. *It's a Wonderful Life. Mr Smith Goes to Washington. The Sound of Music.* Greeting-card movies, not what she had expected from a suspected killer. A long line of books on a shelf. All by Chad Channing. *The Art of Be. Sail Through the Goal Posts of Life! I Make Me Happen.* Self-help tripe. The books' spines were all cracked and worn with handling.

Robin brought massive goblets of chardonnay, filled nearly to the brim, already sipping from one. 'Oh, those,' she said, seeing Claudia inspecting the books. 'You can see how depressed he's been, reading that junk. It lifts him up.'

She handed the wine to Claudia; a trickle sloshed onto Claudia's hand. 'Does it?' Claudia asked.

'It's a comfort blanket,' Robin said, 'that guru whispering in his ear. It's like a conscience-for-hire.'

'This is a very nice place. What's he doing now to keep the mortgage paid?'

Robin shrugged, sat down on the couch. 'Consulting. Bucks's got friends who keep him busy.' A note of bitterness crept into her voice.

'Bucks?'

'That's what his friends call him. Not too many people call him Greg.'

Claudia sat, took a sip of wine, unsure of what to do now. 'Robin. In doing my research, I understand there were three of Bucks' friends at the company who were murdered a few weeks before the Energis story broke.'

Robin nodded. 'Horrible.' But a new wariness was in her eyes.

'Well, I'm sure that must have been very upsetting for Bucks. Did he ever say that anyone at Energis was involved?'

'Like had them whacked?'

Whacked. Not killed. 'Yeah,' Claudia said. 'Whacked.'

Robin took a solid gulp of her wine. 'Those guys were his best friends at work. Bucks was crazy with worry. I didn't really know him well then. He and his friends frequented the place I work, I knew them as really good customers. After his friends died, well, I guess I felt tender toward Bucks, we started spending time together.' She stopped, as though embarrassed about displaying this corner of her heart.

'Where do you work?'

'Club Topaz. I'm a stripper.' Claudia liked that Robin said stripper, not entertainer, not exotic dancer. 'But I'd like to finish college and sell real estate. I like big houses.' She gave a little off-key laugh.

Claudia played her first card. 'See, in my research, I've found who would have wanted those guys dead. And I don't want to scare you, but Bucks might be in danger.'

Robin's eyes widened.

'There's a crime ring in Houston, the Bellinis. They used to be Mafia up north. Have you heard of them?'

Robin grew very still and Claudia knew, suddenly, she had made a mistake. But better to press on, see it through. 'The Bellinis benefited from the Energis double-accounting. They unloaded a lot of stock in the weeks before the stock fell.' She made this up on the fly.

'They're not crooks,' Robin insisted.

'But the Bellini family owned a lot of Energis stock, and . . .'

'So did lots of other people. If you lived in Houston, you owned Energis stock.' It sounded like a platitude that Bucks had taught her. 'Bucks went to school with Paul Bellini. I know Paul. He's a super nice guy, he's not a crook.'

'His dad is. Or was.'

'My mother is a beautician,' Robin said. 'You see me styling hair?'

'Bucks worked with the three guys who got killed, and I'm

249

wondering if he knew details that they knew. But he doesn't know the information's dangerous, you see, he wouldn't necessarily know that the Bellinis were involved in the deaths.' It was a neat little theory, constructed out of nothing, but she wondered if it would resonate with the young woman. A complete lie that had a terrible, recognizable possibility to it.

Robin frowned, the silence drawing out, and then a key slid into the front door.

'He's home,' Robin said. 'Why don't you ask him?'

37

'They shot me up,' Gooch said. 'To keep me quiet, then to get me talking. My arms feel like stone right now and a while back I had a conversation with Mahatma Gandhi. I'm pretty useless.' He opened his eyes for a moment, closed them. He lay on the couch in Charlie's house. 'There's a spiderweb up there Charlie needs to clean. Or am I hallucinating?'

'It's a web,' Whit said. 'I'm not leaving you again.'

'You didn't leave me, I got caught. I was deeply moronic. If it ain't too much to ask, could you check and see if I still have both my balls?'

'You're not missing anything.' But Gooch had been beaten, roughed up badly, blood dried on his lips and ears, and indigo bruises on his torso, along the tender skin that shielded kidneys. A horrible contusion marked the back of his head, under the hair, a hard knot. His skin was clammy, a connect-the-dots spiral of injection points along his arm, and Whit's fear for him turned into a stone-cold rage.

'I'm taking you to a doctor,' Whit said.

'No. What am I gonna say, I got attacked by pharmacists?' Gooch blinked. 'I'm strong. I can process it out. Man, I got shot in the head, sort of, and I'm okay.'

'No,' Whit said. 'Doctor. Now.'

'No,' Gooch said. 'Info. Now. Then doctor.' He closed his eyes.

'Kiko has Eve,' Whit said. 'Bucks works for him now.'

'And someone else is on their side. Whoever killed Paul.' Gooch opened his eyes, blinked once, twice, watched Whit.

'That could have been Bucks. He finds out about the meeting between us and Bucks takes Paul out.'

'And then Bucks steps into command,' Gooch said. 'Command of increasingly little.'

'So how do I get my mom back, Gooch?'

'We can't assume she's still alive, Whitman.'

'Say she is.'

Gooch looked at him. 'You're the brother I never had, Whit. I love you, man, if that doesn't sound stupid.'

'You're a doped-up idiot.'

'Ask yourself if it's time to walk away,' Gooch said in a quiet voice.

'No.'

'Kiko will find out Eve doesn't know where the money is, then he'll kill her,' Gooch said. 'Maybe what's left of the Bellini ring and Kiko's people shoot it out. Kiko can find other buyers in Houston, given time, or sell it himself. This doesn't have a good ending.'

'I can't just let her die.'

'Then we call the police.'

'We don't know where she's being held,' Whit said. 'Even so, do I save her so she can spend her life in prison for money laundering and God knows what else?'

'Man, straighten it out in your head,' Gooch said. 'You can't save her.'

'I'm taking you to a hospital. You need to be checked.'

'Forget it.'

'I'm serious, Gooch, you're out of the game,' Whit said.

'I'm okay.'

'They could have pumped you full of Clorox, man.'

'In which case the blood froth would be a bad sign.' Gooch sat up, blinked. 'I'll be okay. What do you want to do?'

'I want you to go back to Port Leo.'

'No way.'

'This isn't your fight,' Whit said.

'They kidnap me, beat me, drug me. Played Frank Polo music while they did it to drown out any screaming. Made it my fight more than yours.' Gooch attempted a smile.

'Brace yourself,' Whit said. 'If you come with me, you're gonna hear Frank's voice at least one more time.'

Kiko Grace cut into the fat stack of pancakes, shoveled them into his mouth, and pointed the fork at Eve's untouched plate. 'You don't have much appetite, I guess,' he said. 'Shame. This is genuine Vermont maple syrup.'

'I'm dieting,' she said in a very quiet voice, through her bruised and cut lips.

He chewed. 'You're skinny already. Pancakes are good for the soul.' He glanced over at José, rinsing a skillet in the sink. 'Isn't that right, José?'

'Comfort me with apples,' José said, 'for I am sick of love.'

'Your boy Willie S didn't say that,' Kiko said. 'That's in the Bible.'

'You getting smarter every day, boss,' José said.

Kiko pushed her plate of pancakes a little closer to Eve. 'Come on, it's soft food. José made it special for you.'

'I don't want to eat with you,' Eve said. She was handcuffed by her left arm to the chair, sitting up for the first time since they had brought her to the condo.

'Your loss. These are awesome.' Kiko dug back into the stack of blueberry pancakes, apparently taking no offense.

That afternoon José had come into the room they stashed her in, gently climbed on top of her, asked her where the money was. She said she didn't know. He produced a pair of pliers from a back pocket and asked her again. She said she didn't know. So he pried open her jaw, worked the pliers onto a back tooth and tried to pull it out. It broke and the pain lanced her jaw, blinded her thoughts like he'd poured in hot coals. She screamed. He put the shattered tooth in his pocket and asked again. She begged, told him she really didn't know. Her tongue probed at where the tooth had been. He climbed back on her, worked the pliers back in and she fought to keep from vomiting. *Crack*. He broke another back tooth, lacerating her gums; she sobbed, spraying saliva and blood, and he thought she spat on him. José slammed the pliers into her jaw and mouth, tearing her lips, knocking out two side teeth. She screamed that she still didn't know where it was. Then he hit her with his fist, four deep blows, and she blacked out.

She woke up to the awful, sour taste of blood, wretched pain in her jaw, and the jagged stumps of teeth along her gums.

Then José had come in, removed the handcuffs, let her use the bathroom in privacy. Her jaw and face looked like she'd gone nine rounds in a boxing ring. He let her wash her face with a bar of lavender soap he had unwrapped from delicate paper. The bar smelled wonderful and she nearly wept, thinking of Whit and him asking about the gardenia soap she used when he was little. José took her to Kiko's table, blindfold off, which she could not consider a good sign, and pushed her down to eat. The clock said it was close to eleven; night held itself against the windows.

'You know what I want?' Kiko asked.

'What?' she said, watching him chew blueberry pancakes.

'Happy wife. A cure for cancer. Marlins back in the World Series,' Kiko said.

'No, think big. Chicago,' José said from the kitchen. He wasn't eating, but he stood at the counter, drinking a glass of milk.

'Your mouth hurting?' Kiko asked.

'Yes.'

'José, get the lady a pain pill,' Kiko said. José brought her a pill, a glass of water. She palmed it and Kiko said, 'Really, it's okay, we aren't going to poison you.' She swallowed the tablet, the water, hating herself for taking anything from him but God her mouth hurt bad.

'I know a guy. He really digs older ladies. Really.' Kiko mopped a bit of pancake through the maple syrup. 'He's got unresolved mother issues, Norman Bates-level nutzoid, and that's a bitchin' hard-on that don't fade. Therapy can't make a dint in this bad-ass. You don't help me, I give you to him. Actually, I sell you to him.' He chewed, sipped at coffee. 'He'll fuck you no less than a dozen times the first day. Everywhere. Then he'll turn mean, get out the knife. We got these Albanian bosses trying to move south from New York, horn in. One of 'em had a wife. We grabbed her, sold her to my friend. Let him have her for three days. She lost the ability to speak. I put a bullet in her head. Seemed the kind thing to do.'

She said nothing, she didn't want to shiver in front of him.

'So, Eve. When you took the money, the Bellinis came after you. Where did you put it?' Kiko said.

'I didn't take it,' she said. 'Over the years I've had plenty of opportunity to steal from the Bellinis. I didn't do it.'

'They seemed very sure you did.'

Eve took a careful breath. *Play the hand right,* she thought, *and they'll see going after Whit as a no-gain. They'll leave him alone.* She had not even had a chance to say good-bye. 'The most logical choice is that Bucks took the money and framed me.'

'Why would Bucks betray Paul?' Kiko asked almost idly.

'For five million reasons,' she said.

'But you see, Eve, I had an arrangement with Bucks,' he said. 'He was supposed to steal the money for me. The money's gone but it sure ain't in my pocket.'

She watched José inspecting a hand juicer. He made her nervous, futzing in the kitchen like an old woman. 'So Bucks betrayed both you and Paul.'

Kiko shook his head. 'He was highly motivated not to screw me over, Eve,' he said. 'In fact, he would be an idiot if he screwed me over. I know you don't like him, but do you think he's stupid?'

'I suspect he's a hell of a lot smarter than you, Mr Grace.'

Kiko laughed. 'Who's your partner? Bucks says his name is Whitman Mosley. That his real name?'

'No,' she said after a moment. 'It's a fake name. Two of his English professors in college.' The answer sounded inspired. A slowness crept into her limbs, the pain pill starting to kick in, fast and sweet.

'What's his real name? Where is he?'

'Since I didn't take the money, neither did he. He was trying to help me prove Bucks took it. Leave him alone.'

Kiko leaned over and stabbed her with the syrup-sticky fork, deep in the meaty part of her arm. She screamed as the dull tines drove into her flesh.

'Quit lying. He offered to trade the money for you. Made the appointment. So where's the money?' Now his voice was soft. She turned to José he was drying the juicer with a dishtowel, looking bored.

'Whit doesn't have it.' Blood dribbled down her arm. The fork hung from her flesh. He leaned over and shook the fork and agony bolted up her arm, searing every nerve, worming into her bones. She screamed again, nearly fell from the chair. José moved in behind her, pushed her into Kiko's reach.

'Where's the money?' Kiko asked again.

She said nothing.

'I used the fork,' he said. 'I still have a knife.' He held it up, smeared with butter and a loose rope of syrup. 'You want to meet my personal Norman Bates? He'll be on the first flight from Miami if I FedEx your picture and your panties to him.'

She closed her eyes. Oddly she thought of the small, close air of that Montana motel room, thirty years ago, the whiskey-and-hamburger smell of James Powell, his idle threat against her children, the way the gun snuggled into his mouth like it was meant to fit there, dark against the white of his teeth. The heady little rush of righteousness that soared into her heart when she pulled the trigger. And she thought: *I deserve whatever I get.*

She spat in his face. He slapped her and the blast of pain against her savaged mouth nearly made her pass out. 'Let Bucks rob you blind,' she gasped. 'With that money he can hire enough muscle to send you back to Miami with your tail between your legs.'

Kiko thumped the end of the fork. She tried not to wet herself. 'I got serious dirt on him, Eve. Proof he's a murderer, and he's scared to death of me sending it to the police. So you're lying. Mosley's got the cash and you're shielding him.'

She gritted her teeth. 'With that money, Bucks can put a big-ass contract on you, one you can't escape from.'

Kiko tilted his head, studied her with a half-smile. 'I heard you were smart once. Shame to lose the edge, ain't it.' He stood, pulled the fork from her arm. Skin and flesh gave way, blood bubbled from her skin. 'Same question. This time I want an actual answer.' He grabbed the back of her head, brought the fork close to her eye. One of the tines dug into her eye's corner.

She had gone down the wrong road in blaming Bucks. Kiko wasn't rattled. Dumb thinking done fast. She wished she could suck the words back in, turn back time five minutes. He would never leave Whit alone.

But then Kiko looking up past her shoulder, saying, 'No need, man, going slow yields more . . .' and then three pops in rapid succession, three red eyes opening on Kiko's forehead, the hair and flesh shearing away from the skull, Kiko toppling backward against and then off his chair.

José stepped around her, a pistol in his hand, a silencer screwed on the barrel. He prodded Kiko with a foot.

' "Is the chair empty? Is the sword unsway'd? Is the king dead?" ' he said. 'I would say, Eve, the king is pretty fucking dead.'

Eve swallowed against a tide of bile in her mouth, waited for him to raise the gun to her.

'Don't I get a thank-you?' José said.

'Oh, my God,' she said. 'You killed him.'

'It was a choice,' José said. 'You ever do that, Eve? Weigh your choices?'

He waited for an answer.

'Yes,' she managed to say.

'Even for decisive people it's difficult.' José went to the kitchen, got a first-aid kit, grabbed a dispenser of antiseptic soap. He came back, set the gun back in his shoulder holster, and started to clean the fork wound on her arm. She sat perfectly still.

'Now,' José said. 'I'm doing big serious weighing right now. I can either believe you or Bucks. You know the whole infrastructure of the Bellini operations. That's valuable information. I think I'll believe . . . you.'

She continued to stare, glanced at Kiko, syrup still on his lips, the beauty mark by his mouth all bloodied, distorted wide-eyed surprise on what was left of his face. 'Is everyone turning on their bosses these days?' she managed to say.

'I did it because he was a drug-dealing animal. And I'm a good citizen. Consider it a public service.' He laughed softly, bandaged her arm, taped it, lowered her sleeve back over the dressing. 'That'll do for now.'

'But I don't know where the money is.'

'I know you don't,' José said. 'I believe you. Sorry about the teeth, but I did the least I could for him to know you got worked over proper. We have a dentist we can probably get you. If you behave.'

She stared at him.

'I'm interested in a lot more than five million,' José said. 'You know how much drug money is laundered in this country each year?'

She shook her head.

José smiled, gave a little canary chirp of a laugh. He tapped her forehead. Once, twice, gently, almost with respect. 'So you don't know the numbers. But I bet you can help us find a big percentage of it, can't you?'

'What . . .'

'You know all the tricks of the trade, don't you, Eve? How to clean it, hide it. You're a number-rattling little genius.' José gave her a smile. 'You're key to what I need.'

She was going to live then, at least a little bit longer. 'I'll do whatever you want me to. Just leave Whit Mosley alone? Please?' She hated herself for asking but she had to. She had to.

'First things first.' José pulled her to her feet. 'Let's finish the night's work, okay?'

38

Greg Buckman wasn't what Claudia expected. He looked like a stockbroker, trim but muscular, average-handsome with ruddy cheeks, hair thinning early. He wore a white button-down that had gotten dirty in the course of the day, wrinkled suit pants, an old-school rep tie loosened – *a tie on Saturday?* she thought. He looked like a young exec fresh from a one-martini-too-many happy hour, a little bleary, tired, and sour. And he had a nasty black eye.

This was the man Whit thought killed Harry.

The man with Bucks had a Caribbean accent spicing his 'hello' to Robin, dreadlocks neatened back with a red embroidered band, dressed in faded jeans, white T-shirt, and a leather jacket, but he wore a back holster that Claudia spotted the moment he came through the door. The man stayed by the door, not quite like a guard, but like a friend, bored and ready to go find excitement, waiting on his buddy.

'Who's this?' Bucks said to Robin. Staring at Claudia. No hello, honey, how are you. Or hi I'm Greg.

'She's a writer. She's working on a book about Energis,' Robin said. 'But defending the guys like you.'

Claudia stood, offered a hand. Bucks didn't take it. 'I'm Claudia Salazar.'

'Lady, I don't talk about my former employer. At all. Please go.'

She lowered her hand. 'I can help salvage your reputation, Mr Buckman.'

He gave a sharp little laugh. 'I didn't know it needed fixing. I'm asking you to leave. Nicely. You're trespassing.'

'Robin invited me in.'

'Please go.'

'My research assistant died earlier this week,' Claudia said. Second card to play, the one she was afraid of, to throw him off entirely if he knew anything about Harry's death. 'His name was Harry Chyme. He was helping me with research on Energis execs. He got shot in an insurance office near the port.'

Bucks touched his temple as though a migraine were blossoming. 'What part of go did you not get?'

'You're in danger.' She decided to try the approach she'd tried with Robin. 'Harry was tracking information on three Energis employees killed last year. I understand they worked for you.' See how he handled a curveball, see how he reacted under sudden, terrible pressure to the unexpected.

Bucks came close to her, smelling of gunfire. She took a step back. 'I'm sorry about your friend's death. But it has nothing to do with me.'

'You know what it's like to lose a friend,' Claudia said. 'You lost three at once.'

Not a muscle on his mouth or face moved. 'I've not had a good day. You're pissing me off. And anger blinds, it leads to obstacles.'

'Greg, listen to her, you might need to—' Robin started.

He hit Robin. A solid slap that sent her reeling. She fell, skidding across the coffee table, knocking over a candlestick and a small stack of Chad Channing videos.

Claudia had her police pistol out, close to his face. 'Don't move,' she said slowly. 'Hands where I can see them, sir,' she said to the dreadlocked friend, who stayed still and who now wore, to her surprise, an amused smile. He kept his hands away from his jacket but not exactly up.

Bucks said nothing, his eyes big.

'Anger is the road to obstacle, Greg, you are so right about that,' Claudia said.

'Sorry. A momentary loss of control.'

'If you draw,' Claudia told the friend, 'I will shoot him, then you. You got me?'

'I believe I do,' he said.

'Call the cops, MacKay,' Bucks said.

'Is this a 311 or a 911?' MacKay said. But he didn't move toward the phone.

'Robin. Go outside,' Claudia said.

Robin climbed to her feet, a bright little stream of blood dripping from her mouth, her fingertips probing at her jaw. 'Oh, Greg,' she said. More stunned than tearful, too surprised yet to be angry. She flailed an arm at Claudia. 'Hey, put that gun down.'

'I will, when you and I are out of here.'

'A feminist with a gun,' Bucks said. 'Isn't that a contradiction, waving your phallic symbol around?' He'd gotten the cool back in his voice. He circled away from Claudia, putting her between him and MacKay as he moved toward the living room's bank of windows.

'I'll shoot your phallic symbol off with it if you don't shut up,' Claudia said. 'C'mon, Robin.'

'He never hit me before,' Robin said. Digging in her heels, not thinking.

'You never pissed him off before,' Claudia said.

'She pisses me off plenty,' Bucks said. 'I'm picking up the phone, okay? Calling the cops. Robin wants to press charges, she can. But you're trespassing and threatening us, and—' He leaned down to scoop up the cordless phone from its cradle and the windows behind him shattered in gunfire, glass, blinds, and curtain sharding into the room. Claudia dove to the floor, knocking Robin down with her, the redhead screaming, Bucks screaming, the other man screaming.

The dust-stale taste of the sisal rug was in Claudia's mouth and suddenly the thunder of gunfire stopped. She turned her head away from the window, Robin squirming in panic beneath her, and saw MacKay slumped against the far wall, a red smear on the wallpaper behind him, his hand tucked uselessly into his jacket.

Silence now from the guns, from the destroyed windows that faced onto the parking lot. Then a man stepping through them, blunt-faced, stocky, Hispanic, dressed in black T-shirt and jeans. Carrying an automatic rifle. Looking at Bucks' feet, sticking out from under a table.

Claudia fired at the man's chest. And Robin moved under her, trying to bolt.

Her shot went wide, splintering the window frame next to the gunman; he fell back, firing again, but wild. Claudia hustled Robin to her feet, looking back in the bullet-peppered den for Bucks. She shoved Robin toward the back door where MacKay lay splayed. Robin was sobbing.

Bucks was gone. A door slammed shut to her left, Bucks hiding elsewhere in the townhouse.

'Get out! The back!' Claudia ordered. Robin stumbled, opened the door, went out. Not a backyard but a small garage. Trapped.

Then more gunfire erupted behind them. Claudia turned. Bucks, running from a bedroom, laid fire across the shattered windows with an automatic of his own. Claudia slammed the door to the condo shut, jabbed the garage door opener. The door rose with slow suburban solemnity and she pushed Robin down behind a battered Jaguar. But no greeting of gunfire as the door tracked upward, just the heavy swampiness of the night.

Silence. The gunfire ended.

'Run,' Claudia said. 'Get to a neighbor's, call 911.'

Robin Melvin ran toward the gleam of the pool and the clubhouse beyond.

Claudia turned back toward the door. She eased open the door, yelled 'Police! Lay down your weapons!' She listened. No sound. Staying low, she went through the door, keeping her gun trained on the opposite corner.

The room was empty.

She checked MacKay. No pulse. A lock of his hair lay across his throat like a rope, smelling of sandalwood. She moved through the rest of the condo. No sign of Greg Buckman. She headed out of the condo, through the garage, working her way toward the front, then around again.

No shooter. No Bucks. A car raced off across the lot, a late-model black Suburban, ripping across the landscaping and then through the main exit, splintering the wooden rail that didn't rise fast enough. Gone. The license plate began with TJ, the rest of it unreadable as the car vanished into the night.

Then the thrum of a second engine sounded and the Jag tore out of Bucks' garage into the lot. She chased it, yelling at Bucks to stop. He must've gone out a window and circled the condo in the opposite direction from her. The Jag zoomed through the exit. Chasing the Suburban.

Claudia Salazar put her gun down at her feet, dug her police ID out of her jacket, and sat down on the driveway to wait for the police. The distant wail of sirens approached. Her nerves caught up with her now, and her hands shook, a coldness crept over her, and she wondered if Whit still breathed.

39

Sunday morning, at Frank Polo's house, there were no hymns. There was disco. Frank wrapped himself in the cocoon of his own voice, the beat and croon drifting up from the speakers, the one slow ballad he had made into a hit, 'When You Walk Away.' He lay on the couch, a wet cloth on his eyes, a cup of coffee balanced on his stomach. His left foot bopped in rhythm to the song.

'Do you really listen to yourself?' Gooch asked. He stood by the small music collection, which offered mostly Frank Polo CDs.

'Those are promotional copies,' Frank said from underneath the wet cloth. 'We give 'em out at the club. Very popular.'

'Right. No one goes to that club for the women, it's all about the giveaways.'

'Frank.' Whit sat by the singer's feet and took the coffee cup off his stomach. 'I need you to think.'

'Jesus, thinking is the last thing on my mind.' Then what he said struck him as funny and he gave a nervous little laugh. Whit and Gooch didn't laugh.

'When he was a kid, Paul used to lip-sync to my songs,' Frank said. 'He had the attitude of a performer. He could've been so much more.' Sounding genuinely sad.

'He's spilt milk now,' Gooch said.

Frank lifted one corner of the wet cloth. 'Yeah, but he was a sweet kid, once, okay?'

'Paul cut your hand open and tried to have Eve and me killed,' Whit said. 'You're sorry he's dead?'

'No, I'm sorry he turned into such a bastard.' Frank sat up. 'There's a difference. I got to call his mom, I'm dreading that.' He tossed the damp cloth on the coffee table, smoothed his hair. 'With

Eve and Paul gone, there's no senior leadership left but Bucks, and he's MIA, the traitor.'

'How would he know about Paul meeting me? He's on Kiko's side now,' Whit said. 'How would Kiko know, for that matter?'

'Paul told Bucks, simple as that,' Gooch said. He still didn't look good to Whit, his skin waxen. He'd slept fitfully, vomiting this morning, sweating with chills, but still refusing to go to a doctor.

The shootout at Bucks' condo and the triple homicide that included Paul Bellini last night had been all over the morning news, and Bucks remained missing. 'Kiko's people killed Paul and then went after Bucks,' Whit said. 'Double cross.'

Frank stood. 'I should be at Paul's house. Rallying what's left of the troops for a war with Kiko. This is not my style. I don't want to do this.'

'Frank, if my theory's right, you don't want to become the head of the Bellinis. Kiko's eliminating them.'

Frank said, 'Leadership ain't my groove.'

'We've got to find where Kiko hid Mom,' Whit said. 'Think, Frank, please.'

'I want to believe she's still alive, too, Whit,' Frank said. 'But if Kiko killed Paul and Gary and Max, and tried to kill Bucks, why's he gonna keep Eve alive?'

'Because she can hand him the Bellini assets. Transfer funds. There's no one to stop him now from a complete takeover. With what Eve knows, Kiko can force Mary Pat to hand over control of every business, every asset. He's erased the Bellinis' power in a night.'

Frank got up. 'Bucks and Paul knew where Kiko was living, but I didn't. So I put out word on the street. Said I'd pay cash to know where Kiko's staying. There's nothing more I can do.'

'I'll go nuts sitting here and waiting,' Whit said.

'Learn how. Unless you want to call the police.' Frank crossed his arms. 'You find Eve, you're leaving town?'

'Yes. She's coming home with me. For a short while, at least.'

'I think that's an excellent idea,' Frank said.

'Thanks, Frank,' Whit said.

'Lot of ifs there,' Gooch said. 'You boys are optimists.'

'Don't talk like she's dead. Don't,' Whit said.

The phone rang. Frank went to it, said hello, listened, said no a few times, hung up. 'No one's seen Bucks. The rest of the ring isn't meeting at the Bellinis'; there's a cop car on Lazy Lane, probably there to take pictures of the license plates of the cars coming and going. Oh, man, I'm moving to Vegas.'

They sat, waiting, and two hours later the phone rang again and Frank answered it, spoke quietly. 'Yeah. Fine. Stop by and I'll give you your money.' He hung up. Didn't look at Whit, at Gooch, leaned against the little bar counter for support.

'That was a dealer I know. He said Kiko Grace and his bodyguard José are living in a townhouse on Fannin, near downtown. The dealer's got three other dealers working under him. One knew Kiko from Miami, saw him at those condos last week when he did a YSD.'

'What?'

'Yuppie Scum Delivery,' Frank said. 'So this condo, maybe that's where he's got Eve.'

'Give me the address,' Whit said.

'Sure. But then I got to go to the Topaz,' Frank said. 'I should put in an appearance today, calm the girls that we're staying open.'

'No,' Gooch said. 'You come with us, Frank. In case you're setting us up in a trap.'

'Gooch, I love Eve. I'm not gonna let her kid get killed.' Frank touched Whit's shoulder. 'C'mon.'

'Maybe Whit trusts you. I don't,' Gooch said. 'Sorry.'

'You can be a little late for the Topaz,' Whit said. 'And it's safer for you staying with us.'

'Right. What you gonna do,' Frank said, 'ask Kiko Grace prettyplease to give you Eve back?'

'No. I'm going to tell him if he doesn't release her, I'm going straight to the police, with everything I know. Simple.'

'You'll do that even if he kills her.' Frank shrugged. 'His way, he gets rid of a witness. He's probably gonna get rid of you, too.'

'If he lets her go, I stay silent about him killing Paul. Forever.'

Frank shook his head. 'I don't see this conversation going smoothly.'

'I killed a man once, Frank,' Whit said. 'He tried to kill me. He had already killed a woman I loved. I killed him, and I thought guilt would gnaw at me forever, but you know, it didn't. He was a murdering bastard, not too different from Kiko. I was sorry I had to do it, but I did it.'

Frank opened his mouth, then shut it.

'I'm not going to let him kill my mother,' Whit said. 'It's not going to happen.'

'Usually I admire optimism,' Frank said. 'Right now this seems stupidity.'

'But you're going, too,' Whit said.

'Well, I'm stupid,' Frank said.

They left in Frank's BMW. Fifteen minutes later, a battered Jaguar pulled to a stop next to River Oaks Park, then circled around the neighborhood three times, and parked two streets over.

'He doesn't have Eve,' Frank Polo said. 'He doesn't even have a face.'

They stood over the body of Kiko Grace, still sprawled on the floor of the condo's breakfast nook. The whole drive over to the condo, Whit had felt like his skin was on fire, rushing to save his mother, rushing, possibly, to die. Let her see he hadn't given up on her, hadn't abandoned her. He was afraid she thought he had left her to be caught.

But the condo had been empty, the door unlocked, as if the killer didn't mind if Kiko was found.

Gooch moved from room to room, making sure no one else was in the condo.

'Kiko dead. Paul dead,' Gooch said. 'Guessing not a coincidence.' His face was blanched. He leaned against a wall.

'No,' Whit said. 'Dangerous world.'

'You think?' Frank asked. He prodded at Kiko's shoulder with his foot. 'You bastard, where is Eve?'

'Your bravery's a little late, Frank,' Gooch said. But his voice was weak.

Whit said, 'You okay?'

'Fine.' Gooch turned away.

'We need to see if there's anything here that could tell us where Eve is,' Whit said. He pulled on gloves he'd gotten after last night's shooting to finish cleaning Paul's Porsche of his and Gooch's prints when they dumped the car on a residential street. He handed a set to Frank and another to Gooch. 'Don't leave a trace you were here.'

'Maybe she killed him,' Gooch said, 'and she's waiting for us back at Charlie's house.'

Whit handed him his cell phone. 'Call. Or Bucks took her. Getting rid of the leadership on both sides. I don't think Kiko shot Paul.' He moved Kiko's body to one side, peered down the back of the pants for lividity marks. 'He's been dead for hours, probably about the same time that Paul died.'

'You can tell by looking at a dead man's ass?' Frank asked.

'Um, yeah,' Whit said. It wasn't a good time to announce he was a judge and coroner, that he'd seen several gunshot bodies and recognized the timing of postmortem conditions.

'I knew we shouldn't have recruited from the corporate world,' said Frank. 'Those people give me the creeps.'

'Whit, if Bucks killed Kiko, he would have killed Eve, too,' Gooch said. His voice wasn't so slurred now, but Whit didn't like the pallor of his skin or the shakiness in his hands. He watched Gooch dial, but he felt by a sinking in his gut that Eve wasn't curled up in front of the TV at Charlie's.

'What the hell?' Frank pointed at Kiko's mouth. A bit of green protruded from between the lips. Even though most of Kiko's face was raw meat, his mouth was relatively untouched and Whit knelt down, conscious he was disturbing a crime scene but not caring. He peeled back the little tube of paper. It was a twenty-dollar bill. He unrolled it and written in heavy black ink across the money was A PUBLIC SERVICE.

Frank peered over his shoulder. 'What does that mean?'

'I don't know,' Whit said. He carefully rerolled the bill, stuck it back between the dead man's teeth. 'But I don't see Bucks leaving little notes on the body.'

There was no sign of a fight other than half of Kiko's face being splattered on the breakfast nook wall. An answering machine held two messages from a young-sounding woman, in Spanish, asking Kiko to call her, she was better this morning.

The condo itself was sparse; a few pieces of leather furniture, TV with DVD player, a breakfast table, a toaster, and a coffee maker. More like a temporary camp than a home. Whit found a small amount of cocaine in the pantry, double-bagged, tucked behind the cornstarch box. Not a good hiding place. He expected better from Kiko. The outer bag had loosened masking tape on it, as though it had been stuck to the wall and hidden elsewhere. And moved.

Why move it out of the hiding place? To snort. To sell. But then you would hide it again, being careful was part of the job. It bothered him.

Whit tried the redial on the condo's phone, got a Chinese delivery restaurant down the street. Hung up.

'José's not here,' Frank said. 'Kiko's right-hand guy.'

'Probably out mailing résumés,' Gooch said.

'So what do we do?' Frank said. 'Leave and call the cops?'

'Are there more drugs here?' Whit asked.

'Thanks, I'm cutting back,' Gooch said.

'Or cash or records? Anything relating back to them being dealers.'

'No cash that I found, but I haven't looked hard,' Gooch said. 'Ain't thinking they got receipts.'

'Let's look. Quickly.'

'What, you're gonna take the dead guy's money?' Frank said.

'Yes, Frank. Go through his pockets for me,' Whit said. Frank stood uncertainly over the body, as if deciding whether or not Whit was serious.

Whit searched, carefully, through the closet in the first bedroom. Silk shirts, polos, pressed linen slacks, stylish jackets. Of course, the better to hide a holster under. And expensive shoes, all perfectly polished. Kiko probably threw out a pair at the first scuff. He either packed heavy or planned a long stay in Houston.

He checked the rest of the bedroom. The bed was unmade and rumpled. Underneath the bed was nothing but a dust bunny or two. Whit expected firepower to be hidden under there, but nothing. No notes, no papers of any sort. No PDA, no cell phone.

'The other bedroom's empty,' Gooch said. 'All the clothes are gone.'

'Then José took off,' Frank said.

'Then odds are José killed him,' Gooch said.

'Why turn on his boss?' Whit asked.

'Why not?' Gooch said. 'José thinks Eve has the money, decides to take it himself. Kiko's in the way.'

Whit hated the clarity and simplicity of it, because it put them back at zero. 'But she doesn't have it.'

'Are you absolutely sure, Whit?' Gooch said quietly.

'She doesn't.'

'Let's say Bucks delivered the money to Kiko,' Frank said. 'Eve got the upper hand, killed him, took off with the money.'

'No,' Whit said. 'She'd call me. She wouldn't run away from me again.'

Frank said nothing, turned, went back into the den.

Whit went into the bathroom. He glanced through the materials in the cabinet. Nothing unusual. Mouthwash, allergy medicine to deal with the inescapable Houston pollen, shaving kit. He opened the toilet, thinking more coke could be hidden there, that it was the common place in movies but Kiko wouldn't be that dumb.

Or yes he was. A package lay taped inside, heavily wrapped in plastic.

Carefully, Whit pulled it free, laid the package on the floor. Too thin for a cocaine brick. A DVD in a case, unlabeled.

'Let's get out of here, boys,' Frank said as Whit headed back into the den.

'Wait a minute.' Whit slid the disc into the player, set it running. Gooch and Frank watched behind him.

A darkened shot, the camera clearly hidden at a slightly tilted angle. Four men entering a house at night. Bucks one of them. All nicely dressed, young executive types. Two minutes passed. Then Bucks coming out. Carrying a body, dumping it in the trunk of a BMW. Then another. And another, Bucks then getting in the car and roaring away.

'Our smoking gun,' Frank said. 'Thank you, Lord.'

'If Bucks or José killed Kiko, why leave this behind?' Whit popped the disc from the machine.

'Bucks didn't know the disc was here,' Gooch said. He sat down suddenly, touched his chest, frowned. 'And what's it to José if Bucks gets caught for murder?'

'Bucks did know about the film,' Whit said. 'Kiko told me he had Bucks in his pocket. This is how he got him there.'

'Whit.' Gooch clutched at his chest. 'Whit, oh, man . . .' And he collapsed onto the floor, groaning, eyes rolling into whites, a thin sliver of spit oozing from his mouth.

40

Claudia stood over Whit, holding a cup of steaming coffee in her hand, and he wondered for a second if she would pour it on his head.

'You look terrible,' she said quietly. A family was camped in the corner of the intensive care room, and she spoke in a hush.

'Hello to you too,' he said.

She handed him the coffee. It was close to six Sunday night, Gooch lying in critical condition for the whole afternoon.

'Thank you,' he said.

Claudia sat next to him. He didn't look at her.

'Whit.'

'Yes?'

'What's going on?' she said.

'Sitting here with a coffee that my friend brought me,' he said.

'Don't,' she said in a low, harsh whisper. 'Do you know what I've been through?'

'Does it matter if I know? You're mad at me before I've even opened my mouth.'

'Walk with me,' she said. 'There's a little garden outside. I'm going to yell at you, and I don't want to disturb these people.'

'Visiting time is in another fifteen minutes. I can't miss it.'

'Level with me and you won't,' she said.

'I love it when you get all authority figure.' He walked out past her. She followed him.

The evening was damp, rain having ceased its fall an hour ago, and the wet held the air in a swampy embrace. Whit sat down on the damp stone bench. Claudia stood.

'I almost got killed last night,' she said. 'Did you know that?'

'No,' he said, watching her. 'Are you serious?'

'Greg Buckman. A shooter came after him. Nearly got me. A man got killed.'

'But you're okay.'

'Yes, I'm okay.' She sat next to him. He reached for her arm and she stood. 'And you are so not okay, Whit. Not okay at all to me. You sit here like a stone statue, not answering a single reasonable question over the past three days.'

'So ask me.'

Start easy, she decided. 'For God's sakes, what happened to Gooch?'

'He had a heart attack.'

'I don't mean that, Whit.' Claudia thought: *infinite patience right now*. 'He was full of a cocktail of narcotics, morphine, a whole mess of junk. He's been beaten.'

'So much for medical privacy,' Whit said. 'Gooch does love to party.'

'You protecting your mom, Whit?'

'Claudia. Please go home. I don't have anything to say.'

'I nearly got killed trying to help you.'

'I warned you that Bucks was dangerous. I'm sorry. I'm really sorry.'

'He wasn't half as dangerous as José Peron,' Claudia said. 'That's the shooter's name.'

'His name is Peron? Like Evita?'

'Yes. Look at me, Whit.'

Instead he studied his shoes.

'Whit. I love you, you're my dear friend. Whatever you've done, I'll help you. Okay?'

'Okay,' he said. 'I want you to take Gooch back to Port Leo, soon as he can travel. That's how you can help me.'

'Fine,' she said. 'But on the condition you tell me what's happening.'

'First tell me everything that happened to you last night. Please,' he said, taking her hand. She let him, and she told him about finding Robin and Bucks. When she was done he said, 'Thank God you're okay.'

Claudia turned his face toward her, looked hard into his eyes. 'The police found Greg Buckman prowling around a house in River Oaks today. They were already headed there to talk to Frank Polo, who's the manager of a strip club called the Topaz.'

'Oh.'

'The owner of the club, Paul Bellini' – she put an emphasis on the last name – 'got gunned down in a parking lot last night. His Porsche was abandoned near Shepherd and Alabama. It was wiped clean of prints. Oddly enough, there was a van parked not far from where Bellini's body was found. Gooch's van.'

Whit let go of her hand.

'So I'm freaking, I'm calling hospitals, Whit, not knowing if you and Gooch are dead or alive. Eventually I find Gooch here. You haven't talked to the police about all this, have you, Whit?'

'I told the doctors my friend had gone missing for a few hours, turned up beaten and sick. They gave the information to the police. They ran a check, found his van was near the Bellini death scene. They came back and talked to me. I told them I didn't know why his van was there. And Gooch isn't up for much questioning yet.'

'So you lied to the police.' Claudia couldn't keep the outrage out of her voice.

'Tell them what you suspect. I don't care.'

'You came to Houston to find the Bellinis. You sure as hell found them, Whit.'

'So where's Bucks now?'

'They questioned him and let him go. His story is that this José Peron is a hit man hired by disgruntled Energis investors to get rid of him.'

Whit raised an eyebrow. 'They bought that?'

'No. The man killed at Bucks' place, a guy named MacKay, is a suspected drug dealer and hit man himself. But never arrested with cause. They don't have a charge against Bucks, other than fleeing the scene of a crime. His apartment was clean. There's nothing hard yet to connect Bucks to any illegal activity. He drove around Houston all night, slept in his car, then drove to Polo's house this morning. The police are talking with his girlfriend, to see if she'll give him up.'

'Bucks is out there,' Whit said. 'Thanks for telling me.'

'I get the feeling it's not telling, it's warning.' She paused. 'Where's your mother?'

'I have no idea. Dead, probably.'

'Whit.' She touched his knee; he didn't move. 'I'm sorry.'

He said nothing.

'Wait.' Her eyes widened. 'Does that mean you found her? Or didn't?'

'It doesn't matter, Claudia.'

'You found her.'

'Found and lost,' he said. 'Isn't it supposed to be the other way around?'

'What does that mean? She ran away from you again?' Then she said, softly, 'Did you kill Paul Bellini?'

'No.'

'You can tell me if you did, Whit. It's okay . . .'

He crossed his arms, gave her a crooked smile. 'And why is it okay if I killed Bellini? Because he was scum?'

'I didn't say it was okay if you killed him. I said it was okay if you told me.'

'I absolutely didn't kill him. Neither did Gooch.'

'What really happened to Gooch?'

'Gooch can tell you all about it,' Whit said, 'on that long drive home.'

'And you're doing what? Staying in Houston to play high noon with Bucks?'

'Thanks for the coffee, but it's visiting time.' He stood up and walked away. If Gooch was conscious, now was the time to get their stories straight, whispering to each other under the hum of the medical equipment.

'José Peron's mother was killed two years ago,' Vernetta West-brook said. Claudia sat across from her in the hospital cafeteria, sipping coffee. 'He was once on the fringes of the Miami drug trade, a guy who didn't deal anything harder than pot, but after her murder he started taking on the dirty jobs no one else wanted and he accelerated up through the ranks.' She lowered her voice.

275

'Does Judge Mosley know Peron? His Honor like to snort a little coke?'

'No. Tell me about the mother's death. Was she dealing?'

'It's the kind of story the drug czar tells to boost budgets,' Vernetta said. 'Mrs Peron was a high school drama teacher. Staged Shakespeare in the Projects with underprivileged kids, did volunteer work, well-loved in the community. She walked into a drug deal going down in the school lot. She told the boys to get the hell off school property. They shot her four times.'

'They catch the guys?'

'The suspects – two of them, both eighteen – were found floating two days later near the very busy Bahia Mar marina in Fort Lauderdale. Shot in the head. Dumped rather publicly, the police thought, to make a statement.'

Claudia's eyes widened. 'José Peron killed them.'

'He had an airtight alibi. But I talked with the Broward County DA's office and they believe the guys were offed as a favor to José. Then José began his heavier involvement in the organization. It's headed by a guy named Kiko Grace. We got an anonymous tip today that his body was ready and waiting for us, in a leased condo near downtown.'

'So Peron's boss is here and dies around the same time as Paul Bellini.' Claudia felt cold. *God, Whit, did you* . . . No. She could not believe it of him.

'Your judge isn't saying much more than what you told us. That he hired Chyme to find his mother, that he hasn't found his mother, and that his friend Guchinski had nothing to do with Paul Bellini's death. He either is lying or he really doesn't know. Which is it, Claudia?'

'I'm not a mind reader. If he says he doesn't know, I have to believe him.'

'I don't,' Vernetta said. 'I don't have to believe him at all. We'll invite him for a long leisurely chat for hours on end.'

'You won't convince one judge to sign a warrant to arrest a fellow judge without hard cause.'

Vernetta shook her head. 'Mosley's a rural JP, not even a lawyer. He's nothing to the judges here.'

'Why don't you drag in Greg Buckman again? He was friends with Bellini, and Peron and Grace must've wanted Buckman dead if Peron came after him with guns blazing. Leave Whit alone. Buckman's clearly in the middle of this.'

'We've got tit for tat. Kiko Grace comes here, wants to move into Houston drug territory. He whacks Bellini. Bellini's group whacks Grace. Or vice versa, it doesn't matter who died first. They have a short little war and then it's done. Peron shooting for Bucks is the next stage of the war. Let them kill each other. They're a cancer.'

'You have no problem with murder, Vernetta. Assuming innocent people don't get hurt.'

'That's not so. And your pet judge isn't innocent, Claudia. He knows more than he's saying.'

'If Grace is Miami-based, José Peron might head back to Florida and pull forces in here.'

'I hope he goes home. Stays there and runs Grace's ring. You wonder why a guy would get involved in the trade that killed his mother. Shortest line to revenge, I guess.'

'Yes,' Claudia said. But Vernetta had a point. It made her wonder. 'None of your informants have skinny on Peron?'

'He's too new in town. Nothing yet.'

'When Leonard Guchinski's well enough to travel, and assuming he's not charged with anything, I'm taking him back to Port Leo. It's a long drive. He's a friend, of sorts. I can hope he'll talk.' She stood.

'Talk more than your precious judge, at least,' Vernetta said. 'But let me ask you a hard question. Guchinski talks, or Mosley talks to you, in confidence, tells you the truth of what's happened between all these people, what do you do, Claudia? Rat on your friends if they've broken the law?'

'I'll worry about that when I cross that bridge.'

'Girlfriend,' Vernetta said, 'you're running out of road.'

41

Eve no longer knew if it was day or night. After killing Kiko, José had given her another painkiller, bound her, dumped her in the back of a black Suburban, tossed a cover over her, driven into the dark of Houston. She slipped into the emptiness, dreamed of gunfire, heard José jumping back in the car. Then driving, fast, short, lots of sharp turns that made her nauseated, then a long haul on the highway. She fell asleep.

She woke to a radio, tuned to jazz, played soft as a gentle whisper in the dark. José bound her to a narrow cot, then sat by her with a syringe in his hand, sliding the needle under her skin while she protested, pumped her full of chemical bliss that made her head hazy and cloudy and sweet. She was conscious of José coming in once, feeding her a chocolate shake and a package of lukewarm French fries. Then another shot. In the darkness once, cool water sponged on her face, her hands, a kindness, then medicine daubed the back of her mouth, where her teeth had been, across her busted lips. The taste of the medicine lingered a long while. When her thoughts became clearer she remembered Kiko, his face blown away. But mostly she thought of Whit.

Whit. Here and gone. Like the life she should have had. She wanted to cry but her face felt too numb to know whether or not she was weeping. An ache that defied the drugs settled in along her arms, her chest, her jaw, like years of unshed tears letting her know they waited for release. She slept. Awoke in the dark. Listened. Heard voices, a man and a woman.

Her purse lay on the floor, all its contents spilled across the carpet. Makeup, brush, a package of mints. Her gun was gone. And something else. She tried to remember what was in her purse that would matter so much. The room was small, carpet the color of clay, the ceiling old and worn. It had the impersonal dimensions of an office. Boards covered the one window.

She tried to reason it out. They knew she didn't have the money. They found the money? Or had they had it all along? They didn't need her. But they did. They'd kept her alive. Through the fog she remembered he had called her the key. Key to what?

She made a noise in her throat, tongued her numb, parched lips. They were keeping her for bait.

The idea rose up, tumbled back into the mess of her drugged brain. If they wanted her alive, it was because they wanted Whit.

The door opened. José stood in the doorway, smoking a cigarette. He shut the door behind him, crossed to the bureau, extinguished the cigarette in a small plastic ashtray.

'Secondhand smoke's bad for you,' he said. His voice was quiet but not warm.

She said, 'What are you going to do with me?' Her voice didn't sound like her own anymore.

'Feed you. Eggs. Toast. Sound okay? Mouth up to eating, or you want another shake?'

'Depends. Is it my last meal?'

'I told you that you were valuable to me.' Now he smiled, a bully's knowing, taunting grin.

'I don't understand.'

'You're Open Sesame,' he said. 'You're gonna tell us how they do it. How they hide and move the money.'

'They.'

He smiled. 'We'll start with Kiko Grace's organization and his rivals back in south Florida.'

A cold nausea prickled her guts.

'Then the Dominicans in Dallas and New Orleans. The cartels in New York and Los Angeles. You're gonna help us break their backs.' José's voice went low. 'We call ourselves Public Service. We do what the cops can't. Take the war on drugs to the streets. We get in with the dealers. Learn their setup. Then we kill the leaders, gut the organization, take their money and go after the next group.' He leveled a hard look at her. 'Dealers killed my mom.'

'I'm sorry.'

'No you're not. You're not one bit sorry, bitch. What was my mother to you or your kind?'

The door opened. Tasha Strong stepped inside. Beautiful face stern. A gun in her hand, barrel lowered.

'Tasha?' Eve blinked. 'Tasha?'

' "O tiger's heart wrapp'd in a woman's hide!" ' José quoted, making guns with his fingers, grinning at Tasha.

'Don't give her more of a headache with that crap,' Tasha said. 'Mouth better, Eve?'

Eve managed to nod.

'She's been tending to you. She worked Paul's side, I worked Kiko's.' José smiled. 'Tasha lost her brother to a drug gang. It tends to gnaw at you, knowing that the police alone can never beat these people. So we work together. Dozens of us.'

Eve glanced over at the spill of her purse. The CD Whit took from Tasha. It was gone. 'The cooked books . . .' she said.

'Those files that listed other revenue sources for Paul on the CD? Faked. By Tasha and me. Paul gave her access to your house so she could check your finances, see if Frank had been doing any more stealing. But that was a chance to copy those fake files to your hard drive after she copied your real financial files without anyone knowing. False trail for the authorities to follow if you got caught or killed right away. She already planted those files on the computers at the Topaz after you vanished. We didn't want the Feds grabbing the Bellini money before we could. But that's not a worry. Now that we have you. See? We plan as thoroughly as you do.'

She closed her eyes. 'You want me to help you, but I can't. I don't know how other rings clean their money.'

'You know the tricks. The processes. Like, I'm intrigued, the exchange place for Kiko's money being done at what appears to be a simple insurance company. You cleaning money through insurance policies?'

'Yeah.' Suddenly there was no point in not telling him. 'You buy a life insurance policy, overseas, then cash it out a few months later and transfer the money back into the country. You don't get watched as closely. It's a loophole I found. You can move millions in short order and there's no question of legitimacy.'

José patted her cheek. 'Sweet lady, you're exactly what we need to destroy the worst people in this country.'

'I said, I can't.'

'You got a choice,' he said. 'Help us, give us what we want, crack open the vaults for the major dealers in this country, or watch Whit Mosley die. Slowly. Painfully.'

Tears of anger, frustration, welled up in her eyes. 'But Whit's not a drug dealer, he's not Kiko or Paul.'

'Definitely. He's a judge, a justice of the peace down on the coast,' Tasha said.

Eve gave a sharp little laugh. 'A judge.'

'I had a chance to kill him when I killed Paul, and I didn't,' Tasha said. 'You owe me one. Don't forget it.'

'I don't consider your partner a good guy,' José said. 'He's a guy who could cause us a lot of trouble. And if you want him to keep breathing, you do what you're told.'

'Eve,' Tasha said. 'I kissed Paul, slept with him, listened to him cry about his dad. Then I killed him. We won't show Whit one moment of mercy if you don't help us.'

'Don't hurt him,' Eve pleaded. 'I'll do whatever you want.'

They left her alone in the room, an old office at one end of the warehouse, walked to the other end of the warehouse.

'You think she'll cooperate?' José said. 'With what she knows, she could accelerate our schedules.'

'No,' Tasha said. 'We need her son. Whit.'

'Son?'

'Look at him, look at her, José. It's obvious. If he was just her business partner she wouldn't plead for him like that.' Tasha shook her head. 'She's been in the business for thirty years and was never caught. She's forgotten more than most people know. She could lead us down blind alley after blind alley, slow us down without us even knowing. We need Whit where she can see him hurt. Hear him scream.' Tasha touched José's shoulder. 'Weigh his life against all the lives we save doing this. The innocents. The kids. He's nothing compared to them. He's the guarantee she'll work her best.'

'But the police are looking for me. I don't know if I can hunt him around Houston. We don't even know if he's in town.' Frustration in his voice.

'You want him as bait to get her to deliver what we need,' Tasha said. God, men could be dense at times. She already had a plan. 'It works both ways. Use her as bait to get him.'

'Only works if we can find him to have a conversation,' José said. 'Eve won't want to get him anywhere close to us. She won't talk.'

Tasha frowned at this hard, unappealing truth. 'Try Frank Polo,' she said. 'He's dumb as a stump but maybe he knows how to find Eve's son. His number's on my cell phone.'

'Just call him up and ask him where Whit is?'

'Make it worth his while. He's gonna be signing autographs on the unemployment line with Paul dead. Or maybe tell him he gets Eve back if he helps us.' Tasha went back in to feed Eve, make sure she ate. When she came out of the office, José was clicking off her cell phone and smiling as though he'd won the lottery.

'I just had me,' José said, 'one brilliant idea to kill two birds with one stone.'

Monday afternoon thin rain fell from the sky, clouds wandering in from the Gulf, and the wet lot of Club Topaz, closed, was empty. But it was where Robin agreed to meet Claudia. Robin sat in Claudia's passenger seat. Claudia handed her a coffee, one of those cinnamon-toffee-mocha latte creations that was sweeter than a box of candy.

'Her name is Tasha Strong,' Robin Melvin said. 'Tasha dances here. Nice girl but a little uppity. Paul was all crazy about her.'

'Have you seen her since Paul died?' Claudia asked.

'No. She's probably scared to death. I sure am,' Robin said.

'These aren't good people, Robin. I know you have feelings for Greg Buckman—'

'No. I had hopes.' She said the word like it left a bitter taste in her mouth. 'I knew he wasn't the nicest guy on the planet but I thought, if he and I could get away from these people, he would be better. All that goal stuff he says. He wants to be better. But I'm not sticking around for the home improvement anymore.'

'Can't change 'em, Robin,' Claudia said. Tried not to think of Whit.

'Clearly not.' Robin poked at her puffy lip. 'I never, ever, had a guy hit me. Not once. I swore I would never put up with that *Lifetime*-movie shit. And he did it, and I was so surprised I acted a fool. I'm sorry.'

'It's okay, don't apologize.'

'But I want to help. I don't know anything about any illegal stuff, okay? I told the police that about a dozen times. They don't believe me, they think Bucks must have talked plenty on the pillow.' She lowered her voice. 'He never did. But Bucks wanted me to watch Tasha. So I'm guessing she knew bad shit about him and Paul. I searched her changing room, where she keeps her stuff. Nothing odd. A few pictures.'

'Pictures.'

'In a drawer. Of a boy. From being a baby to teenage years. Kind of looked like her, maybe was a brother. But the pictures were old, creased with handling. Not new.' Robin cleared her throat. 'Funny thing for a girl to keep, family pictures, in the place where she takes her clothes off. Most girls don't.' She sipped at the hypersweetened coffee. 'I love my mom, we're close, but she thinks I'm a cocktail waitress. I wouldn't have her picture around in the changing room. Like she was looking at me in my getups.'

'Was there a name or date on the back of any of the photos?'

Robin closed her eyes. 'Yeah. Darius. On one of the baby pictures.' She opened her eyes, looked at Claudia. 'If Tasha doesn't know anything I don't want the cops crowding her. Cops keep wanting me to make a deal, like I'm holding back info to annoy them. Bucks wanted me to watch her because she was close to Paul, and he didn't like that. But since she was closer to Paul, she might be able to help the cops. And then they'd leave me alone.'

'Describe her to me, tell me where she lives,' Claudia said, 'and I'll have a talk with her.'

'Would you?' Robin said. 'We weren't real close, so I don't have her contact info, but Frank would.'

'Frank Polo, right?' His name had cropped up before, the singer turned nightclub manager. Eve Michaels' boyfriend.

'I'm not ashamed to say I love disco,' Robin said. 'Bucks hated it. But it's happy music. And Frank's really a good singer.'

'Tell me about Eve Michaels.'

Robin shrugged. 'Eve? She's a bookkeeper for Paul, I think. Nice but distant. Tasha liked her, seemed interested in Eve's work. Tasha wanted to get off stage, move into the business side of the club. But Paul never would have let her, you have to *see* her. She's gorgeous.'

'Did you like Eve? Is she nice?' It suddenly and oddly mattered to her, if this was Whit's mother, that she have at least one redeeming feature.

'Nice as long as you didn't get in her way. Cross her, you'd be missing a liver and she'd be licking her lips. I was a little afraid of her.'

'You have her and Frank's address? My sister was always a big fan of Frank Polo's,' Claudia said. 'I'd like to get an autograph before I leave town.'

42

Whit said, 'It's time we reported Eve as officially missing.' He hadn't slept much in the past two nights and he rubbed at his unshaven face.

He and Frank Polo sat in a little diner off Shepherd, not far from Rice University, themed for fifties nostalgia. The jukebox played a mournful tune, appropriate for a nearly empty restaurant after the lunch rush. Frank didn't respond to his suggestion as the waitress approached them. They both ordered omelettes.

'When I was famous, we lived on breakfast food. You're tired, you want comfort, but you can't get full up. You never want to be stuffed when you're on stage for a living. Did you know I was famous once?' Frank said to the waitress, who was a cute college girl with a little silver ring piercing her pert nose.

'I didn't,' she said.

'I used to be a singer,' Frank said. The waitress gave an indulgent, polite-but-I-don't-care smile and took their menus.

Frank waited till she was out of earshot. 'And tell the police what, Whit? That José has her? We don't know he does, we don't know where he is. Some cop named Gomez already stopped by to see me about her. I told them she took off, I don't know where, gave him her cell phone number. The cops are going to think she's running.'

'But the police could look for her and José.'

'And when they find her, they'll stick her in prison and you'll never see her again.'

'I don't believe—' and Whit's cell phone rang. He clicked it on.

'Whitman Mosley.' It wasn't a voice he knew, a baritone, strong and steady. 'Your mother's alive. Thought you'd want to know.'

'Who is this? José Peron?'

'We're going to keep her for a little while, then we'll give her back to you. Alive and well. Unless you call the cops. Then we have to be mean, and we don't want to be. Mean is not what we're about.'

We. José was not acting alone. 'I want her back, right now.'

'Sit tight. Be patient. We'll take good care of her, then we'll give her back. We'll arrange a meeting between us.'

'I don't believe you.'

'Believe or not,' the voice said. 'We could have killed her with Kiko. We didn't. Take that as serious reassurance.'

'Let me talk to her.'

'What will you discuss? Her money-laundering skills? Her killing the guy in Montana all those years ago?'

Whit's mouth went dry. 'How did . . .'

'Behave, she lives. Don't, she dies. We'll be in touch very soon.' And the caller hung up.

Whit told Frank the gist of the conversation.

'What the hell does that mean?' Frank said. He wiped at his puffy eyes with the back of his hand. 'Why would they want to keep her?'

'José . . . if it's him, he must want info on the Bellini operations. But he won't let her go. He'll kill her.' *Montana. José knows about Mom shooting James Powell in Montana. And that I'm her son. Because he took Harry's notes off Harry's body. He killed Harry.*

The weight of the knowledge made him very still. He didn't look at Frank, didn't look at his plate.

'So you're going to the cops?' Frank asked.

'He says he'll kill her if I do that.'

'Then we have to listen to him. Not endanger her.'

'Frank. I can't.'

'Yes, you can and you will,' Frank said. 'We play by their rules, we get her back.'

'I need to know where José is, Frank. Where he has her.'

'I can't work wonders. Finding the condo they hid out in was tough enough. But I'll put out word again. Money for information.'

'Let's say José's the power behind all this. He kills Kiko. He kills or has Paul killed. He tries to kill Bucks. Why? So no one else is chasing after the money? That only works if he *has* the money, Frank, if he doesn't want to be chased himself. I'm thinking he killed Harry and Doyle and stole the money.'

Frank shook his head. 'How would José know where the exchange was?'

'He followed Eve. Or, worse, Bucks told him. The police should compare the bullets in Kiko to the bullets in Harry Chyme and Richard Doyle.' Whit finished his coffee. 'José stuck that money into Kiko's mouth. If he was stealing the money, why bother with gestures and symbols? He's got his own agenda.' The waitress brought their omelettes, hash browns, grits with a warm little puddle of garlic and cheese on top. They began to eat. Suddenly Whit laughed.

'What?' Frank asked, buttering a biscuit.

'This is so freaking normal and domestic,' Whit said. 'Like if Eve had taken me with her when she took off, I probably would have had a lot of breakfasts with you by now.'

'I would have been a crappy stepdad,' Frank said. 'Be glad she left you behind.'

'Because abandonment is so awesome.'

'Get over it,' Frank said. 'Actually, you seem pretty well-adjusted. Except for hunting down your mom. You got a problem letting go?'

'No.'

'You need your mom for what? To complete you as a person?' Frank said. 'You and Bucks are more alike than you know.'

'Excuse me?'

'Him and his self-help tapes. It's all to reassure himself that if he screws up it's not entirely his fault, he can make it better with a quick fix. You finding Eve, it's all about fixing you, Whit, not her.'

'At the beginning. But not now.'

'I know she wasn't around,' Frank said. 'But I'm sure she loves you.'

'She's a thief and a crook.'

'So? She's not a nutcase like Bucks or José. Put a premium on sanity.'

Whit thought of Eve tending his wounds, of remembering he liked pepperoni pizza, of warning him to save himself.

'Do you love her?' Frank asked. 'I'd like to know.'

Whit put his fork down. 'I don't want to talk about it. But I want you to get Bucks where I can talk to him alone.'

'Bucks?'

'Bucks is the key.'

'He won't meet with you,' Frank said. 'Plus, the cops have got to be watching him. You want the cops knowing you're in deeper than you are, seeing you with him? Whit, they'll haul you in as a material witness. Offer a deal with you to testify against me, your mother, Bucks, whoever.'

'I'm going to give the police the movie of Bucks carrying those bodies, anonymously, but as soon as I do, Bucks is behind bars and I can't ever get to him.'

'Arresting him, you could have more pressure put on him.'

Whit leaned forward. 'Call him. Tell him I have the movie.'

Frank's eyes went wide. 'You crazy?'

'I'm dead serious. Tell him. Bucks knows where José would hide. Maybe that's why José tried to kill him.'

'Your mother wouldn't want this,' Frank said. 'She'd be wanting you to head your ass back home.'

'Bucks and I have a common enemy now in José,' Whit said.

'It's a deal with the devil. I won't do it.' Frank pulled a twenty out of his wallet, tossed it on the table. 'My treat. Think about my suggestion about getting Bucks arrested. There's your game plan, son.'

'Think about what I said, Frank. We need Bucks.'

'Jesus and Mary,' Frank said. 'You didn't answer me. You love her?'

'I don't know her in the conventional sense you know your family. But still, I do know her. Or I want to believe I know her. Maybe I'm fooling myself.' Whit shook his head. 'Love her? I must.'

43

Frank Polo left the diner, watching Whit drive off in Charlie Fulgham's borrowed Lexus. Whit was so like Eve in certain ways. Resolve. Smarts. Single-mindedness. Frank drove around an extra twenty minutes before heading home, stopping at lights, watching his back. He wasn't quite sure who he was looking for in his rear-view mirror. He imagined cops, lantern-jawed guys who'd give him the tough eye or a woman cop with a lesbian-short haircut who'd take him downtown, call him Mr Polo, be excruciatingly polite while panic tore his guts and ribs in half. See what he was made of, sitting there in their interrogation room, the cops lobbing a suggestion or two about his involvement with Paul Bellini beyond being the Topaz's manager, about his knowledge of any criminal activities about the family. Asking where Eve Michaels was. Probably good he'd had to move the money he'd taken from the club back into the club's accounts. It made him clean. Christ, Paul had done him a favor.

'What you gonna do to me?' Frank practiced saying in his mind to his imaginary interrogators. 'Make me give the Grammy back?' That was always a hell of a line to keep in your pocket, it made people know that they weren't nearly as cool as you were. The Grammy, he still had that, up on a mantel in his bedroom. Usually one of the last things he saw before he went to sleep.

For a change, there were no police cars parked near the house. No lawyers waiting to talk to him, and no Bucks. He had gone to the hospital straight from Kiko's with Whit and Gooch, but stayed in the background, not letting anyone know he was with the other two. Thank God he hadn't come home that night to find a furious and panicked Bucks waiting for him, anxious for help.

He got out of the car, headed up to the front door. The woman was waiting for him in the eaves of the porch, dark-haired, mildly pretty, with a serious and intelligent face. Frank froze, the keys in his hand.

The man in front of her looked older than the pictures of Frank Polo Claudia remembered, vaguely, from her older sister's record covers. He'd been short for a singing star, big black hair in a seventies flip, gaudy with chains and the requisite long-pointy-collared shirt slit open to the belly, big-heeled shoes, pants tighter than skin. This man was still short, but quietly dressed in comfortable gray slacks and a plain blue shirt, hair cropped short without a bit of gel. But there was the too-big diamond on the ring, the hint of gold chain under the modest collar.

'Yes?' he said. A little fear in his voice, the barest inflection. Because she was unexpected and he was tense, expecting attack or trouble from a new angle.

Claudia had given long thought on how to work this. 'Mr Polo? I'm looking for Tasha Strong. I understand you have her address or phone number. She's unlisted.'

'Who are you? A cop?'

'No. A friend is worried about Tasha and asked me to find her.'

'See me at the club, I don't have the dancers' contact info at home.' He fumbled for his house key on a thick ring.

'I'm also looking for Eve Michaels.'

'She's out of town.' Not looking at her.

'Where could I find her?' Claudia asked.

'I don't know.'

'You don't know what town she went to?'

'You have ten seconds to get off my porch,' he said. 'Then I call the cops.'

'Eve Michaels is missing, isn't she? Won't one more investigation fill up your date book, Mr Polo?'

He crossed his arms. 'Eve and I had our differences. She left town for a while. Satisfied?'

'She got a cell phone?'

'Not for strangers to call.'

'I'm not exactly a stranger. I'm Claudia Salazar. I'm a friend of Whit's and Gooch's.' She watched his face; he gave no reaction to their names. 'Is Eve dead? Did the Bellinis kill her? Or José Peron?'

'I don't know what you mean,' Frank said. 'Eve wanted time alone.'

'Time away from her son? Whit's her son, isn't he?'

Now he studied her and said, 'I can give you her cell phone number if you want.'

'That would be great, thanks.'

'I don't have it memorized,' he said. 'You know how it is, you press the speed dial code. My phone's inside. You're welcome to come in.' Suddenly friendly, the frost gone. 'Or wait out here.' Like knowing he'd been too friendly.

'I'll come in. Thank you.'

'I was about to make coffee,' Frank Polo said. He stopped, tossed his suit coat onto the chair, closed the door behind her. 'You want a cup? You could even try Eve's cell phone from here.'

She pasted on a warm smile. Get him talking; people nearly always told you more than they thought they would. 'That'd be great. My sister's a big fan of yours.'

'Oh. Well. Thanks,' he said. Thanking her for her sister's devotion to disco seemed strange, but then what else was he going to say? She wondered, a moment too late, if saying her sister rather than she was a big fan was an insult. But Frank Polo didn't seem to care. 'Whit know you're here?'

'Yes.' It seemed the prudent answer. Claudia followed Frank to the kitchen, watched him putter with filter, grounds, and water over the brewer. He turned to her, leaned against the counter, and smiled again.

'I'm a bad guy, Claudia. I told you a little white lie,' Frank said. 'Eve didn't leave because of an argument. She left because of Whit.'

Claudia waited.

'Him being her kid, looking for her. Finding her. It upset her. Deeply.'

'I'm sure it was a shock.'

'For me, too. I didn't even know she had a kid.'

'She has six of them. All boys. Whit is the youngest.'

'Six? God Almighty.' The coffee maker gurgled in the quiet. 'If you're Whit's friend, maybe you can help convince him to give her a little space.'

'She didn't leave town because of Paul Bellini?'

'Why would she?'

'Things could be a little tough at the office now. You both worked for him.'

Frank took down two coffee mugs from a cabinet, gave her a blank smile. 'Technically, I work for a holding company that owns Topaz.'

'Owned by Tommy Bellini, a mobster.'

Frank shrugged, put out milk, sugar, sweetener. 'Former mobster. Tommy's a good guy who, in his past, did bad things. It doesn't make him a bad person if he's good at heart.'

'My actions don't matter because I define myself as good?' Claudia said. 'Sorry, that excuse chafes me.'

'We all have our life philosophies.' Frank poured coffee into her mug, pushed the sugar bowl toward her. 'Look, she doesn't want to have anything to do with Whit, okay? I know those words hurt. The poor kid, it breaks your heart.'

'She leaves town right at the same time that Kiko Grace and Paul Bellini are murdered?' Claudia shook her head. 'I'm wondering, what triggered all this bloodshed, Mr Polo?'

'I don't know who Kiko Grace is.'

She watched him, sipped the coffee. 'Kiko Grace is a drug lord from Miami. He was found shot to death the day after Paul was. Two major crime figures gone in short order. Now something or someone set that off. Maybe Eve.' She put down her coffee.

'You must be looking for work to keep your mind busy. Are you another PI? Or a lawyer?'

'I'm a police investigator down in Port Leo, where Whit's from. But I'm not here in any official capacity. I'm here as his friend.'

'You could have told me that from the beginning,' Frank said, almost reproachfully.

'I didn't want you to run from me being a cop,' she said. 'But I'm not going to lie when you ask me, either.'

'I'm not allergic to cops,' Frank said. He smiled. 'The Bellinis have lots of cop friends. Always have.'

'Great,' she said. 'For my own curiosity, or a memento for Whit if Eve doesn't want to see him again, would you have a picture of her I could keep?'

He seemed to weigh his options. 'For Whit? Let me see.' He set his coffee down, wandered off down a hallway. She didn't like him out of her sight, but it was his house, she knew the risks of stepping inside. She noticed a picture of Frank and a woman hanging on a dining room wall, beyond the kitchen.

The woman was pretty, must have been drop-dead gorgeous in her shallow youth, fine-featured, high-cheekboned, thin lips parted in an honest smile for the camera. She looked normal, nothing bent or broken within her that would make her leave her family, her children, run off with an embezzler, perhaps kill him, then join a crime family. She didn't look like a mom who'd bake cookies for the PTA but she looked like a mom who'd let you eat ice cream until you got sick. Whit looked like her, Claudia could really see the resemblance, across the eyes, the mouth, the cheekbones, and she bit her lip, her heart full for Whit.

Frank Polo came back into the kitchen, holding a small photo. She stepped back into the kitchen to meet him and he handed her the picture. 'Took that last year on a trip to Cozumel. It's a good likeness of Eve.'

Claudia took the photo. The same woman, wearing Capri pants and a white blouse, turquoise jewelry at her throat, smiling in bright sunlight. 'You know, her name isn't Eve. It's Ellen.' The woman named Ellen should have had a life with her sons. As she looked at the picture, an acid dislike for Ellen Mosley settled in her mouth.

'Ellen. It doesn't fit her. Too Sunday-school teacher.'

'Where is she, Mr Polo?'

'I told you I don't know.'

'I find it hard to believe that if she left because of Whit, she didn't tell you where she was going.' But her voice stayed friendly.

'She didn't want Whit strong-arming it out of me,' Frank said.

'I know you know,' Claudia said.

'Trust me,' he said. 'I don't. Having your unwanted kid show up is enough to make a woman like Eve run for cover. There's nothing else to it.'

'All right,' she said. 'Does that mean you're not going to give me her number?'

He went to an address book, wrote down numbers and an address, handed them to her.

'Tasha Strong's phone number and address. Eve's number. Good luck.' Tasha Strong's address was on Telephone Road, a major thoroughfare near Hobby Airport.

'Greg Buckman,' she said. 'You know him, too.'

He let three beats pass. 'Yes. Worked at Energis, the jerk. Bad freaking influence on Paul.'

'A bad influence on a mobster.'

'Paul's not a mobster. No matter what you think. But Bucks, he's a greedy, mean bastard.'

'Yet, when Bucks nearly gets killed the other night, he comes running to you. To this house,' Claudia said. 'It's odd.'

'He probably thought Paul would be here.'

'But Paul was dead by then. See, if Bucks killed Paul, he sure wouldn't have come to your house afterwards and sat waiting for you. He'd leave Houston.'

'People are idiots,' Frank said. 'Haven't you noticed? I haven't really talked to Bucks since Paul died.'

'Because the police are watching you all.'

'Are they? No one's at my door or window,' Frank said. 'And like I said, it's been nice talking to you.'

'Bucks could turn, cut a deal. Say you and Eve are more to the Bellinis than family friends. With Paul dead, the structure may crumble and crush you underneath it.'

'Sweetheart,' he said. 'I'm not doing a half-assed plea deal. Because I didn't do anything wrong. I'm going on with my life. I got to get my throat into shape, practice my arpeggios and finger snaps and hip swivels.'

'I'm glad you have your priorities.'

'You want to help your friend. You know, I like Whit. I know it's tough. Losing his mom. I loved my mom. She was the best person, next to Eve, I've known. Don't look surprised. Eve is a wonderful person. You don't know her.'

'Thanks for the coffee,' Claudia said.

'If Eve calls,' Frank said, 'I'll leave it up to her whether or not she wants to talk to you. Since you're Whit's friend. You got a number where I can reach you?'

'Yeah.' She set down the purse on the counter, dug inside for paper and pen, pulled them out. Wrote down her cell phone number. Handed it back to him.

'You seem like a nice young lady,' Frank said. 'I know Whit's your friend and you want to help him. Can I give you friendly advice?'

'Sure,' Claudia said, not wanting to burn this bridge quite yet.

'Stay out of this. It's between a mother and son. Or two people wondering if they can be a mother and son. Let them sort it out.' He gave her his best smile. 'You still want an autograph? For your sister?'

'Sign it to me. I'll make her jealous. I don't suppose . . . well, you're famous. Would you have a photo of yourself on hand?'

'I always do,' Frank said.

Claudia drove away from the house, sure his eyes were watching her from the window.

From her car seat, a thirty-years-younger, open-shirted Frank Polo smiled at her, the words TO CLAUDIA, YOU'RE MY GROOVE! YOUR FRIEND, FRANK POLO scrawled beneath his then-perfect chin.

Frank watched her leave. Nice young woman but clearly not the kind who would give up. He closed his eyes, rested his forehead against the cool of the glass.

He wanted Eve back so bad. Whit was right. The best answer was to deal with one more devil.

44

'José Peron has Eve,' Frank said. 'He therefore has the money.'

Bucks sat across from him at the dining room table Monday night, hands steepled in front of his mouth. 'I knew it.'

'Greg,' Frank said, and Bucks looked up, a little surprised at the use of his first name. No one but his parents and Robin, who wasn't even talking to him now, ever called him by his given name. 'You're the dirty guy here. The police know that you're dirty because José tried to hit you. They'll keep digging until they find evidence to truly connect you with José, Kiko, or Paul. It's over. Your only hope is that money. You can do anything, go anywhere with it. Brazil. Ecuador. Thailand. Places where cash shuts folks up and they never ask questions.'

'You want me to have the money?'

'I just want Eve back if she's still alive,' Frank said. 'That's all.'

'Because you care,' Bucks said.

'Because I love her,' Frank said. 'You don't have much time. Robin's not gonna keep her mouth shut for long once the police start leaning on her.'

'Robin doesn't know shit.'

'Son, women always know more than you think they do. Look at Tasha. I heard she's taken off. Because she knows too much about Paul and she don't want the police bugging her. Or us whacking her to keep her quiet.'

'I'm not whacking Robin.' Bucks found, to his surprise, he was really missing her. She wouldn't talk to him. He had never felt so alone in his life, even with Chad Channing's reassuring words playing in his head for company.

'You act like you still have choices.' Frank shook his head. 'The police can haul you in at any minute, lean on you hard if you're not cooperating with them about why José tried to kill you. Paul's dead. And you're the one doing the dirty work for him and for Kiko both. Trying to play them against each other has left you on the bottom, son.'

'I didn't . . .'

'Save it,' Frank said. 'I can guess what went down. How long do you live if Paul's guys knew you'd helped Kiko?'

Bucks swallowed. 'I didn't have a choice, Frank, I . . .'

'It seems to me, though,' Frank said, like he didn't care about excuses, 'you and I are the ones that truly suffered.'

'What?'

'I've lost the woman I love. You've been through hell.'

Bucks looked like he hadn't slept in two days. He'd shaved, but missed spots, and one scraggly bit of stubble lay along the edge of his cheek. The immaculate grooming was slipping. 'So why are you even talking to me, Frank? If I screwed Paul so bad, why do you want me to have the money?'

'You in jail is a bad thing. Not just for you. For everyone. The pressure on you to talk will be huge. And any friends of Kiko, they believe you killed him and that's why José tried to kill you, well, they'll whack you in jail. Simple as a phone call.'

Bucks raised an eyebrow. 'But that would take care of the problem of me.'

Frank cleared his throat, tented his hands under his chin. 'How about a private little deal between you and me? You take care of José, you get Eve and the money back. You give half the money to me and Eve, you keep the other half for yourself, and nobody ever knows you screwed over Paul. I'll keep my mouth shut.'

'I didn't kill Paul.'

'I don't think you did. You know they found Gooch's van where Paul died?'

Bucks said nothing.

'Wasn't in the paper. I know that from Whit Mosley. Now, what does that suggest to you?' Frank said quietly.

'Whit killed him.'

'Getting Gooch back.'

'I'm not gonna kill Whit Mosley because he killed Paul,' Bucks said. 'I'm out of the ring. I don't do revenge.'

'Then get rid of Whit because he can bring you down. Keep you from the money. If Eve's dead, he has no further reason to try to deal with you. Eve is his mother.' Frank watched Bucks blink. 'So Whit, eventually, will tell everything to the cops. That you tried to have him and Eve killed, you kidnapped his friend, you're in with drug dealers. But if you and I have Eve, the money, and plane tickets, our worries are pretty much over.'

'You act like you know where José has the money,' Bucks said.

'Oh, I do.' Frank pulled a Sig Sauer out from under the table, leveled it at Bucks. 'But you get rid of Whit for me. He's willing to meet you because he thinks you know where José has Eve. And José called him, told him Eve was still alive.'

'Why do you want him dead?'

'I want Eve with me, not her kid. He's a judge down on the coast. She goes with him, she gives up our life together, and I'm not letting her go.'

'Wow, you're a really romantic old fart. So where's the money, Frank?' Bucks asked, the low growl coming back into his voice. 'Tell me or no deal at all. You want Whit dead, that's sweet with me.'

'They're at an old warehouse off Mississippi,' Frank said. 'I know the dealers in this town, the big ones who like to come to the club, and I got more eyes than a fly. Our time's running out, son. You take Whit with you, he'll fight these guys to save his mom, you get the money, we get Eve. But make sure Whit doesn't make it out alive.'

'Can I state the obvious?' Bucks said. 'I could risk getting killed, take the money myself, and why should I worry about saving Eve?'

'Because, if you don't, I'll tell the cops you killed Kiko.' Frank watched Bucks. Frank knew that Bucks probably thought José had the movie, had taken it after killing Kiko, because if the police had found it, then his Brooks Brothers ass would be behind bars, getting warmed up to be a jail boss's new bitch. Bucks didn't know Whit and Frank had both seen the movie.

'But I didn't.'

'But you had every reason to, didn't you, Bucks?'

Bucks tented his cheek with his tongue. Frank waited. Let the greed and the fear work their magic. It wasn't that different from dealing with music promoters. If you appeared quiet and relaxed, not desperate to sing, even if every fiber in your body was screeching *please, God, book me, please let me get up onstage because I know they will love me* then the other person usually blinked first. Frank never wanted a real agent, not when he had Tommy to cut the infrequent deals. He had watched and learned.

'All right,' Bucks said. 'You got a deal. Get Mosley here.' He gave Frank a wicked little smile. 'Chad Channing always said you should turn enemies into friends if it shortens your to-do list.'

'Gomez will kill me for pulling this stunt,' Vernetta said, changing lanes to get around a stalled bus.

'You don't work for him,' Claudia said.

'No,' Vernetta said. 'But he'll kill my boss, and then, with his dying breath, my boss will shoot me.'

Tasha Strong lived in one of the many complexes near Hobby Airport, along Telephone Road. The complexes lay in a steady necklace, with withered yards and peeling paint. Monday evening was settling in for another long stretch of unease. Claudia had hijacked Vernetta at the Harris County Courthouse as she got off work, insisting that Vernetta come with her to find Tasha Strong.

'He won't shoot you. He'll fire you. Think positive,' Claudia said.

'I'll see if the Bellinis are hiring,' Vernetta said. She pointed at one decrepit apartment building. 'Love what they've done with it. A Chinese gang here took over a wing of one of these complexes, ran a whorehouse and peddled dope out of it. They had elementary school kids as their gofers.' She shook her head. 'If I don't sound caustic, I'll cry.'

'Here. This is the address.'

'Gomez and his team already tried to get in touch with her,' Vernetta said. 'No dice.'

'Yes, but we're not the scary police, are we?'

'You are. You've scared me since you came into town,' Vernetta said. She pulled into the parking lot, past three hard-faced working girls. The bored ladies watched them ease into a slot and walk across to the stairs, up to apartment 325.

Claudia knocked. No answer. But she could hear the soft strains of a radio playing on the other side of the door.

'Tasha? Tasha Strong?' she called softly. 'I'm a friend of Robin Melvin's. She's worried about you. Please open up.'

The door opened. An old woman stood there, dressed in a faded pink robe and a maroon baseball cap. 'Tasha don't live here,' she said. 'Sorry.'

'Hello, ma'am. Do you know where we could find her?' Claudia said, ignoring the woman's blunt manner.

'No,' the old woman said. 'She's gone for good.'

Claudia and Vernetta looked at each other, then at the old woman. 'I'm sorry, ma'am, when did Tasha leave?' Claudia asked after a moment.

'Who are you?'

Vernetta and Claudia both showed their official IDs. 'Oh, God,' the old woman said. 'She's in trouble, I'm sure of it, but she won't help herself get out and she sure won't listen to me.'

'We can help her,' Vernetta said.

'Come inside, then,' the woman said. They came inside the apartment. It was small but clean, although there was a clutter of a tea mug, tissues, a rumpled newspaper. A cane was next to the door and the woman used it as she headed back for a chair. 'Gettin' over flu,' she said. 'Shouldn't be contagious any more. Sit.'

'Are you Tasha's mother?' Claudia asked.

'Grandmother,' the woman said. 'Mrs Annie Strong.' She sat. 'I don't hold with lying, and I haven't slept well since the police called looking for her. Tasha asked me to lie for her, and I can't do it no more because you folks are gonna keep knocking on my door.'

'What lie did she want you to tell?'

'First Tasha told me that if anyone came looking for her, say she was dead. Not to say she moved, or gone on a trip, but dead. Killed in a car accident in New Orleans, that was her story. Showed me what looked like a death certificate she'd faked up. I said you're crazy, girl, what kind of trouble you in?' Mrs Strong shook her head. 'That's a tall order to give me, after I done half the raising of her. I told her I'd tell people she'd left town, but not that she was dead.' Mrs Strong spit out the last word.

'So where is she?'

Mrs Strong shook her head. 'I don't know. She ain't lived here in years.'

'She gave this as her address to her employer.'

'Huh. She got her community college degree, she moved uptown fast. Left me in the dust. Came to see me when it suited her.'

Claudia remembered Robin's mention of the photos. 'Does Darius live here?'

The old woman closed her eyes for a moment. 'Darius, he really dead. Five years ago. Out playing basketball down the street with a group of boys who dealt. Other group of boys shot at 'em all. Killed Darius. He was fifteen.' She leaned against the door. 'Fifteen-year-olds killin' each other for crack. Tasha, got everything in the world going for her, she tells me to tell the world she's dead because she's in bad trouble she won't let nobody help her fix. Like I could bear her and Darius both dead. It would kill me. I can't pull off such a lie for her. I ain't doing it. No. Ain't doing it. You find her. Please.'

'She's running because of what happened to Paul Bellini,' Vernetta said as they drove away.

'But why would a woman whose brother was killed by drug dealers take up with a drug lord?'

'She didn't know Bellini's business.'

'She knows enough to be scared, so she's asking her grand-mother to do clumsy lying for her,' Claudia said. 'Can you ask HPD to look for her?'

'If she's a witness, or she's charged in a crime. But if she's left willingly and doesn't want to be found, well, you hire another PI to find her.'

'What?'

'If she's left willingly . . .'

'No,' Claudia said. 'You said *another PI*.'

'Yeah. I was thinking of your friend Harry. Like him looking for Eve Michaels.'

Frank Polo said something about another PI, when she was getting ready to leave his house. Another, like he'd known of a first one. Harry. Perhaps Whit had told Frank about Harry. Of course. Yes. Probably.

The thought irritated her brain like a thorn prick. Whoever killed Harry had stripped him of his ID. Possibly of his notes on the Eve Michaels case; none of those had been found by the police, and she knew Harry kept his notes with him. There was a simple way to test her theory. 'Have they identified all the prints at the Chyme/ Doyle murder scene?'

'I don't know. Gomez would. I don't even know if they have suspect prints to compare to.'

'How quickly could Gomez get prints done?' she asked.

'Why?'

'That photo of Frank Polo that's on my back seat,' Claudia said. 'Let's put it under the powder, see what shows.'

45

At ten on Monday night, the front door of Frank and Eve's house stood open, a rectangle of glowing light in the darkness. Whit stepped inside.

Frank's phone call to him had been quiet and calm: *Bucks is here and wants to talk. We have a plan. Make no mention you have the film, he doesn't need to know. Come alone.* And so Whit had walked past the doctors and nurses and families facing down death at the ICU, left a sleeping Gooch behind and driven to Frank's house in Charlie's borrowed Lexus.

'Come on in,' a voice called from the den. Unhurried, relaxed.

Whit walked into the den and Bucks sat at the edge of the couch. Pistol in hand, but pointed down at the floor. His suit was rumpled, his tie gone, the black eye Whit gave him in full bruising bloom.

'You want your mom back?' he asked.

'Where is she, you bastard?' Whit said. But calm.

'Frank knows,' Bucks said.

'So where's Frank?'

'I'm here, Whit.' Frank stood in the doorway.

'Truce,' Bucks said. 'Because we're all buddies now. We're all on the same side. Got a proposal for you.'

Whit waited.

'You could have brought the police,' Bucks said. 'You didn't. I could kill you. I won't. We got to trust each other. At least for the next few hours.' He smiled. 'I admire your steadfast focus.'

'Give me a minute to come up with a compliment about you,' Whit said. 'Maybe an hour.'

'Peace treaty, okay? I know you don't have the money.'

303

'So why help us now?' Whit glanced over at Frank. 'Need good deeds for extra credit?'

'José's the bad guy,' Bucks said. 'We get your mom, we get the money, and then we're all fine.'

'And we all go our separate ways.'

'Yes, Whit. And never open our mouths. You want mommy with you, right, not dead or rotting in jail or worrying about getting whacked. I want a nice little house on a beach that doesn't extradite.'

'Where is she?' Whit said.

'A warehouse off Mississippi Street, not far from the Port. Used to be used by a South American importer who brought up fake pre-Colombian art, Guatemalan weaving, hippie crap,' Frank said.

'You know this how?'

'Frank got a paid tip.'

'It cost me a thousand in cash, Whit,' Frank said quietly. 'A regular dealer who is a good customer at the Topaz and liked Paul told me. José's started to put word on the street he wants to deal the coke. The information is valid.'

'I'd like to talk to this informant,' Whit said.

'He doesn't want to talk to you, though. You can appreciate that, can't you, Whit?' Frank said.

'Be cool, Whit. That warehouse, if they don't have Eve there, we force them to tell us where she's at.'

'So our solution is simple,' Whit said. 'We call the police, have them raid the warehouse, arrest everybody.'

'That will get Eve killed. Or in prison for the rest of her life. You don't get your mom either way. Remember, José knows about your mom and . . . Montana, Whit,' Frank said. 'You don't want José caught but cutting a deal with prosecutors, that hurts your mom.'

Bucks asked, 'What about Montana?'

Whit said, 'Never mind.' He watched Frank.

'No police,' Bucks said. 'José and I got our own issues to settle. He killed Paul, right?'

'Whit, it's simple. We attack the warehouse. Rescue Eve, force José to turn over the money. José has the money, Whit. You were right, it's the only explanation. He's got it all. He killed Doyle and your friend Harry. We get Eve and then we all part ways.' Frank crossed his arms.

'And the two of you are millionaires,' Whit said.

'You too, if you want,' Bucks said.

'But your mother is safe, Whit. She can be with you,' Frank said. 'The police don't have anything hard on her. And if they do, we can hide her for a long while with that money. You won't lose her again.'

'I don't want any of that cash,' Whit said. 'None of it.'

'I like you more and more,' Bucks said.

'So what's the plan?' Whit said. Getting into bed with the devil.

'You and me,' Bucks said. 'We go there, kick ass, save your mom.'

'I'll stay here,' Frank said.

'No,' Whit said after a moment. 'You come with us.'

'I want to, Whit,' Frank said. 'But I'm not a young man, I'm not good with guns.'

'You're coming with us, Frank,' Whit said. 'End of discussion.'

Three a.m. Tuesday morning, and they were on the 610 Loop, and Frank Polo sat in the back of the Jag, fighting down the temptation gnawing at him. Bucks drove, Whit sitting next to him. It would be easy to blast Whit's head open, nuzzle the warm, bloodied gun barrel against Bucks' neck, get him to pull over, kill him, take the Jag and head down to Galveston Island. Wait for the bank to open in the early morning light. Open the big safety-deposit box where he'd hidden the five million. That was a siren song that played constantly in Frank's ear. But now was the time for self-control. To be cool.

Because the money without Eve was nice but not what he wanted.

If Frank thought about Eve too much, he would cry, and he hated that. He hoped it had ended quickly for her if she were dead. Painlessly, a single bullet in the brain. He knew she wouldn't have screamed or begged, if she could help it. She was stone-solid, stronger and better than him, just as he had told Whit. But he believed she was alive. He wished it hadn't unfolded this way; it wasn't supposed to. His plan was to frame Bucks cleanly for killing Richard Doyle, plant a little of the cash in Bucks' condo, a hundred thousand to make him look guilty, urge Paul to have Bucks whacked and then, within a year or so, part ways with the Bellinis, head to the West Coast, quietly vanish with Eve. But Paul decided to send Eve to the meeting and screwed up everything. Life twisted back on you, but a smart guy could make it work out in the end. It was the kind of self-boosting thought Bucks lived by, but it was true.

Five million in cash to see him through retirement, an extra bit to finance cutting a new record. Dance beats were back in. Tony Bennett, after all, still wowed the kids. He could be Tony Bennett with a beat. Have sexy backup dancers. Wear a suit that made him look cool and trim. Eve in the front row every night in Vegas, clapping for him. He could see it.

But saving Eve, maybe that wouldn't work. All this was going to do was to get Bucks killed and Whit caught and maybe dead. Because that was his deal with José. Trade Whit and Bucks for Eve.

That was okay. Because if José won, Bucks and Whit were dead, and if Bucks and Whit won, they'd see José had no money. But they wouldn't, couldn't blame Frank. Bucks would still have to kill Whit. And Frank would kill Bucks, do it all in front of Eve so she'd think he'd avenged her son's death. That'd be good.

Now he was halfway to free. Free, if he didn't dwell on Richard Doyle begging him not to shoot, saying he was a father; didn't think about the PI giving him a glare of such defiant bravery Frank almost couldn't pull the trigger, didn't remember how he'd wanted to vomit after he'd killed them, then how he wanted to scream at the top of his lungs as he drove away with five million in cash, knowing he and Eve would finally be on their way.

The plan hadn't worked out exactly right, but it was going to work out tonight if he didn't lose his nerve.

He watched the back of Whit's head. Even the guy's head reminded him of Eve, that slight tilt of it when he listened. Eve could never know he was behind her son's death. He'd comfort her when this was done, take her shopping, get her a puppy, whatever she wanted.

Frank started to hum his favorite of his hits, 'When You Walk Away,' thinking that Bucks and Whit, each trying to out-macho the other in the face of what was coming, weren't doing nearly a good enough job watching their backs.

A few cars streamed past them on the mighty highways, constellations of lights spread across the coastal plains bleared by fog and mist.

'At another point in our lives, Whit,' Bucks said, 'we might have been friends.' Bucks drove easily, fingertips barely on the wheel of the Jag. The night traffic was intermittent along the 610 Loop. Bucks had a tape playing in the console, but it wasn't music. A low, thin, cajoling voice of a man on the tape: '. . . and when you visualize your goal, you actualize your goal. That's how you make the life you dream . . .' – dramatic pause – '. . . the life you lead.'

Frank sat in the back seat. Mad about coming, scared, Whit thought, but making a real effort not to show it. Whit glanced back at Frank. He hummed, gazing into the night. Gave Whit a wan smile.

'Friends. Yes. Perhaps as babies,' Whit said.

'How's Gooch?' Bucks asked.

'Better.'

'Him I like,' Bucks said. 'I could've used about a dozen of him with Paul. Kiko wouldn't have messed with us then.'

'But Kiko had you on his side,' Whit said. 'What else did he need?'

'That was an extremely temporary arrangement,' Bucks said.

'You betrayed your best friend,' Whit said. 'You won't have a qualm about shooting me and Frank and Eve if this rescue works out. So understand this. I took precautions. A lot of them before I stepped into the snake pit tonight. And if I get screwed over, so do you.'

'Precautions,' Frank repeated. A thin little smile came and went on Bucks' face, like Whit was trying a high-schooler's bluff in hopes of being cool.

'The only precautions you need to worry about,' Bucks said, 'is doing what I tell you.'

'Wrong,' Whit said. 'You're not in charge.'

'I know the warehouse,' Bucks said. 'You don't. You want to walk straight in and get your ass shot off? Listen to me and I'll tell you the layout.'

Whit waited.

'These warehouses, the Bellinis used one like it before, a few blocks over. The layouts are all the same. It has two bays for the trucks, has a glass door on the side, there's a little office space off from the storage area. Probably that's where they're keeping Eve. We go in through the office door,' Bucks said. 'Frank, too, if he wants to go, if he's got his dick screwed on now.'

'Your dick's on now, right, Frank?' Whit said.

'Ha ha,' Frank said.

'Walk right in,' Whit said.

'No,' Bucks said. 'Probably have guards watching the lot. We'll take care of them first.'

'Take care of,' Whit said.

'Shoot if we have to,' Bucks said. 'You want your mommy back, right?' He didn't quite make it a sneer. 'You know, you must create your own moral center, Whit. You can't get that from your parents.'

'Then what?' Whit said. 'Storm the door?'

'No. Go in quiet if we can. Shoot anyone we see we don't like. Grab Eve, grab José, grab the money if it's there. If it's not then José's my worry, not yours. He'll talk.'

Whit was silent. He wondered how close a coffin would feel. If you were really, truly dead it was a mercy if you couldn't know the tight quarters of the casket, the bare inch of air between your lips and the coffin silk. Then wondering if he could stand by and watch people get shot. Not innocent people. But still. He couldn't. Not in cold blood. So he would have to change Bucks' plan. 'What if we get caught?' Whit asked.

'Don't be dense,' Bucks said. 'They kill us.'

Bucks turned onto the Clinton exit off 610, turned right onto Mississippi. The warehouse was one in a long chain of dreary industrial buildings, the lamps giving off faint light.

'That's it,' Bucks said. He drove on by, four blocks, then turned into a small office building. Two cars were parked far back in the shadows, men inside them. Waiting.

'Oh, shit,' Frank said. Whit's guts turned to slush.

'This wasn't part of the deal . . .' Frank said.

'I took precautions, too, boys,' Bucks said, and in the moonlight his smile was ugly.

'You don't need to know names,' Bucks told Whit and Frank as the men stood in the cold of the night behind the office building. But Whit could guess. One man looked like the guy who'd shot at him on the chase on the 610 Loop, owlish eyes watching Whit with the careful regard of an accountant. Frank had said he was called the Wart. Two other men, one heavy, the other lanky and wearing dreadlocks. Associates of the dead MacKay, Whit guessed, looking for a little payback. No one said hello.

'Too many,' Frank said to Bucks. 'Too much. Not what we discussed.'

Whit thought: *too much for what, we need all the strength we can get.* 'Jesus, Frank, quit worrying about how much money's left at the end.'

'Frank, hush and let the men work,' Bucks said. 'Guys. Here's the drill.' He explained they wanted Eve alive, they wanted the money, mostly they wanted José Peron, who was responsible for MacKay's death and who had stolen five million from its rightful owners. 'We've got a goal, men. A goal we can reach.' His voice deepened and Whit realized he sounded like the low murmuring on the tape in his car, talking in the same empty cadence of blank reassurance. He described how they would approach the lot, fast and silent. If José and Eve weren't inside, they'd take what was of value and leave. 'Keep an eye open for any DVDs. José stored info on them I need. I'll pay a bonus for any you find.'

In the dark, behind Bucks, Frank nudged Whit.

Bucks turned to Whit. 'You want to go first? She's your mama.'

'That's fine,' Whit said.

'Don't worry, Whit,' said Bucks. 'I'll be right behind you.'

They moved down a maze of alleys that reeked of dog piss and uncollected trash. Too many of the offices and warehouses had been empty for too long, dragged down in the latest economic stumble. A cloying mist hung in the night. Whit had the gun Gooch had given him, another gun tucked in the small of his back, and a small knife strapped above his ankle, all from Charlie's weapons collection. But the heavyset Jamaican walking by him toted an assault rifle, and he felt unprepared.

'This is it,' Bucks said. The six men hung back in the alleyway, surveying the parking lot of the warehouse. A high fence, topped with barbed wire, separated the lot from the adjoining side road. An office light gleamed through the glass door. Three cars were parked nearby; Whit recognized one. A little red Honda. Tasha Strong's car that she'd driven over to Frank and Eve's. He started to speak, thought, and stayed quiet.

They waited ten minutes. No movement or sound in the lot.

'No guard,' Whit said.

'We go over the fence, then through the side truck bay, the service door. Quietly. I got skeleton keys. Surprise them. Surprise is critical,' Bucks said.

They waited another two minutes; no sign of movement.

'Trevor, Wart, go,' Bucks whispered and the thin Jamaican and the Wart hurried forward. Trevor lifted the Wart up high; Wart started cutting the stretch of barbed wire at the top of the fencing. Trevor balanced Wart on his palms, and the ribbon of wire curled away as Wart moved down the fence.

Then Trevor boosted Wart over the fence. He eased himself down on the other side, carefully, then dropped to the asphalt. Whit, Bucks, and Heavy Jamaican began to scale the fence, Trevor helping them. Frank hung back.

'Frank, shake your ass up here,' Bucks said.

Frank started to climb, tentatively.

Whit was over the fence, trying to be silent in making his jump down, when the shadow bulleted out from the other side of the lot, beelining toward Wart, who was crouched over, waiting for the rest of them.

Whit said, 'Oh, no,' loudly, as he dropped to the pavement next to Bucks and the bullet, a sleek Doberman the color of night, launched itself at Wart. The dog took him down in the shoulders, hammered him to the concrete. A horrible tearing noise rose from their struggle; a spray of blood shot across the asphalt. Teeth sunk into flesh and ripped with ingrained precision.

Wart screamed once as the dog yanked him around by the neck, as fangs found new hold. Bucks and Trevor fired. The dog yelped, twisted, then Bucks put a bullet right in the dog's skull. Wart lay there, groaning, cupping his hands under his chin, the blood welling.

Whit turned and the second dog was arrowing right for him, eyes locked to his throat, snout down, ten paces away and Whit fired, the silencer Bucks had attached to his gun making a soft-bark sound, firing once, twice, catching the dog in its leap, the bullets tearing dogflesh from ribs and it fell, thudding into him, knocking him to the ground. But dying. Whit climbed out from under the dog; it made a last, feeble attempt to snap, to fend off the dark, then shivered into stillness.

'They know we're here now,' Bucks said. 'Rush it, full frontal.' He and the Jamaicans charged the office door, Whit kneeling by Wart. He was fading, gone as Whit touched his wrist, the carotid and jugular torn, his throat nothing but wound, the neck broken. His eyes were still open in shock at the sudden, end-it-all turn.

Whit glanced back over at the fence.

Frank was gone, fled into the dark of the alley.

Whit turned and headed for the building; a couple of sharp pops from Bucks' gun shattered the door glass, loud in the quiet of the industrial park. Bucks reached inside, flipped the locks.

They were in, Heavy taking the lead and Whit coming in last.

The entry office was dimly lit, an empty desk, a mountain of old newspapers scattered around the room. The smell of gasoline – rich, unexpected – filled the air. Two gas canisters stood on the side of the desk. Whit stopped. The canisters were full but capped. Waiting to be used or moved.

Bucks gestured down the hall, and Heavy Jamaican bolted down it, laying a spray of suppressing fire, tearing chunks out of the wall and ceiling. At the end of the hall a metal warehouse door stood shut.

'Wait,' Whit called, 'they're torching the warehouse?' But Heavy and Trevor and Bucks were blasting the door, charging into the warehouse proper, and now there was an answering hail of shots, an intense staccato of bullets and screams.

He barreled down the hall, after Trevor and Bucks, and went through the door. A storm of gunfire met his ears, battle in full rage, shrieks, the horrible sound of metal impacting flesh.

They had been waiting for them. Two men, taking cover behind boxes twenty feet beyond the door, emptying rifles, Heavy stumbling as blood erupted from his chest. No sign of Trevor but then the men behind the boxes screamed, fell. Bucks charged past a wall of boxes and gave out a bloodcurdling yell. More gunfire erupted to Whit's right, from two different guns. A moment of quiet. Then bullets shot by his head and Whit dove down, skidding on the concrete floor, crabbing for cover behind a set of crates near the door, Spanish scrawled along their sides. Bullets ripping into the wood.

He heard his mother scream his name.

46

'Whit!' Eve screamed. 'Get out!'

Whit stayed down on the floor, his gun close to his head. She must have seen him come through the door; he hadn't seen her. He heard sobbing. Then he heard a soft cussing. Bucks, in pain, angrily moaning.

But no more shooting. Over in thirty seconds that felt like thirty hours. He closed his eyes, forced himself to breathe quietly.

'Whit,' a voice called. José Peron's. 'Come out now. Or I shoot her.'

'He'll shoot me anyway,' Eve said. Her voice calmer now, ordering him. 'Get out!'

Whit risked a look past the crating. The warehouse space was huge, but most of the shooting had taken place in an open area within thirty feet of the door. Wooden crates stood stacked, haphazardly, and José and his group had quickly retreated behind the boxes. A forklift sat idle in a corner. A small space had been cleared behind a tower of boxes, and worn chairs and a desk were grouped there.

Heavy lay in a heap by a desk, half his face gone, two men Whit had not seen before dead near him, heads and chests bloodied messes. Heavy had kept shooting after he went down, probably taking the two men with him, and the concrete floor was scarred and chipped with bullet hits. Whit could not see Trevor, but Trevor wasn't shooting and he hoped the man had found cover. Tasha Strong stood over Bucks, a gun locked at his temple, relieving him of his pistol. Bucks bled from a leg wound, had his palms open in surrender. And José stood, looking to Whit's right, listening like a wolf for the scrabble of the rabbit in the grass.

Whit aimed at José, who didn't see him but stepped behind the forklift. No clear shot. Whit ducked back behind the crate.

'I'm counting to three, then I'm shooting your mother if you don't come out, toss the gun out, arms up,' José said. 'One. Two.' Counting fast.

'I'm counting to three,' Whit shouted, 'and if you don't release Bucks and my mother, I'm calling the rest of our team outside and telling them to start your office fire for you.'

'Excellence!' Bucks yelled, then groaned. 'That's real excellence!'

'Shut up,' Tasha said. 'Shut your ever-running mouth.'

'Where's my movie?' Bucks said. 'José, you bastard . . .' A shot rang out and Bucks shut up.

'Do you not know what be quiet means?' Tasha said.

But José had stopped his countdown. 'Let's all be cool. Where's the money, Whit?' he called. 'You tell me and I'll let you and your mother go.'

Whit said nothing. *He thinks we still have the money. But that's crazy, he has it.* No, clearly he didn't, and the realization froze Whit's blood.

Frank, running from the fence once Bucks changed the plans. Frank being more than a coward. Maybe Frank hadn't gotten any tip from the street; maybe Frank cut a deal with José to deliver Whit and Bucks. He could hear Frank's voice, smooth, into a phone: *Yeah, say you know about Montana, that'll prove to him you really have his mom.* José wanted Eve to help him, get the rest of the Bellini money for them, and she wouldn't do it. So give them Whit because Eve would help them if they had a gun to his head, give them Bucks to tidy up the last of the loose ends, and Frank was set. That's why he objected to the extra men Bucks brought. Frank thought tonight would be a walk-in and exchange for all intents and purposes, some separate deal cut between him and José.

Whit had thought José knew about Montana because he killed Harry. But whoever killed Harry could have coached José. Frank never knew about Montana until he saw Harry Chyme's notes.

Frank's left us with guns pointing at each other's throats while he has the money.

Whit eased back from the crates. The stack stood five feet high, next to a long wall of shelving, and he abandoned his original position, ducked down, tried to move silently under the shelving, his pistol in front of him.

'Whit!' Eve yelled.

'You. Shut it down,' Tasha said. A hard slap. 'Scout,' Tasha called. The little nickname she'd given him back at the club, a thousand years ago. 'Come on now. Make it easy on her and you, okay?'

Then silence.

Whit knew that in the sudden quiet, José was hunting him. Moving into the maze of crates, not waiting for him to show himself. He moved further back along the wall, heading south, and in a bit of open space he spotted Trevor. Dead on the floor, eyes glassed, a puddle of brainy gunk underneath his head. He'd come around in a swath through the boxes, caught the two guys shooting at Heavy, killing them, before catching a head shot.

An assault rifle lay by his side.

Whit inched over, knowing he was putting himself into the open. But he didn't see Tasha, didn't see José. He carefully picked up the rifle, pulled it close to him, crabbed back behind a crate. It was wicked, an AR-15 he guessed, the kind popular in law enforcement and the military, a sixteen-inch barrel. Maybe thirty rounds in a magazine, he thought Claudia had told him once. No idea how many Trevor had used, the rifle could be empty. He checked the selector lever; it was set on auto.

Near him was a set of metal stairs that led to a catwalk that cut straight over the warehouse space. At the level of the catwalk an array of fluorescent lights, dimmed but active, gleamed.

Climb up there and he would be a dove in the sky, an easy target. But he was getting backed into a corner. He could dash across the remaining open space of the warehouse that he could reach, pray they couldn't see him in time . . . and then what?

He heard footsteps. A soft tread. Coming his way.

In the dim light he backed into the stairway, trying not to clang the rifle barrel against the steel. Looking back he spotted red metal behind him, beyond the stairs. More canisters of gasoline, stacked near another set of crates. Weird, why gas where they had their drugs? Why weren't they getting the cocaine out of here and onto the street as fast as they could? Perhaps the coke was gone. But no, these were the pottery crates that Kiko had smuggled the goods in. Eve had said the dope was in pottery. But hardly a crate opened, the drugs staying put.

Tasha and José didn't want to deal the cocaine. They were going to burn it. Hence the gasoline and flammables in the front office.

Or he could. They were going to kill him and Eve. He could not hide longer than perhaps another two minutes.

He made his choice. He was going to kill people now, including himself, and he fought down the sharp throb of fear and regret in his chest. Because there was no other route, no other way. At the least José wouldn't get away.

Whit closed his eyes, thought of his father, his brothers, Claudia, Gooch. Eve. Said his good-byes.

He opened a canister, gently tipped it over, let the fuel glug out onto the floor.

'Whit. Come out, now.' Twenty feet away from him. 'You give us the money, we'll let you go. We're really not the bad guys here.'

Whit upended another container of gasoline, then a third and a fourth, scurried back from the spreading puddle. The smell rose like swamp gas; José had to know what he was doing. He backed up into stairs that led to the catwalk that crossed the space. Looked up, saw the fluorescents, still dimmed.

'We're not the bad guys,' José repeated. 'We're doing good. We're all about stopping the drug dealing, man.'

Whit stopped, counted the lights, wondered how much they would spark. Either from the electricity being shorted or bullets hitting metal.

José's voice drew closer. 'We call ourselves Public Service, Whit. We rid the world of this scourge of drugs. Your mother's joined us. Willingly. Isn't that right, Eve? She's nodding, Whit. We could use a resourceful guy like you on our side. Don't be afraid. "True nobility is exempt from fear." What we do is truly noble. Let's talk.'

Ten feet now.

'If you join us—' José started.

Whit fired the assault rifle at the canisters, stacked by the fuel he'd poured. They blossomed into flame. Then he spun and ran up the steel steps, fired a long burst at the ceiling, at the array of fluorescents.

The lights shattered, sparking from the gunfire, plummeting into the spreading gasoline. Debris hit his shoulder, cut his arms. He reached the top of the catwalk and heard the *whoo-humph* of the gasoline catching in full fury, felt the sudden heat beneath his feet. The lights flickered in the other half of the warehouse and running hard along the catwalk, harder than he ever had, he saw his mother. Handcuffed to a folding chair, Tasha shoving her toward the office door, José screaming below him, caught in the flush of fire, screaming, screaming, and then not.

Bucks limped after the women, his pants leg torn and bloodied. Whit ran down the stairs at the other end of the catwalk, thinking *Christ was I stupid, the fire moves faster than me* and then he was on the floor, the crates erupting into fire as more canisters exploded, the warehouse's very air seeming to ignite. He dropped the empty assault rifle, grabbed Bucks' arm, hurried him through the splintered warehouse door. Heat rose like a storm surge behind them.

They ran through the outer office into the thin rain of the night. Eve lay on the ground, Tasha standing over her, forcing her to her feet.

'Stop!' Whit yelled. He grabbed the Sig tucked into his pants, tried to bring it to bear.

Tasha spun and fired at them as they came through the busted door and Bucks howled, staggered, fell to his knees. Whit jumped from the concrete steps, no place for cover, fired at Tasha. Missed.

And then Tasha had her gun at Eve's head.

'Scout! Back off!'

The heat flooded the air behind him, rising to an inferno. He aimed the gun at Tasha, at her shoulder. Eve dragged her feet, dragged the chair she was bound to, trying to slow Tasha, pull her off balance.

'Let her go,' Whit yelled.

'You let me walk!' Tasha shouted. 'Or she dies!'

He moved faster toward them.

Eve screamed, 'Whit, run!'

Tasha aimed at Whit, fired as Eve swatted at her arm, and the bullet cracked inches past his head. But Eve and Tasha were too close together for him to shoot.

'Get away from my mother,' Whit shouted.

'You let me walk,' Tasha screamed and Whit said, 'Fine. Fine. Go.'

'What?' Tasha screamed. Disbelieving.

He turned the gun up, away from her, palms open. 'Go. But don't kill my mother. Please.'

'Don't do to me what was done to you, okay?' Eve said.

Tasha backed away from them both, and Whit thought *what are you doing, she's guilty as hell, don't let her go* but letting her go meant saving his mother. Tasha ran. Whit hurried to Eve's side, put himself between Tasha and Eve. Tasha bolted to her Honda, barreled the car through the closed gates, windshield breaking, metal screeching, but then on the street and careening away.

Eve was sobbing. 'You came for me. You came for me.'

He held her for a moment. Then raced back over to Bucks. Blood welled from his chest, from his mouth. He checked Bucks' pulse. Faint. Fading. Inside the warehouse a series of explosions shuddered. Fire department, police would be here any second.

Bucks opened his eyes.

'Did . . . I get?' Bucks said, looking hard into Whit's eyes.

'We'll get an ambulance, Bucks, okay? Hold on.'

'Did I get . . . the money?' And then his eyes went vacant, empty as a useless platitude.

Whit closed Bucks' eyes and pulled the Jag's keys from the dead man's pocket.

'We got to go, Mom. We got to go.' He steadied his mother's arm, shot the handcuff off the chair. He hurried her through the now-broken gates, ran her back through the alleys to where the cars were hidden. One car was already gone. Frank and a hot wire, he decided. They got in Bucks' Jaguar, and Whit tore out of the lot, headed down Mississippi toward Clinton. In the distance they heard the rising whine of a fire engine.

'Whit,' she said. 'Oh, God. I love you.' She clutched his arm, wouldn't let go.

'Mom, let go, I got to stick-shift and I'm not good at it,' he yelled and it made her laugh, a long hysterical laughter that put her low in the seat as he shot the Jag onto Loop 610.

'Where . . .' she asked.

'We're leaving town,' he said. 'We are leaving Houston, Mom, right fricking now.'

'But Frank . . .'

'Frank is a lying, murdering piece of shit,' Whit said, and Eve went silent. She held onto his arm, shivering, crying, squeezing his arm like she couldn't believe he was there. He steered the battered Jaguar onto I-10 West, toward Austin and San Antonio.

She spoke again when Houston was well behind them, the road an empty black band except for the occasional eighteen-wheeler, the gleam of the truck stops of Brookshire ahead on the horizon. He held the steering wheel in a death grip.

'The money. So where is the money?' she said. 'I can't help but want to know.'

He glanced over at her and now he could see the wreck her mouth was, her lips badly cut, her jaw a solid bruise. 'Frank has it. Has had the money all along.'

'Oh, Christ. Frank. No.'

'It doesn't matter, Mom, it doesn't matter, okay? It doesn't matter. We're safe now.'

She started to cry. 'Don't let them take me away from you, Whit, okay? Don't let them take me from you.'

47

They arrived in San Antonio by seven in the morning, and found a small motel. She didn't want to be alone so he got a room with twin beds and while she showered he drove to a nearby Target, waited for it to open, and bought them cheap jeans, sneakers, underwear, shirts, duffel bags. When he got back to the hotel she was clean but sitting in her dirty clothes. He showered while she changed and then he drove her to a nearby emergency room.

The doctor was a young Pakistani woman who gave Whit a fierce, accusing glare as she inspected his mother's bruises. 'What happened?'

'My boyfriend beat me up,' Eve said. 'My son came and rescued me.' She gave Whit a little smile.

'My word,' the doctor said, checking in her mouth. 'He pulled out two teeth, broke two.'

'With pliers,' Eve said.

'You should file charges,' the doctor suggested.

'Perhaps later,' Eve said.

'I beat him up,' Whit said.

'Good for you.' The young doctor cleaned and stitched up Eve's lip, gave her painkillers, and made an emergency appointment for them with an oral surgeon on call with the hospital.

While the surgeon worked on Eve's damaged teeth, Whit sat in the waiting room, watching the Texas Cable News channel. The report on the fire came third on the update. Two people found dead in the parking lot of a warehouse, investigators sifting through the rubble had found at least two more remains. It appeared to be arson and one of the dead had been identified as Gregory Buckman, a former Energis executive who had become of interest to the police after a recent attack at his home. A second man, as yet unidentified, had been mauled to death by two Dobermans, who were also found killed. Police suspected, the announcer said, that the killings and fire were drug-related.

They would find nothing left of José. He closed his eyes. Killing José, strangely, didn't bother him. It was almost as if he hadn't done it. Eve had told him about Public Service, what José had told her, and he could not shake the thought that, in letting Tasha go, he had released a woman who, however misguided, was trying to do good. Justice wasn't often a straight line, but he wasn't sure what he had done was justice any more than what José or Tasha had done.

The oral surgeon took his time with Eve and when she came out she was groggy, her mouth padded with cotton, armed with pills.

'That wasn't fun,' she mouthed. 'Need to sleep.'

So he took her back to the hotel. She lost herself in a heavy doze. He checked the voice mail on his cell phone. One from Vernetta Westbrook, one from Arturo Gomez, five from Claudia. He called her.

'Where are you?' she said.

'I found my mom. In San Antonio.'

'Whit, is Frank Polo with her?'

'No. They're not together anymore. She left him.'

'We found a partial of a fingerprint of Polo's at Harry's murder site,' Claudia said. 'Actually, on the underside of Harry's rental car bumper. If he was wearing gloves he probably tore the latex taking off Harry's plates. The police are looking for Polo. Whit, you can't protect this man.'

'I promise, I'm not.' He paused. 'We'll come back to Houston in a few days. She got hurt, I had to get her medical attention.'

'Is she okay?'

'Yes. Frank Polo roughed her up.' A cold rage settled in his bones. Frank's prints at the murder scene. That devious little bastard. 'Claudia, I want to tell you everything. I'm not sure I can. Because I have to take care of my mom first.'

'When you come back to Houston, you have to talk to the police and the DA's office. You understand that.'

'I'll call right now and set up a time to meet,' he said. 'How's Gooch?'

'Continuing to improve. Continuing to not cooperate. And Greg Buckman is dead.'

'Really?'

'You don't know anything about that, do you, Whit?' There was a coldness in her voice he'd never heard before.

'No,' he said, watching his mother. 'I don't.'

'Come home, Whit.'

'This is over now,' he said. 'I will. Claudia. Thank you.'

'I'm going back to Port Leo today, Whit. Without Gooch. I can't take off more time. Call me when you get home.' And she hung up without a good-bye.

He thought of calling her back, but instead called Charlie Fulgham's cell phone. 'Are you back home?'

'Yes. Should I not be?'

'Your house is safe now. Are we all still your clients?'

'Still got my three dollars in my pocket,' Charlie said.

'Buy some legal pads, Charlie. Fast.'

'I don't want to talk to the police, Whit,' Eve said. It was Wednesday morning, and she was curled on the hotel bed. She'd taken another Vicodin but it hadn't kicked in hard.

He sat down next to her, touched her shoulder. 'Where would Frank run?'

'Anywhere, if he's got five million. I really don't know.'

'Don't lie to me, Mom,' he said. He touched her swollen jaw. 'You and Frank strike me as people with contingency plans. Where is he?'

'I told you, Whitman, I don't know.'

'He put you in mortal danger when he could have cleared your name in an instant. He ran when it was time to save you,' Whit said. 'He doesn't really love you.'

'He loved me,' she said. 'Just not enough. Like how I loved you when you were little. Just not enough.'

'There is no parallel,' he said. 'Please.'

'Why didn't you tell me you were a judge?' she said, surprising him.

He kissed the top of her head. 'I didn't want to scare you off.'

She managed a smile. 'I'm proud of you. Really proud of you, honey.'

He felt a little kindle of pride that died instantly. 'Sure. You should be. I killed a man. Let a criminal walk free. Lied to one of my best friends, lied to the police. I'm a real pride and joy, Mom.'

'But you saved your mother,' she said. 'You saved me.'

'We're going back to Houston tomorrow.'

'Okay,' she said, suddenly surrendering. 'I'm ready.' She closed her eyes, sleepy again. 'I'm actually very clean, you know.'

'Charlie's going to represent us. If needed.'

'That should be good for laughs,' she said and she went back to sleep.

The manifesto from Public Service appeared in six newspapers nationwide Thursday morning, including the *Houston Chronicle*. They claimed responsibility for the deaths of five drug lords, including Paul Bellini and Kiko Grace, and three others in Los Angeles, Philadelphia, and New York in the past month. Two of the dead had been found with rolled-up money in their mouths, a signature of the group. The manifesto was both a scathing indictment of the government's war on drugs, for not being tough enough, and against the drug trade, for its relentless waste of human lives, police efforts, and money.

The statement held a chilling promise: 'We target the casual buyer, for you are the cash cow of the drug trade. If we see you buying drugs, even simply a joint to share with a friend, we will shoot you.' And ending it with ' "God defend the right!" – William Shakespeare.'

Whit wondered where Tasha was, if she had written the letter. Or if José had before he died. The TV pundits had a field day on this twisting new front on the drug war.

When Whit met Charlie at his house, Charlie hugged Eve, shook Whit's hand, and pointed to the letter in the paper. 'This, sweeties,' Charlie said, 'is called manna from heaven.'

Two hours later they sat in Gooch's private hospital room, an artful arrangement by Charlie. Whit and Eve sat next to Gooch's bed; Arturo Gomez, two of his detectives, and Vernetta Westbrook on the other side of the bed.

'My clients will cooperate fully,' Charlie Fulgham said. The party-loud shirt from his stand-up routine was gone, replaced by a gray Armani suit, fitted to the millimeter.

The police officers all looked at Charlie like they knew him. And didn't like what they saw.

Gomez started. 'All right, Mr Mosley—'

'Actually, you should refer to him as Your Honor,' Charlie said. 'Judge Mosley is a highly respected magistrate.'

Gomez surrendered on the point. 'Can you fill in the gaps for us, Judge Mosley?'

'It's really simple,' Whit said. And he told them: he had hired Harry Chyme to find his mother. Harry told them that she was in Houston, he believed, living under the name Eve Michaels, and he and Gooch came to Houston to find her. They never heard again from Harry, but after making inquiries at a club Harry said her boyfriend managed, found Eve.

'She agreed to meet us at Pie Shack,' Whit said, and this was the risky part. Gooch could go to jail for this when he had saved their lives, saved the life of the young hostage the gunman had taken.

'But Ms Michaels was followed there,' Charlie said, stepping smoothly in. 'By gunmen possibly related to this Public Service group. Vigilantes mistakenly seeking to harm Ms Michaels due to her connection – via Frank Polo – to Tommy Bellini's businesses. We certainly know that Public Service had declared war on the Bellini family, right or wrong.'

Gomez grilled all three of them, but they stuck to their story with relentless precision: they ran, like everyone else, and in fact went into hiding because Eve was afraid the Bellinis or these gunmen were after her.

'If the Bellinis did illegal activities,' Eve said, 'I didn't know about it. I was the accountant for five of Tommy Bellini's companies, and they are all perfectly legit. If his son started dabbling in the drug trade or screwing around with his father's companies, it has nothing to do with me.'

'What's the relationship of the Alvarez insurance firm to the Bellinis?'

Here Eve threw them a bone to chew. 'I know Tommy loaned money to the Alvarez family when their company was in bad shape, about to close. He was a silent partner. They sold a lot of life insurance. But they did their own accounting; I had nothing to do with them as a business.' She paused. 'They always seemed like a nice family.'

'But you lived in a house owned by the Bellini family.' This from Vernetta.

'That was provided to Frank Polo. He was an old family friend. So was I. That's not illegal.'

Whit's throat thickened as Vernetta said, 'Mr Guchinski's van was found at the Paul Bellini murder site.'

'The Bellinis grabbed me when I stopped by Eve's house to pick up her things,' Gooch said. 'She didn't want to go back there, she thought Frank Polo would force her to stay. Paul and his guys beat me up, detained me.'

'Paul Bellini wanted Mom to trade for Gooch. They knew about the shooting, they were afraid Gooch and I were involved with Public Service,' Whit said.

'They tried to get me to give them details on Public Service, but I didn't know jack. They pumped me full of drugs, thinking if I were looped I'd talk,' Gooch said.

Whit said: 'Paul told me we could meet. We did. He had Gooch in the trunk of his car. He thought I was bringing my mother to him, but of course, I wasn't. I drove Gooch's van. Paul and I were talking and he was shot. He was clearly dead. I ran and took his car, because the shooter fired at me, twice, and I couldn't abandon Gooch. We took off.'

'And didn't call the police,' Vernetta said.

'I asked Whit not to,' Eve said, 'because I was afraid, and because he's a judge and I didn't want him to lose his job.'

'I take full responsibility for that decision,' Whit said. They asked more detailed questions about Paul's shooting, and Whit answered truthfully.

'Of course, you could charge Judge Mosley with fleeing a scene of a crime,' Charlie said. 'Of course, in doing so, he saved his own life and that of Mr Guchinski.'

'He didn't report the crime,' Gomez said.

'At his mother's request. They'd already been traumatized by one shooting, Detective. And Paul Bellini and his thugs were already beyond help. Charge them if you like, but then my clients will stop talking.'

Gomez made a noise in his throat.

'The death at the Greystoke,' Vernetta said. 'Detective Tarrant here is in charge of that investigation.'

Tarrant was a thin woman, hair pulled back in a modest ponytail. 'A man matching Judge Mosley's description retrieved a van from the parking valets. Two rooms were abandoned there, belonging to an Emily Smith.'

'We were at the Greystoke,' Eve said. 'But I don't know any Emily Smith. I was going to meet Frank there; I wanted a public place because I was afraid of him. But we didn't stay. Whit left because he wanted to see a friend of his, a police officer from his hometown. To explain to her what we'd been through. After Whit left, I thought I saw one of the gunmen from the diner, a man in dreadlocks. I left the hotel and called Whit on his cell phone. Whit rushed back and picked me up. I decided then to leave town. He took me home. Frank was there. I thought it best that Whit leave us to talk, and at my request, he did. Frank was calm as we talked, but he drank a bunch of wine and became violent. He beat me, knocked my teeth out. He drank more, passed out, and I went to San Antonio.'

'Where'd you stay?' Gomez asked.

'In my car. After a couple of days I called Whit. He came and got me.' Her Mercedes was back in its garage at the house, where it had been since Gooch was caught, and they had dumped Bucks' Jag a mile from the burnt-out warehouse late last night.

'After my mother left town,' Whit said, 'the Bellinis left us alone intentionally or were occupied with attacks on them by Public Service. We didn't know what was happening.'

The detectives watched them in silence. Whit thought he saw a tug of resignation in Vernetta Westbrook's eyes.

'Your Honor,' she said, 'you told Claudia Salazar you thought Greg Buckman killed Harry Chyme and Richard Doyle. You never explained why.'

'Frank Polo suggested it to me, I'm sure now in an effort to put attention off of him. This isn't complicated.'

'My clients were innocents caught up in the cross fire between the Bellinis and Public Service,' Charlie said. 'Ms Michaels has offered her full cooperation with the fraud examiners in the DA's office, if they want her help in identifying possible points where illegal Bellini funds became legitimate revenue.'

'But I get immunity, and so do Whit and Gooch,' Eve said. 'I can help you sift through every Bellini financial record if you want to go after them. Otherwise, you're on your own and you'll find it, I suspect, very difficult to make a case against Tommy and Mary Pat Bellini that gets you their assets.'

Gomez and Vernetta exchanged a glance.

Charlie said, 'You can try and make a case against my clients, on rather circumstantial evidence, or you can get unparalleled access into the Bellini finances. And also build a case against Public Service, who are nothing more than self-proclaimed domestic terrorists. Choose your headlines, ladies and gentlemen.'

'I wish you'd stuck to the stage, Charlie,' Vernetta said.

48

'Daddy? Did you hear what I said?' Whit said. 'I found Mom.'

Whit broke the news as gently as possible to Babe, sitting at their breakfast table. Irina stared at him as though he'd announced he had cancer himself.

'What?'

'I found her over a week ago. That's why I've been in Houston. We came back this morning.'

Babe blinked, took a deep, fortifying breath. 'Ellen?'

'She wants to see you,' Whit said. 'Would you like to see her?'

'Whit,' Irina interrupted. She moved from her chair, a sickly smile of shock on her face, to stand behind Babe, put her hand on his shoulders. 'Your father, this is too much for him.'

'I'm okay.' Babe patted her hand. 'It's okay.' He closed his eyes, passed a hand over his face. 'Do I want to see her?' But not asking the question of anyone but himself.

'When I asked, you said yes. You said you wanted to ask her why she did what she did,' Whit said.

'How the hell did you find her?' Babe said.

'Long, long story. For later, Daddy.'

Babe's lip trembled. He put his hands over his face.

'This was a bad idea,' Whit said. 'But if you wanted to make peace with her before . . .'

The hands came down. 'Peace. Yes,' Babe said with sudden, hard resolve. 'I would like to see her. Bring her in.' He gave a jagged little laugh. 'Why not? Life's too short.'

Whit went out to the car where Eve sat. She followed him into the house, touching the side of the door, glancing around as if cataloging every change the house had weathered in her absence. She walked into the kitchen behind Whit.

'Hello, Babe,' Eve said.

Babe stared at her for several long moments. 'What's with your hair?' he finally said.

'I went red,' she said.

'It don't suit you,' Babe said. He ran fingertips over his chemo-bald head. 'But then I got a new look, too.'

'Dad, maybe Mom would like a cup of coffee. Would that be okay?' Whit said. 'Can you be trusted around hot beverages?' Trying to deflate the tension.

'I'm not fixing breakfast for this woman,' Irina, usually the voice of calm reason, announced. 'Whit, your papa doesn't need this upset, for God's sakes . . .' Then a torrent of Russian.

Babe whispered, in the babyish Russian he knew. Kissed Irina's cheek. 'We moved the coffeemaker while you've been gone, Ellie. It's on the other counter. Help yourself.'

Eve didn't move. 'I won't stay. I'm sorry I left you, Babe. I want you and the boys to know that it had nothing to do with you. It was me. The situation . . . was such I thought it best I not come home. So I chose not to. I'm sorry for the pain I caused you. The boys.' She stopped, ran a finger along her lip. 'I'm sorry. I don't know what else to say. Two words don't sound adequate. I know.'

Silence. Babe cleared his throat. 'You know, they didn't stop crying for a real long time. Wondering why their mama would leave them. Do you have any idea what you tell small kids why they matter, why they're still worthwhile human beings, why they're still lovable when their own mother can't be bothered to love them? I took them to Disneyland six months after you left. For two weeks. I thought it would help. Me herding all six of them, trying to pretend rides and candy and Mickey Mouse could make up for you gone. Jesus, we go, they don't see anything but moms with their kids. I was cruel trying to help them.' Now his voice trembled. 'I don't hate you for ripping my heart out. But what you did to my boys.' His voice broke. 'Treating my sons as disposable is unforgivable.'

'I'll ask for their forgiveness,' Eve said. 'Yours is a separate issue.'

'You don't want my forgiveness,' Babe said. 'You show your sorry face in time to stand over my grave and decide you want to play mom thirty years too late.' He shook his head at Whit. 'Whit, you lose one, you go find the other?'

'I'm not trying to replace you, Dad, for God's sakes.' Whit took a calming breath. 'I'm trying to help you both. You're my parents. Make your peace. Please.'

'Whit,' Eve said. 'Your father is your parent. He's the one who took care of you.' She stood. 'You raised a very fine son, Babe.'

'Who gives a rat's ass what you think?' Babe said.

'Screaming was not the point of you and Mom talking,' Whit said.

'Sure was for me. I said what I wanted.' Babe got up from his chair. 'She's dead to me.'

'She is back in our lives,' Whit said. 'She is not dead.'

'If yelling makes you happy, Babe,' Eve said, 'yell away. I deserve it.' She dabbed at her eyes with her sleeve.

'And I thought the chemo made me puke,' Babe said.

'Tell me, sweetie,' Eve said to Irina. 'Now that he's retired, what does he talk about? Because I never heard a single word other than oil business, golf, oil, golf, and oh yes, oil with a hint of golf. It was enough to drive you nuts. Did you know he wouldn't change a diaper? Six kids and he wouldn't change a single diaper.'

Irina said, very quietly, 'I don't know you, Ellen, and I don't want to.'

'We're staying in the guest house,' Whit said, his chest full and hot. He had never seen the look now on his father's face, dead love resurrected into absolute, unforgiving hate. 'Just for tonight.'

'No,' Babe said.

'Yes,' Whit said. 'I pay rent. You don't have to see her if you don't want.'

'I won't stay here if it's going to upset him,' Eve said. 'You know, I did want to apologize. I don't care if you believe me.'

'Since when do you care about occupying the high ground?' Babe said. 'Tell me, Whit, did she hug you the moment she saw you?' He gave a jagged laugh. 'Does she think she's still in the will?'

'Dad, she came. That's all that matters.'

'Yeah, right. You're not gonna drive a wedge between me and my sons, Ellie,' Babe said. 'Especially in the last five minutes of my life. You hurt my boys again, I'll kill you.'

'I owe Whit my life. Hurting him is the last thing I would ever do.' She turned for the door, waited for Whit. 'I won't bother you again, Babe.'

'Give him time,' Whit said.

'Yeah, he's got time to spare,' Eve said. The day had bloomed into bright sunshine and they sat on a deck at the Water's End, an old bar on the beach. The other patrons were tourists and winter Texans, a quiet group.

Eve didn't sip her beer. 'Put me in a trailer; I'll tell everyone I'm from Michigan. I'll fit right in for the next month or so.'

'There's a plan.'

'This secret between us,' Eve said. 'It's a nasty thing, isn't it? Living with what you know and you don't tell?'

Whit sipped his beer. 'Yes. I've been outlining my resignation letter in my head.'

'Why? What good does resigning do? Stay on the bench, keep doing good.'

'I can't. I killed for you.'

'In self-defense. Screw the law books. Saving your mother is instinct.' She tasted her beer.

They had survived – both the mob and the possibility of prosecution – but he felt emptied. His mother smiled a lot at him. Like she was seeing herself in him, truly, for the first time.

Whit saw the bar door open, Claudia step outside onto the deck. She headed straight toward him, toward Eve.

'A family reunion,' Claudia said. She didn't pull up a chair, but she gave Eve a quick, dismissive glance, then looked back at Whit. 'It's been a few days since we spoke.'

'How are you?' Whit asked.

'Did you lose my phone number in the past week?' she said.

'I only got back this morning.'

'This is your mother,' Claudia said. Statement, not question.

'Yes. Eve Michaels. Mom, this is my friend, Claudia Salazar.'

Eve offered her hand. Claudia let three beats pass then she took it, with the barest politeness.

'Whit speaks so highly of you,' Eve said.

'Does he,' Claudia said. 'I used to be able to say the same about him. Until he threw away everything he stood for.'

'Really,' Eve said. 'I suspect he stands for something greater than you know.'

'I'm sitting right here while you talk about me,' Whit said.

'I know what you are,' Claudia said to Eve. 'I don't believe for two seconds that you were Tommy Bellini's simpleminded accountant who didn't know squat.'

'Claudia. I totally understand why you're upset,' Whit said.

'It's okay, son,' Eve said. 'What am I, Claudia?' Her eyes were a little bright. 'Tell me.'

'A woman who would let her son ruin his life to save her own sorry ass.'

'That's enough,' Whit said. 'You don't know the truth . . .'

'Because you've told it all, right, Whit?' Her voice was low but it was worse than if she was shouting.

'Whatever you believe about me,' Eve said, 'is true. Not that Whit and I care, do we, honey? We're a team.'

Claudia's jaw trembled. 'I have nothing to say to you.' She glared at Whit. 'Do you ever think about Harry?'

'Yes. All the time. I hope the police find Frank Polo really soon.'

'Frank Polo. Because he was the one bad guy in the picture, right, Whit?'

'I didn't know he killed Harry. I didn't.'

'But you *knew* this group of people were connected to his death. You knew and you said nothing.' Every word like a small little explosion between them.

'I told you about Greg Buckman,' Whit said, keeping his voice low.

'You didn't tell anyone the whole picture. All you cared about was protecting your mother. I can't prove it, but I know it. You walked away from every value you once held dear, Whit. Like this woman walked away from you and your family. I guess the acorn doesn't fall far from the tree, even when the tree hauls ass.'

'Nice that you have this moral clarity about my life,' Whit said.

'You know, Harry has a mother too. Two sisters, an ex-wife. People who loved him. He was worth about a dozen of . . . her.' She jerked her head at Eve.

'Can we please discuss this later?' he said.

'Why? Are there voters here, Your Honor? Maybe I'll keep my opinions to myself. Maybe not. I don't know yet. We still have to work together. For now. But I don't like it.'

'I'm grateful to you for trying to help me,' Whit said. Aware now of people on the deck starting to stare.

'Screw your gratitude. You made your choice, Whit. And I'm making mine. It was nice knowing you, once.' Claudia turned, walked out. She tried to slam the bar door but it was hinged to shut slowly, and even the angry yank she gave it couldn't overcome the mechanism. She stormed out.

'People are very territorial about you, Whit,' Eve said, but her voice was subdued.

'Yes.'

'She cares about you.'

'She did.'

'She will again,' Eve said.

'I don't think so,' Whit said. 'Or it will be a long road for her and me.'

She touched his hand. 'What have I cost you, son?' Eve asked.

Suddenly he thought of Lance Gartner, that boy dead from heroin in the bay, his mother's pleas for Whit to change the death certificate. *I can't go against the law,* he had said, and a sudden hard shame rose in him. Whit took a long swig of his beer. 'It's okay, Mom. It's okay.'

He took Eve back to the guest house. He poured good cabernet and she went into the guest bathroom, came out smiling, holding a bar of soap. 'Gardenia,' she said.

'Isn't that what you used?' He had bought it as a surprise for her.

333

'Yes,' she said. 'Thank you.' He drank wine while they made phone calls. Five of them, with Whit talking first. To Whit's brothers. Teddy hung up on her when she started to speak and did not answer when they called back. Mark talked to her for nearly an hour. David and Danny weren't at their homes, and Whit simply left them short messages saying he had important but good news and to please call, anytime, night or day. Joe talked to Whit but said no on talking to Eve. At least for now. Give him time.

Eve sipped at her wine. 'I didn't expect hugs right away.'

'No.' Whit felt as tired as he'd ever been. 'You want to watch a movie?'

She studied a long line of DVDs on the shelf. 'Who is Monty Python?'

'British comedy. Hilarious.'

She'd moved on to the next section of films. 'I don't much like Woody Allen. He whines a lot.'

'He's self-deprecating. It's an art.'

'*Caddyshack*,' she said. 'That one I like.'

So he put in the movie, one of his favorites, and they sat on the couch and finished the bottle of cabernet. He laughed where he usually did and so did she.

When he was putting up the disc she said, 'Did I tell you that if any of the boys ever came looking for me, I figured it'd be you?'

'Why?'

'Fiercely independent. Strong. Like me,' she said. 'No holds barred about getting what you want.'

He was suddenly unsure if this was a compliment or not.

'I love you, Whit.' She kissed him with a quick, almost embarrassed smack on the cheek. 'You know that, don't you?'

'Yeah, I love you, too,' he said, the words and the idea still a little strange. They stayed up late, hoping for Joe or Teddy or the twins to call back, her opening a bottle of zinfandel, him drinking more, and finally he dragged himself back to bed, happy and dizzy-sick and wondering exactly what the rest of his life was going to be like.

He awoke suddenly, hearing the soft little click of the front door shutting, a wetness on his cheek. The linger of a kiss. The scent of gardenia.

He sat up in the darkness, the guest house too quiet, knowing it was empty. He glanced at the clock: 3:34 A.M.

Whit went to the guest bedroom. She was gone.

He hurried out the front door and up the driveway. Eve stood at the curb, one of his duffel bags packed and sitting at her feet.

'Where are you going?' he said.

She turned. 'Oh. Honey. I hoped you wouldn't wake. I shouldn't have kissed you good-bye. But I had to.'

'Where the hell are you going?'

'I have unfinished business. The less you know, the better.' She drew a hand through her hair. 'I'll be back soon.'

'You don't leave in the middle of the night if you plan on coming back.' His voice rose; he suddenly felt as scared as a child, and he forced himself to calm down.

'I don't fit in with your life, Whit. I don't. I do love you, but . . .'

'Bullshit. Bullshit. I'm calling you on your bullshit, Mom.'

'I'm grateful for everything you've done for me. But I need to do this. Alone.'

He saw it then. 'You know where Frank is. With the money.'

She glanced down the darkened street.

'Did he call you? After what he did you'd go back to him?'

'Of course not. But I can find him.'

'Who gives a shit about that money, Mom? You're here. You're home.'

'But it's five million, honey. Five million.' She gave a quick little shrug. 'Probably four by now, knowing Frank, but still . . .'

Whit shook his head. 'You aren't going to do this to me again.'

Out of the dark a cab from a Corpus Christi taxi service rolled up and stopped three houses down. Of course. She wouldn't give the cab this address; the headlights might wake him up.

She tried to smile at him. 'Whit, honey. Let's not have a brutal little scene. You can either let me go or tie me up, but I'll go eventually. That's the hard, bitter truth. Love me, but don't change me into what you'll love better.'

'Mom—'

'And I want to change you, and I can't. You don't want what I call life. You're going to look at me every day and see the bad things you did. Don't be more like me. Be like your father. Your brothers. Even Claudia.'

'I can tell the police about James Powell,' he said, desperation rising in his voice. 'There's no statute of limitations on murder.'

'Go right ahead.' She gave her little shrug. 'He threatened to kill you and your brothers if I didn't do what he said, so I killed him. You want me to confess to a crime, there you go. I'm not one bit ashamed of it.'

'Mom. You killed him for that money.'

'Believe what you want. Do what you like. Lock me up, throw away the key.' She leaned over, kissed his cheek again. 'Stay good, baby.'

'Please don't. Please don't do this,' he said.

She leaned down, picked up her duffel. She didn't look back, didn't wave. He watched her get into the cab, vanish into the dark.

Eve who became Ellie

I'm breaking one of my own rules now, because I'm close to a beach. Beaches are okay for me now. To the police I'm a city girl. The Mosleys think of me as a beach girl. But Whit won't come looking for me again, and he won't find me if he does.

The beach here at Princeville is absolutely pristine, and the tourists are mostly honeymooners, nice kids, a few golf widows sunning and reading fat novels. The beach here is far prettier than the ones in Texas, but it's so pretty it almost doesn't seem real. A dream. So it seems safe.

Here I am Ellie again, now Ellie Masters. Eve fit like a suit faded from fashion, so I shed it. I stayed a while at a small hotel on the south side of Kauai, waiting, thinking, until I found a condo for rent by a landlord living in California. Retired lady, she and her husband moved here, then he died and she moved back to San Francisco to be close to her grandkids. I hope she decides to sell and I bet she'd like cash. God knows I do.

Jacksonville, Florida, was where Frank landed; it was where he spent summers as a kid, visiting grandparents, and he always spoke fondly of it. See, he broke the first rule. I traced him there via a false ID he thought I didn't know about, he'd gotten it a few years ago from the same guy who got me the Emily Smith cards. Mistake number two. I found him in a beachside house, a modest little bungalow, and walked right up to him on his back porch one cold night and, before he could say I'm sorry, put the bullet in his face. No hello, no good-bye you sorry piece of trash. Not in the mouth like James Powell but right between the wide, lying eyes. Frank was surprised. I was surprised he had as much brain as he did voice. But he was never stupid. My mistake.

The money was hidden in the house, in six different places. I took it and then phoned the Houston police, anonymously reported that I thought I'd seen Frank Polo, who they were looking for, at the Jax address and hung up. My second good deed for the day.

Frank had laid low, hadn't spent more than a few thousand, and I headed down to Miami, caught a plane to the Caymans, and started re-cleaning the money back through a series of accounts. Finally I put half in an account for me. Half in an unnumbered account for Whit. Mailed him a note with the bank name, the account and access numbers, and 'I love you.' Nothing else. I hoped he wouldn't give it away or refuse to touch it or call the police about it like a high-minded idiot. I sort of tied my boy's hands; he won't tell the police now because it's too many questions, and the money can help make up for all the trouble I caused him and his brothers their whole lives.

I don't have to work, what with my cash settlement from Frank, but I get restless sitting around so I took a part-time job in a little coffee shop/bookstore in Hanalei. It's a hippie town near Princeville. The young people here all have dirty feet and it's not the kind of Hawaiian destination anyone from my previous lives would pick. So I am the world's oldest barista and I sell travel books and bestselling paperbacks to the vacationers. The dirty-feet kids all like to read Beat Generation writers. They don't know what life lived running is, trust me. But most of the customers are tourists who come in once and only once, and the other clerks are nice but aren't nosy. I say I'm from California, where it seems half the world is from, and it's answer enough.

But every day is a terrible temptation.

The bookstore owner, Doris, a really sweet lady, set up an Internet access on a couple of computers in the store. Thought it'd sell more coffee, and it does; the hippies love it. They come in and e-mail their parents for more money.

But when the store's not busy, I sit down and I open to a search engine and I want to type in Whit's name so bad I could cry. I want to know he's okay. But I'm afraid, every Web site you visit on that machine is recorded in a file somewhere in the world, I'm sure of it, and having made myself vanish again I don't want to risk it. I would for him and him alone. Because if I know he's okay, will that be enough? Will I keep from e-mailing him? Or phoning him? Did he get the two-plus million out of the account? Is he having fun with his share or did he give it all away to charity out of pointless guilt? I won't ever know.

The temptation is like hunger, hell, starvation of the worst sort. Because you imagine that the barest crumb would keep you going.

But I don't. For weeks and weeks, I don't. Then I get an idea. I log on using Doris' account (her password was 'doris,' for God's sakes), go to the Web site for the *Corpus Christi Caller-Times*. I don't search by Whit's name on the archives, I search for 'justice of the peace.' How many are there in the Coastal Bend? Not many, right?

I find articles on him. Still in office, conducting a death inquest on a homicide over in Laurel Point. A mention in a story on Babe's passing, dated two weeks ago. Babe gone. Whit grieving bad, I know, I'm aching to hold him now.

So Whit's safe. He stayed in office. I didn't ruin him. He's tough like me.

But it made me miss him more, bad enough where I felt sick and I went home early and lay on my bed. I could buy one of those prepaid call cards. Pay cash. Make it impossible to trace. Let him know I'm okay, hear his voice for a minute.

But no. He let me walk away when I needed to and it's not fair, me opening the door again. Let it be shut. Let me be strong to keep it shut. He doesn't need me.

At night I rent the movies. *Caddyshack* and Monty Python and all those Woody Allen ones full of jokes only New Yorkers and Whit get. I pretend he and I are sitting together, sharing popcorn, watching the movies. It is all I'm gonna get now.

And it has to be enough.

Acknowledgments

In writing this book, I relied on the particular help and expertise of Peter Ginsberg and Genny Ostertag; Lieutenant Gray Smith, Narcotics Division, Houston Police Department; John Leggio, Media Relations, Houston Police Department; Ted Wilson, Chief, Special Crimes Bureau, and Roe Wilson, Division Chief, Post-conviction Writs, both of the Office of the District Attorney, Harris County, Texas; and Dr William K. Thomson. Any errors are entirely of my doing, not theirs. I also owe thanks to my mother and stepfather, Liz and Dub Norrid; Matt Manroe; and Trish Kunz for kindnesses to me during the writing process.

No one writes a long book alone, and my most special and heartfelt thanks go to Leslie, Charles, and William for their loving support and encouragement.

Some of the Houston locales in this book are real; others are entirely fictional. Everything else in the novel – characters and events – is a product of my imagination.

If you have enjoyed *Cut and Run* don't miss:

A KISSGONEBAD

The first novel in Jeff Abbott's highly acclaimed Whit
Mosely series. Coming soon in Orion Hardcover.

ISBN: 0 75286 094 1
Price: £9.99

1

When the Blade (as he secretly called himself) felt blue, he liked to relax behind the old splintery cabin, where his three Darlings were buried, and feel the power of their vanished lives pulse through him. It was quiet in the shade of the laurel oaks, and on lonely evenings the Blade pretended that his Darlings lived with him, with their cries and pleadings and wet, fearful eyes. His kingdom was small, twenty feet by twenty feet, and he ruled over only three subjects. But he ruled over them completely, life and body and soul.

Today, with his portable tape recorder playing a worn Beach Boys cassette and the clear harmony of 'God Only Knows' drifting up into the oaks, he sat down between two of the unmarked graves: one of the mouthy carrot-topped girl from Louisiana who had fought so hard, the other the young woman from Brownsville who had cried the whole time and hardly deserved to be a Darling at all. He had selected a new Darling, a prime choice. But fear made his spit taste like smoke, because he had never wooed near Port Leo, much less wooed anyone . . . famous.

He had followed her for a daring ten minutes yesterday, sweat tickling his ribs, idling near her in the grocery store while she shopped with the big-shouldered boyfriend who had brought her to Port Leo. The Blade didn't like the boyfriend named Pete, not one bit, although he liked to think about all the mischief that Pete had been up to, starring in those nasty movies. The Blade had eavesdropped in the grocery, pretending to inspect the jug wines while the couple selected beer. She fancied Mexican beer, one that folks drank with a lime slice crammed down the neck of the bottle, and he wished he knew its taste; but Mama didn't let him drink.

3

The Blade hoped they would talk about sex, being their vocation, but Pete and his Darling talked about grilling shrimp, the rainy autumn, how irritating his Godzilla-bitch ex-wife was.

His Darling's voice sounded edgy, and impatient. *I'm tired of us sneaking around this town and you pissing off these dumbasses. Let's go to Houston to write your movie. I'm in big favor of Plan B.* The hint that his Darling was making a movie, here in Port Leo, tightened his throat with desire. The boyfriend muttered no. Then she'd said, *Jesus, let this crap with your brother go.*

The sweet agony of being close to her flamed into fear. He'd grabbed a gallon of cheap cabernet in terror and bolted for the checkout lines, crowded with new winter Texans. He'd fled to the cereal aisle and shoved the jug behind the Cheerios and waited until his Darling and her boyfriend left the store before venturing out.

They hadn't seen him, known him.

Pete was writing a movie? He didn't think that the films those two did involved screenwriting. Didn't they just point the camera, clamber on the bed, and do their artful moaning and thrusting with all the sincerity of professional wrestlers?

Last week he had driven into Corpus Christi when he learned that his soon-to-be Darling did movies, of an extremely dubious sort. He frequented adult bookstores, driving the two hours to San Antonio or the thirty-odd miles to Corpus Christi, avoiding the few establishments that were too close to Port Leo along the ribbon of Highway 35, never going to any single store too often, paying with bills worn thin from lying under Mama's mattress. He never asked the clerks for recommendations – he didn't want to be remembered – and tried to fit in with the faceless men who wandered the too-brightly lit aisles of the porn stores. He was unremarkable: just another lonely guy with eyes only for the bosomy models on the video covers.

His research uncovered that she had acted in only a few movies; she had directed far more. He almost felt proud of her. On his last jaunt, off the sale table, he bought a video she had headlined five years ago, her last acting job. She went by the name Velvet Mojo, an appellation the Blade found tasteless. The tape was called

4

Going Postal. He suspected the post office would receive a satirical treatment. Perhaps even a deliciously violent treatment. But the movie disappointed. No violence. And while his Darling was versed in erotic tricks involving stamps that made his tongue go dry, her friend Pete performed with her, which seemed . . . wrong. The Blade watched them couple again and again until the world's edges grew soft and his mind napped. He heard Mama cursing. When he awoke, he felt bleary and offended. She deserved rest with the pleasure of his company.

He could save her from this sordidness. He would.

That little shady spot under the odd bent oaks, it would be perfect for her. But winning her would be tricky. Wooing other Darlings and avoiding suspicion had been easy. Louisiana and Brownsville and Laredo were far away. She was within a mile or so. And he would have to wait. He could not truly enjoy her now, but he could in a few days. His hunger sharpened, and he imagined her lips, speckled with her own blood, tasted of copper and strawberries.

The Blade stood with resolve. He would make her his. But first he would have to make sure that no one cared if she was gone.